Dear Reader,

I never wanted to write about a millionaire heroine. And I haven't. But there are some characters who've really stuck with me...characters who feel like they have more to say, more to do. Parker Welles was one such character. You might remember her from *The Next Best Thing*, Lucy's blunt and good-natured best friend. For some reason, I just wasn't able to forget Parker, who seemed so content to be on her own, raising her son, writing those sappy children's books.

I also couldn't seem to get over Gideon's Cove, Maine, the setting for *Catch of the Day*. So many of you wrote to me, wondering what happens to Maggie and Malone, and I'm very flattered that you loved them enough to want to see them again! I wondered, what if I took away Parker's money and career and sent her up to the coast of Maine, to a little town where she doesn't know a soul? What would she do? How would she handle things? Could she spend the summer reinventing herself and create a happy life for her son? And what if the man sent to help her out is the last guy whose help she'd want...James Cahill, her father's attorney.

James has watched the Princess, as he calls her, from afar for some time now. Perfect Parker has never needed anything from him...until now...and James is determined to make her see him in a new light.

Somebody to Love is a story about discovering your true worth, and finding out what you can do when your back is against the wall. And it's also about who we truly are, despite outward appearances, and what we really want. Home. Love. A future. What more could there be?

I hope you'll love Parker and James, and if you've read *Catch of the Day,* I hope you'll have fun seeing Gideon's Cove again.

Enjoy the book!

Kristan

KRISTAN HIGGINS

Somebody to Love

HQN™

Recycling programs
for this product may
not exist in your area.

ISBN-13: 978-0-373-77658-0

SOMEBODY TO LOVE

Acknowledgments

As always, I am so grateful for the lovely friendship and tremendous dedication of my agent, Maria Carvainis, for her unwavering efforts on my behalf. Many, many thanks to my wonderful team at Harlequin: Keyren Gerlach, Tara Parsons, Margaret O'Neill Marbury and Michelle Renaud, the incredible gang in Marketing and Digital, all the lovely sales reps and especially Donna Hayes, who makes running a huge corporation look easy and does so while wearing incredible shoes.

Much love and thanks to the endlessly capable Kim Castillo of Author's Best Friend and to the brilliant Sarah Burningham at Little Bird Publicity, ever cheerful, ever helpful, ever lovely, both of you!

For their input, thanks to Huntley Fitzpatrick, Shaunee Cole, Kelly Morse and Karen Pinco. You guys are fun, smart and gorgeous, all of you. To the merry band of writers better known as CTRWA, thank you for the love and support. Love and thanks to Jackie Decker, my BFF and sister-in-law (the Holy Rollers and Ark Angels were her ideas, so blame her). Thanks to my mom for telling us the story of Mickey the Fire Engine so many times when we were small...the thrill has yet to fade! Huge thanks to my brother-in-law, Brian Keenan, Esq., for his input on legal issues (any mistakes are mine, all mine). Claire Shanahan Bacon named Beauty, Parker's dog, and the dog's personality grew from there. Maura Fehon was my lovely and hardworking summer intern—thank you, honey!

I am very blessed to be able to claim so many writers as dear friends, but this time around, thanks especially to Robyn Carr, Susan Andersen, Jill Shalvis, Cindy Gerard, Joan Kayse and Elizabeth Hoyt. And thanks especially to Robyn for letting me steal a certain salty expression Lavinia uses. You'll know it when you see it.

Thank you to my two wonderful kids who only grow more delightful, and to my sainted husband, who is the love of my life, even after all these years... especially after all these years.

And you, dear readers, for the letters and notes which bring me such joy...thank you from the bottom of my heart.

Somebody to Love

This book is dedicated to my daughter Flannery, who is my treasure, my joy and my heart.

CHAPTER ONE

"*AND WITH THAT, the six Holy Rollers—Golly, Polly and Molly, Ike, Mike and Spike—took off their magical roller skates for the last time. Their job on earth was done. They'd earned their beautiful, sparkly angel wings and could stay in heaven forever...and ever...and ever. The end.*"

Parker Harrington Welles suppressed a dry heave, closed the book and tried not to envision smothering the fictional angels, no matter how much she would've enjoyed it.

Don't kill us, Parker! squeaked the imaginary voices in her head, their voices helium-shrill.

I can't kill you. You're immortal. Unfortunately. One of the huge downsides of writing the series—the little pains in the butt talked to her. Another downside—Parker talked back.

Seven or eight little hands shot up in the air.

"Please write more Holy Rollers books, Miss Welles."

I'd rather bathe in my own blood, kid, thought Parker. "No, sweetie, the Holy Rollers are in heaven now," she answered. "This is the last book in the series. But you can see them in a movie this summer, don't forget."

Today at her son's preschool, the Holy Rollers, a book series so sickeningly precious it made *The Velveteen Rabbit* look like a chapter out of *Sin City,* was officially done. Though they had made Parker moderately famous in the world of kiddie lit, had been translated into sixteen languages and had print runs in the gazillions, there was no getting around the fact that their author hated them.

Hate *is such an angry word!* chorused the child angels. *We love* you, *Parker!* Honestly, they were a Cartoon Network version of a Greek chorus, always popping into her head with unwanted advice.

"Did you write *Harry Potter?*" was the next question, this one from Nicky's friend Caitlin.

"No, afraid not, honey. But I love those books, don't you?"

"Sometimes I get the Warm Fuzzles, just like the Holy Rollers," Mariah said, and Parker nearly threw up in her mouth. Had she really invented that term? Had she been drinking at the time?

"Are you rich?" Henry Sloane asked.

"Well," Parker answered, "if you're asking if I make a lot as an author, the answer is no. All the money I get for the Holy Rollers goes to a charity called Save the Children."

"That's for kids who don't have enough food," Nicky said proudly, and Parker smiled at her son. It was the one good thing about the book series. Parker didn't need the money, so right from the get-go, she'd donated all proceeds to the charity, which took away some of the nausea.

"But you live in a mansion," Will Michalski stated with authority. "I've been there. You have twenty-nine bathrooms."

"True enough," she said, a twinge of discomfort flashing through her.

"It's a mansion. It's a castle! I want to live there when I grow up!"

"Are you going to write another book?" asked Amelia.

Excellent question. Parker might not love the Holy Rollers, but new ideas hadn't exactly been pouring out of her. "I hope so."

"What's it about?"

"Um, I'm not quite sure yet. But I'll let you know, okay? Any other questions? Yes, Ben."

After another half hour, as the questions dwindled into what color wings Golly should have, the teacher finally stepped in.

"Miss Welles has to get going, I'm sure," she said. "Kids, can you say thank-you to Nicky's mom?"

"Thank you, Nicky's mom!" the kids chorused, then rushed her, hugging her legs, the payoff for reading *The Holy Rollers Earn Their Halos* out loud.

"Am I staying with Daddy this weekend?" Nicky asked as they walked to the car.

"You sure are," Parker answered. She stroked her son's dark hair. Ethan's weekend had come awfully fast, it seemed. She gave her son a kiss, then bent to buckle him into his booster.

"I can do it myself," Nicky said.

"Right. Sorry, honey." She got into the driver's seat and started the car.

A weekend alone. Parker tried not to sigh. She really needed to find another idea for a series. The Holy Rollers had been born as a spoof, sure, but they'd been her job for the past six years. Aside from staring at a blank computer screen and possibly watching a Gerard Butler movie or three, she had no plans.

"You should sleep over, too," Nicky suggested, practically reading her mind. "We could have popcorn. Lucy said she's making me a cake."

"The woman can bake, that's for sure," Parker said. "What kind?"

"My favorite kind. With the frosting and the coconut. I can eat seven pieces, she said."

"Did she, Nicky?" Parker cocked an eyebrow. Truth wasn't a strong point for her little guy these days.

"I think so. She maybe said five. But it was a lot."

Nicky continued to chatter about the joys that lay ahead of him for the weekend: eating cake; a sail on Ethan's boat; more cake; sleeping with Fat Mikey, Lucy and Ethan's cat; possibly taking a bath with Fat Mikey; having cake at midnight; and finding the pirate's cave that Mackerly, Rhode Island, supposedly possessed. Like his grandmothers, Nicky had been born with the gift of chat.

As she pulled onto Ocean View Drive, Parker frowned a little. The preschooler's comment about living in a mansion had struck a nerve. Lately, she'd been thinking of moving, concerned over the idea that Nicky would be thought of as the rich kid. It hadn't helped her; trust funds were hard to get past for a lot of people. But Grayhurst had been in her family for four generations, built by her great-great-grandfather at the turn of the century, and though she'd grown up in New York City, Parker had moved to Mackerly permanently after she'd gotten pregnant. She had a lot of happy memories of childhood summers—tea parties with her three cousins, learning to sail with her father. Ethan lived in town, and she'd wanted Nicky to grow up knowing both his parents, even if they'd never been married. But two people, living in a mansion in which they really only used a few rooms…it didn't feel right.

The place was gorgeous, though, she thought as they pulled into the driveway. Silhouetted against the aching blue of a June sky and bathed in the golden sun of late afternoon, the gray stone building looked like a stately grande dame gazing out contentedly over the acres of manicured lawns, flower beds and mature trees. Frickin' huge, but beautiful.

Ethan and Lucy, Parker's closest friends, were already here, holding hands as they sat on wide front steps that led from the driveway to the enormous entryway. Ethan jumped up to open her door as she pulled in.

"Daddy!" Nicky yelled, scrambling out of the car.

"How's my guy?" Ethan asked, scooping him up.

"So," Lucy said, "are congratulations in order?"

"I am officially done with the Holy Rollers. Let the good times roll."

"Good for you, Parks," Ethan said, kissing Nicky's cheek. "You proud of Mommy, Nick?"

"Yup. What's for snack? Is cake for snack?"

"No cake till after supper," Lucy said. "Unless your dad decides otherwise."

"Decide otherwise, Dad!" Nicky commanded, cantering ahead.

"Parker, do you have plans tonight?" Lucy asked. "I figured the boys could have some time alone, and we could hang out."

Saved! "I would love that! We can break open some of my father's wine and gossip about Ethan's flaws all night."

Lucy reached for his hand. "He's driving me crazy. I'm thinking marriage was a huge mistake."

"My God, it's like you're reading my mind," Ethan said. "Shall I call an attorney?" They grinned at each other.

"Guys, I just ate, okay?" Parker said, cocking an eyebrow. The tiniest swirl of envy threaded through her. Lucy and Ethan were crazy in love, and yep, Ethan was the father of Parker's child. It wasn't as freaky as it sounded. Or maybe it was, and Parker was in denial.

"We brought the itinerary for our trip," Ethan said, standing back to let the ladies go in first. "Figured you'd want a copy."

"Great!" Parker said firmly. "I'm dying to see it."

Her friends had gotten married in February, but they hadn't had a honeymoon yet; instead, they were taking Nicky to California as soon as preschool finished. San Francisco, Muir Woods, Yosemite. After that, Ethan would be occupied with the reopening of his restaurant, so the timing seemed perfect.

It was just that it was for three weeks.

Three weeks without her boy.

"Daddy!" Nicky galloped back and grabbed his father's hand. "Come see my room! I cleaned it yesterday. Mommy made me. She said it was a sty. Where pigs live. I found Darth Vader's head!" He tugged his father up the curving staircase.

Parker and Lucy went through the house to the kitchen, Parker's favorite place in the house. "I brought us sustenance," Lucy said, holding out a bag. "White-chocolate macadamia cookies."

"Satan, get thee behind me." She took out a cookie— heck yeah, still warm!—and took a bite. Bliss. "Do you know I've gained eleven pounds since last year? You hit thirty-five, and bam, all those things you ate in your twenties launch themselves onto your ass." Parker raised an eyebrow as Lucy laughed. "You'll see."

"I already see," her friend said. "So what? You're a size eight now? The horror, the horror."

"Oh, I hit double digits some time ago. Let's never speak of it again."

"You bet," Lucy said.

Marriage agreed with her, Parker thought. Lucy'd had it rough; widowed before her first anniversary years ago. Jimmy, her husband, had been Ethan's older brother; Ethan and Lucy had been college friends; the shared loss brought them closer together. About six years after Jimmy died, Ethan and Lucy had finally hooked up.

And somewhere in there, long before Ethan and Lucy had anything romantic together, he'd dated Parker for about two months. The guy had been great on paper, save for one minor detail: he'd been in love with Lucy. Parker always thought it funny that more people hadn't seen it. She broke up with him—it wasn't terribly hard; they'd already seemed more like old pals than anything—then found out six weeks later that she was pregnant. They'd shared Nicky from the beginning.

She took another cookie out of the bag and ate it. "Holy halos, these are good. Shoot me if I eat another. Where's the itinerary? It's color coded, right? Tell me it's color-coded."

"Of course it is," Lucy said, unfolding a three-page spreadsheet.

"So you'll be in San Fran for three days?"

"Four." Lucy pointed. "See? San Francisco's in pink."

"Of course." Parker bent over the paper, grateful for Lucy's organizational skills. She'd know where her son was every minute.

Ethan came into the kitchen and helped himself to a cookie. "Parker, what are your plans while we're away?" he asked. "Got anything lined up?"

"Oh, I might bop out to Nantucket and see some old pals out there. Go into the city. Maybe visit my mom. You know." She reached for another cookie.

The truth was, she hadn't made any solid plans. The idea of having her son four *thousand* miles away made her want to sleep at the airport, in case something went wrong. *Which it won't,* the Holy Rollers assured her. *Lucy and Ethan are the best! Plus, it'll be good for Nicky to see what a healthy adult relationship looks like!*

Take a bite, Parker thought. So she hadn't been in a relationship since Ethan. So she'd yet to go on a second date with anyone in five years. So what? She tended to attract emotionally unavailable men, anyway. Married men, engaged men, sociopaths, that sort of thing. Better not to date at all. The fact that she'd spent a lot of time watching gritty TNT dramas and eating Ben & Jerry's should not be construed as jealousy. It was more like a filling of the gap.

A gap that would now be uninterrupted for three weeks.

When Ethan broached the vacation idea back in March, it had seemed like a fabulous idea…Parker, on her own, free to do whatever she wanted—sleep past 5:00 a.m., for example, as Nicky was like a rooster about mornings. Find that elusive new idea for a book series. Just because Parker had been born with a trust fund didn't mean she wanted to build a life around shopping for handbags.

But as the spring progressed, she did nothing. What if something happened with Ethan's restaurant, and the trip had to be canceled? What if a new book series came to her, and she was on fire to write it, the way she'd heard other authors describe? She should probably stay home, in case something came up.

It didn't. And now with ten days to go, the time alone seemed to loom like a mine shaft. She didn't even have the Holy Rollers to keep her busy, and the fact that this even caused a twinge was deeply disturbing.

"I was hiding! No one found me! I beat you all."

Nicky charged into the kitchen with Elephant, his favorite stuffed animal.

"Nicky, you can't hide without telling us, remember?" Parker said. "It's not a game that way."

"But I always win," her son pointed out.

"He has a point," Lucy said.

Parker grinned and knelt down. "Kiss me, mister. I love you."

"I love you, too. Bye, Mom! Bye, Lucy!" He bolted out of the kitchen.

"That's my cue. See you, girls. Have fun tonight." Ethan kissed Parker on the cheek, then went out to the foyer with Lucy, where Parker presumed he would kiss her goodbye a little more intensely.

For a second, she wondered if Lucy was here out of… well…sympathy. Once, she, Ethan and Lucy had been three single friends. Now, instead of three, it was two and one.

So? Get a boyfriend, Golly advised. Since the release of the final book, it seemed to Parker that the Holy Rollers were aging in her imagination. They were depicted in the books as being about eight, but here Golly was already trying on mascara.

"Right. A boyfriend," Parker answered. "I need that like a stick in the eye."

She headed down to her father's beloved wine cellar, complete with a stone tasting room—fireplace and all. Thousands and thousands of bottles, including the bottle of Château Lafite supposedly owned by Thomas Jefferson. Or not. Harry was quite a liar.

She hadn't seen her father for a while now; the last time was when he'd held a wine-tasting dinner down here with a few sycophants from Wall Street, his omnipresent personal attorney and one of the Kennedy clan, who was up for reelection. Her orders were to bring Nicky down to be introduced, then bring him back upstairs. And stay upstairs with him. Not that she'd have stayed even if asked. Which she wasn't.

Well. Here was that nice 1994 Domaine de la Romanée-Conti Harry had bragged about. Eight grand a bottle, far less than the 1996 vintage. Surely Harry wouldn't mind if his only child and her best friend drank that, right? He had a whole case, after all. She wouldn't tell Lucy how much it cost. Lucy was a little scared of Harry. Most people were.

Parker went back upstairs, uncorked the wine and let it breathe a little. Got out some goat cheese and grapes, some of those crumbly crackers. It was so great that Lucy had decided to hang out. Maybe too great. *You've got to fill these empty hours somehow,* Spike said.

"Hush," Parker said. "You're dead to me. Go. Fly off to heaven." She poured two glasses of the wine and set the cheese plate on a tray.

"Who are you talking to?" Lucy asked, coming back to the kitchen.

"Spike."

"Oh, dear. Well, listen. The books were very, um… entertaining. And they did a lot of good for a lot of kids. To the Holy Rollers." Lucy clinked her glass against Parker's.

"May they rest in peace," Parker said, taking a healthy sip of wine.

Six years ago, Parker had been sitting in the office of a Harvard classmate, hearing for the fifty-seventh time that *Mickey the Fire Engine,* the children's story she'd written, wasn't good enough.

"I'm sorry, Parker," George had said. "It's a little familiar."

Familiar? Mickey was wonderful! And really, what the heck? She had a double degree from Harvard in literature and ethics. Half of her graduating class seemed to be writing romance novels; Parker had fifty-six rejections to her name. Make that fifty-seven. Mickey was full of sincerity and good messages—having a purpose, commitment, courage, second chances. With all the schlock that was out there, it was hard not to feel bitter.

"Got anything else?" George asked, already glancing at his watch.

"Yeah, I do," Parker said. "How's this? A band of child angels are sent to earth to teach kids about God. Right? They haven't earned their wings, though, so they roller-skate everywhere—they're the Holy Rollers. Do you love it? All they eat is angel food cake, and they live in a tree fort called Eden, and whenever a regular kid is up against a tough moral decision, in come the Holy Rollers and the preaching begins." She rolled her eyes. "It's *The Crippled Lamb* meets *The Little Rascals* meets *The Exorcist*." She sighed and stood up. "Well, thanks for your time, George. Good to see you."

"Hang on," he said.

The next week, she'd had an offer and a contract, and she and Suze, her old roomie from Miss Porter's School, had come to Grayhurst to celebrate, eat whatever Harry's chef felt like cooking them, swim in the indoor pool and laugh at life's ironies. The second night, they'd gone to Lenny's, the local bar, and there was Ethan Mirabelli, who'd flirted with them equally, despite Suze being gay and built like a professional wrestler. When Ethan had asked for Parker's phone number, Suze had given her a heavy elbow to the ribs, her way of indicating approval. And the rest, as they say, was history.

Parker and Lucy took their goodies into the front room

and were laughing over Lucy's in-laws' propensity for dropping by during certain intimate moments. "It's like they know," Lucy said. "Honestly, some days I think they have the apartment bugged."

"They might," Parker agreed. Her phone rang, and Parker glanced at the screen "Oh, speaking of difficult parents, it's my mother. I bet she has a husband for me."

"Goody! Put her on speaker so I can hear, too!" Lucy clapped like a little kid.

Parker clicked on. "Hi, Mom."

"Darling, I have someone for you!" Althea Harrington Welles Etc. Etc. sang out.

Parker pulled a face for Lucy. "Hooray! Don't even worry about us meeting—just start planning the wedding."

"Sarcasm is the lowest form of humor, haven't you heard? Anyway, his name is…oh, well, I don't remember. But his last name is Gorman, as in Senator Gorman from Virginia? His *father*. Those charges were dropped, by the way. Isn't it exciting, sweetheart? I'm thinking The Caucus Room for your engagement announcement party, the National Cathedral for your wedding, reception at the senator's home on the Chesapeake. It's stunning. I looked it up on Google Earth."

"Just tell me when to show up in the big white dress."

"Can I be matron of honor?" Lucy whispered.

"Definitely. Mom, Lucy's here."

"Lucy?"

"My best friend?"

"I'm aware, dear. Hello, sweetheart."

"Hi, Mrs.—um…Althea," Lucy said.

"Lucy, maybe you can make her take this seriously. She's so obsessed with that child, she hasn't noticed she's getting old! Honestly, my only daughter, never married."

"It's awful," Lucy concurred, grinning. "I tried to fix her up with my mute assistant at the bakery, but she said no to him, too."

"I'd rather date Jorge than a senator's kid," Parker said. "His tattoos are amazing. That one of the crucifixion? So lifelike."

"Fine. Make fun of me, girls. Oh, did you see my Facebook? I'm auditioning for *Real Housewives* out here. Maury thinks it's a great idea."

Parker mimicked a scream, then said, "That's great, Mom. So you think you might come visit next month?"

"I'm not sure yet. Maury has this thing. How's Nicky?"

"He misses you," Parker said, playing the guilt card.

"Well, you kiss that beautiful boy for me, all right? And seriously, sweetheart, think about the Gorman heir. I hate to think of you in that hideous old house, all alone except for your toddler."

"He's five and a half, Mom."

"Oh. Well, when does one stop being a toddler? Anyway, it's not my point. My point is— Oops! Maury's ringing in. Kisses to my grandson! Nice to hear your voice, Lisa. Bye, Parker! Talk soon!"

"Bye, Mom." Parker sighed. "More wine, Lisa?"

Lucy laughed. "I like your mom."

"I'd like to see her more, that's for sure," Parker grumbled.

Just as they'd finished their first glass of wine and were debating on whether to Google the Old Spice man or Ryan Gosling, they heard the crunch of tires on the long gravel driveway. "Think Nicky forgot something?" Lucy asked, going to the window and pushing back the silk drapes. "Eesh! It's your father. And his entourage."

"Oh, bugger and damn. Do we have time to hide?"

"I think *I'm* allowed to hide," Lucy said. "You probably have to say hi."

"Don't you dare go anywhere," Parker ordered.

A flare of nervousness—her trademark reaction to Daddy Dearest—flashed through her stomach. Almost automatically, she smoothed her hair and glanced down at her attire. Since she'd been at Nicky's school as Parker Welles, Author, rather than Nicky's Mom, she'd dressed up a little...beige silk shirt, ivory pencil skirt, the fantabulous leopard-print shoes. Good. A little armor.

She joined Lucy at the window and looked out. The driver of the limo opened the back door, and Harry Welles emerged into the sunlight, followed closely by Thing One and Thing Two, his minions.

Technically, Grayhurst was Harry Welles's home, though he lived in a sleek and sterile duplex on Manhattan's East Side. He only came to Rhode Island to impress clients or when he couldn't avoid a family event. He was the third generation to run Welles Financial, once a conservative financial-services firm, which Harry transformed into the kind of Wall Street playah that was often picketed by students and teachers' unions. He never traveled alone—flunkies like Thing One and Thing Two were part of Harry's makeup.

The three men came up the walkway and into the house, Thing One and Thing Two trailing at a respectful distance behind him, like castrati guards in a harem.

Her father scanned her, unsmiling.

"Hi, Harry," she said, keeping her tone pleasant. "How are you?"

"Parker. I'm glad you're here." Her father glanced at her friend. "Lucy."

"Hello, Mr. Welles. Nice to see you again."

Harry took a deep, disapproving breath—well, it

seemed disapproving. "I have something to discuss with you, Parker. Is Nicky here?"

"He's with his father this weekend. But I can run over and get him." There was that pesky, hopeful note in her voice. *If you don't like me, at least like my kid, Dad.*

"No, that's just as well. We need to discuss a few family matters." He looked pointedly at Lucy, who smiled sweetly and, bless her heart, didn't move a muscle. Harry's eyes shifted back to Parker. "How's Apollo?"

"Still alive."

"Good." Pleasantries finished, he strode down the hallway. "Join me in the study, please," he added without looking back.

"Miss Welles, your father would like you to join him in the study," said Thing Two somberly. The man held a long and meaningless title at Welles Financial, but so far as Parker could tell, his job was to echo her father and occasionally slap him on the back in admiration. He fell into step behind Harry, keeping six or seven paces behind.

"Parker. Always lovely to see you."

And then there was Thing One.

It was his customary line, usually delivered with a raised eyebrow and a smirk, and she hated it. Yes, Thing One was attractive—Harry would never hire an ugly person. The whole cheekbones and perfect haircut and bored affect...okay, okay, he was hot. But he knew it, which detracted significantly, and that line—*Parker, always lovely to see you*—blick. Add to the fact that he was a Harry-in-the-making, and his appeal went down to nil.

Thing One didn't work for Welles Financial; he was Harry's personal attorney, having replaced the original

Thing One a few years ago—why change a perfectly good nickname? He lived somewhere here in Rhode Island and did things like…well, Parker really didn't know. Occasionally she'd have to sign a paper he brought by. Otherwise, he seemed fairly useless, glib, smug and so far up her father's butt she wondered how he could see daylight.

"Thing One," she murmured with a regal nod. Miss Porter's hadn't been for nothing.

"It's James, since you can't seem to remember. I also answer to Mr. Cahill."

"Thing One suits you so much more."

He gave her a sardonic look, then turned to her friend. "Hello, Lucy," he said. He'd met her at a number of Nicky-related events—God forbid Harry come alone. "Congratulations on your wedding."

"Oh, thank you," Lucy said, looking a little surprised that he knew. Parker wasn't. Harry was hardly a doting grandfather, but he did keep tabs on Nicky's life. Or had his people keep tabs, as the case might be.

"After you, ladies," he said. He looked somber. Parker was more accustomed to seeing him in full-blown slickster mode, kissing up to her dad, glad-handing whoever was around him. A small quiver of anxiety ran through her gut. Something was…off.

As they walked down the hall, Parker rubbed the tip of her ear. It was itchy. Stress eczema, probably, brought on by dear old dad.

Harry never did any real work in the study. So far as Parker could tell, he used it to impress and intimidate his colleagues. The room was beautiful, though, filled with first-edition books, Tiffany windows, a state-of-the-art humidor and a desk the size of a pool table. Harry sat in his leather chair now, his thick gray hair perfectly cut, his suit Armani, his eyes cool. Around his arm was twined Apollo, her father's pet ball python.

Yeah. You are your pet, right? Apollo was maybe four feet in length—Parker didn't spend a lot of time looking at him, as he gave her a hearty case of the heebie-jeebies. Nicky, though...in case living in a mansion wasn't cool enough, he loved to impress his friends with Apollo, whose glass cage, it must be noted, was always locked. Didn't want to have a python slithering around the house, no indeed. The gardener was charged with feeding him and cleaning his cage.

"It's so Dr. Evil," Lucy whispered, giving Parker's hand a squeeze. She went to a window seat and curled up there, nearby, but at a distance.

"So, Harry," Parker said, that nervousness flaring again. She sat in one of the three leather chairs in front of the desk. Things One and Two stood to one side, like soldiers at a funeral. "How are things? Are you here for the weekend?"

"No. And things have been better. Is my grandson almost finished with school?"

"Yes. Then he's going to California with his dad and Lucy."

Harry glanced at Lucy. "Glad to hear it."

"Glad to hear it," echoed Thing Two, scratching his stomach. Parker waited for Thing One to chime in, too, but he remained silent, his arms folded.

Harry gazed at his pet, then kissed the snake's head. Parker tried not to flinch. That snake would make some very attractive shoes. Otherwise, he was her rival for Harry's attention. Well, hardly her rival. Apollo was ahead by miles. Her father looked at his minions. "Gentlemen, have a seat."

Thing One and Thing Two obeyed, taking the seats

on either side of her. She glanced at Lucy, who gave her a nervous smile of solidarity. There was definitely something in the air, and for the life of her, Parker felt a little bit as if she was about to be sentenced.

She wasn't far off.

"Well, there's no easy way to say this," her father said, stroking his snake.

"No easy way," Thing Two murmured.

Harry didn't look up from the snake. "We're broke. You have to move."

CHAPTER TWO

JAMES CAHILL, also known as Thing One, closed his eyes. Granted, Parker Welles was not his favorite person, but even so. Hearing it put so baldly…uncool. Her friend gave a little squeak. Otherwise, there was silence.

He glanced at the princess. She didn't move for a second, then tucked her hair behind one ear, the tip of which was growing red. Otherwise, she just sat there, her profile to him. She crossed her legs. Said legs were flawless—long, smooth, perfect. Not that he was allowed to look at them—she'd put him in his place quite a while ago, and yes, she was being informed of her financial ruin, but man, those legs were incredible.

"Broke?" she said, then cleared her throat.

"That's right," Harry answered, petting the snake. "You've heard of broke, I assume?"

Now, James knew that Apollo was some kind of security blanket for Harry; easier to break the news to his only child if he had something else to look at. Their whole vibe was always wicked uncomfortable; James hated having to go to Welles family events, but if Harry invited him, he'd come along. It was the least he could do, given what Harry had done for him. Didn't make things fun, though.

Parker took a deep breath, her breasts rising under her silky shirt. Nice. *Focus, idiot.* The perils of being a straight guy in the room with a beautiful woman. Even one who loved putting him down.

"What happened, Dad?" she asked, her voice more gentle than James had ever heard it. And "Dad." He couldn't say he'd ever heard her call him anything but Harry in the six years he'd been working for the guy.

Harry shifted Apollo to his other arm. "Just a bump in the road. For now, there's no more money."

"No more—"

"James, fill her in."

"James, why don't you fill her in?" Vernon echoed, parrotlike.

Right. Time to earn that salary. "Okay, well, it's a little complicated," he began.

She gave him a razor blade of a look. "Try me. I'm a Harvard grad."

So much for her soft edges. And God forbid he forget that her blood ran crimson. James himself had gone to Boston University; once, he'd flirted with a Harvard girl and told her he went to BU. "Where's that?" she'd asked, because if you went to Harvard, other schools didn't exist.

She had, however, gone home with him.

"Magna cum laude," Parker added.

"Should I kneel?" he asked. Harry snorted, and Parker's mouth tightened. Not cool. James hadn't meant to make it seem as if it was boys vs. girl here. Even if it kind of was.

Parker's friend cleared her throat. "Um, Parks, you want me to, uh, get started on dinner?"

"I'd rather you stayed," Parker said. Her tone was locked into rich-girl drawl. "Please continue, Thing One."

Yes, Majesty. "It seems that Harry got mixed up in an insider-trading deal."

She looked back at her father, who was stroking his snake. "Oh, Harry."

"Let him finish," Harry said, not looking away from Apollo.

James shifted in his seat. "Harry made a sizable investment in a company on which he'd had inside information—"

"I know what insider trading is," she said.

"—and that was obviously unethical, but more to the point, the results weren't what the information promised." Okay, here came the hard part. "To cover the losses to investors, your father needed to, ah, liquidate certain assets."

She blinked, and James felt a pang of sympathy for her as realization dawned in her eyes. "Which assets, Harry?" she asked, her voice calm.

Harry looked at the python. "Your trust fund."

She looked at her hands, her mouth tight. "Granddad set that up for me."

"Well, I've been managing it most of your life," Harry snapped. There was a pause, and the grandfather clock in the corner ticked ominously. "Nicky's, too," Harry added in a softer voice.

James couldn't help but wince. It had to hurt, hearing your father had sold you down the river. Your kid, too.

"You stole your grandson's trust fund, Harry?" Her voice was harsher now.

Harry's lips pressed together. "I'm the administrator of the Welles family trust, Parker, as you're well aware. I liquidated it temporarily."

"Liquidated it temporarily," Vernon echoed, smiling like an idiot. James had almost forgotten he was here.

"*How* temporarily?"

"Yo!" came a voice. A shaggy-haired guy wearing overalls stood in the doorway. "Hey there, gang, sorry. Is this the Welles place?"

"It is," Harry said.

"It's awesome, man! Really nice! So, like, we're the movers? Gonna start in the game room, okay?"

"Billiard room," Harry muttered.

The mover laughed. "Totally! Colonel Mustard in the billiard room with the candlestick! Dude, is that a snake? Nice! Okay, better get going. This place is frickin' huge! See you later!"

Parker's mouth was open. "They're taking stuff already? I— Wow, Harry. You don't mess around."

Her face was pale now, and James wished he could, well, make this easier for her somehow. "Parker, anything that you bought for you or Nicky or the house is yours. Everything else, I'm afraid, falls under Harry's assets, which the Feds have seized. The investigator is aware that you're living here, and you have a little time to, ah, pack."

"My God." She squeezed her little finger and glanced at her pal, who was frozen.

"It'll be okay," Lucy murmured automatically.

Harry cleared his throat. "Obviously, Parker, having these vultures pick over our belongings is not my choice. I'll get everything back."

"Really," she said faintly.

"Eventually. I'm a little…constrained for the immediate future."

"A little constrained indeed," Vernon said.

That was one word for it. James rubbed his forehead. Wicked headache coming on.

"So." Parker shook her head. "About my trust fund,

and Nicky's. Don't you need my signature to just…empty it? There must be something left."

Nope. There was nothing, and Harry had only needed James himself to file the paperwork. Poor planning on her part, that was for sure. At any time since her eighteenth birthday, she could've taken full control of that money. When her son was born, same deal.

She never had.

"Your signature wasn't required," Harry said. "Nor was your consent."

"Your consent was not required," Vern said, nodding cheerfully. There was a crash and a curse from somewhere in the house.

Parker took a deep breath "Wow, Harry. So it's *gone?* That was a lot of money."

"Yes, Parker!" Harry barked. "I'm sorry to say you'll have to make do for a while. Until I can recover some losses."

"How long will that take, do you think?"

Again, Harry's eyes sought out James.

Shit again.

"That's undetermined right now," James said. "Your father is being sentenced Monday morning."

Parker's hand went to her mouth. "Oh, Dad." Twice in one day. "Can I do anything?"

"Like what, Parker?" he asked.

"I—I don't know."

"I'll be fine. I have a great team."

"A great team!" Vernon agreed.

Lucy got up from the window seat and went to Parker's side. Took her hand. Good girl, James thought. Parker would be needing her friends, and so far as he could tell, Lucy here and the Paragon of Perfection otherwise known as Ethan Mirabelli were her closest. Or so it seemed from those dreaded family events he'd attended.

"It's really nothing," Harry said. "I'm not even sure I'll have to serve any real time."

James was sure. Oh, yeah. Harry was looking at somewhere around five years. His case wasn't the clusterfuck that some Wall Streeters had been involved in of late, but it was a clear-cut case. And after Bernie Madoff and the Occupy movement, there wasn't a judge in the country foolish enough to go easy on a case like this.

"As I said, you'll have to move," Harry added. "I'm hoping you'll take Apollo."

You know, James had to wonder sometimes what the hell was wrong with Harry. He loved the guy, yeah. But he was a pretty big idiot around his daughter. And yep, here it came.

Parker's voice hardened. "Take *Apollo?* You're worried about your snake, Harry? How about your *grandson?* The one you robbed? Where should I take your *grandson,* Harry?"

"I'm sure his father would take him."

"I'm not living away from my son!" she exclaimed. Her ears were burning red now.

"You can both live with us, Parker," Lucy said. "We'll figure something out."

"No! Lucy, thank you. But no. Harry, Ethan and Lucy just got married. I'm not moving in with them! What about your apartment? You could sell that and—"

"Parker," James said as gently as he could. "The SEC has seized all your father's assets. The apartment, this house, the place in Vermont…everything."

She glanced out the window. "There goes the Steinway. Holy crap." She swallowed, then looked at James, her expression bleak. "When do I have to be out?"

"They'll leave your rooms for last," he said. "You have till the end of the month."

"This month?"

"This month," Vernon confirmed.

She squeezed her pinkie again. "Okay," she said, biting her lip. "Well, that's... I was actually thinking it might not be a bad idea to move to a smaller place."

"Smaller place. Not a bad idea," Vernon echoed, and James resisted the urge to duct-tape his mouth shut.

"Let me go call Ethan, okay, Parker?" Lucy said.

"Okay," Parker said distantly.

"Look," Lucy said more firmly. "You're not alone in this. Okay? I have some money put aside, and you'd do the same for me. We're family."

Harry made a rude snorting noise.

"Shut up, Harry," Lucy snapped. "You should be grateful she has friends when her own father does this to her."

Score one for Team Lucy.

"Thanks, Luce." Parker said. "But it's fine. I'll be fine. But sure, go call Ethan. Fill him in."

Whereupon the Paragon would no doubt charge up the driveway on his white horse and rescue the mother of his child. Which, no doubt, Parker would love. James sighed.

Harry was staring at the python, and James thought, not for the first time, that if he gave his daughter as much attention as he gave the snake, things would be a lot less chilly in the Welles family.

"So my trust fund's gone," she said. "The stock market's not too bad these days. How's my portfolio doing?"

Harry still didn't look at her. "Anything you had through Welles Financial is now unavailable."

"Unavailable?"

"I'll get it back, Parker!" Harry snapped. "You have what's in your checking account at the moment. Do you have anything in savings?"

"No! You told me the stock market was better than… well, what am I saying? You're a felon. I took advice from a felon. Good God. I guess I should've stuffed some cash into the mattress." Parker gave a shaky laugh.

Clearly the news was catching up with her. She ran a hand through her long hair, the strands falling back into place. Smooth, silky hair that— *Been there, worshipped that,* his conscience chided.

"I can believe you took my money," she said. "But I can't believe you stole Nicky's. That's really low, Harry. Even for you."

"It was necessary," he barked.

"For what? For covering your ass?"

James held up his hands. "Okay, okay, let's just…let's try to calm down. This is a lot to take in. Your father made a mistake—"

"How much did you lose, Thing One?" she asked abruptly.

James hesitated.

"Oh. I get it," she said, and if looks could kill, James would be lying in a bottomless puddle of blood right about now. "So you knew. Well. Do go on."

"You have six thousand dollars in your checking account, and since that's in your name only, it's free and clear."

"I have to make a phone call," Harry said, unwinding his pet and putting him back in the case. "Vernon, come with me, please. I need the information on the drug-company stock. Parker, James can fill you in on the rest."

"There's more? Are you going to beat me with a rubber hose, Thing One? I can't wait."

James waited till the study door closed, leaving him alone with Parker. And Apollo.

Nope, not alone. The mover was back. "Okay if we start on the dining room? Packing up that china's gonna take a while. It's really nice! Expensive, I bet."

"Go for it," Parker said. When he was gone again, she looked at James. "Is Harry really going to jail?" she asked, and James had to say, it wasn't the question he imagined she'd ask.

"Yes. He went to the D.A. and confessed this morning, so that's why it hasn't been in the news yet. Monday morning, though…"

She gave him an odd look. "He confessed? That doesn't seem like him."

James looked at his hands. "Yeah." There was that ticking noise again.

Parker sighed. "So, all this other stuff…Granddad's boat and the paintings and Grandma's china…it doesn't belong to us anymore?"

He turned to face her. "Anything in this house that you personally bought stays with you—your clothes, artwork, your car, anything you bought for your son—but the rest will go to refund what Harry's clients lost."

"So I have no savings, no portfolio, no trust fund, and we have to move. Is that it in a nutshell?"

"Harry was able to secure another five thousand in cash for you." James reached into his briefcase—a gift from Harry—and handed her an envelope, which she took automatically. "You have some jewelry that's yours, right?"

"I guess so," she said. James knew exactly what she had, as it was listed on the insurance forms. Nothing spectacular—some aging pearl necklaces, a few antique stickpins from her grandmother. All in all, maybe worth another couple grand. Parker wasn't the type to drape herself in diamonds or redecorate or buy a sports car—she drove a Volvo Cross Country that was a good five or six years old. She didn't even travel that much. She was more like the Welles family of yore—quieter, old-money New England wealth.

Harry was the new breed—make sure the world knew how much you had by spending every cent.

And even though she'd handed him his nuts on a platter a few years ago, he couldn't help feeling really shitty about the whole situation. "I know this is a lot to take in," he said gently, and she cut her eyes over to him. Yikes.

"I suppose there was no way you could've given me a heads-up, Thing One."

"No. I'm sorry. Attorney-client privilege."

"Hope that lets you sleep at night."

"Moving on," James continued, "you do own the house in Maine."

"Which house in Maine?"

Rich people. Honestly. "Your great-aunt Julia Harrington left you a house when she died six years ago. Ring a bell?"

She frowned. "Oh, my gosh, right. I was just about to have Nicky when she died. Where is it? I never did make it up there."

James kept his expression neutral. How do you forget about inheriting a house? "The house is in Gideon's Cove," he said, handing Parker the folder. "North of Bar Harbor." He knew the town…or he did once. His bachelor uncle owned a bar up there, and James had spent a couple of summers with him as a teenager.

"So I could sell that, right?" Parker asked, her expression brightening a little. "Sell the house and have a nest egg?"

"You could," James said. He didn't know which house was hers, though he had a copy of the deed. If he remembered, Shoreline Drive had some nice places on it.

"Fine." She was quiet for a minute. "I'll go up there when Ethan and Lucy take Nicky on vacation, slap on some paint and get it listed with a real-estate agent."

"Sounds like a plan," he said. His own experience was that life was rarely that easy, but for her sake, he hoped it was.

"You reminded her about the house?" Harry asked, striding back into the room.

"Yes, sir," he answered.

"Good. Parker, James knows the area. He'll go with you and check out the property." Right. She'd love that. God save him.

"He'll go with you," Vernon agreed.

"No, he won't," Parker said. "But thanks all the same, Thing One."

"Don't be foolish," Harry said sharply. "You'll need help."

Parker turned to James, her eyes about as warm as Apollo's. "Thing One, my father is so very kind to offer your services, but no thank you."

"Fine," Harry said. "Do whatever you want. You always do. We'll be in touch."

"Harry," she began, standing up. There was the pinkie squeeze again. "Are you sure I can't do anything for you?"

"I'll be fine." He flashed her a toothy smile that was so far from sincere it made James wince. Then Harry strode back out, looking every bit the master of Wall Street he used to be, Vernon murmuring on his heels.

And James, he well knew, was expected to follow. He stood up, then turned to Parker, who was staring at the snake. "I'm really sorry about all this, Parker," he said. "I'll do whatever I can to help."

She gave him a look they must've taught her at her fancy prep school. *I'm sorry, and you are...?* "Save the ass kissing for my father, Thing One."

Sigh. Some people never changed. "I mean it."

"So do I."

Okay, enough with the princess act. "I *am* good for some things," he said. "As you might remember. Carpentry is one of them."

"Really. How fascinating. Bye-bye, Thing One. And tell my father I'm not taking that snake."

James stood there another minute, torn between guilt—his favorite pastime—the desire to help her in some way and the fact that he could see down her shirt a little bit from here. Fantastic view.

You don't take anything seriously, do you? his father's voice demanded in his head.

Hard to deny. "I loved the last Holy Rollers book, by the way," he added.

"Then your IQ is even lower than I thought."

He couldn't help a smile. Parker looked away. "Call me and let me know what happens on Monday," she said.

"Will do." He picked up his briefcase and turned back to her. "See you in Maine."

She shot him an icy look. "Not if I see you first. The gun laws are pretty clear about intruders on private property." He said nothing. "Go, Thing One. Your master awaits."

James obeyed. There was nothing else he could do.

For now, anyway.

CHAPTER THREE

IN THE TWO WEEKS since her father's bombshell, Parker thought she'd done a pretty good job of holding it together. She was a mother…you don't get to walk around cursing like Job or crying. And Lucy had been amazing that first weekend, helping her through the initial shock, going through the house, determining what could reasonably be called Parker's as the movers tagged and wrapped her family's belongings.

Not a lot was Parker's outright. Her Mac, of course. A few pieces of furniture, a couple of paintings, a few little things for the house—a vase, some throw pillows, nothing tremendously valuable.

"You know I'll help with money," Lucy'd said at least fifteen times. "I have Jimmy's life insurance, and—"

"I appreciate that," Parker said. "But you know what? It's okay. It's shocking, sure, but Ethan's got a nice bit tucked away for Nicky's college, and I can flip the house in Maine and have a little money and write some more books. Or get a job doing something else."

She smiled firmly, trying to forget that she'd A) ignored her father's advice to major in economics and had instead double-majored in two such ridiculously unemployable fields that she actually woke up covered in a cold sweat one night—English was bad enough, but Ethics? *Ethics?*—and B) she hadn't had a new idea for a book series since the hideous Holy Rollers had been conceived. It was *such* bad timing that she'd given the little suckers their wings and halos. She could've milked them forever.

But honestly, after the initial shock, it was a little hard to feel as if a great injustice had befallen her. For thirty-five years, she'd had more privilege and wealth than ninety-eight percent of the world. When she'd watched the footage of the Occupy Wall Street gang, back before she was broke, she couldn't help thinking they had a point.

And now the point had been made. Now, she was normal. Better than normal, according to Lucy—she had a little over eleven grand in her bank account, no debt and a house on the coast of Maine. By Paris Hilton standards, she was destitute; by normal-people standards, sitting kind of pretty.

"I'm going to miss coming over here," Lucy said as she folded a sweater. "Guess I'll need to find another friend with a mansion."

Parker smiled, appreciating Lucy's attempt to keep things light, not to mention her help at packing. Lucy was very organized. "Good luck with that."

"How does Nicky seem to be doing?"

"Well, you know how he is. One minute, he thinks it's great that we're moving, the next he forgets why we're packing. I don't think he's really wrapped his brain around the idea that we won't be coming back to live here. But I was thinking of moving anyway. It's easier than explaining why my father's in jail."

"He told Ethan that Grandpa Harry was in a time-out."

"Yeah, that's how I put it. He had to go away and think about playing by the rules and being greedy." She winced. "Nicky still took it pretty hard. But Harry'll probably be out on good behavior and all that in a couple years." Years. Crikey.

"And how are you doing with that, Parker? I know you and your father aren't really close, but still."

"Yeah. But still." She gave Lucy a quick look. "I don't know. I feel bad for him on the one hand. On the other, he deserved it. Then again, I've lived off family money all my life, and I never really looked at where it came from. So anyway, it all belongs to the Feds now."

"It must be hard, though."

Parker swallowed. It was hard. The people from the SEC had been here last week, and they'd let her keep a few sentimental things—a model of a duck that her grandfather had carved, the little white vase her grandmother had let her fill with flowers from the garden. "Well, I did snag a few bottles of wine from the cellar."

"Priorities."

"Exactly. And it was nothing really expensive."

"So tell me about your cottage in Maine. Am I wrong to think Bush compound? Sort of like this place, but with gray shingles?"

Parker snorted. "I don't know. I only met my great-aunt a couple of times. You know my mother, always dragging me off to a new stepfather. When we did see family, someone was always having a nervous breakdown. There were no picnics, no bonfires, no uncles who dressed up as Santa. One of my few memories of Aunt Julia is that she told me to start smoking or I'd get fat. I was probably about thirteen at the time." She gave Lucy a rueful smile.

"Jeesh, Parks! How come you're so normal?"

"I'm probably not," she admitted, tossing some socks into her suitcase.

"So you barely see your relatives, but you inherit their summer homes."

"Yes. It's our own form of guilt and family obligation and to make up for decades of bitterness, alcoholism and neglect."

"Weren't you curious about the house?"

Parker shrugged. "Well, I was nine months pregnant when Julia died. Then that colic—remember? I could barely say my own name for six months. The truth is, I kind of forgot about it." Parker zipped up a suitcase. "I did a Google search of the address, but all I got was a spot on a map; no satellite pictures available. Apparently I have a second or third cousin up there, according to my mom. I left a message on what I think is her machine."

"Well, it's great that you'll have someone close by."

"I know. I did see pictures of the town, and it's really pretty, Luce. Like a postcard…lobster boats and pine trees. And I do know the house has a water view, so how bad can it be?"

"Right. I bet it's beautiful."

"So I'll zip up there, spend a little money, flip it, zip back down here, find a place for us to live, and we should be all set before Nicky starts kindergarten." She folded a cashmere hoodie. "It'll be fun. It'll be good for me."

"And what about a new book series? Think you'll get some writing done up there?"

The million-dollar question. "I hope so. I figured my father's crimes would hurt sales, right? But no. The opposite, and now my publisher is all over me for another idea before the notoriety fades. Can you believe that?"

"Well, that's good, I guess. That you're wanted."

"Yeah." It *was* good; it was just a little disheartening to picture writing another sappy series, rather than that elusive, noble, touching *Charlotte's Web* kind of masterpiece she'd been hoping to pull off. *Attitude is everything,* the Holy Rollers chided. "I'm really excited to get started."

That's better! the HRs cheered. They'd aged to about twelve and giggled a lot these days.

"So I was thinking," Lucy said, shooting her a little smile. "No kid for three weeks…you should have a fling."

Parker snorted.

"No, no! It'd be great! A summertime romance with some hot sailing dude or a fisherman. I'm thinking George Clooney in *The Perfect Storm*—"

"His character dies."

"You can do a little swimming, eat some lobster, do whatever else they do in Maine, but live a little, Parker. Find a summer hottie and get it on, girl! What do you say?"

"I cannot believe I'm hearing this from you, of all people. Princess Purity turned pimp."

"Listen, you're the one who admitted to watching Neil Patrick Harris's Emmy speech eight times."

"I'm up to eleven, actually. And I'm convinced I could turn him straight."

"Yeah, okay, we all have that dream. But a fling would be great, Parks! Come on. Who was the last guy you slept with, Parker?"

"No comment."

"Oh, crikey! Was it Ethan?"

Parker winced. "Nope. No, it wasn't."

"It was. Oh, my gosh. Ethan, who is now married to your best friend." Lucy grabbed another sweater and folded it. "That's both sick and sad."

"Please stop pimping me. It's so unlike you."

"Right. Remember that singles thing you made me go to last year? Who was pimping whom?"

"What's pimping?" Nicky burst into the room.

"Yes, ladies, what is it?" Ethan asked, raising an eyebrow.

"It's a grown-up thing," Parker said. "It involves, um, baby making."

"Gross," Nicky said.

"Exactly," Parker agreed, looking at Lucy with a smile.

Fling, Lucy mouthed.

"Daddy couldn't find me," Nicky said, jumping on the bed and rolling amid Parker's clothes like a puppy. "I was in the pantry, and he couldn't find me."

"I didn't know we were playing, Nick," Ethan said. "You're supposed to answer when I call."

"Okay. Sorry." Her son began trampolining on the bed. "Guess what, Mom?" *Bounce!* "Daddy says—" *bounce* "—our plane leaves—" *bounce* "—in four—" *bounce* "—more—" *bounce* "—hours!" He jumped off the bed with a thud. "And I might get some peanuts from the waitress."

Parker's throat tightened. She ran a hand through Nicky's hair, which was still baby-soft. *Don't change too much while you're gone.* "You'll have so much fun, sweetheart."

"I know it. You should come, too."

"Well, I'll be up in Maine, so I'll have a vacation, too. And Daddy will bring you up there when you get back. It's really pretty. We can eat lobster. Maybe go sailing."

"Okay. Kiss Elephant." He held up his stuffed animal for a smooch. Parker obeyed, then gathered her son in her arms, breathing in his salty little-boy smell.

"I love you, Nicky," she whispered.

"I love you, too, Mommy," he said. Then he wriggled out of her arms, seeming to see her suitcases for the first time. "We won't live here ever again?" he said, his voice quavering.

"No, honey. I'm sorry."

"Then I want a house just like it."

"We'll have a smaller place. Like Daddy and Lucy's."

"I want *this* house. I'm gonna come back here and live!"

"Nicky, pal," Ethan said, "this house is really big. It's meant for lots and lots of people. But the new house will be yours and Mommy's. And you can help pick it out, right, Parker?"

"Definitely." She gave Ethan a grateful look.

"I want it to be purple." Nick folded his arms across his chest.

"I love purple," Parker said.

Ethan glanced at his watch and gave her an apologetic look. "We really should get going."

This was it. Three weeks—twenty-three days, if one was counting, and Parker definitely was—without her son. She picked him up again and held him tight, relishing his strong little arms around her neck. "I love you, Nick. I'll call you every night. And we can use Skype."

"I'll call *you* every night," Nicky said. "And every morning. And in the daytime, too."

"Anytime you want," Ethan said. "Lucy, can you take Nicky down to the car?"

"You bet." Lucy hugged Parker. "Love you." She lowered her voice to a whisper. "Fling."

"Sure," Parker said. "You guys have fun, okay? It's the trip of a lifetime."

"Bye, Mom! Elephant says bye, too!"

"Bye, Elephant! Bye, Nicky! I love you!"

Then Lucy took Nicky by the hand and led him down the long hall. *Don't worry, Parker,* chimed the Holy Rollers. *No one can replace you! You're the mom!*

"Parker." Ethan took the shirt she was folding—and folding and folding, apparently—and put it on the bed. "I know this hasn't been easy. And you've been a rock. But I know it's been…a lot."

His eyes were so kind and nice that Parker could feel her own filling. Dang it. "It's a little overwhelming," she whispered.

"I know. But you're not alone in this. I love you, Lucy loves you, you gave my parents their only grandchild, and they think you walk on water. You have all of us." He kissed her forehead. "Especially me."

Not for the first time, Parker wished things had been different with her and Ethan. The guy was damn near perfect. "I do know that, Ethan. And I appreciate it. Things aren't that bad, really. It's just been…fast. But I'll flip the house up there and we'll be fine."

He looked at her another minute. "Okay." He squeezed her shoulders and let her go. "I'll call you when we land."

"Thanks."

"Have fun in Maine."

"I will. I really will. It'll build character."

"You have plenty of character." With that, he hugged her again and left. A minute later, she heard the echoing thud of the front door closing.

Alone in an eight-thousand-square-foot house.

Once, when she was seven, she'd roller-skated down the big hallways and into the vast kitchen, where Bess, the cook, had given her a slice of rhubarb pie. Most of the year, the Welles family—Althea, Harry and Parker—had lived in New York, in an apartment on the Upper East Side, but Grayhurst had always felt more like home.

When she was very small, her grandfather had still been alive, and she had some cherished memories of a man with a deep voice who smelled like Wintergreen Life Savers. For a few magical weeks each summer, they'd come here and be together, Harry around for dinner, Althea making sand castles on the beach. Her three cousins, all girls, would come over to play, and they'd spy on the grown-ups, and make forts in the endless rooms of Grayhurst. Her dad had taught her to sail, and she and Althea played tennis after dinner.

But when she was ten, her parents divorced, and summer was never the same. Harry became a stranger, and Althea married Clay, the first of Parker's stepfathers, less than a year afterward. Per court order, she'd visit Rhode Island for a week or two in the summer, sometimes foisted off on her aunts, then spending a torturous few days alone with Harry, who'd work most of the time. Then it would be off to whatever summer program was the in thing that year—a summer at sea, another at the Sorbonne, one in Scotland with other daughters of rich people. And don't get her wrong. She'd had some great times, seen some beautiful places.

But those summers here, at Grayhurst, before she realized what kind of man her father was, before her mother had become a serial trophy wife…those summers had been the best. Her fifth birthday party had been here, and there'd been a white pony. When she was nine or so, she'd had a sleepover, and the gardener had rigged up a screen in front of the indoor pool, and Parker and five friends had bobbed around on inner tubes and watched *Jaws*.

And this was where she'd brought Nicky home after he was born. She'd rocked him in her grandmother's

Morelock chair and looked out at the sea. How could she not love the place where she learned how to be a mother?

Now Nicky's beautiful room would be someone else's. The dining room where they'd once tied a rope and played Tarzan, the topiary in the back where they'd had so many lunches, the back parlor where she and Lucy had spent many a girls' night, laughing until they cried... all someone else's.

Well. Self-pity wasn't going to get her car packed up. The moving truck was coming to take her clothes and most of the stuff to storage—Nicky's bunk bed, the big white sofa she had in her office, the collection of Holy Rollers books in their many translations. The photo albums and framed pictures of Nicky's artwork.

All her life, Parker knew, she'd had the cushion of not just a trust fund, but the security of being a Welles of the Rhode Island Welleses. John Kennedy had once sailed his boat here and stayed for dinner, as he and her grandmother were childhood friends. E. B. White had played tennis on Grayhurst's courts with her grandfather.

Now, for the first time, Parker was truly on her own. It was oddly thrilling.

She'd use what she needed to spiff up the house in Maine and turn a cushy profit—what, maybe a couple hundred grand? Not bad for a woman who was broke.

And you know what else? Maybe Lucy was right. Lady Land had been long ignored. Maybe a little summer romance would be a good thing. Heck yeah! She had twenty-three days on her own. Might as well live a little.

But now, she'd go downstairs, uncork a bottle of her father's cheapest. She'd take it out onto the back terrace and enjoy Grayhurst's view for the last time. And maybe, since no one else was around, she'd have a good cry. And skate down the halls one more time.

CHAPTER FOUR

AFTER EIGHT HOURS in the car, Parker finally saw what she was looking for: a white sign surrounded by pansies and the words *Welcome to Gideon's Cove, Population 1,411.* "Finally," she muttered, slowing the car. Maine was flipping enormous, and one didn't really understand *how* enormous until one had to drive the entire length of the thing. But she was here at last. Hopefully, in a few moments, she'd be opening the door of her inheritance, pouring a glass of wine and running a hot bath. *You deserve it!* cheeped the female Holy Rollers, who were much more in tune with this kind of thing than the boys.

"You said it, sisters," Parker muttered. She'd been talking to them the entire drive. Just one more reason to be grateful she was here.

The downtown of Gideon's Cove consisted of a tiny library, two churches, a town hall and about four storefronts. A bar with a neon Bud sign in the window. There was a cheerful little diner; it seemed to be the only restaurant in town. Parker grimaced. It was cute, but not exactly a tourist mecca—no T-shirt stores, no ice-cream shop, no fried-clam shack. How robust could the real-estate market be in a town with 1,400 people?

The road ended at the harbor parking lot. Parker pulled into a space and looked out at the view. Okay, yes, it was beautiful here. The cove was edged with a ragged line of gray rock and pine trees, the water a deep cobalt accented by choppy waves. A small fleet of lobster boats—six or eight of them—bobbed in the darkening blue of the evening. Beyond the cove was the Atlantic, and clouds tinged with pink and lavender rested on the horizon.

Gorgeous. And somewhere close by was her house.

The Harringtons had been wealthy, too—not like the Welles family, but sedately comfortable. Althea had gone to Bryn Mawr and grew up in Westchester; Aunt Julia had been from the Boston side of the family, and had lived in a musty but respectable town house. Parker had only visited a few times, so her memory was dim. A house on the coast of Maine…surely it had potential.

Unfortunately, her GPS didn't acknowledge the existence of Shoreline Drive. Wouldn't hurt to find someone to ask.

Parker got out of the car, her lower back creaking a little, stretched and inhaled deeply. Then gagged. Bugger! What was that *smell?* Sure, Gideon's Cove was a fishing village, but there was fish…and then there was *this*. Briny, fishy and rotten, thick enough to practically taste. It must have had something to do with the corrugated-metal building past the harbormaster's building.

A few more breaths, and the smell wasn't quite so repulsive. The wind was stiff and salty, so at least there was that. And though it was a beautiful evening, no one seemed to be around. Seagulls hovered on the breeze, and waves slapped against the white hulls of the boats. The wind shushed through the pines. Farther away, Parker heard some music, a baby crying. Mostly, though, it was quiet.

Aha. There was someone—a man motoring in from one of the lobster boats. He pulled up to the dock, jumped neatly out and tied off the boat, then came up the ramp toward her. Perfect. A local who could give her directions. "Hi," Parker called, waving in case he missed her.

He stopped in front of her, then nodded.

Oh, Mommy! The word *fling* jumped rather forcefully to mind. She glanced at his left hand. No ring. Perfect. Lucy had urged her to have a fling, and the gods of Fling had sent this guy. How was that for convenience? Black hair. Light blue eyes. Laugh lines. Welcome to Gideon's Cove indeed.

He didn't say a word. Just looked at her. Perhaps he was mute.

"Hi there," she said again, sticking out her hand. "I'm Parker. I'm visiting for a few weeks."

He nodded again and shook her hand briefly, his hand strong and calloused. "Malone."

Dead sexy, just the one name. "Nice to meet you."

He didn't answer. Which was fine—he didn't have to speak. He could simply stand there, looking hot. Okay, but yes, it was going on a little long. So. How to proceed? Truth was, Parker was a little—very—out of practice on the boy-girl front. Too bad Fling Material didn't say, *Hey there, blondie, welcome to town. Let me buy you a drink and show you around! Maybe we could have a fling, because I find you very attractive.*

Yeah, no. He didn't seem to be the talking type. But he hadn't left, either. "So," she said. "Right. Well, I'm looking for my aunt's house. Julia Harrington. She lived on Shoreline Drive."

He didn't say anything.

"Do you happen to know where that is?"

"Ayuh." He said nothing more for a second, then, realizing perhaps more was required, cleared his throat. "About a mile out of town, that side of the cove." Malone pointed. "Take a left out of the lot, then a quick right, and there you are."

His voice was rough, and he dropped his *R*s even more than they did in Rhode Island. It worked. "Thanks," Parker said, her voice perhaps a little breathy. *Go ahead, ask him out,* Spike advised. *He's a guy. He'll say yes.*

Her ears were itchy. "Well, um, I'm sure I'll see you around. Small town and all." *That was not asking him out.* "And thank you, Malone was it? Malone." *Still not asking him out.* "So...I'll see you around?" Jeesh. So out of practice.

But no, no, looky here. He was smiling a little. Heck yeah! Maybe she wasn't so bad at this after all.

"Good night," he said.

Nope. She did suck. She would've said good-night, but he was already walking away.

That was terrible, the Holy Rollers said in disappointment. They were right. She was very bad at asking men out. This hadn't always been the case, but it was sure true now, wasn't it? Tall, Dark and Silent had simply appeared, all tousled and manly with those rough and calloused hands that, come on, probably knew their way around the female anatomy, because really. How many gay lobstermen were there?

"All right, settle down," she told herself, getting back into her car. Talking aloud, the writer's affliction. "Let's get home before we start jumping the locals."

Home. That had a nice sound to it, yes indeed.

Julia's house was at 97 Shoreline Drive, and Parker drove slowly, checking the numbers on mailboxes and doors. The road wasn't much wider than a driveway. There were a few very nice houses—two Victorians, a Greek Revival—but they grew smaller and more sparse as the road curved with the rocky shoreline, leaving

behind the snug little town surprisingly fast. The last
house was 66 Shoreline Drive; otherwise, there was nothing, other than a decrepit little shed that appeared to be
about to fall into the ocean.

Hang on a sec. The road led to a small peninsula that
jutted out into the cove, and Parker glimpsed a clearing
in the pine trees. Heart rate kicking up a few levels, she
wound down the road, then slowed to a stop. This had
to be it; it was the end of Shoreline Drive. An iron gate
barred the driveway, flanked by stone posts and a small,
tasteful sign—Welcome to the Pines at Douglas Point.
Number 66 was a ways back; this had to be 97.

Heck yeah!

She turned off the engine and got out of the car. Lucy
had joked about the Bush compound, but Parker wasn't
sure the Bushes could afford this place. The house was
gorgeous. Smaller, much smaller, than Grayhurst, but
absolutely stunning. The driveway led up through the
pines to what had to be a fifteen- or twenty-room stone
house. Slate-shingled roof. Iron lampposts. Though the
light was fading from the sky, Parker could see mul-
lioned windows galore, huge beds of white and red impatiens, hydrangeas, mountain laurel and ivy…the place
was like a park! Good Lord, in ten minutes, she could be
inside, wine and bath a reality!

"Thank you, Aunt Julia!" Parker breathed. She
couldn't *wait* to see what it looked like. Was it furnished?
She had an air mattress, just in case, but given how well
kept the outside was, she'd bet it was full of solid old
furniture. Maybe there was a caretaker; it sure looked
that way. Weird that she owned the place and had never
been sent a bill or anything. Then again, maybe her ac-
countant had taken care of it. Still, she should've known
if someone was on the payroll.

Whatever. She wasn't complaining. You know what? She'd have a party before she sold it. Nicky could wear his little tux, and she'd wear that ice-blue Vera Wang, and they'd send out invitations—*Parker Harrington Welles and Nicholas Giacomo Mirabelli warmly request the honor of your company for the weekend at the Pines at Douglas Point, Gideon's Cove, Maine.*

"Okay, okay, let's get inside," Parker muttered. There was a code box; she flipped it open. State-of-the-art. Getting back into the car, she reached into the glove compartment and pulled out the envelope Thing One had given her the day he told her she was broke. There was the deed, there was his business card, there was a key... but no code. Dang it! She pulled out her phone and found *Thing One* on her contacts list. It went right to voice mail. The one time she actually needed something from him, and he was unavailable.

"Hi, Thing One, it's Parker. I'm here in Gideon's Cove, and I have the key, but I don't have a code for the gate. Would you please call me as soon as you get this? Thanks."

Her irritation with her father's minion faded as she looked back at the house. It was *so* pretty, and far less imposing than Grayhurst. Good Lord, she could get at *least* half a mil for this place, probably much more, and hey, maybe she could even hang on to it and rent it out—

"Problem?" came a voice, and Parker jumped and whirled around. It was Fling Material—um, Malone—sitting in a somewhat battered pickup truck, and ten minutes apart hadn't diminished his appeal. Unless he was stalking her, which, though a flattering thought, was somewhat terrifying.

"Oh, hi again." She held her phone up to her ear. "Just talking to my lawyer," she lied, in case he was a serial killer. "But I found it fine, thanks. See you around. Have a good night."

"You're at the wrong place."

Parker blinked. "Excuse me?"

"Julia Harrington's is back there." Malone nodded behind him.

"Where back there?" Parker asked.

"That little place you just passed."

Parker looked back down the road. There was nothing except the shed. She glanced at Malone. He nodded.

No. That couldn't possibly... Oh, no. Uh-uh. Her stomach twisted abruptly.

That wasn't a house. It was a shack. A falling-into-the-ocean *hut*.

"That?" she squeaked.

"Ayuh."

No. No, no. *That* house had boards over the windows. It was...crooked somehow. It couldn't have been more than five feet from tumbling down to the rocky beach below. Square-footage wise, it wasn't really a house at all! It was the size of her bedroom back home.

Odd little noises were coming from her throat. She swallowed and turned to the lobster guy. "You sure?"

"Julia Harrington's?"

"Yes."

"I'm sure, then."

Bugger! Bugger and damn. Parker took a deep breath, then another.

"You need anything?" Malone asked.

"Um...a different house?" He didn't respond. "No, I'm...fine. It's okay. Thanks for checking, though."

He nodded and put his truck in gear.

"Wait! Malone, is there a hotel in town?"

He shook his head. "Used to be a bed-and-breakfast, but it burned over the winter."

Well, tie her to an anchor and throw her in an ocean full of hungry sharks.

"Good night, then," Malone said, then was gone, his taillights disappearing around the corner. Good news was, he hadn't murdered her. Bad news was...oh, crap! This beautiful house wasn't hers, and that...that... *tenement* appeared to be.

Parker got back in the car and sat for a minute. *It's a fixer-upper!* chirped the Holy Rollers. "Easy for you to say," she snapped. "You're imaginary. You won't be picking up a hammer and helping, will you?" She threw the car in Reverse and backed out the driveway. "I really wanted you!" she called back to the Pines. Yes. She wanted a house with a name. Call her shallow, but bugger, she did *not* want to live in a shack, even for a few weeks.

Ninety-seven Shoreline Drive was on the ocean side of the road; the hill was steep as it rose from the harbor, and it was clear why there weren't many other houses around—most of them had probably fallen victim to storms over the years.

The shack sat on cement pilings, a two-foot gap between the earth and the house. No basement, clearly. She walked around the house slowly, the grass up to her knees. Were there mice in there? Probably. She shuddered. She hated mice. Her father liked to dangle them over Apollo's cage before dropping them to their doom.

Upon further inspection, she saw that the shack was, or had once been, an actual house, like something Nicky would draw—a square box with a triangle on top. The gray shingles had warped, pulling away from the side of the house like eyelashes, and great shards of paint peeled from the once-white trim. The roof was patchy and battered, complete with crumbling chimney, but at least there was some form of heating, she guessed. All the windows were boarded, and the aluminum screen door was off its hinges, leaning against a rusting front door. Clearly people had tried to break in over the years—there were dents all around the door handle, and the small windowpane was broken.

A cluster of lilac trees was in full bloom. "Good sign, right?" Parker asked, her voice a bit unfamiliar. The HRs agreed that yes, it was indeed a positive indicator.

There was a wooden stairway down to a small dock, but it was nearly full dark now, and Parker was not about to break her neck figuring out whether or not the stairs were sound.

"Bite the bullet," she said aloud. "Time to go inside and view your inheritance."

The key Thing One had supplied fit fine. Had he known this was her house? Had Harry? Think they might've given her a hint at what lay ahead?

Parker turned the lock, which slid open after some wiggling. The door was warped, however, and stuck fast, so she shoved harder, using her shoulder. Once, twice, three times, and bam, it opened.

Pitch-dark inside. She groped on the wall for a light switch and got lucky. Someone had turned on the electricity—or it had never been turned off—and a harsh yellow light momentarily blinded her.

Permanently blinded might've been better.

Parker closed her mouth, then opened it to swear, then realized that she didn't know a word bad enough.

Aunt Julia had been a hoarder.

Faded boxes and stacks of crumbling newspapers lined the hallway so there was only a tiny path leading into the house. The smell was so thick and dry Parker choked. There was so much crap everywhere, it was hard to take in—pots, pans, candlesticks, yellowing plastic containers, paper plates, old fabric, swollen paperbacks, a set of encyclopedia, plastic dolls. Cripes! And this was just the hallway! Parker lifted her gaze to the cracked plaster walls visible above the hoard to the cracked plaster ceiling. God. The place was a wreck. She tried to take a calming breath, choked and pulled up her shirt to cover her mouth—or muffle her scream, she thought darkly. *It's only stuff,* Spike said. *Check it out a little. See what you got.*

Good advice, good advice. To her left was a bathroom, the door open. Pepto-Bismol-pink tub spilling over with…stuff. But there was a sink visible, and a toilet, thank the Lord. First things first.

You're not really going to pee in there, are you? asked the female Holy Rollers. *When was that last cleaned?*

"Where else should I go?" Parker answered. "Outside?"

A girl had to do what a girl had to do, especially after two coffees on the way up. Still, the horror of the situation was not lost on her. An eyeless doll lay in the bathtub, just in case the place wasn't creepy enough. The toilet flushed, but when Parker turned on the faucet to wash her hands, nothing came out. Fine. She had Purell in the car.

Across from the loo was a bedroom, she guessed— too much junk to open the door all the way. Praying no bats were currently living inside, Parker poked her head in. There may have been a bed, but it was hard to tell with all the boxes. Clothes, some still on their hangers, lay abandoned and forgotten. Shoes, hats, a box full of

ceramic kittens, bags of yarn, books, macramé plant
holders.

A second bedroom held more of the same.

She sidled down the hall, trying not to touch anything,
toward what proved to be one big room, the kitchen on
one side, what had once been a living room on the other.
Another single lightbulb hung from a wire in here—
still worked, showing piles of plastic bins filled with old
clothing, more newspapers, sewing bric-a-brac. There
was a fishing pole on the counter, couch cushions in
front of the refrigerator, which looked to be from 1950,
rounded and hulking. The oven was green, its door hanging open as if in a scream—Parker could totally relate.
More boarded windows that probably overlooked the sea.

Sometimes it's darkest before dawn! the Holy Rollers
chirped, patting her shoulder, and Parker envisioned herself backing over them with the Volvo. Platitudes were
not going to help. A fire—a big one—might.

How was she going to have Nicky come up here?
How was she going to sell this place? Until this moment,
Parker hadn't realized how much she'd been counting on
a real house. This was all she had to her name, other than
the $11,202.57?

Oh, crap, she was hyperventilating. And who knew
what she was breathing in?

"It's okay," she said aloud. "We can do this. It's bad,
yes, sure, but that's okay. This will be really fun. We can
do this."

She could. She was a strong person. Right? She could
lift heavy things, and she'd cleaned bathrooms and stuff
before. Not that she really had to—there was always the
housekeeper or cleaning service—but she'd done it. Zil-
lions of people cleaned out garages and stuff, and she
would, too. It would be deeply satisfying. Yes. Maybe

she'd write a book about that, sure. *Learning Life Skills Really, Really Fast.*

Good. There. She was calmer now.

Suddenly, there was a fluttering of wings, and Parker screamed and ducked. A bird! In the house! A mourning dove, a glorified pigeon. "Get out!" she yelled, causing the bird to panic. It flew back and forth, hitting the walls, thudding sickeningly. "Stop!" she yelled. Bugger, it was coming at her! Parker covered her head and twisted and turned down the little path, bumped into a dressmaker's dummy, the bird fluttering right over her head, that horrible, panicked trilling…gah! It hit her in the head, its feathers hideous, its little talons…

Then Parker was outside. Hunched over, she dashed to her car, got in and slammed the door, panting wildly. "Bugger!" she yelled.

Little Pigeon loved the lady's hair. It was so cozy there! With a smile, he dug his little claws into her scalp and hunkered down.

She was still shuddering. Good thing she'd just gone to the bathroom, or she would've wet herself.

As her breathing calmed and the shaking of her limbs quieted, Parker made a mental list. Her eyes burned with tears, but that was stupid. Crying wasn't going to help. Tomorrow, she'd see about…well, hell. Getting a Dumpster, to start. And some giant rubber gloves, and maybe a hazmat suit.

Tonight, however…tonight, she'd be sleeping in the car. She had her comforter packed in the back, along with a few bags of groceries and her suitcase. She'd eat some Wheat Thins and sleep here.

She cracked the windows. It had turned chilly—of course, they were what, fifty miles from Canada? But the air felt clean and pure, and Parker sucked in great lungfuls, that faint tang of fish nothing compared to the closed-up stuffiness of the house.

And the stars were brilliant, blazing overhead in a clarity Parker had never seen before. The waves sloshed against the shore, and across the cove, the lights of the town glowed and winked as if welcoming her.

She'd make this work. She had twenty-three days to make this work.

But, even though she tried hard to keep such thoughts at bay, she couldn't help remembering that a month ago, she'd stayed in a suite at the Peninsula Hotel in New York City with her son. Her publisher had taken them to dinner to Nobu to celebrate the release of the last Holy Rollers book, and after that, she and Nicky had gone up to the Top of the Rock, just the two of them, so he could see the view.

Tonight, she was sleeping in her car.

It was almost funny.

CHAPTER FIVE

THOUGH HE VISITED the great state of Maine at least six times a year, crossing the Kittery Bridge never failed to make James feel as if someone had hammered a nail in his eye. Ever since he was twelve years old, Maine had been a place to escape from, not Vacationland, as the license plates proclaimed.

Dresner, his hometown, was not on the agenda. Rarely was, even though—or because—his parents still lived there. The town had grown up around a paper mill that had long moved operations to some third-world country, but the bitter tang of chemicals still hung over Cahill family events.

Last night, James had stayed at his sister's, set his phone to go off at five-thirty, since Gideon's Cove was another two hours away. Whether or not Parker wanted his help—and she didn't—she was getting it.

Gideon's Cove had been a cute town back then. There'd been a diner, he remembered, and a pretty girl about his own age who waited tables…he'd hung around, hoping she'd notice him, but she'd had a boyfriend, it turned out. Still, he'd managed to lose his virginity with a very, ah, generous woman about a decade older than he was. Chantal. *Very* nice woman. Just the thought of her had James grinning. Yep. All guys should get started out that way.

Speaking of women he'd slept with, it occurred to

James that he hadn't called Leah. Not that they had an actual relationship…a hookup now and then, but still.

James pulled over on the side of the road and took out his phone. *One missed call—Parker Welles,* the screen said. Cell-phone service was spotty up here, so no surprise there. The surprise was that she called him at all. He listened to the message, frowning. He didn't know anything about a security system or code. When he'd called his uncle to tell him about his plans, James asked him if he knew the Harrington place. "Ayuh," Dewey had said. "Needs a little work. I'll make sure the electric's on." Nothing about a security system.

Well. He'd be there in an hour. He could figure it out then. Besides, making Parker wait had its own appeal. And he did owe Leah a call.

"Hey, Leah, it's James."

"Hi there, stranger! How are you *doing?*" she said, her cheerleader-style exuberance making him hold the phone a little farther away from his ear. She was cute, but best in small doses, which explained why they only saw each other about once a month.

"How are you?" he said.

"I'm awesome! What's *up?* You wanna get together this weekend?"

"Well, actually, I'm in Maine right now, and I'll be here for a while. Six or eight weeks. Figured I'd let you know."

There was a pause. "Oh," she finally said.

It was impressive, how much could be packed into a two-letter word. They must teach it at woman school. "Yeah. So, just wanted to say bye and have a nice summer and all." James pressed his thumb against his eye socket, bracing for the relationship talk.

"What about…you know? Us?"

Ah, mooseshit. Was there an *us?* Because he'd seen Leah, a very pretty redhead who liked to play pool and flirt, maybe six or seven times since they'd met at a wedding on New Year's Eve, and if there was an *us,* it was pretty anemic. There was him, and there was her, and the two of them intersected at a bar once in a while, which generally led to more intersecting in bed, which had always seemed like enough.

Until this moment.

"Well, I have to be in Maine this summer," James repeated.

"For Harry?"

"Yep. So I figured I'd call, tell you I wouldn't be around. And after the summer, I really don't know where I'll be jobwise." There. Mission accomplished.

"You want some company up there? I love Maine!"

Mission not accomplished. James sighed and closed his eyes. "Well, I'll be busy, Leah. And it's far. Way up the coast. But it's been fun hanging out. Good luck with everything." He winced. He didn't mean to sound like a dick. They just taught it in guy school.

There was a lengthy pause, then a sigh. "Fine." Another pause. "Where are you staying?"

"A town called Gideon's Cove. Harry's daughter has some property up there."

"Harry's in jail, right?"

"Yeah. But his daughter needs a little help. Real-estate stuff." James never liked talking about what he did, just in case what he *didn't* do came out. *Well, I sit in my office a lot. Shot thirty-nine Nerf baskets in a row one day. I was really stoked.*

Another pause. "Well, try to have fun," she said, her voice a little brighter. "And thanks for calling, James! That was so thoughtful."

Atta girl. Leah was sweet. Not tremendously bright, but good-natured and fun. It'd been really easy, hanging out with her. And easy was good so far as he was concerned. "You take care, Leah."

"You, too, James. Give me a call when you're back, if you feel like it."

"You bet. Take care," he repeated.

There. His condo was sublet for the summer. Leah had been informed. Stella, his secretary, had told James not to worry; she'd been about to quit anyway and become a jujitsu instructor. The guys he played basketball with on Saturday mornings had taken him out for a beer as a farewell. No point in telling Mary Elizabeth about work…she pretty much only cared if he brought her a present.

His parents could wait.

So. On to Gideon's Cove to see Parker. Maybe she'd be glad to see him.

Right. And the ice-skating in hell was fabulous this time of year. But she was Harry's daughter, and James owed him more than he could say.

Six years ago, James had been stuck on the tarmac in L.A., where he'd interviewed for a job—one of 204 prospects, apparently. He'd been out of law school for a year and had yet to get a job offer, and panic was setting in. His father was sixty-two and business was slow; his brothers were just getting by. The law was supposed to have been a sure bet for James, a guaranteed decent salary, and making money had always been the goal.

At any rate, James had been upgraded to first class—the girl at the desk had liked his "smies," whatever those were. James was enjoying the extra four inches of legroom when a man sat in the seat next to him, growling about the inconvenience of having to fly commercial. Harry Welles, legend of Wall Street, in the flesh.

A guy who probably had a whopping-size legal department.

James introduced himself, made wry comments about the joys of air travel, spent his last hundred bucks on a bottle of champagne—which Harry had declared cheap swill—got the guy to laugh and a few hours later found himself with a job offer. Not a corporate position, though. Harry's longtime personal attorney had announced his retirement; would James like the job? On retainer for personal and family business, no other clients in case Harry needed him. It would be mostly real-estate dealings, as Harry owned a couple dozen corporate buildings, maybe some trust and estate planning. When Harry had named a salary, it was all James could do not to hump his leg. For that salary, he would've done anything. He needed money, a lot of it, and fast.

So James had become a glorified clerk, turning his attention to getting through loopholes so Harry could build a bigger boathouse, changing the terms of the lease on a commercial building. He set up a trust fund for Harry's unborn grandchild. Paid off Harry's occasional mistress. And became, it seemed, Harry's closest friend.

It was odd; Harry had colleagues and clients and employees, he had connections, but he didn't seem to have friends. And though James knew Harry had a daughter, he never talked about her. But from that first day on the airplane onward, Harry seemed to anoint James as the chosen one. He'd summon James to the city, take him out for dinner, tell tales of his early career. Took him to ball games. Slapped him on the back and told him he was doing a great job, even though the work was mindless and dull. One night, when Harry'd had too much to drink and James was seeing him back to his huge apartment in the city, Harry had said, "If I had a son, I hope he woulda been like you, kid."

Strange, given that Harry had only known him a few months. And stranger still that for all the time he'd spent with Harry, he'd never heard him talk about Parker. James knew she existed, of course. But she was never discussed.

And then, on the eighth day of the sixth month as Harry's attorney, when James had sunk eighteen Nerf baskets in a row and was in a heated mental debate between roast beef or turkey avocado, his cell phone rang. It was Harry. "James, my daughter had her baby. Can you swing by the hospital with the paperwork?"

"Hey, congratulations, Harry! Boy or a girl?"

"A boy."

"What's his name?"

"Hang on. Mona! Did my daughter tell you the baby's name?" There was a pause. "Don't know. Can you get over there?"

"Sure! Absolutely."

"Great. Tell my daughter I'll get up there when I've got some free time. And I'll see you here in the city next week. Knicks game, don't forget." With that, Harry hung up.

James stared at the phone. Granted, his own parents weren't perfect, but they wouldn't miss out on seeing a new grandchild. Parker was Harry's only child, and this was her first baby, as James knew from the trust-fund paperwork.

Ten million dollars at birth, another ten at age thirty.

So much money, it felt fake to a kid from a blue-collar mill town in Maine.

And so James, then twenty-five years old, had taken

the papers to the hospital for Parker's signature. Uncomfortable about Harry's apparent lack of interest, he stopped at a toy store and bought a stuffed animal, a large gray rabbit with floppy ears. That's what people did for babies, after all. He was an uncle, and even though he wasn't close to his brothers' kids, he knew enough to send a toy on birthdays and Christmas.

He got to the hospital, found the maternity floor, went down the hall to room 433, and there was Parker Harrington Welles. She was all alone, holding what looked like a large burrito with a blue cap, and her face was so soft with wonder that James literally stopped in his tracks. Kinda fell in love right then and there.

Then she looked up, and there was no kinda about it.

"Hi," she said quietly, a question in her eyes. Right, because he was a stranger, and she'd just given birth.

"Uh…hi." His mouth was suddenly dry. "Um…I'm James. James Cahill. I'm your father's attorney?" *And you sound like the village idiot.*

She blinked, and her face went completely blank. She looked back down at her baby, who made a little squeak. "So you're the new Thing One."

"Excuse me?"

"You replaced Sol?"

"Yeah. Yes. I replaced Sol. Uh, I have some papers. For you to sign. For the baby's trust fund." He closed his eyes briefly. "Congratulations, by the way. Um…cute baby." Not that he could see anything from the doorway, but that was what you said to women who'd just popped a kid.

She adjusted the baby's cap, then looked at James. "I take it my father's not coming."

Ouch. "Well, he—he wanted to, but he's stuck in the city."

Her face didn't change, but for one second, something flashed across her eyes. Her *beautiful* eyes. Crap, he was like a twelve-year-old with his first crush. But man, her eyes were beautiful. Blue or green, he couldn't tell from here. Didn't matter. She was gorgeous. Long, straight blond hair, perfect mouth. Even in a johnny coat, she was frickin' glorious.

Then a guy brushed past him, going instantly to Parker's side, and reached down to touch the bottom half of the burrito. "How's he doing?" he asked, and Parker smiled up at him. The father of the baby, clearly.

"Still sleeping," Parker said. "Your parents were great, by the way."

"You won't be saying that when they show up four times a day," he answered.

"Well, I think they're sweet."

"And they think you walk on water. Thanks for the middle name. That was really…" The guy's voice choked up, and it was only then that he seemed to notice James, standing there like a lump.

Parker nodded at him. "My father's attorney."

James stepped forward and offered his hand, which the guy shook. "James Cahill. Congratulations."

"Hi. Ethan Mirabelli. New dad." He grinned broadly, clearly delighted with his title.

"Mr. Welles sends his best and says he'll be up as soon as he can. He's, um, very sorry he couldn't make it." James swallowed. Lying for the boss. Yikes.

"Really. He said that?" Parker asked coolly.

"Yes."

She wasn't fooled. Gave him a knowing look, then touched her baby's cheek.

James suddenly remembered the bag in his hand. "Oh, here. For the…little one." He passed it over to the dad, who pulled the rabbit from it and smiled. "It's bigger than he is," he said. "Hey, Nicky, look. It's a bunny." The baby slept on, unimpressed.

"What can I do for you, Thing One?" Parker asked.

"Right." He approached the throne—there was definitely a regal sense about her—and held out the papers. She passed the baby to the guy, Ethan, who immediately kissed the tiny head.

James cleared his throat. "Sign here, and then initial here...." Her hair smelled so good, all clean and flowery. *Don't go there, idiot,* his conscience advised. *Right, right,* he agreed. Her skin was perfect. Beautiful hands.

She signed with brisk efficiency and didn't look at him when she gave the papers back.

"Lucy was wondering if she could come by," Ethan said.

"Absolutely," Parker answered. "I already told her that."

"You're not too tired?"

"Are you kidding? I feel like a superhero." She grinned up at the baby's father.

"You *are* a superhero," he answered, smiling back.

A nurse came in. "How's it going, Mom?" she barked.

"Great," Parker answered.

"Good! I need to check those stitches, then I'll leave you in peace."

The dad went over to the chair, murmuring to the burrito.

James, idiotically, didn't move. He was having trouble thinking. Those eyes were so...the whole face, so...

"Thing One? I'd rather not have you see my episiotomy," Parker said. "If you don't mind, of course."

Shit. "Right, no. Sorry. Congratulations, you two," he said and, with that, got out of there. Went home and did a Google search, saw her books. Ordered a bunch. Sent them to Mare. Got a pleasant thank-you note from her about a month later. *Thank you for the rabbit you gave Nicky. It was very thoughtful. Best, Parker Welles.*

Harry didn't visit his grandson until the baby was three months old. He asked James to come with him, stayed at Grayhurst for forty-five minutes, then informed Parker that he and James had a business dinner. "You sure you don't want to stay a little longer?" James had murmured in the great front hall as they put on their coats. Harry had held the baby for approximately thirty seconds.

"My daughter's a little intense," Harry had said tightly. "Baby's a good-looking boy, though, don't you think?"

"Oh, definitely," James answered. Thus ended the conversation, and while James was curious, he knew better than to bite the hand that fed not just him, but Mary Elizabeth, as well.

From that point on, Harry began sending James to family events. Even when Harry did show up, he'd call James and ask him to come, as well. No matter how much James tried to subtly protest, to hint that family was family, Harry was insistent, and so James ended up at quite a few Nicky-related events—christening, birthdays—always on the edges, always uncomfortable.

Parker would greet him and say goodbye. That was about it. She was civil, though she continued to call him Thing One, and after a while, James adopted a somewhat wry attitude at those dreaded family gatherings. He worked for Harry, the end. But he'd watch Parker, see that she made her kid's birthday cake herself, clearly adored him, made sure he thanked James for whatever gift he'd brought. She treated Ethan's family warmly, even though she never did marry the guy. And she worked for a living, writing those books, giving all that money away. Not your typical trust-fund baby.

And then there was that one time—

"Watch it, idiot," he said as a driver with Massachusetts plates blazed by at an easy ninety miles an hour. "And you, idiot," he added to himself, "should really think about something else. You're here to help Harry's daughter flip a house. No more."

CHAPTER SIX

ONCE UPON A TIME, there was a family of chipmunks who found a lovely, clean place to live for the winter. They climbed inside and got all snugly and fell asleep. Then, alas, someone started their home, which was actually the engine of a car, and they were pulverized in their sleep. But they went to animal heaven, so it wasn't a total wash.

The Holy Rollers sighed with deep satisfaction. "Save it," Parker muttered, putting aside the red notebook she always carried in case inspiration struck. Chipmunk puree would probably not sell, no matter how much her publisher wanted a new series. As for herself, she would not be recommending an overnight in a car anytime soon. Not comfy, no, sir. She'd woken at the horrible crack of morning and had been, quite honestly, avoiding going inside the house again. But it was now 7:14 a.m. Couldn't pretend she was working on a story, couldn't avoid the day ahead of her.

She checked her phone; too early in California for Nicky to call her, of course—it was still practically the middle of the night there. Thing One hadn't bothered calling her back, she noted with irritation. Of course, he'd probably found another job by now, since Harry was in jail.

The thought that Harry was actually in prison gave her pause. She'd called him twice so far; both times, the conversation had lasted less than three minutes. Harry was as busy in prison as he'd been on Wall Street, it seemed. No time for that pesky daughter of his. He had, she admitted, asked after Nicky. At least there was that.

At that very minute, her phone chimed, startling her so badly that she dropped it. *Harrington, L.,* the screen said. "Hello?"

"Yeah, hi," said a horrible voice. "Is this Pahkah?" For a second, Parker thought it was the guy from last night—Malone—but of course, he wouldn't have her number.

"Excuse me?" Parker said, running a hand over the back of her head. Her hair was matted.

"Ah you Pahkah?"

"Oh! Um, yes. I'm Parker." Man. That was some accent.

"This is Lavinnyer Harintin."

Lavinnyer…aha! The caller was her distant cousin! Lavinia Harrington.

"Hi!" Parker said. "Right! How are you?"

"Word has it you're here in town," Lavinia said.

"I am. I got in last night."

"Where'd you sleep?"

"Um…in the car."

Lavinia laughed, a dark, horrible sound that ended in a hacking cough. "Is that right? Quite a shit-nest you gawt there, isn't it?"

Parker tried to smile. "That's a pretty accurate description."

There was a sucking sound…Lavinia had to be smoking, and with a voice like that, had been smoking three packs of Camel cigarettes a day since the age of four months. "Welp," she said, exhaling, "you wanna meet sometime this week? Seems like we should lay eyes on each other."

"That'd be great," Parker said. Honestly, she had no

idea where to start with this house, and Lavinia could probably give her some names and places.

"Wanna come to the diner for breakfast tomorrow?" Lavinia suggested.

"Sure," Parker said. A real breakfast with eggs and bacon. Beat the two Nutri-Grain bars she'd had an hour ago.

"Know where it is? Joe's?"

"I passed it yesterday."

"Good. See you tomorrow."

Parker got out of the car carefully; if she'd been stiff yesterday, she was practically crippled today.

Eyeballing the house in front of her, Parker decided it looked even worse than last night, if possible. It had a water view, yes. The cove spread out before her, Douglas Point to the north, the harbor to the south. So that was a plus, the view. The house…eesh.

Well, nothing to do but face the music. She got her toiletries bag from her suitcase and, pushing through the long grass, went inside. Her bird friend from last night seemed to be gone, thank God. She left the door open just in case.

Clearly she'd need to rent a Dumpster and buy some seriously sturdy trash bags. Almost everything in here would need to be thrown away. She winced, picturing trash stuffed in her beloved Volvo. But cleaning the house out would show her what she had to work with, at least. Maybe it could be a jewel. She really needed it to be a jewel.

She went into the bathroom and turned on the faucet. Right. No water. Sighing, she brushed her teeth dry and combed her hair, trying not to touch anything in the bathroom. This would be first on her list of things to scour.

She turned to leave, figuring she'd put on a clean shirt

in the car, rather than inside, when she felt something at her ankle…a tickle.

She looked down. Nothing there. Just an itch, she decided, from being in this house of crap.

Nope, there it was again, right under her ankle bone. A mosquito? She shook her foot. Nothing.

Then, horribly, the tickle moved. Moved *up*.

"What the hell?" she hissed, shaking the leg of her jeans. If that was a cockroach, she'd die.

The tickle moved up again. Faster this time, toward her knee.

"Shit!" Parker said, flapping her pants. "Get out!"

The tickle was now past her knee…and it had a lump. It was a lumpy, warm tickle.

"Nooo!" Parker shrieked, jumping up and down. The lumpy tickle zipped around to the back of her leg, then across her *ass* and around to the other side, and with that, Parker ripped open her pants and there it was, a *mouse* in her *pants*. Its eyes were huge and terrified and Parker heard a scream rip through the air—*her* scream—and the tiny rodent—rodent!—leaped, practically flying through the air, and landed in the pile in the tub.

Parker ripped off the jeans, dimly hearing herself shrieking, and ran out of the house, through the grass and right up onto the hood of her car. "Bugger! Bugger! Jeesh!" she yelped. Her jeans were clutched in her hand. What if there were more in there? What if a whole family of rodents was in her jeans right now? *Once there was a family of mice who loved to snuggle up against the warm flesh of an unwitting human.* She whipped the pants against the car, cracking them against the hood again and again and again, shrieking at the remembered feeling of tiny claws. On her leg. Her skin. On her *ass!*

"Hey, Parker" came a voice. She kept cracking. "Parker?"

She looked up, her breath stuttering in and out of her chest.

Thing One. Thing One was here.

"Hi," he said, as if she wasn't murdering her jeans against the hood. "How's it going?"

"There was a mouse in my pants."

He raised an eyebrow and smiled. "Lucky mouse."

Her breath caught. Wrong thing to say. Wrong. "It's pretty traumatic to have a *rodent* in your pants, Thing One," she snapped. "Unless you like that sort of thing."

"Oh, hey, sorry, princess," he said, approaching her car. "Didn't mean to make light of your tragedy."

"There was a *mouse* in my *pants,*" she blurted. "It's bad enough, okay? I mean, do you see that house? That's mine! I own it! And I was doing fine, I wasn't panicking or anything, even when that fricking *bird* flew into my hair last night but a *mouse*— I...I can't have Nicky here! That place is infested!"

"Okay, okay," he said. "Settle down. You are aware that you're not wearing pants, right?" Another quirked eyebrow. "Not that I'm complaining."

She looked down at him, her throat working. She could murder him and throw his body in the water. Or she could put on her pants. She took a shaky breath. "I'm not...eager to put them back on. In case the mouse had cousins."

"Well, here. Let me check." Thing One took the jeans from her and turned them inside out, then shook them vigorously. Checked the pockets, too. "Nothing."

"I saw it. It was there. It ran all the way up this leg, then across my butt, then God knows where it was headed." His mouth twitched. Did he think this was funny? This was not funny! "It's not funny, Thing One."

"Well. It's gone now." He looked down. She suspected he was smiling. Idiot.

"It's in the tub," she said, giving the jeans a last shake before pulling them on. "You can go find it. Maybe it'll crawl up your pants and we can compare notes."

"How was your trip up?" he asked, and really, what kind of a question was that when they were sitting in front of a hovel?

"It was lovely, Thing One. This house, however, is a sty."

He looked at the house for a long moment, then back at her. "Well. Good thing I'm here, then."

Right. It suddenly dawned on her that he was *here*. A familiar face, at least. Something moved in Parker's chest. She looked away, but no, there was the mouse-infested house. The harbor. Better. Nice view.

"All right. Let's see what we're up against."

Thing One went into the house, and Parker heard a few clunks and thunks. She sat on the hood of the Volvo, her panic fading gradually into the occasional shudder. A rodent running up her leg...*there* was a sensation a person wouldn't forget, right up there with an episiotomy.

Her father's attorney emerged a minute later. Now that she wasn't screaming, she noticed he looked...different. It took a minute to figure out why.

He wasn't wearing a suit. First time ever she'd seen him out of— Well, this was the first time ever she'd seen him in jeans and a T-shirt, that was for sure.

Parker looked away and cleared her throat. "So what are you doing here, Thing One?"

He sat on the hood next to her. "Since I'm devoting

the next few weeks to overhauling this dump, Parker, you think you could call me by my real name?"

"I seem to have forgotten it." There. She was getting her old vibe back. Good.

He smiled slowly, his dark eyes crinkling. Dangerous, those eyes. "Again?"

"Is it John? Jason?"

"It's James. James Francis Xavier Cahill."

Goose bumps broke out along her arms. It was chilly. Or something. "So what are you doing here, James?"

"Your father asked me to come up."

Right. James was an obedient pet; she'd give him that. She didn't say anything for a minute, just pulled her knees to her chin and wrapped her arms around her legs. "How's he doing?"

"He's okay."

She'd bet her left arm James got more than three minutes on the phone with her father. She sighed. "So. This place. Did you know how bad it was?"

He shook his head. "I called my uncle this morning to ask about a security code, and he told me it was kind of a dump. I didn't think it'd be this bad, but I can help you out."

She really needed the Army Corps of Engineers, from the look of it. "So law school trained you to overhaul a house, Thing One? I know you're good at emptying trust funds, but carpentry?" There. Hopefully that would erase the edge he'd gained from having seen her hysterical and in her panties.

He gave her a look of his own. "Nothing I did was illegal, Parker. Your father had the right to do what he wanted with those trust funds, because you gave him that right. You signed papers letting him have full authority over every penny. And even if I'd wanted to say something—which I did—attorney-client privilege prevented me."

"Wow. You're a great guy. Maybe my dad will give you a sticker."

He ignored that. "At any rate, my father was a builder. I worked on a construction crew summers when I was in college. Do you really want to kick me out because you don't like me?"

She felt her jaw locking. She'd be an idiot to send him away.

He took her silence as protest. "Look. Aside from hauling all this crap to the dump, you'll need to reshingle the entire exterior. The roof needs to be replaced, the gutter's hanging off the front, the chimney is crumbling. I'm guessing there's dry rot under the linoleum in the kitchen, the cupboards are pulling away from the walls, and the stairs down to the dock are a death trap. The back door frame is warped. You probably need some significant rewiring, not to mention a new paint job inside." He paused. "I happen to find myself free this summer."

"Where would you stay?" she asked.

"Here."

"Here? Where here? In the Harbor Suite?"

"Actually, we can get a lot of this stuff cleared out pretty fast. I already have a Dumpster being delivered today."

He did? "How'd you do that?" she asked.

"My uncle lined one up."

This summer was supposed to be about doing things on her own, a fresh start. The plan had been to take sheets off aging but lovely furniture and paint the sunroom. The plan was to meet George Clooney before his boat went down in a hundred-foot wave, have a fling, then welcome Nicky for a few weeks of blueberry picking and sailing.

It was not to have her father's minion living with her.

But she hadn't realized what she was up against. "Well, you can't stay here. What about your uncle's place?"

"He lives in a one-bedroom apartment over the bar. I can get more work done if I'm here."

She didn't comment.

"Oh, come on, Parker," he said, his voice low and scraping. "It's not like we're strangers."

She felt the tips of her ears practically burst into flame. Took a calming breath. "Fine. Stay. Thank you. You can report to Harry and ease your conscience over helping my father rob my son. I can't say no, because I'm desperate and broke. But I don't like it."

"Well, how's this?" he said, his voice amiable. "We'll acknowledge that if the situation were different, you'd kick me out. You'll barely tolerate me, and only because your back is against the wall and you had a mouse in your pants. Deal?" He gave her a smug smile.

Parker unclenched her jaw and glanced at her watch as she got off the hood of the car. James followed suit. "I'm going to the hardware store."

"You can have the bigger bedroom."

"You're too kind."

"I get that a lot." There was that smile again. Parker ignored it and started the engine. "You know where the hardware store is?" he asked.

"I'll find it," she ground out, throwing the car into Reverse.

Not going as planned. No, sir.

CHAPTER SEVEN

WELL, SHE WASN'T HAPPY. He hadn't expected her to be. But man oh man alive, this place was a mess. Three hours in, and James had thrown away a good ton of crap. He paused outside to wipe the sweat from his forehead and breathe in some fresh air. The Dumpster had been delivered right after she'd left, thanks to Dewey, who knew everyone. James had put quite a dent in the piles of crap in the house, starting with the bigger bedroom. The princess had slept in her car last night, he guessed, based on the comforter in the front seat. Probably wouldn't want to do it again.

A car pulled into the driveway, and a very luscious redheaded woman unfolded herself from the driver's seat. "Jamie Cahill! How you've grown!"

Holy shit. "Chantal?" Couldn't be anyone else.

"Your uncle told me you were back. Don't you dare say you've forgotten me."

"Are you kidding? I think of you every night."

She laughed, and James smiled. Time hadn't simply been kind to Chantal; it was in love with her. She'd been beautiful at age twenty-five; at fortyish, she was unbe*liev*able. "It's great to see you," he said. "Please, God, you're single."

"Sorry, baby boy. I'm married—to a much younger man, I might add—and I'm a mommy, even. A little boy named Luke, six months old. I'm nursing." She raised an eyebrow, inviting James to look. And what was a guy to do but obey? He dropped his eyes to Chantal's generous endowments, showcased in a very tight and low-cut blouse.

"Lucky kid," he murmured.

"I won't bore you with pictures, but he's the love of my life. Okay, just one, since you begged." She held out her phone and showed James a shot of a drooling, fat-cheeked baby. "And here's another one. Isn't he beautiful? Looks like his daddy."

"Cute," James said. All babies tended to look the same to him, but then again, he didn't spend a lot of time staring into cribs or strollers or whatever.

"Oh, you look good enough to eat!" Chantal exclaimed. "Give us a hug." She wrapped him in a soft embrace. And hey, she patted his ass, too, making him laugh. Still had quite the effect, Chantal. "So," she said, releasing him, "you called Harbor Realty, and guess what I do on the side? Real estate. It's your lucky day."

"In so many ways," he murmured.

"Show me what you got. In the house, not in your pants," she said. "Which isn't to say I don't remember you fondly."

"Okay. Harry Welles—you heard of him, right?"

"Another Wall Street scumbag, from what I hear."

"Yeah. Well, he bankrupted the family, and all his daughter has left is this house. From her mother's side of the family. Julia Harrington was her great-aunt."

"Wow. Millionaire to shack-owner," she murmured as they walked toward the front door.

"Yeah. So she needs to flip it as soon as she can." He opened the door for Chantal, who recoiled.

"I'll pass on the inside for now," she said. "I'm guess-

ing crappy insulation, maybe four entire electrical outlets and plenty of wildlife."

"You're psychic."

"So how much money can your client spend on it? If
we put on an addition, a master suite with sliders and a
deck, a big bathroom with a Jacuzzi, gourmet kitchen,
build a big patio into the hillside here, outdoor fireplace…we can get a gay couple in here faster than you
can say, 'Bar Harbor is unaffordable.'" Chantal licked
her red-painted lips in anticipation.

"She has about ten grand," James said.

"Well, shit, then." She sighed. "There are back taxes
on this place, did you know?"

"No," James said. Crap. If he'd known that, he
could've paid them off. Why Parker didn't, he had no
idea. Then again, she didn't even remember that she
owned the house.

Chantal nudged a piece of trash with her foot. "Julia
was broke, and no one in Town Hall ever had the heart to
go after them while she was alive. Sorry to say, Harry's
daughter will have to pay about fifteen years' worth of
taxes. Guess it slipped through the cracks until now."

"What if we did a teardown?" James asked.

Chantal shrugged, pursing her full, red lips. "Nah.
Waterfront property up here isn't worth a ton, because
who the hell wants to live in Washington County, right?
It's too far from everything."

"Right," James acknowledged.

"And this is what we call a postage-stamp lot. You
can get two acres of waterfront over on Mutton Chop
Bay for next to nothing. Judy Phillips has been trying to
sell a parcel for three years now. Not one offer." Chantal tipped her head and folded her arms under her chest,

making her breasts swell, then glanced at James to make sure he noticed. How could he not? She winked.

"So what's your advice, Chantal?"

"Well, her best bet for a quick sale is to make it pretty. Strip it down, slap on some new flooring, new roof, new shingles, paint the inside. Market it as a tiny jewel of a hideaway. Maybe we can get enough to cover the back taxes and give her a little nest egg besides, *little* being the operative word here. The place isn't even winterized. But curb appeal, you hear? Make it adorable. You might get a family or a retired couple looking for a cheap summer home."

"Okay. We'll shoot for that. Thanks, Chantal."

"You're welcome." She gave him a sunny smile. "How's your family? Dewey says everyone's doing about as well as can be expected."

"Yep. Everyone's fine."

She shaded her eyes and looked him up and down. "You turned out awfully nice, James Cahill."

"And you're just as beautiful as I remember."

"Aw. Give me a kiss. On the cheek, now. I'm extremely faithful to my young stud of a husband."

"How'd he get so lucky?" James asked.

"He knocked me up. Let me know if I can help, okay? I'll probably see you at Dewey's, and you have my number."

"You bet. Thanks for coming out, Chantal."

"Nice to see you again, honey," she said. She got back in her car and backed out of the overgrown driveway. No sign of Parker, who'd been at the hardware store for a couple hours now. Or she'd fled.

In the truck he'd borrowed from Chuck, one of his basketball buddies—who'd been more than happy to take the Lexus off his hands for the summer—was James's own stuff. Some tools, left over from his summertime work as a construction worker, not from his father, God knew—Frank Cahill wouldn't give James a staple, and James wasn't dumb enough to ask. A few boxes that he'd found in Grayhurst's attic. He wasn't sure if Parker had meant to leave them or not, but the Feds hadn't wanted them.

And his laptop. The old résumé would need brushing up. Unfortunately, there seemed to be more unemployed lawyers in the world than Chinese, and getting a job that paid him what Harry had…not gonna happen.

Speaking of Harry…James reached into the cab of the truck and pulled out his cell phone. A few minutes later, he had Harry on the line.

"How you doing, boss?" he asked.

"Not bad, James, me boy," Harry said. His jocular tone told James that someone else was nearby, so Harry would be keeping up appearances. "Where are you?"

"Up in Maine. About four hours away from you, give or take."

"I appreciate you going up there."

"No problem, Harry." Playing along with Harry's mood—because it was one of his few talents—James added, "You've paid me enough to go to the Black Hole of Calcutta for the summer, let alone the coast of Maine."

Harry burst out laughing. "True enough, true enough." He paused. "I'm trying to get in touch with some of my former associates about a job for you, kid."

Whatever James had done to earn Harry's affection, he didn't know. "I'll be fine. You don't have to worry about me."

"Well, I'll let you know if something turns up. How's my daughter?"

"She's okay." James paused. "The house isn't worth much."

"No?"

"No. And it's a mess."

Another lengthy pause. "So what's the plan?" Harry asked. There was some noise over the PA about visiting hours.

"Well, we'll fix it up as best we can, try to sell it." He paused. "You doing okay, boss?"

There was a long silence from the other end. "It's not bad," Harry said in a low voice. "I have a lot of time on my hands. Not much to do. Plenty of time to consider my sins, right?" He gave a halfhearted chuckle.

"I guess so," James said. "Did you get the books?"

"I did. *Shogun* and *Moby-Dick,* huh? Trying to educate me? Afraid I'll join a gang while I'm in here?"

"Yep. I also figured you could use them as weapons if a riot broke out."

"Good thinking. All right, I should go. I have a meeting. Take care of yourself, son. Talk soon." With that, he hung up, sounding much like the corporate wheeler and dealer he'd been.

A meeting. That was good. One good thing about prison—Harry would have to sober up.

Well. Back to work. Parker's room was almost clear.

He had to admit, it was more satisfying than Nerf basketball.

"OKAY, FOR MOLD KILLING, this here's what you want, little lady," said Ben, one of the three senior-citizen gentlemen who'd pounced the second she'd walked into the tiny hardware store.

"Mold killer. Got it. Thank you so much, really."

"Oh, my Lord, it's a pleasure," Rolly said. "Pretty

ladies who don't know nothin' about home repair…it's what we live for."

"You guys are angels."

I resent that, said Spike. *A totally overused word.*

"You're sweet, dahlin'," said Stuart. "It's our pleasure. You ever painted a room before?"

"I haven't," she admitted, and the men charged the paint-chip wall.

Almost three hours after she entered the hardware store, Parker left, the three guys carrying her packages to the Volvo. "Oh, Rhode Island," said Ben, glancing at her plates. "I went to Providence College."

"A wonderful school," Parker said, making him blush.

"You need any more advice, we'll be happy to help," Stuart said.

"I absolutely will, and thanks a million, boys. Really."

She realized she was smiling as she started the car. The guys had advised on mousetraps—the thought made her cringe, regardless of this morning's little incident, which she'd relayed to her new pals to their howling delight. They'd shown her what she'd need: sponges, brooms, mops, bleach and lots of it, Murphy's wood oil, razor-blade scrapers, gallons of Windex, six pairs of thick rubber gloves, two pairs of work gloves, mega-size trash bags. Not only that, but the boys had a box of doughnuts from Joe's Diner—no Starbucks up here, that was for sure—and they'd made her eat two, bless their hearts.

Parker had never been in a hardware store before. Nope. It was her new favorite place, though—all those mysterious thingies, the pleasant smell of metal and wood smoke from the stove in the middle of the store. All those solutions for her troubles.

Glancing at her watch, she saw that, at last, it was late

enough to call Nicky. She pulled over to the side of the road. Cell service, thank heavens.

"Mommy! Guess what? I *love* sourdough bread! I *hated* it yesterday, and now I love it! You have to smear it with jelly. That's when it gets good. Guess what else? We're going to the Golden Bridge today! And some gardens…Lucy's making me go but I want to see the jail! It's on an island and me and Daddy—"

"Daddy and I."

"Daddy and I are gonna go to jail like Grandpa, but I'm gonna break out! And I'm gonna bring Elephant, and he's gonna break out, too. And guess what? I'm gonna jump in the water and swim all the way to Maine, Mommy! We'll take you out for lunch."

Man, her boy was the best kid ever. Parker felt a bit as if she'd swallowed the sun, so warm and bright his chirpy little voice made her feel. "Well, don't swim yet. The house isn't quite ready, and you have to go see the giant trees and rocks, remember?"

"I know. But I miss you."

The vise that had gripped her heart since Nicky left tightened a notch. "I miss you, too, sweetheart." *I miss you so much I cried in the car last night.* "I can't wait for you to get here. It's so pretty. I can see lobster boats from the house." Well, she could if the windows weren't boarded up. "And there's a really cute diner where we can go out to eat."

"Do they have sourdough bread?"

"I don't know. I'm going there tomorrow."

"Did you know there are *earthquakes* in Fran Francisco?" Nicky said.

Parker smiled again. "I did, actually."

"I'm gonna lay on the floor—"

"Lie on the floor."

"—and see if I can hear one. Here's Lucy! Bye! I love you! I got you a present! It's a necklace and it's a rainbow."

"Bye, baby. I love you! I'll call you later," Parker said.

There was a smile in Lucy's voice. "He's on the floor. Every time a bus goes past the hotel, he tells us to get in a doorway. Go brush your teeth, okay, pal?" she said to Nicky. "So how are you, Parker? What's it like up there?"

"Oh, it's pretty. It's very pretty," Parker said.

"And what's the house like?"

"Well, um, it's right on the water. It's pretty small, very cute. It needs some work. But it'll be great." No need to worry her two best pals on their vacation. She'd save the stories for later, when the horror wasn't so fresh.

"How's the real-estate market up there?" Lucy asked.

"I haven't checked yet. It's on my list." *Right after I kill Snuggles the Mouse, of course.*

"And how about that summer romance?" Lucy asked. "You up for that?"

Parker paused. "Well, I happened to meet a very attractive lobsterman yesterday."

"No, sir! That's great! Do I smell a fling?"

They chatted a few minutes more; Lucy said Ethan was in the shower, so he'd call her later. And even though Parker knew she'd be talking to her son again that day, she couldn't help feeling a little lonely as she hung up. The three of them in San Francisco, her alone in Maine. Such were the perils of joint custody.

Well. She wasn't completely alone. She had Thing One, heaven help her. That was going to be…difficult. It wasn't so much that he worked for her father, or even that he hadn't warned her about the trust-fund issues, because yes, Parker could see that legally, he was stuck.

It was that—*Go ahead, this is good,* advised Spike—

even after all these years of her father's neglect and vague disapproval, she would've given a lot to have one-tenth of the affection Harry Welles offered so freely to James. Maybe James was the son he'd always wanted. Maybe James reminded Harry of his younger self. But just once, it would've been nice if her father had called *her* up and asked her to come for dinner or play a game of squash or go to one of his single-malt nights.

Stupid, that even after all these years, she still wanted her dad. Not the man Harry had become, but the man he'd once been, who'd pushed her on a swing and let her sit in his chair at Welles Financial and answer his phone.

Well. That guy had taken a bullet to the heart when she was ten years old.

"Old news, my friends," Parker said. She started the car and glanced across the street. Gideon's Cove Animal Shelter, the sign said. And quite unexpectedly, she found herself turning into the driveway. There was a gray-shingled house and a small outbuilding from which the sound of barking could be heard.

"Hello there!" called a young woman as Parker got out of the car. She came over, wiping her hands on her jeans. "Can I help you?" She glanced at Parker's Rhode Island plates. "You must be Julia Harrington's niece. Hi, I'm Beth Seymour. Sorry. Small towns. We know every-one's business."

"Parker Welles. Nice to meet you."

"You looking for a pet?" Beth asked.

"No, I just stopped. I've never had a pet before." Except Apollo, if you could count that thing. She won-dered briefly what had happened to it. Harry probably gave it to a minion. Or ate it.

"Come on in, since you're here," Beth said. Crafty woman. Parker followed. She was *not* going to get a dog.

Or a cat—Lucy had a cat, and it was always leaping onto Parker's lap and sniffing her lips, which Parker found quite repulsive. Why she was even standing here was a mystery.

"Pets take a lot of work. I won't lie," Beth said, opening the door of the outbuilding. "But the love they give you…it's worth any price."

Nice sale line. "So what have you got here? Not that I'm really looking." *You could be!* sang the Holy Rollers. *Pets can fill those giant voids in people's lives!*

"Well, we try to be a no-kill shelter," Beth said, "but times are kind of hard, and donations have been down. We have a lot of animals, sad to say, and we're running out of room. The vet's coming to put a couple to sleep today, actually."

Shee-it. Parker could picture a chunk of resolve crumbling like sand. "That's really sad."

At the sight of their caregiver, several dogs leaped to their feet, barking joyfully. Or savagely. Parker couldn't tell. "This girl's going on to her great reward today." Beth stopped in front of the first enclosure and pointed to an orange tabby cat. To Parker's eyes, it already looked dead, its filmy eyes half-open, fur dull and uneven. "She's twenty-one, can you believe it? Her owner died two weeks ago. At least they'll be in heaven together."

It's true, the Holy Rollers confirmed.

"This girl is the other one we have to let go." Beth knelt down in front of the next kennel. "I'm so sorry, honey," she crooned. "Don't be scared."

Parker looked in. A brown-and-white dog sat in the corner, as far away from the door of her cage as she could get, trembling. Parker couldn't see her face, but her fur was long and feathery.

"You think she knows?" Parker asked, shoving her hands in her pockets. "She looks scared."

"No. She's always like this. Bob Castellano—have you met him yet? No? Well, he was behind someone out on Route 119, and they pushed the dog right out the window. Didn't even stop! Can you believe that? She had a broken leg and two broken ribs, not to mention a bunch of cuts and bruises. She's all mended now, but no one wants her. She's too shy."

"Guess you can't blame her."

"Yeah. She's been with us four months now."

"Think she'd bite? Since she's so scared?"

"I've never even heard her growl. She's too afraid." Beth stood up and sighed. "So. She'll be put down later on, too, poor thing. But down here, we have kittens. Christy and Will Jones are taking two of them, but there are two left. And we have this very cute little pit-bull mutt—he's an absolute sweetheart."

Parker didn't move. Thrown out of a moving car, huh? Unbelievable. Well, it was one of a thousand horror stories, she was sure. She couldn't afford a pet, no matter how sad its life had been thus far. And she didn't know anything about dogs. She liked them, often stopped to admire one here and there, but she didn't know how to train one or take care of it.

Even if she wanted to have a dog, she had nowhere to put the thing. Parker wasn't sure where she herself would be sleeping tonight. Most likely, the car once again.

"I'll take her," she said.

Fifty bucks later—really, not so much—with another fifty in dog supplies—collar, leash, shampoo, food, heartworm pills, brush—Parker went slowly into the dog's cage. The poor thing bowed her head and looked away as if certain Parker was about to kick her.

"Hi," Parker said, squatting down. "Want to come home with me?" The dog didn't move, but she didn't flinch, either, when Parker reached out and petted her neck, working her way up to the dog's cheeks, which were as soft and plush as velvet. The dog didn't resist, but didn't look at her. "I won't hurt you, sweetie," Parker murmured. Slowly, as if picking up Nicky while he was asleep, she lifted the dog into her arms. No resistance.

"Looks like she found her forever family," Beth said.

The Holy Rollers sighed in deep satisfaction. Spike even wiped away a tear.

"What will you name her?" Beth asked.

Parker looked down at her new best friend. Not the most attractive dog, with her drooping ears and sorrowful face. She had a bald spot behind one ear, and one of her eyes didn't open quite as much as the other. Her head seemed too big for her body. Parker looked at Beth and smiled. "Beauty."

CHAPTER EIGHT

JAMES WAS FILTHY and exhausted by the time Parker finally found her way back to the house. He watched as she got out of the car, then turned and lifted something out. It was a dog, some kind of spaniel mutt, maybe twenty pounds, curled into her arms. She set the animal on the ground and clipped on a leash.

"Aw. We have a dog now?" James said.

"*I* have a dog now," Parker said. "Thing One, meet Beauty. Beauty, Thing One."

"Hi, Beauty," James said. The dog tucked her head behind Parker's knee and peed, not even bothering to crouch, trembling, unable to even look at him.

Parker tilted her head and gave James a smile. "You have that effect on women, I guess."

He returned her smile. "Not all women."

Her ears started doing that sunrise thing, getting all pink, then red. Then she popped the trunk and lifted out a bag. "I bought out the hardware store. Think you could grab a few things so we could get to work?"

"Sure."

We, huh? She walked past him, her dog scuttling along, half-crouched, as if James was about to karate-chop her on the head. Parker, on the other hand, looked pretty damn good in those jeans, all long legs and perfect ass. And how was it that she smelled good...well, okay, sure, she smelled like dog, but also a little bit like…whatever it was she smelled like. Lemons or something. Flowers. Who knew? She smelled good, dog or no dog.

Just before she got in, her cell phone rang. "Hey, Ethan!" she said, her face lighting up. "No, I talked to them a little while ago. How are you? You did? Cool! Hang on a sec, the cell-phone service out here is horrible. Let me go down to the dock. Yes, there's a dock, and no, it's not what you're picturing."

She set her bag down and went around to the front of the house, the dog slinking beside her through the long grass.

And here was the thing. It *irritated* him. First of all, he'd spent the past few hours shoveling garbage on her behalf, and like some little kid who'd gotten an A on his paper, he wanted to show her. *Think you could grow a pair, guy?* his conscience asked. Secondly, message received. The Paragon calls, the minion can wait. Not that Ethan Mirabelli was a bad guy, based on James's interactions with him over the years…friendly, successful, great father. That was the problem.

And third…she was down on the dock, and he hadn't checked that out yet, and who knew if it was sturdy? What if she fell in? She was standing on it, and it hadn't sunk, but he'd been too busy getting the water turned back on and clearing out her room to get to it.

She was laughing now. She sat on the dock crosslegged, looking every bit the upper-crust, beautiful, graceful woman she was. Oh, a little hair toss. Too bad the Paragon wasn't able to see it.

"You're an idiot," James told himself. He went back inside—plenty more crap to shovel—and got to work.

But he checked on her every thirty seconds or so, just to make sure she hadn't fallen in.

WHEN SHE HUNG UP with Ethan, Parker felt considerably cheered. The fact that he'd called made her feel less out of the loop. One thing to check in with your kid a couple times a day, another to have Ethan call her just to say hi. Maybe Lucy had told him she'd sounded lonely—and she'd tried not to, honest—or maybe, and more likely, Eth was a prince.

For about five minutes last summer, when Lucy had decided that she should marry some guy who wasn't related to her dead husband, Ethan and Parker had thought about trying to be more than friends and parents of the same kid. After all, they laughed at the same jokes. They were both attractive. Once upon a time, they'd gotten it on with satisfactory physical results and a beautiful child. They were both single. Why not, right?

But whatever chemistry had once been between them had faded, and one kiss was enough to make them each rub their mouths with the backs of their hands. "You gave me cooties," Ethan had said, and they'd ended up baking brownies and playing Scrabble.

It was too bad, in a way, because Ethan was pretty damn perfect. If he could clone himself and excise the part that had loved Lucy since he was nineteen years old, she was pretty sure he could be the One.

"What do you think, Beauty?" Parker asked. The dog had followed her without protest, James being the more obvious threat, but she wouldn't make eye contact. Slowly, Parker put her hand out and stroked the dog's cheek with one finger. So soft. "Good girl," Parker said. "Good girl, Beauty." The dog sidled closer to her, and a strange, sweet feeling filled Parker's chest. She'd like to find the person who'd thrown her dog out of a moving vehicle and kick him in the nuts. Wearing her sharpest Jimmy Choo heels.

Parker looked up at the house and sighed. Time to get to work. There was Thing One, looking at her from the window— Hey! He'd taken the boards off the windows! Fantastic.

"Come on, girl," she said to Beauty, standing up and heading up the short flight of stairs. The back of the house was barricaded by more junk—a table, boxes, a couple of plastic chairs, a tire—so she went around the front, the dog walking so close to her legs that Parker almost tripped.

She went inside and lurched to a halt.

"Holy halos, Thing One," she breathed.

The hallway that yesterday she'd had to sidle down was completely empty. Wood floor. Grimy walls, a hole near the ceiling, but the entire hallway was cleared. She went down to the kitchen. "My God! You did all this?"

"Yeah," he answered.

"You… Wow. This is amazing."

The kitchen was much improved. There were still plastic boxes of who-knew-what, but the trash and cardboard and newspapers were gone. And it smelled *much* better, thanks to the salt air blowing through the windows.

She glanced out the window at the Dumpster that now graced the side of the house. It was already about a quarter full. "That's a lot of crap," she murmured.

"I kept some things I thought you might want. Over there on the table."

She glanced over, then did a double take at the glass case on the floor by the wall. "Is that Apollo?"

James shrugged. "Think of him as mouse control. I already gave him one."

"Really?"

"That's what he eats."

"Well, we can't keep him in the kitchen. He gives me the willies."

"Yes, Majesty. He can stay in my room."

Whoops. She did sound a little imperial there. "That would be great. Thank you."

"Here's the deal," James said. "The fridge works, but it needs to be scoured. It's not the most efficient thing in the world, but it'll keep things cold. The oven is shot and I think your mouse and all his friends live in there, so we should ditch it. My uncle knows a used one you can buy pretty cheap. The cupboards are bolted on, so if we tear them off, it'll rip out chunks of the walls. The best bet is probably to clean and paint them. You'll need a new subfloor and linoleum or tile in here, but the floors in the rest of the house are wood. Clean them up, slap on some polyurethane and you have character. New roof, new shingles, cut down some of the scrub around the house, fix the stairs to the dock and the real-estate agent says you might be able to pay off the back taxes and get a little besides."

"Back taxes? And how much is a little?"

"Depends on the offer you get."

Crikey. She didn't really want to hear the actual figure. "Think I'll have enough left over to buy a house in Rhode Island?"

"Not even close."

A strand of panic laced through her. Parker took a deep breath. And another. Looked at Apollo, who stared back impassively.

You can only do what you can do, the Holy Rollers chimed. True enough.

She looked around the kitchen, which still had yards and yards of crap in it, then back at Thing One, who was looking at her, arms folded, face unreadable.

"Thank you, James," she said.

His expression softened. "You're welcome."

His eyes were dark, dark brown. Best not to look for too long. She cleared her throat. "I guess I'll get to work on my room."

"You do that."

She went down the hall, opened the door and got another shock.

The room was completely empty. All that stuff…the clothes and boxes and lamps and macramé and Christmas ornaments…was gone. The room was bigger than it had appeared when crammed with junk; the windows were open and somewhat battered screens were in the windows. It smelled clean. It *was* clean.

"Your bed is being delivered later on." His voice made her jump. He'd followed her down the hall.

"What bed?"

He shrugged. "I figured you were too much of a princess to sleep on the floor, so I ordered you a bed. Nothing special. Just a frame and a box spring and mattress."

"James…" Her cheeks burned, and she swallowed.

He smiled. Oh, that was dangerous.

Parker did not find Thing One particularly appealing, though she could recognize that he was attractive. He just didn't *do* anything for her. No, those sulky good looks and arrogant bone structure…yawn. He looked like a Gucci model or a bored playboy. Not her type. Not at all.

Until he smiled. He had a wide, generous smile, almost too wide if there was such a thing, and his eyes crinkled far more than a young man's should, and heck *yeah,* she felt it in Lady Land, uh-*huh.*

And given that they were apparently stuck together for the summer—and as James Cahill was the last guy she'd slept with—this was a very dangerous thing indeed.

CHAPTER NINE

TWO YEARS AGO, the thought of sleeping with Thing One had never crossed Parker's mind.

Really.

Since the day she'd met him, Thing One had *bugged* her. Intellectually, she knew that it wasn't his fault that Harry had sent him to the hospital the day Nicky was born. Just doing what the boss said, following orders, covering for Harry's complete and utter lack of interest. Whatever the case, roughly five hours after she'd given birth, a stranger had been standing in her hospital room. Not her father.

She knew that Harry had viewed her decision to A) have Nicky and B) not marry Ethan as a personal slap in the face, but Parker had honestly thought that once he saw his first—possibly only—grandchild, he'd thaw. He'd never viewed her books as much of an accomplishment—well, she couldn't fault him on that. But a baby, come on. Surely he'd be thrilled to meet his grandchild.

But no. He'd sent a stranger. The fact that the lawyer had thought to buy a stuffed animal only reinforced the fact that Harry had sent nothing but legal documents. No flowers—apparently one didn't reward one's wayward daughter for having a bastard child—and nothing for her beautiful, perfect, miraculous baby other than Nicky's cut of the family trust. Thing One's presence announced—shouted—the fact that her child wasn't important enough for Harry to leave work…Harry, who once stopped a meeting with the head of Goldman Sachs because his nine-year-old daughter had come to his office to tell him she won the school spelling bee.

And then Thing One had kept *on* showing up, sent by Harry or accompanying Harry, and while Parker knew that it was at her father's behest, it still drove her crazy. Obviously, Harry couldn't bear to be around her, even with Nicky there. Thing One was at Nicky's baptism, his first birthday, his second birthday. If Harry summoned the rest of the family to a party, which he did once a year—the better to rub their noses in his superior wealth—Thing One would be there, too.

That first day in the hospital, she'd almost felt sorry for him—he was so awkward and uncomfortable. But then he tried to cover for Harry, lying about how her father was so sorry he couldn't come—as if Harry had ever apologized for anything. It made it worse, knowing that a stranger knew how low she was on her father's list of priorities. And then, Thing One turned rather glib, a Harry Junior, almost, and that line, *Parker, always lovely to see you,* was so sarcastic. She knew she was nothing but another duty given to him by Harry.

Before long, Harry was calling Thing One "son" and inviting him to those pretentious wine-tasting dinners with his cronies or taking him out on Granddad's wooden sailboat. Mostly, though, Parker was more irritated with herself than with Harry. He hadn't sought out her company for years; why would he now? Her father had missed her graduation from Miss Porter's, though he did make it to her graduation from Harvard and spent the time schmoozing senators and Kennedys. He never came to her book signings. Even when she signed at

Barnes & Noble in New York City and there was a line out the door, he didn't show up.

On the occasions that Harry did interact with her son, Parker had to admit, he wasn't bad. He'd ask Nicky questions about what he wanted to be when he grew up—standard awkward adult fare—as compared with Gianni Mirabelli, who'd get down on his arthritic knees and pretend to be a horse or teach her son how to make the perfect meatball. But once, Parker came upon Harry and Nicky in the study, coloring, and a warm, hopeful feeling had rushed through her so fast, though what exactly she hoped for wasn't clear.

A month later, she invited her father to come to Nicky's graduation from swimming class; her boy had won the Eel Award for fastest swimmer. Wonder of wonders, Harry's assistant called back to say yes, Mr. Welles would come, and Parker really thought maybe a new era was about to start, now that Nicky was old enough to warrant her father's interest.

Harry didn't show. But there was Thing One, expensive suit, calfskin briefcase, as if Nicky wouldn't notice the difference.

Sleeping with Thing One? Please. It never even crossed her mind.

Until her cousin Esme's wedding.

Harry had two older sisters, Louise and Vivian. They, in turn, had three daughters, Esme, Juliet and Regan. When Parker was young, the four cousins would play together during the summers at Grayhurst, unaware of the tension between the adults.

But then her parents divorced, and Althea took Parker to Colorado, only to send her back East for boarding school in Connecticut. During term breaks, Parker would sometimes stay with one of her aunts, who lived on the same street in giant homes that weren't big enough for them, and listen to them complain about her father.

Harry was a legend on Wall Street. The Welles fortune, founded first on shipping, then on mills, had dwindled significantly in the 1960s as manufacturing went overseas. By the time Harry was a teenager, there was a little money, but they were hardly the Kennedys or the Hiltons. Enough for membership in the country club and college for Harry and his sisters, a very modest trust fund to get each one started as adults.

Then Harry decided to swing for the bleachers. He took his trust fund, asked his sisters if they wanted in—they declined; Harry was just out of Wharton and what did he know? Harry sold his car, schmoozed every client his father had, hit up every friend for a loan and stepped up to bat. He took every cent he'd managed to get his hands on and bought up stock from a little company that dealt with a technology no one had ever heard of.

Turned out Apple Computer did okay. Harry was featured on the cover of *Forbes* magazine, a baseball bat over one shoulder, a cocky grin on his handsome face and the headline Play Big or Go Home. Welles Financial, founded by Parker's great-grandfather, went from a stodgy, trustworthy investment firm to an enormous force on Wall Street, and Harry became filthy rich.

His sisters had their modest inheritances; beyond that, if they wanted more—and they did—they had to come to Harry and present their request, be it jobs for their husbands or the money for an addition to keep up with the Joneses. Harry might or might not grant said request; his sisters hadn't trusted him back in the beginning, and he made them pay, and they hated him for it. Didn't stop them from asking, though.

And so Parker was an outsider, too, by association.

Her cousins became an impenetrable clique, her aunts joined forces to disapprove of her, and Parker found herself thinking of them as the Coven. When she had to come to stay, Juliet, Regan and Esme made sure she was left out of the conversation, took potshots at Althea and her marriages, mocked Parker's hair, clothes, shoes. Her aunts weren't much better. Once, she overheard them discussing Althea's latest divorce from Parker's second stepfather, who was a lovely man; Parker had been devastated when he'd left. "Who'd want Althea *and* a sulky teenager?" Louise asked, laughing.

"Sulky's the least of her problems," Vivian said. "Juliet thinks she might be doing drugs."

"I wouldn't be surprised," Louise answered. "She'll probably end up overdosing in a nightclub bathroom somewhere." There was a pause and the clink of ice as Louise took a sip of her Long Island iced tea.

Parker became even more of a freak by getting pregnant out of wedlock—and staying pregnant—and choosing to be a single mom. The books put her over the edge.

Family gatherings…eesh. Parker once described them to Ethan as *Flowers in the Attic* meets *Jaws*. Generally, she avoided them like a robust case of Ebola, but once a year or so, she had to make an appearance, and Esme's wedding was one such affair.

Parker was a bridesmaid, pretty much because Harry was paying for the wedding, an obscene affair at the Rosecliff mansion in Newport. Esme and Aunt Vivian had wheedled and whined to Harry for weeks before he finally played Santa and said of *course* he'd pay for his niece's wedding. Apparently, Esme had been yearning to get married at Rosecliff since her conception, and she'd gleefully spent Harry's money hand over fist: flowers and hairstylists, a twenty-thousand-dollar dress, yada yada yada.

None of that made Parker welcome. She'd spent the rehearsal dinner largely being ignored and pretending not to mind. She hadn't been invited to help Esme get ready the morning of the wedding, either. Nicky was with Ethan, so Parker had gone to Rosecliff alone. She figured she'd do her bridesmaid duties, endure the reception, then leave as soon as she could.

"Thanks, Chuck," she said to the driver of the car service her father kept on retainer. "I'll be maybe three hours, okay? I'll text you when I'm ready to go."

"You bet, Miss Welles," he said.

"Sure you don't want to be my date?" she said, tipping him a twenty.

"Very. No offense."

She laughed. "I hear you, pal. See you later." Heart sinking a little, she got out of the car. "I am a wonderful mother," she said as she approached the mansion. "I am a very successful author." *Preach it, sister!* the Holy Rollers chorused. "And no one can make you feel inferior if you've had enough to drink. Or something."

Without your consent! the angels corrected in their tiny, scolding voices.

Inside was the Coven—Esme, the bride, and Juliet and Regan as co–maids of honor—huddled together in a preceremony clump. Her aunts made disapproving noises about Parker's timing, though she'd arrived ten minutes before they'd told her to.

"You look exhausted," Aunt Vivian said, frowning. "Are you sick?"

"No, I'm fine, thanks," Parker said. "Esme, you look beautiful."

"Thanks. Um…so do you?" the bride said, staring at Parker as if she had a third arm.

Parker smiled determinedly, took her bouquet and walked down the aisle, her eyes searching for her father. One thing they had in common—they hated family events. She didn't see him, but then again, there were four hundred wedding guests.

In the receiving line, Juliet took her shots. "Parker, did you bring your husband? Wait, are you married? I always forget." As if they hadn't seen each other the night before.

"Nope. Not married."

"And how old is your son again? It is a boy, right?"

"Nicky's three."

"Are you seeing anyone these days? It must be hard, because who wants a single mom?"

Finally, the reception began in earnest. Parker glanced around for a safe haven, hoping to see a friendly face somewhere. One of her uncles—Louise's husband—had always been nice, but the last time she'd seen him, he'd hugged her a little too long, his hand a little too low on her back.

Still no Harry. He wouldn't miss a family wedding— or the chance to remind people who paid for it—and last she knew, he was coming. For a second, she indulged in the fantasy that she and her father were close. That they'd sit together today, that he'd dance with her and tell her she was the prettiest girl in the room. He'd come to Grayhurst after the wedding and play Candy Land with Nicky, read him books until her son fell asleep. Then she and her dad would watch something manly on TV, because Harry loved war movies. *Saving Private Ryan.* She'd make popcorn.

Right.

She should've brought a date. Ethan would've come, and Lucy would've loved to have babysat. She could've hired an escort, like in that movie she'd fallen asleep on a few weeks ago. But needing armor and actually admitting you needed armor were different things.

A drink, however, was definitely in order.

"Hello," she said to the bartender, smiling. "I would like a very strong martini with three olives and a smidge of brine."

"Belvedere okay?" he asked.

"How about Stoli Elit? Got any of that?" she said. It was her father's favorite.

"You have good taste," he said.

"Got that right, buddy," she answered, grinning. She gave him a fifty as a tip, knowing half her relatives would fail to tip him at all. Rich people. Sucky tippers.

The martini went down as it should, icy cold and so smooth she barely noticed.

"Parker! What are you doing, just standing there?" It was dear Cousin Regan, dragging her fiancé behind her.

"I'm taking it all in," Parker said.

"You haven't met Rob, my fiancé, have you?" Regan asked.

"We met last night," Parker said, nodding at him, the poor guy. "Hello again."

"So, like, *our* wedding?" Regan said. "I'm thinking Manhattan? Like…the Pierre? Right, Rob?"

Parker nodded, feigning interest. This would be Regan's third engagement, and if it followed suit, it should be over in, oh, about an hour. Regan enjoyed upstaging other people's weddings.

"And how are your little books doing?" her cousin asked, nudging Rob with her elbow.

"They're doing great. The last one came out at number five on the *Times* list," Parker said.

"Rob, Parker writes those strange little books about the angels," Regan said in mock explanation. "They're very…um…precious?"

"So glad you like them," Parker said. "Excuse me for one second." No point in hanging around Regan, who'd recently posted a vicious review of *The Holy Rollers and the Blind Little Bunny* on Amazon. She'd forgotten to use a screen name, however. Or maybe she hadn't.

Regan's whisper, loud enough to ensure she was heard, followed Parker. "Those books? They, like, make you want to *hurl*. And her mother? On her *fourth* rich old man. Seriously."

The thing was, Regan couldn't say anything about her books that Parker didn't already think herself. The books were a joke, it was true. That they were bringing Save the Children some serious money didn't matter to the Coven.

As for Althea, well, it was also true.

"How about another one of these?" she said to the nice bartender.

She sidled through the crowd, saying hello here and there, making her way out of the throng. She had to stay; if she left, it would be an admission of defeat. But hey. She could have a quiet moment. The thing about having a three-year-old…the only time he didn't talk was when he was asleep, and the questions these days! *Why, Mommy? Why? Why? Why not? Why?* She smiled. Maybe she'd give Ethan a call, see how their wunderkind was doing. So much for not wanting to talk to anyone. A friendly, nice person…she would *love* to talk to a friendly, nice person. But these mean people? They sucked.

Seemed as if the martinis were having the desired effect. That bartender knew what he was doing, yes, sir.

She wandered into the foyer—well, *a* foyer, because this place was huge. It was less crowded here, and oh, perfect. A small, secret staircase leading up to the second floor.

Parker went up, not spilling a drop of martini because hey! She was a Miss Porter's grad, thank you very much! Stellar education *and* social graces. Also, the drink was nearly gone.

At the top of the staircase was a long hallway blocked by a velvet rope. Parker sat down a few steps from the top. From here, she could see not only the foyer, but the guests going in and out of the ballroom. Esme, despite being Bridezilla, was beautiful in her crystal-beaded dress, and certainly, as settings went, it didn't get better than Rosecliff, if you liked ostentatious excess, which the Welles family certainly did. Everyone was dressed to kill, and laughter and squeals floated up.

Oh, bugger. A dark-haired man had spied her staircase and was heading up. Parker looked into her purse, planning to make that phone call and avoid conversation. But the man stopped.

"Parker. Always lovely to see you."

She winced and looked up. "Thing One. How are you?"

"Fine, thanks."

"Is my father here?" she asked, hating that he would know and she didn't.

"I'm afraid he can't make it."

For God's sake. Her father was blowing off his own niece's wedding. The Coven would have a fit. Parker was used to it—Thing One: Emissary—but Harry usually put in an appearance with the extended family, the better to lord his power.

"Anything you need, Parker?"

"No thank you."

"Not even this?" He handed her an icy glass and sat next to her. "I asked the bartender what you were drinking."

"And to think I never liked you," she said with a small smile. He raised an eyebrow. "Thanks, Thing One."

He had a drink, as well, and sat down next to her. Like every man there, he was wearing a tux, which was… good. Not many men looked worse in a tuxedo, and Thing One was no exception. He was quite attractive. Not to her, of course. But he looked…good.

Wicked good.

She took a sip of her drink.

"Having a nice time?" he asked, giving her a sidelong glance.

"Oh, absolutely. You?"

"You bet." This was their first one-on-one conversation since…since Nicky was born, come to think of it. "So how have you been, Parker?" he asked.

She smiled as she sipped the martini. "Do you care, Thing One?"

"Of course. I'm paid to care." He grinned at her, and Parker had to laugh.

"At least you're honest. If there is such a thing as an honest lawyer, that is." He had a nice smile. Hell.

"I get the idea that you're somehow persona non grata around here," he said. "Why is that?"

"No clue."

"Probably because you're prettier than anyone else."

Parker rolled her eyes. "Save the ass kissing for my father, dear boy."

He shook his head and looked into his drink, the smile playing around his mouth. "Beautiful women. So cruel."

"Smarmy men. So common."

"Now you're just reinforcing my point." He reached into his breast pocket and pulled out a long, slender box tied with a silky black ribbon. "Happy birthday from your dad."

Oh, hell. Bugger and damn. She swallowed carefully, not looking at Thing One.

Because yes, it was her birthday. No one had mentioned that fact when Esme's wedding date had been set, and Parker hadn't wanted to bring it up. She wasn't sure that her aunts knew when her birthday was.

She wasn't sure her *father* knew when her birthday was.

Parker took the package from Thing One's hand and untied the ribbon.

Inside the box was a fountain pen made of some glossy blue stone. It was heavy and beautiful, and there were two cartridges of peacock-green ink. She could use it for signings. The kids would love the ink color, and her signature would look like calligraphy, coming out of the brass nib.

It was perfect. "My father did not pick this out," she said, not looking at him.

At least he didn't deny it. She turned her head to look at him. His eyes were brown. She'd never noticed that before. There was a warm, tugging sensation down in Lady Land. Thing One had nice brown eyes. He'd brought her a present *and* a martini. And had she mentioned the tux?

"What's your name, Thing One?" It was James. She knew that. She just didn't want him to know she knew it.

"James."

"James what?"

"James Francis Xavier Cahill." He smiled as he spoke, and she felt the tug harder this time, her stomach tightening, knees tingling.

"Thank you for the beautiful pen, James Francis Xavier Cahill."

"You're welcome," he said.

That was a *good* smile, vodka goggles or not. A great smile. That was a smile involving his whole face. Yep. With vodka goggles—quite possibly without, she'd never really let herself dwell—Thing One was *smokin'* hot. Really thick, dark brown hair. It would be hard to check for deer ticks in hair like that. Okay, that was the mother part of her speaking…also maybe the vodka part. *Let's shift gears, shall we?* Parker asked herself. *No need to waste a perfectly satisfactory ogle thinking about ticks.* Hair that would look excellent if it were all tousled and rumpled. There. Much better. His eyes were, shoot, she couldn't think of the word for them, but they were smiley. Smiley eyes with very nice crinkles around them. One of his incisors was a little bit crooked, and for some reason, that made his smile even better.

"How old are you, James Francis Xavier Cahill?"

"Twenty-eight."

Five years younger than she was. She could've babysat for him. She wouldn't have *minded* babysitting him, now that she thought about it…when he was around eighteen, let's say, and she was twenty-three. Weren't there porno movies about that kind of thing?

He seemed to read her dirty mind, because he smiled again, just a little. Then his eyes dropped to her mouth. Heck yeah! So he was having kissing thoughts, too. And from the looks of it, his mouth would be excellent for kissing, full and generous.

Kind. That was the word she was looking for. He had kind eyes.

He reached out, slowly, and tucked a wisp of hair behind her ear, and without further thought, Parker leaned in and kissed him.

She was right. His lips were smooth and warm and it was so, so nice, simply having her lips against someone else's, someone not her child—crikey, it had been a *very* long time. And James let her kiss him, the gentle pressure of his mouth just enough to let her know he didn't mind. A lovely kiss. Perfect. Made Lady Land feel kind of wriggly and warm, and oh, hey, look at this, she was frenching him, and that wriggly feeling leaped and twirled and surged.

He didn't mind at all, apparently, because the next minute, he was kissing her back. She could taste whiskey on him, and oh, God, he was good at this, kissing was so underrated, there should be kissing apps for phones or something. Her fingers slid through his thick, wavy hair, and his arms slipped around her and pulled her closer. The heat and the gentle scrape of his five-o'clock shadow, and oh, man, that *mouth* against hers…this guy would graduate top of his kissing class, no doubt.

Her heart was thudding, lust thick and hot in her veins, drowning out rational thought. Parker ran her hands down his neck, his shoulders thick with muscle—*nice,* Thing One!—then slid her hands under his tuxedo jacket and felt the heat of his skin under the thin cotton of his shirt.

From down below came the sound of someone laughing.

"Know what?" she said, tearing her mouth off his and

standing unsteadily. "Come with me." She grabbed his hand and practically dragged him up the rest of the stairs, shoved aside the velvet rope and towed James down the hallway, opened the third door on the right, and bingo. A bedroom, thank you very much.

James pushed her against the wall and kissed her again, and it was so welcome, so wonderful, being kissed like that, as if the building could burn down around them and it would be more important to keep kissing, hard and hot and fierce. His hands slid down her sides, to her ass, pulling her against him, and damn if her legs weren't already shaking.

His mouth had moved to her neck, his dark hair brushing her cheek, and Parker felt such a wave of...longing and tenderness and gratitude and a melting sweetness. He *wanted* her. There was no doubt about that, and she turned her head and kissed his jaw, just under his ear, making him groan a little.

Then he straightened up and looked at her, leaning his forehead against hers. "You really want this to happen?" he asked, and his voice wasn't quite steady, and that sealed the deal.

"Yes," she said. Then she pulled him close and pulled his shirt from out of his pants and slid her hands up his hot skin.

He unzipped her dress and didn't ask any more questions.

No, sir. No indeed.

As PARKER WOKE UP—holy halos, she'd fallen asleep with a near stranger—her first thought, aside from "Parker, you slut," was "Dear Lord, don't let me be pregnant." Yes, they'd used a condom. And she was on the Pill, not that she'd needed it for contraception; her gynecologist recommended it as prevention for ovarian cancer. Whatever. Chances were, she wasn't preggers.

Next thought was "Please don't let him wake up."

James Francis Xavier Cahill was *beautiful*. His cheeks were flushed, giving him a boyish look, and one arm was up over his head. How had she not noticed how delicious he was before this day? He looked like a fallen angel. He looked beautiful. He looked…eesh…young.

If she could get out of here without talking to him, that would be fantastic, because what the heck do you say after you, the somewhat inebriated older woman, drag a man, the hot young stud, into a bedroom, basically tear off his clothes and shag him silly? She barely let him speak. May as well have commanded him to *do* her.

Not that he seemed to mind.

Her dress, his shirt, her shoes, his tie, were all strewn around the room. So classy. Parker grabbed her panties and dress and slunk into the bathroom attached to the bedroom—excellent for trysts, these mansions— and looked at her reflection. Her mascara was smudged, her lips pink and bee-stung, her cheeks pink. Eyes were dreamy.

We're so disappointed, said the Holy Rollers.

We're not, said Lady Land. *Thank you! That was rather spectacular, yes?*

Yes.

Nevertheless, this was a huge mistake! Thing One? For God's sake! What was she thinking? She was thinking Stoli Elit, that's what she was thinking. Stoli Elit, a bad case of poor little rich girl and James Cahill's smile. Bad, bad combo. So bad. So naughty. *Dirty,* even.

The thought of what they'd done…what he'd done to her…and the noises it evoked…the feelings that had prac-

tically— *Okay! Stop! Let's get moving here, shall we?
Before the Coven finds us?*

She dressed and ran a wet facecloth under her eyes,
dampened her fingers and slicked her hair back into
its twist once more. There. She looked normal—for a
woman who'd spent the past hour against the wall, on
the bed and yes, on the floor. With her father's attorney.

Oh, this was bad.

She'd slip out of the room and call her driver and get
out of Dodge. James could wake up and do whatever he
wanted, but a face-to-face encounter? Bad idea.

She opened the door and jumped. There he was, right
in the doorway.

"Sneaking out?" he said.

"Oh, no, no," she stammered. "Nope. No. Just…fresh-
ening. Freshening up, that is."

He had his pants on, and his shirt, though it was un-
buttoned. Oh, *Mommy.*

"Are you going back to the reception, or making a run
for the border?" he asked, giving her a quick once-over.

Border. "The reception. Esme's my cousin. I'm a
bridesmaid."

"And will you acknowledge me down there?"

The question caught her off guard. Parker found she
was pinching her pinkie. Hard. "Um, of course."

"Really?"

There was something a little…dubious in his eyes.
"Yes, James."

He grinned, and once again, it hit her, the force of
that incredible smile. "Is there any chance you'll sit with
me during dinner? Because as much as I love the Welles
family…"

"They're piranhas," she said.

"They're piranhas," he agreed. "So?"

Wow. When she'd imagined the reception, she'd pictured a few painful hours with the Coven; James of the beautiful smile was much, much more appealing. "Sure. I'd love to." Her ears felt hot. This was almost like a date.

"Great." He was looking at her mouth again, and Parker felt her knees wobble. "Any chance I can drive you home?"

"There's always a chance," she murmured.

"I'll take it," he said. God, he was *darling!* How had she missed this? "Want me to go out first? So your evil cousins don't bust you?"

"That would be great. Thank you."

Five minutes later, James was once again impeccably dressed. He stood in front of her, looked at her for a long minute. "See you down there," he said, and there it was again, that smile.

"Okay." She bit her lip, then, on impulse, gave him a quick kiss on the cheek.

His smile grew. Then he winked at her and left the room, closing the door quietly behind him.

Parker sank down on the bed and let out a long breath.

So. Okay, it wasn't as if this was her first time, obviously, not with a three-year-old son. But the whole earth-moving experience…she hadn't had a whole lot of that. Sex had always been nice. Very nice. Fun. And sure, it had been a while. She hadn't had a—oh, hell, a *lover,* though her mind cringed away from the word—since Ethan.

That had been four years ago.

Holy halos.

So maybe it was just a long abstinence with only the pulsating showerhead for company on nights she couldn't sleep, but holy heck, sex with James Francis Xavier Cahill had been unbe*liev*able. Heck yeah!

Parker realized she was smiling. Apparently, the best sex of a woman's life did that to her. James the Cutie-Pie, Purveyor of Said Experience, did that to her, and the thought of that smile, that slightly crooked tooth, the way his eyes looked so happy when he smiled…her knees were feeling wriggly again.

She sighed. Dreamily, for heaven's sake.

But for one second, she let herself feel dreamy. Moony. Dopey. Meltish. It was kind of wonderful.

Guess she'd misjudged Thing One. Strike that. James. James was *nice*. Wasn't he? He was hot, sure, but he also seemed kind of… And he'd made sure she'd… Maybe they'd…well. She didn't want to get ahead of herself.

"Okay, team," she said aloud. "Time to rejoin the masses."

She took another look at herself, hoped that while she definitely had a certain glow, no one would be able to tell she'd been *done*—the inhabitants of Lady Land gave a hot squeeze—and left the bedroom. There were the stairs—*hello, stairs, thank you so much*—and she started down.

And there, in the foyer, was her father, laughing with James.

Parker stopped, squeezing her pinkie hard. Harder, even, till the tip was numb. For some reason, her heart was sinking, and fast.

"Harry," she said, her voice pleasant. "Didn't think you were going to make it."

"Parker," he said. "Hello."

James glanced at her with a little smile, then murmured something to her father, and for one horrible second, she thought he was telling Harry that they'd done the deed, and Harry would clap James on the back and congratulate him or something.

"Happy birthday, by the way," Harry said.

Oh. Maybe that was worse, having James need to tell her father when she was born.

"Thank you." She lifted an eyebrow, something she'd mastered at age seven after watching her father stare a minion into tears.

"James, there's someone I want you to meet," Harry said. "Parker, we'll see you in there."

"Okay," she said, watching as Harry put his arm around James. The two men walked away, but James looked back. Held up his hand and mouthed, *Five minutes*.

The thing was, she knew how long five minutes could last.

"Parker, where have you been?" It was Aunt Vivian, and she was pissed. "Dinner is being served! Would you please come in here? It's Esme's special day. Would it kill you to remember that? Honestly."

And so she ended up with the Coven, after all. The only person at the table with an empty chair next to her.

Five minutes became ten. Ten became twenty. Salad was served. "Isn't Uncle Harry ever going to come over?" Esme whined. He was halfway across the room, glad-handing someone and roaring with laughter.

"Look at that lawyer of his," Juliet said. "He's such a social climber. I'm surprised he hasn't tried sleeping with you, Parker." The cousins burst into laughter, and Parker, who hadn't cried for a long, long time, felt suddenly terrified that she was about to burst into tears.

"Would you please pass the butter, Regan?" she asked.

"Do you really think you need it?" Aunt Louise said, and Parker was actually grateful for the change in subject.

The five minutes had stretched into thirty-three.

She was an idiot.

Don't say that, Parker, the Holy Rollers chimed. *We think you're really smart!*

Not smart enough, apparently, to realize that she'd skipped happily into yet another cliché, even worse than *Wedding Guest Picks Up Guy* or *Poor Little Rich Girl Feels So Alone.* No, this one was worse. Juliet was absolutely right. This one was *Guy Sleeps with Boss's Daughter as Part of Plan to Move Up Corporate Ladder.*

Idiot.

She spent forty-seven minutes at dinner, hoping her expression was pleasant, glancing over occasionally as her father worked the crowd.

Thing One stayed obediently at his side.

Then she texted her driver, went home, took a very hot shower and practically scrubbed off her skin with the loofah.

She got a text a little while later. You still around? Can't seem to find you.

It was now one hundred and twenty-six minutes after the five he'd said. Well. Better to learn this now. She opted not to respond. Sat there and watched *Dexter* instead.

He called an hour later and left a message. "Hey, Parker, it's James. Would you mind calling me? I think there's been a misunderstanding. Talk to you later."

Oh, yes, there'd been a misunderstanding. One hundred and twenty-six of them.

The next day, when Ethan dropped Nicky home, she asked him to stay for dinner before he had to head for the airport. No skipping the armor this time, because if Parker was right, Thing One was going to put in an appearance.

Ethan and Nicky were playing T-ball on the back

lawn when James showed up. Parker watched through the window as he came up the long walk, flowers in hand. He ran a hand through his hair before ringing the doorbell.

She opened the door.

"Parker," James said. "Always lovely to see you." He paused. "Everything okay here?"

"Everything's fine, Thing One. What brings you by?"

"Well, you disappeared before I could find you yesterday." He held out the bouquet. Roses, irises, gerbera daisies and, smack in the middle, a package of Alka-Seltzer.

Damn. She'd been feeling a little polluted all day long.

"Listen, James," she said, shooting for cool but not icy. Icy would imply that she was hurt. "I'm very sorry that I overindulged yesterday and, ah, jumped you. It won't happen again."

"Parker—"

"It won't happen again. I'm actually embarrassed, and I apologize for my behavior."

"You—"

"Unfortunately, we're about to eat dinner. So, I guess I'll see you the next time Harry tells you to come by."

Thing One's smile was gone. "Look, I'm sorry I didn't get to—"

"It's fine. I understand. You have certain duties. It was a business event for you."

His eyes narrowed. "Do I get to say anything here?" he asked.

"I'd rather you got in your car and left, to be completely honest."

"Because if I did get to say something," he went on, "I'd say I'd like to see you again, take you to dinner, get to know you better."

She could picture it. He'd woo her or whatever, smile his crinkly smile, make her fall for him, then, as soon as humanly possible, ask Harry if he'd give his blessing, which Harry would certainly give. Finally, a son. He and James would play golf together on the weekends and be masters of the universe during the week, because sure, James would get promoted—you don't bag the boss's daughter and not move up to Senior Vice President, after all. James would be an official prince in Harry's kingdom, wouldn't have to work so hard to impress her father, not as the son-in-law, no, sir. All James would have to do would be to shag her once in a while, father a kid or two, and he could kick back and relax, his future assured.

"What do you say?" he asked when she remained silent.

Much to her surprise, Parker felt the sting of tears in the back of her eyes. "No, thank you, James."

"Why not?"

She shrugged and looked past him. "I'm your boss's daughter."

"Yes, I remember."

She snapped her gaze back to him. "So, if you think you're going to get closer to him by screwing me, you're wrong."

His eyebrows rose. "That's *not* what I was thinking."

"No, of course not."

"If you recall, you kissed me first."

"Yes, I recall, James. I also recall three very strong and delicious martinis, okay? I wish it hadn't happened, and I'm promising you, it won't happen again."

James opened his mouth to say something, but at that moment, Nicky came careening into the foyer. "Mommy? Mommy? Mommy? Can I have some Goldfish? The eating kind?" Then he noticed James in the doorway, the flowers still in his hand. "Hewwo," he said, not having mastered the *L* sound just yet.

Parker didn't answer, just put her hand on Nicky's head.

James dragged his gaze off her and looked at her son. "Hi, Nick."

"You remember Grandpa Harry's lawyer, right?" Parker said. *Because that's all you're ever going to be in this house, pal.*

Ethan joined the little crowd. "Hey, how you doing, James?" he said. The men shook hands. Ethan looked at the flowers, still in Thing One's hand, then at Parker's face. "Nicky, let's go throw rocks in the water, okay, buddy?"

Parker cleared her throat. "No, that's okay, Ethan. He was just leaving. Drive safely, James."

"Dwive safewy, James," Nicky echoed.

James looked at her another second or two. "Okay. Enjoy your night."

There was a lump in Parker's throat as she closed the door. She was stupid. Stupid, stupid, stupid.

"Nicky, can you go get me a grape?" Ethan asked.

"Sure, Daddy!" Nicky said, racing off to the kitchen.

Parker looked at Ethan, forced a smile.

"Flowers, huh?" he said, leaning in the doorway.

"Yep. You know. Kissing up to the boss's daughter. So is salmon okay? I thought I'd grill it, make a salad. Or we could have what the chef left on Friday. Just need to heat it up."

"You want to talk?"

"About what?"

"About the fact that James brought you flowers and you pretty much set the dogs on him?"

"I don't have dogs."

"Come on, Parker."

"There's really nothing to talk about."

"You sure?"

"Heck yeah."

Ethan gave her a long look but said nothing more.

She spent the next week on edge, waiting for something that never came. James never called her. Never emailed, texted or dropped by. He followed instructions, in other words; proof that she was right—he wasn't going to get anywhere by being with her. If he really wanted something different—not that he actually did, but if—he would've surely tried again.

But he didn't. She saw him a few months later, when, instructed by Harry, he dropped by with some mutual-fund papers she needed to sign.

He never mentioned anything about their hookup.

And even though it was what she'd asked for, it was oddly disappointing.

CHAPTER TEN

PARKER WAS SHOWERING. Not ten feet from his bedroom, Parker Welles was naked and wet.

Okay. Probably not the most productive way to start the day. She'd already blown him off in spectacular fashion once in his life. But she was naked and wet and near, so these thoughts were apparently unavoidable.

Since yesterday, when she accepted that she really did need some help here, Parker had been very civilized, oh, yes. She always was. Nope, he was not allowed to see behind the curtain, as it were.

Except for that one time at her cousin's wedding. Damn. When she'd leaned in and kissed him on those stairs, he actually froze for a second, convinced he was hallucinating the whole thing. But no. The memory of what had followed would live on the trophy shelf of James's mind till the day he died.

And afterward, when he was convinced she was having not only second thoughts, but third, fourth and fifth thoughts, too, she agreed to hang out with him. She kissed him on the cheek. Which, in its own way, meant more than even the unbelievable shag.

Then he'd run smack into Harry at the base of the stairs. *Hey, Harry, I just finished doing your daughter. How's it going?*

So what was he supposed to do?

He figured he'd take his lead from Parker, and she'd

been her usual frosty self with Harry. Then Harry had taken him off to meet some Rhode Island senator, and yeah, maybe it had been more than a few minutes. But he hadn't expected her to bolt, either. Texted her, got no answer. Maybe something had come up with her kid. But Harry was power-drinking and, as usual, wanted company. James called Parker; no answer. When Harry insisted on going back to the city because of a Sunday-morning brunch he couldn't miss, James went with him, knowing his boss was sloppy, feeling that mix of pity and love he always did when Harry overindulged. And now, maybe, he was taking care of not only his boss, but of Parker's father. Drove all the way back to Rhode Island so he could see her the next day.

Whereupon he'd gone over with flowers and found that he'd become dog shit. Then again, he may well have been dog shit all along. He might've just been the guy picked up by the bridesmaid. No one could measure up to the Paragon, after all. A point driven home by the fact that Parker had the guy right there in the house with her.

Not that James really wanted to try to measure up. He'd never pictured himself married, never wanted kids. But the first time he'd ever seen Parker Harrington Welles, staring at her baby as if no one on earth had ever had a baby before, her face so rapt and gentle...something had sneaked up on him in that moment and sucker punched him and reminded him of what he didn't have, and hadn't had for a long time.

Somebody to love.

He loved Mary Elizabeth, of course. But that was different.

Then, at The Wedding, he'd felt it again, that sucker punch when she kissed him on the cheek, a moment of believing that Parker…well. Whatever. She didn't. She'd made that abundantly clear.

So why was he lying in bed, thinking about her? Because he was an idiot, that was why.

The water shut off. James surmised that if he leaped out of bed at this very second, he could probably catch her in her towel. But no, she was quick. The bathroom door opened; her bedroom door closed. He rolled out of his own bed and pulled on some jeans and a T-shirt and went into the kitchen.

A few minutes later, Parker joined him, the little dog slinking at her calves. "Hey," she said. "I have to run, but I poured boiling water over these mugs last night and washed them three times." She glanced at him, not quite meeting his eyes. "And luckily, I brought my Keurig, so there's coffee if you want it."

"Good morning," he said.

Her ears went red. "Hi. Sleep well?"

"I did. You?"

"Yes, thank you." She cleared her throat. "I'm meeting my cousin this morning at the diner. Should I bring something back for you?"

"That'd be great."

She nodded, pulled her wet hair into a ponytail. "So you really think we can get this place up and running by the time Nicky gets back East?"

"Yeah, definitely," he said. So long as he worked twenty hours a day or so. "It won't be what he's used to, but it'll be livable."

"He won't care. He'll be so excited about the dog. And the ocean, too. He swims like a fish." She paused. "As you know."

"This water's too cold for swimming," James said. "It's not like Rhode Island."

"Well, he's five. Hypothermia only deters adults." She smiled a little, then grew somber. "I was thinking last night about how to pay you," she began.

How about in sex? You could pay me in sex, most definitely. "You don't have to pay me."

"Don't be ridiculous. Of course I do."

Right. The help must be paid. "Your father already took care of it," he lied. "Now, get to the diner. Don't you have someone waiting for you?"

"Yes. Um, I guess I'll leave the dog here?"

"Sure," he said. "We can bond."

"Good luck with that." Her smile hit him in the chest like a line drive.

Three weeks together before her kid came up. Three weeks alone with Parker Harrington Welles. He didn't know whether to laugh or shoot himself.

To PARKER'S SURPRISE, Joe's Diner was mobbed; for such a tiny town, she wouldn't have guessed there'd be a line. Then again, it was the only place in town, from what she'd seen yesterday. The smell of dark-roasted coffee and bacon greeted her, practically making her knees buckle. That pizza last night hadn't been anything to write home about...and then again, there was James watching her, which was proving to be quite uncomfortable.

All that work he did—for her—well, Harry was paying him, but still, that smile of his brought up some very conflicted memories.

Because you were slutty, chided Golly.

"You have a point," Parker said.

"Morning," said a rough voice, making her jump.

Oh, yes. *This* was more like it. Fling Material. The guy with one name. Malone, that was it, in all his blue-collar glory. "Hi," she said. "Hi again. Great to see you. How are you? Malone, right? You were very, um, helpful the other night."

He stared at her. Not smiling. A little scary, even. Parker swallowed and tried again. "So, Malone, I think I owe you a drink, since you straightened me out on my little property issue and all. Which I can't say I appreciate, really. I would've much preferred the first house."

So out of practice on this boy-girl stuff.

Maybe it's not so bad, Spike commented. *He's smiling.*

It was true. A little, anyway. "You going in?" he asked.

"Yes, yes." Parker pushed through the door of the little diner and turned back to Malone. "Um, I'm meeting my cousin Lavinia Harrington. I don't suppose you know her, do you?"

"Last booth on the left." He nodded, then turned as someone slapped him on the shoulder.

Last booth on the left. A woman—or possibly a man—sat there, studying the menu. She looked up as Parker approached. "Pahkah?" Lavinia Harrington looked like she sounded—somewhat ravaged. Deep, leathery face framed with frizzy white hair.

"Hi," Parker said, squeezing past a buxom woman holding a baby. "It's really nice to—"

"Hurry it up, girl. Sit down."

Parker obeyed, sliding into the red vinyl seat. "So, you're Lavinia," she began. "I'm not one-hundred-percent sure how we're related, to tell you the truth."

"Could you hush up for a few? There's a surprise planned."

"Oh. Sorry." Rather a strange welcome. She looked around at the diner, which was gleaming and adorable, like a piece of Norman Rockwell. Every seat was filled—families in booths, people sitting at the counter, babies, toddlers, old folks— Oh, hey, there were the Three Musketeers from the hardware store yesterday. She waved, but they didn't see her.

At the counter directly across from Parker's booth was the stacked woman and her baby, who was dressed in blue. Six months, Parker guessed, all drool and smiles. God, Nicky had been so cute at that age! The mother wore a low-cut blouse, and a young guy next to her stared appreciatively at her wares. Aside from him, everyone seemed to be looking out the window and murmuring excitedly.

"Here she comes, here she comes," announced a woman about Parker's age. "Act normal, everyone!"

"Maggie, Maggie!" said the toddler next to her. "Maggie coming!"

"Shh," the dad said. "Be cool, Violet, sweetheart."

Like everyone else, Parker watched as a woman approached the diner, a yellow Lab on her heels, two grocery bags in her arms. "Okay, Octavio," she said, pushing through the door. "I can't believe we ran out of bacon and eggs when I could've sworn—" She stopped in her tracks. Her gaze flicked around the diner, eyes wide. "Where did everyone come from?" she asked. "Mom! What are you doing here? Did someone die?" Her voice trailed off as her eyes stopped on Malone.

Parker sighed…not with happiness, like everyone else in the place. Indeed, the woman with the toddler had tears sliding down her cheeks—hang on, she was twins with this Maggie person, apparently. The busty woman tilted her head on the young guy's shoulder and smiled. Indeed, everyone was smiling.

And here it comes, Parker thought. Sure enough,

Malone, who was clearly *not* going to be her summer fling, got down on one knee and held up a small black velvet box. Yep. She just asked that guy out. The one on bended knee.

"Jeezum crow, Malone," Maggie squeaked. A grinning man wearing a white apron stepped forward and took the grocery bags out of her arms.

"Well?" Malone said, a smile playing on his face. Everyone in the diner laughed—clearly some insider joke.

"Well, what?" Maggie said, a wobbly smile working its way through her tears.

Malone seemed to groan a little, and another laugh went through the crowd. "All right, then." He paused, took a deep breath and soldiered on. "I love you, Maggie, have for a long time, and I'd be real glad to wake up next to you every day for the rest of my life. You and the dog, that is." Another laugh, and now Malone's face was gentle. "Will you marry me?"

"Oh, that was great. Yes, absolutely, yes, Malone, I thought you'd never ask." She half laughed, half wept, and Malone rose and kissed her, and everyone cheered.

Oh! We have the Warm Fuzzles! the Holy Rollers crowed.

You sicken me, Parker thought. Still, the HRs had a point. It was all lovely. Her eyes were even a little wet, too, and several people were openly weeping. The twin was hugging Maggie now, and the toddler was jumping up and down. An older woman holding an infant was crying, as well. The whole place was congratulating the happy couple, slapping Malone on the back, kissing Maggie. Young people, old people, in-betweens…seemed as if the whole town was there.

For one brief second, Parker tried to imagine this scene happening to her. Yeah. No. She wasn't really the

Warm Fuzzles type, despite having invented the nauseating term.

Across the booth, Lavinia coughed, an alarming
sound, then nodded as if satisfied. "We been watchin'
these two for some time," she said in her rusty voice.
"Malone asked us all to come, wanted his daughter here.
She's from away. But he figured Maggie'd like that.
Seems he was right."

A party seemed to be breaking out—orange juice and
champagne were offered, and a few people were coming
in and out of the kitchen with goodies. A thickly built
waitress plunked a plate of Danish pastries down in front
of her, and Parker snagged one. "Think I could get some
coffee?" she asked. "I'm dying for a little caffeine."

"Help yourself," she said, making her way through
the crowd.

"I'll get it, this being your first time and all," Lavinia
said, sliding out of the booth.

Parker looked around, the only stranger here, it
seemed. Rolly gave her a wave, but he was on the other
side of the diner, talking to a young man with Down syn-
drome. Parker looked at the little jukebox at her table.
Oldies but goodies. Tried not to feel awkward.

*Little Maggot looked around. He didn't know any
other maggots on the entire roadkill. If only he was
better at making friends!*

"Hi there!"

Parker looked up at the bride-to-be and Malone, who
nodded. "Sorry, the service kind of sucks this morning," the woman said. "Because this guy here, he told
everyone we know to show up. And I had *no* idea. How
is that possible, I ask you? I mean, I know everybody,
right? Except you. Hi, I'm Maggie, and I know you're
Julia Harrington's niece. Sorry to be babbling. I'm a little

overwhelmed. Because I'm engaged." She bit her lip and looked at the ring herself, then kissed Malone's cheek. "It's so beautiful, Malone. I love it."

She showed off the ring. Three-quarters of a carat, maybe, fourteen-karat gold. Parker's mother's last engagement ring had been five carats, framed by a ring of twelve smaller diamonds, set in platinum and big enough to choke a seventh grader.

"Congratulations," Parker said. "It's beautiful. I'm Parker. In town for the summer." *Sorry I had dirty thoughts about your fiancé.*

"Where are you staying?" Maggie asked.

"At my aunt's house."

"Oh." Maggie gave a little grimace. "Um, that's a beautiful spot. Welcome to Gideon's Cove. Anything you need, stop by. I know everyone. So does this guy here. Oh, my God, Malone! Are you sure you want marry me? Given how much I talk?"

He nodded once. "I'm used to it." Put his arm around her shoulders and kissed her temple.

Dang, they were cute.

"Hey, lovebirds," Lavinia said. "You meet my cousin? Parker, the happy couple."

"Yep, we met," Parker said, gratefully taking the cup of coffee.

"So when's the wedding?" Lavinia asked.

"Two weeks!" Maggie said. "Malone already got the license and everything, because he wanted Emory to be here, of course."

"Way to go, Dad!" a young woman called amid the hum of conversation.

"Think you could do the flowers?" Maggie asked. "Even with such short notice?"

"'Course I'll do the flowers," Lavinia said. "I'll do them for free if Malone sleeps with me, just one time."

Malone grinned but didn't answer.

Maggie laughed. "I guess we'll pay. I'll come by this week, okay? It was really nice meeting you, Parker."

"Same here."

The couple moved on, as everyone in the place clearly wanted to hug and congratulate them.

"Nice," Parker said. "Very romantic."

"Ayuh. So. Welcome to town. Nice to meetcha. You saw your inheritance. What's the plan?" Lavinia asked. She took out a cigarette, lit it and took a drag.

"No smoking, Lavinia!" Maggie called.

"Damn." Parker's cousin stubbed the ciggie out on her *palm* and tossed the butt out the window.

"Didn't that hurt?" Parker couldn't help asking.

"Naw. My hands are tough."

Parker took another sip of the surprisingly good coffee. "Well, my plan is to…I don't know. I thought I'd slap on some paint and sell the place, but I didn't know how bad it was."

"It's a shit-snarl."

"Yes indeedy."

"Got enough money to really spiff it up?" Lavinia asked.

Parker paused. "I have a little. I don't know how far it'll go."

Lavinia pursed her lips together, causing a hundred wrinkles to radiate from her mouth like anemic rays from a sickly sun. "I heard about your problems."

"Did you?"

"Oh, ayuh. News travels fast. Especially when it's on CNN."

"Right."

"How many years did your father get?"

"Six. Time off for good behavior."

Her cousin grunted. "Deserved it, from what I hear. Sorry for you, though."

"Well, it's not so bad." Besides, even if it was bad, she'd been raised not to discuss money, sex or religion. "So, Lavinia—"

"Call me Vin," she said.

"Okay, Vin, um, how exactly are we related?" Parker asked. "We've never met, have we?"

"Nope. Your mother's my cousin on the Harrington side. Althea and I, we spent a little time together as kids some summers, back when my father still owned the Point."

"What point is that?"

"Douglas Point. The big place north of yours."

"That was yours? You lived there?"

"Ayuh. Till my mother and father divorced. Then my father sold it a few years later."

"Wow." Althea had never said anything about summers in Maine.

Lavinia looked out the window. "So how is your mother these days? We didn't really stay in touch."

"She's…she's fine."

"She ever remarry after your folks split up?"

Parker couldn't suppress a smile. "Oh, yeah. A few times."

Lavinia smiled back. "Is that right? Well. Tell her hello from me."

Parker knew that the Harringtons originally harkened from Maine, but her mom had grown up in Westchester County, New York. Back when her parents were still together, big family gatherings had only included the Coven. No second cousins from the Harrington side had ever been mentioned; only those few awkward visits to Great Aunt Julia up in Boston.

"Got any help for overhauling the house?" Lavinia asked, interrupting Parker's thoughts.

She took a deep breath. "Um, yes. A family friend."

"Well, you'll need it. God knows how long it's been since the place was cleaned out. Julia stopped coming here probably fifteen, twenty years ago." She squinted at Parker. "You need a job this summer? Make a little extra cash? I could use the help with Maggie and Malone's wedding. Usually hire a high school kid part-time in the summer, but the job's yours if you want it."

Heck yeah, she wanted it. "Sure. That'd be great. Thank you." Her first real job. Holy halos.

"Great. I gotta grab a smoke. Come by Wednesday. Three doors down. You can't miss it."

Lavinia left, and Parker glanced at her watch. She should get back to the shack, bring James some sustenance. Help clear stuff out. But maybe she'd call Nicky first. She glanced at her watch. He might be up. It was five-thirty in California.

Parker's chest constricted. Nicky felt so far away—he *was* so far away. The fact that she hadn't heard his voice last night, didn't know what he'd had for dinner, hadn't toweled off his hair after his bath…dang. Crying in a crowded diner full of strangers—not fun.

Malone sat down across from her, and Parker jumped a little. "Hey there," she said.

"Everything okay?" he asked, his voice a quiet rumble.

She was about to deny it and found herself telling the truth instead. "I miss my kid. He's with his dad in California for a few weeks."

Malone gave a brief nod. "My daughter lives most of the year in Oregon with her mother."

"Is that your daughter over there?"

Malone looked, his face softening a bit. "Ayuh."

"She's gorgeous."

"Don't talk about it." He smiled a little. "How old's your boy?"

"Five and a half."

"Tough to be apart when they're small."

She tried a smile. "Yeah. Well, he'll actually be coming up when they get back. So. Three weeks to go."

Malone nodded again. "Hang in there."

"Oh, I'm fine," she lied. "But thanks, Malone. And congratulations again."

She got up from the booth and waited at the counter as the gap-toothed cook made a ham-and-egg sandwich to go. He refused payment, telling her everything was on the house today.

Nice to be in a place where she was anonymous. Not one mention of the Holy Rollers, or Harry—except from Lavinia.

The sun was shining, a brisk wind coming in off the water, the waves slapping sharply against the wooden pier. The lobster boats bobbed merrily at their moorings, and a seagull strutted down the sidewalk in front of her, the breeze ruffling its feathers but not its composure.

Upon further inspection, Gideon's Cove had a bit more to it than at first glance. There was a lovely brick town hall, the police station, a bar called Dewey's and Lavinia's flower shop—called Lavinia's Flower Shoppe. Parker peered in the window and saw that it was crowded with little souvenirs and fake flower arrangements. A half inch of dust was on the sill. Well. She'd make herself useful.

After that, the town became mostly residential. There were some beautiful old houses in the Federal style with handsome front doors and widow's walks, rhododendron and lilies blooming in the yards. But the town quickly gave way to blue-collar, with two-family homes and small bungalows as the hills rose around the cove. At the top of one street, Parker could see Douglas Point. Hard to believe that had been in her family and her mother never mentioned it. Then again, Althea was hazy with details.

Aunt Julia's place wasn't visible. Maybe, given Thing One's extra weight, it had fallen into the sea.

Either way, she should probably go back home. To the hovel.

CHAPTER ELEVEN

FOUR DAYS LATER, as James ripped shingles off the roof, he had to admit he'd been wrong in thinking Parker would be a wuss when it came to hard physical labor. Grayhurst had had a cleaning crew, a gardening service, a handyman on call 24/7 and a personal chef who delivered meals daily. But there was Parker, hacking down the weeds along the stairway to the dock like a member of a chain gang. Cut-off jeans that showed her long, gorgeous legs. The jeans were the ones the mouse had run into, and she'd said there was no way in hell she was giving the rodent another chance. A shirt from Joe's Diner; apparently, Miss Welles hadn't packed—or didn't own—a proper T-shirt. A Yankees hat, the only thing marring her golden beauty. Well, she couldn't help it. Had spent most of her childhood in New York.

Nope, Parker had dug right in, shoveling the remainder of her aunt's belongings into trash bags, sorting through what could go to the Salvation Army—not a lot—and what was recyclable. If she had to ask him how to change the head of the sponge mop, well, it was kind of appealing.

She talked to her kid probably four times a day, which James thought was a lot. Then again, he probably talked to his parents four times a year, so what did he know?

She whacked at the weeds again, swinging the scythe like a golf club, then stopped to throw Beauty a stick. She glanced up at James, saw him looking and gave a quick wave, then looked away.

Yeah. Even though they'd been together for five solid days, there was little change in their relationship. She was polite. She was a good worker and listened when he told her how to do something. She had a decent sense of humor. Still called him Thing One occasionally. Didn't seem to be moping about her lost fortune, though she got quiet sometimes, maybe missing her kid.

In other words, she was as out of reach as ever. They talked about the house. The dog. The town. Maybe fifteen or twenty minutes of conversation a day. She spent more time than that by far on the phone with her kid. And the Paragon. And Mrs. Paragon.

Whatever. He had his own work to do, ripping the decaying shingles off the roof. Sweat dampened his hair, and he wiped his face on the sleeve of his T-shirt. Gideon's Cove was experiencing a rare heat wave the past day or so, with temperatures into the nineties. Humid, too. And the blackflies…he'd forgotten about those bloodthirsty little suckers.

He turned as a truck slowed in front of the house. Probably one of Parker's fan club, the old guys from the hardware store, who'd been dropping by daily to check on her progress. She had those three wrapped, that was for sure. Called them the Three Musketeers, which made the old guys shuffle and blush as if she'd knighted them.

It wasn't one of the Musketeers. It was his oldest brother, Tom, a good twenty pounds heavier than he'd been two Christmases ago when James had last seen him. Red-faced, and not from the sun.

"Hey," James said, shading his eyes to be sure. Ayuh. That was Tom, all right.

"Hey, James. How you doing, bud?"

"I'm good. You?"

"Can't complain. Talked to Dewey last week. He said you were here for the summer."

James climbed down from the roof, wariness prickling at the back of his neck. He was the only one of the five Cahill kids who'd graduated college, let alone gone on for a law degree. The only one who'd made it out of Maine, too. His brothers didn't drop by or give him a call for the hell of it.

"Kids are good?" James asked. He hesitated, then shook his brother's hand. From down by the water, he could hear Parker's scythe hacking into the long grass. He hoped she stayed there.

"Kids are great. Maybe you can swing by and visit this summer."

"Uh, yeah. That'd be nice." Except Tom had never once invited James to his house before. "So what brings you up here, Tom?"

"Oh, I had to do something in Machias. Figured I'd swing by." Machias was an hour south, but James didn't point that out. Tom leaned back against his truck door, all casual interest, and nodded at the house. "Got your work cut out for you, huh?"

"Yeah. Just trying to get it up to code, pretty much."

"You gonna reshingle the sides next?" Like their father, Tom was a carpenter.

"Yep. Rebuild those steps, too."

Tom nodded sagely. "So listen. I have a proposition for you."

Ah. That made more sense. Tom was here for money.

His brother folded his arms across his chest and stared out at the harbor. "There's this very cool opportunity to be a part owner in the old lumber mill. Remember that place? Down by the river?"

"I remember," James said.

"So me and my buddies, we were thinking we'd buy it, renovate it, put in some really nice shops on the first floor, right? Cheese shop, wine, upscale shit. Then up above, we'd have luxury condos."

"Sounds great." It sounded idiotic. Dresner was a dying city. There was more call for a soup kitchen than luxury condos overlooking a river polluted by forty years of industrial waste. Cheese shop? Come on.

"So I'm looking for a little capital to get started." He paused. "I'd pay you back with interest and all."

James took a slow breath. "I'd love to help you out, Tom—"

"No one's asking for help. This is an investment opportunity. Thought you liked that shit." There was already an edge in Tom's voice.

"I wish I could help you," James said. "I really don't have the money."

Tom pushed off his truck, his face growing even redder. "Yes, you do, you little prick. You've been working for that rich asshole for years now—"

"In case you didn't hear, my boss is in jail."

"—and don't tell me you didn't get a king's ransom for burrowing up that guy's butt."

Nice. "I did. But it's all tied up, and you know it, Tom."

His older brother glared. "Fuck you."

"Tom, look, even if it was a great idea—"

"Oh, now it's a crap idea?"

"—I honestly don't have the money. It all went to Beckham."

"And we wouldn't have needed Beckham if it wasn't for you! You fucked everyone over, didn't you? When your own family needs something, forget it. But here you are, playing house with your boss's daughter, aren't you? Having fun living off her money?"

"Tom, look at this place. Does it seem like she's got money?"

"Thanks for nothing. I should've known. And don't show your face in Dresner. Mom's enough of a mess without you. Asshole."

Ten seconds later, Tom screeched out of the driveway. He gave James the bird as he gunned the motor. Then he was gone.

Forget the roof. There was a crowbar; there was the long side of the house. James grabbed the heavy metal tool, jammed its wedged end under some shingles and began ripping them off with a vengeance. Sweat poured off his body, soaked his hair, stung his eyes. The wood screamed in protest, but he didn't stop. Just ripped the shingles off the side, no matter that they'd been petrifying there for two generations, just shoved the pry bar underneath and jerked up and ripped them off like scabs.

He didn't even notice Parker come up from the beach until she walked right past him, her dog as always tight against her calves.

"Hello, sweaty day laborer," she said with a grin.

"Hey," he grunted.

"Was someone here? Thought I heard voices."

"Nope."

"You hungry?"

"Nope."

She gave him a look, but he kept ripping shingles. "Okay, Thing One. I'm going for a swim."

"Fine."

She went blithely into the house. James continued jamming the crowbar under the shingles, relishing the screech as they tore off.

Then her words sank in.

She couldn't swim in Maine water. It was practically ice-cold. Fifty-two, fifty-five degrees? Maybe? It was high tide, too, so it'd be even colder. He tossed down the pry bar and stomped inside, folded his arms across his sweaty T-shirt and stood outside her door, ready to lecture her.

Then the door opened, and he forgot what he was there for.

She was wearing a bikini.

"You want to come?" she asked.

His mouth opened, but no sound came out. Skin. There was a lot of skin. And...curves. Breasts. Shoulders. Legs. His mouth went dry. She gave him an odd look, then scooped up her hair and secured it with an elastic, and his eyes slid down to her rack, because my God, that was a fantastic—

"I know. Cellulite. I've gained eleven pounds this past year." She stared down at her torso, then sighed. "Oh, well. Maybe I can swim some off. Come on, Beauty." She grabbed a towel and headed through the kitchen.

Her ass was...well, he was unable to summon actual words at the moment, as there was no blood flowing upward. And that scrap of fabric—*red* fabric—thank you, Jesus. Hard to believe she'd kissed him once, and speaking of hard, she was so beautiful and perfect and *luscious,* bad enough that he'd had to listen to her shower every morning, and—

But wait, wait, wait.

She couldn't swim in that water.

"Parker," he croaked, but she was already halfway down the stairs, the long grass billowing in the breeze, the dog's feathery tail in the air.

"Parker!" he called, banging out the back door. "That water's really cold."

"And I am really hot," she said. *Tell me about it.* "I've been working like a dog. Right, Beauty?"

"It's too cold for swimming," he said, running down the stairs. "Hypothermia cold, Parker. Don't go in."

"Oh, come on. People swim in it all the time."

"Not up here they don't." He reached the dock, which was bobbing vigorously, as the tide was coming in hard, slapping against the buoys that held the thing afloat. If he didn't watch it, he'd fall right in.

"Well, I'm going swimming." She draped her towel over one of the old wooden porch chairs she'd dragged down here. "Beauty, want to come? Come on, girl!" With that, Parker executed a perfect swimmer's dive from the dock, the dog sailing in right behind her.

She didn't surface. He could see her white skin under the water…but no, that was just sunlight. Where was she? Where the hell was she? "Parker!" James stripped off his shirt. "Parker!"

Then her blond head popped up, way too far away from the dock. She pushed her hair out of her face. "Oh, bugger!" she called. "You were right! It's freezing!" She grinned at him, then saw her dog. "Beauty! Good girl! Good puppy!"

"Parker, get in here. You'll freeze."

"I do feel like I'm dying. But eleven pounds, Thing One!" With that, she began swimming in long, hard strokes away from the dock.

James bit his thumbnail. Yes, granted, she'd swum on the Harvard team. There'd been two pools at Grayhurst, one inside and one out. But there were no tides in swimming pools, and they weren't fifty-two degrees, and they weren't strewn with buoy lines. What if she got tangled on one? "Parker, don't be an idiot," he called, jamming his hands into his pockets.

She didn't hear him. Kept swimming. Another yard. Another. She was an entire football field away now. No signs of slowing. Damn it all to hell. If he jumped in after her, could he catch her? Probably not. But once she went under, he'd be a lot closer—

Finally she stopped, and the dog swam right up to her. It had a stick, which Parker threw back toward the dock, and the dog zipped right around to find it.

"Time to come in, Parker," James yelled, sounding like a parent. Then again, she was acting like an idiot child. Like—

"It's really not bad once you get used to it," she called.

"That's what they all say, right before they freeze to death."

She laughed. He was chewing his thumbnail again.

Finally, she turned in the right direction, diving under the surface of the water in a dolphinlike move, then popping up for breath a few yards closer. Swam efficiently, closer, closer. James didn't take his eyes off her the entire time.

Then, as she was climbing back onto the dock, she slipped and fell back with a splash, and before he was quite aware of having moved, he had her by the arm and was hauling her up, slopping frigid water against himself, her skin as cold as if she were dead.

"Easy there, Mr. Lifeguard," she said, stepping back and smoothing the hair off her face. "I'm fine."

"Don't make this a habit. It's too cold. It's stupid, Parker."

"I think I *will* make it a habit, Thing One," she said, squeezing the saltwater out of her hair. "I love to swim, I own a house on the water, and you're not the boss of

me." Goose bumps covered her skin, and her nipples—
Shit. Women were not fair, because a perfectly good case
of righteous anger was turning into lust.

Without another word, he turned and stalked off the
dock.

Time to rip some more shingles.

CHAPTER TWELVE

ONCE UPON A TIME, there was a baby shark named Swimmy. He asked his mommy, "Does God still love me, even though I eat the other fishies?" and his mommy said, "Who cares?" and ate him, and Swimmy was delicious.

Okay. So the writing wasn't going that well. Parker put aside the red notebook, which now contained eleven ridiculous and aborted story attempts, considered tossing it off the dock and sighed. Well, maybe her new series would get the green light. Two days ago, against her better judgment, she'd sent her agent and editor a series proposal. The Ark Angels. How did all those animals get along on Noah's Ark? Why, it was all thanks to a clever lion cub, a singing fox and a crafty kangaroo. *Glee* meets the Bible meets *Animal Farm. We thought it was super awesome, Parker!* the HRs chorused. Parker figured it was close enough to the Holy Rollers in its preachy, simpering style, so she had high hopes that the powers-that-be would love it.

But she hadn't been feeling the mojo. Not that she'd loved the Holy Rollers, but the books had come easily to her. *You're welcome,* said Spike, who now looked to be a thuggish sixteen. *About time we got some recognition around here.* He tucked a cigarette behind his ear.

"No smoking," she said. He stubbed the ciggie out

against his palm, Lavinia-style, and lifted an eyebrow. Teenagers.

She got up and headed inside. Thing One was still ripping and tearing stuff, apparently having his period. She may as well start dinner.

Once all the crap had been cleared from the kitchen, Parker had scoured it. The linoleum was torn in a few places, but otherwise, the room had a sort of cheap charm. Shabby chic, maybe? There was a kitschy little table, one of those chrome-and-vinyl models from the sixties, white with bits of gold, and a couple of usable chairs. Parker had excavated a strange plastic tomato statue; it wore a top hat, had long eyelashes and sported a cane, which, upon further inspection, turned out to be a smiling green worm. She put it on the table and smiled. Looked kind of cute.

Grayhurst's kitchen had consisted of granite and marble and steel with rare-wood cabinets and knobs designed just for the house. The knives were German, the china French. The table had been an original Frank Lloyd Wright.

Well. Those days were over. Sparkly vinyl and plastic tomatoes were more her speed now. And the linoleum, while still cracked and yellowing, was clean, at least. Things were moving in the right direction.

The swim had been great, though James had a point. That water was freaking *cold.* But swimming had always made her feel calmer and happier. Nicky, too, she'd noticed. He'd love the water here, her little eel. She'd been on Skype with him earlier during a quick run to the library; they were at a gorgeous lodge in Muir Woods. Nicky had looked bigger to her. Then again, that might be her imagination. They'd only been apart for five days.

Hard to believe. It felt like five months.

The sound of screeching wood came from the opposite side of the house. James, still hard at work. The noise was like a knife in her eye. Maybe the lad was hungry. She'd see if he had any preference for dinner. Seemed like the least she could do.

Going outside, she saw that James was still shirtless.

Oh, that was...that was good. That was *nice*. The guy browned up fast, that was for sure. His hair was wet with sweat, and half of the shingles on the side of the house were gone. His muscles bunched and corded as he worked. Beautiful arms, lean stomach, the muscles over his ribs shifting hypnotically with his movements. A bead of sweat ran down his neck into the little hollow at the base of his throat.

He glanced at her without stopping. Right. She should speak. She swallowed. "Hey."

"Hey," he answered.

"Are you mad at me?" she asked. "For taking a swim?"

He did stop then. "No. Just had a crappy day."

Parker felt a pang of guilt. She didn't know much about Thing One, granted, and she'd definitely been keeping conversation terribly neutral. But here he was, working like a dog for her. And when she'd gone swimming, he'd been rather adorably anxious.

"Want some dinner?" she asked. "I'm cooking."

His eyes were very dark. Ethan's were brown, too, but a lighter color. James, though. James had eyes that were so brown they were almost black. A person could look into those eyes and just about get lost.

"Sure," he said, then went back to ripping off the shingles.

Crappy day, huh? Well, she'd make him something nice. She'd been to the market this morning—not the tiny one in town, but the bigger one about half an hour away—and had stocked up. In the sunny kitchen, she rinsed some spinach, sliced tomatoes, put the water on to boil the pasta. James came in to shower, and it was hard not to imagine him in there, all soapy and wet. And tanned. And naked. And wet. And naked.

"Down, girl," she said to herself, causing Beauty to flop to the floor. "I wasn't talking to you, sweetie," Parker added. The little dog had been trained by someone, it was clear. She didn't put a toenail out of line, as if afraid of being beaten, poor sweet thing. "You're such a good girl," Parker said, giving her a strip of salami. She was rewarded with a slight swishing of the dog's tail.

Dinner wouldn't be too fancy, but it smelled heavenly. She opened a nice bottle of Meursault, stolen from Grayhurst's wine cellar, then brought everything down to the dock and set it up, picnic-style. She poured a glass of wine for herself and sat down, looking out at the water.

The harbor was smooth now, the smallest ripples lapping gently against the rocky shore, and the sun was beginning its descent, filling the horizon with gold, turning the clouds to cream. A piping plover ran along the shore, stopped to peck at something, then ran some more. Always in such a hurry, those little birds.

The dock shifted, and Parker looked over. James had changed into jeans and a white polo shirt and looked like an ad for Ralph Lauren.

"Didn't know you could cook," he said, looking down at the spread.

"Surprise. I like cooking. Have a seat, James." She patted the blanket, poured some wine and handed him a glass. "Thanks for all your hard work today."

"You're welcome. Thanks for dinner."

"You hungry?"

"Starving."

They ate, plates in their laps, looking over the water, not talking. The tide was going out, exposing a few rocks, and a line of cormorants swam over and clambered up, spreading their wings to dry. A few lobster boats motored in. There was Billy Bottoms, the white-haired man who looked as if he belonged on a postcard; Parker had met him at the diner a couple days ago when she was picking up lunch. Then came the *Twin Menace,* which belonged to Maggie's brother, she'd learned. The *Ugly Anne* came in last, and Malone lifted a hand in greeting. She waved back.

"So why the bad mood today?" Parker asked.

"Family stuff." James set his empty plate next to him.

"Do you have a lot of family around here?"

"I have three brothers and a sister, all in Maine. My parents still live in the same house where I grew up."

"Here in Gideon's Cove?"

"No. About an hour and twenty minutes west of here."

"Are you guys close?"

He paused. "Some of us are."

"And Dewey, who owns the bar, he's your uncle, right?" she asked.

"Yep. My mother's brother. She's one of seven. My dad has three sisters."

She didn't mean to interrogate him, but big families fascinated her. She'd only had her parents and the Coven, after all. "You must have a lot of cousins, then."

"Nineteen."

Parker smiled. "Sounds fun."

"It was," James said.

Was. Not *is.* He didn't explain, though. "I always wished I had more cousins," she said. "Four girls about the same age. It wasn't pretty."

"I remember," he said.

Ah. Right. At Esme's wedding, when they'd done a lot more than talk. Parker felt her ears heat up. Could be the wine.

It was getting dark; clouds had gathered off Douglas Point, and the wind kicked up a little, lifting her hair. A rumble of thunder rolled in the distance.

Parker's phone cheeped. She looked. Oh, goody! A message from Ellen! Maybe her agent already had some interest in the Ark Angels.

Hey, Parker, sorry to say, they took a pass on the Ark Angels. It didn't seem to have the same sincerity as the Holy Rollers. Back to the drawing board! Don't worry. We're all confident that you're almost there! Just go with the flow, and something will hit you. Sooner is better, okay? Hope you're having fun in Maine! Talk soon.

Well, bugger. Bugger and damn.

"Go with the flow"? She'd been waiting for the flow for some time. There was no flow. And "the same sincerity"? The Holy Rollers had *no* sincerity! *Mickey the Fire Engine,* which had been rejected by both her agent and publisher all those years ago…*Mickey* had sincerity. He was an extraordinarily sincere fire engine.

"Everything okay?" James asked.

"Sure. Yes." She looked out at the water. "Actually, no. My publisher didn't like my new series idea. So that's not good."

"But you're a big hit, aren't you?"

"I was."

The phone cheeped again. Aw. Ethan had sent a picture of Nicky, standing in front of a giant redwood tree.

Parker's throat tightened at the sight of her son. There was another attachment, this one a drawing of two humans with giant heads and skinny legs. One had long hair, and one had spiky hair. They were holding the hand of a smaller giant-head person. Nicky had labeled them Daddy, Lucy, Me and written, "We Love You, Mommy."

Crap. Her eyes were wet.

"You okay, Parker?" James asked.

"I miss my son," Parker said, swallowing. The words didn't do him justice. It felt as if a part of *her* was missing, that's what it felt like, as if she was killing time until her real life started when he came back, and crikey, time had slowed to an absolute crawl.

"He'll be here soon, right?"

"Eighteen days."

"Eighteen days," James repeated, looking at her.

"I've never gone more than two without seeing him," she admitted.

"Must be tough."

"Yeah. For me, anyway. Nicky's having the time of his life. Swimming in the Pacific, seeing Muir Woods, horseback riding." She shook her head. "Then he gets to come here, to this…shack."

"It's shaping up, Parker. It'll be fine by the time he gets here."

She set her plate down, glanced at James and his kind, dark eyes. For a second, she almost admitted what was on her mind, and a fear that had cropped up more and more in the past six months: that Nicky would ask to live with Lucy and Ethan full-time, and if he said that, it would kill her.

"What if I can't sell this place?" she asked. "I mean, even if I can, there won't be too much left over, and I don't have that many marketable skills, Thing One. I was a double major in English and Ethics. Should've listened to my father and gone into finance."

"Look where that got him," James said.

Parker picked a splinter from the dock. "You know what the kicker is? Those miserable little Holy Rollers would've made me a ton. The movie comes out this summer—*The Holy Rollers in 3-D!* and they put that exclamation point there as part of the title, as if it wasn't already dumb enough. And now, I can't write anything, I can't come up with anything decent, I'm completely and utterly stuck."

Crap. Why was Thing One always around during her weaker moments? Swallowing, she pressed her lips together and looked away. The sky had clouded over, and it was darker in the west. Another growl of thunder came from the far distance.

A second later, she felt his hand on hers. Warm and calloused and...comforting.

"Everything will turn out fine, Parker," he said. "This summer's just a bump in the road."

Please, God, that was true. She nodded, not trusting her voice.

"You're a Harvard grad, as you like to remind me. You'll find a job. And your son loves you. That won't change."

She glanced at him—he was looking at her steadily, and those deep, dark eyes were kind. She gave his hand a quick squeeze. "Thanks."

He didn't look away.

No one looked at a person that way anymore. They checked their phones, or scanned the horizon, or glanced around. But Thing One kept looking at her. Kept holding her hand, too.

"I'm glad you're here, James," she admitted, and her voice was a little husky.

"Me, too." His thumb moved over the back of her hand, and suddenly, Lady Land perked up. Those eyes… that whole face, in fact…that warm hand…

He leaned a little closer, and her heart rate tripled. She remembered what it had been like to kiss James Cahill, and her legs tingled. Remembered his hands on her, against her skin, his mouth on her neck, on her—

Then a bolt of thunder cracked right overhead, Parker jumped and Beauty leaped up and streaked for the house. The first fat drops of rain smacked down on the dock.

Moment over. Sign from God.

"Well," Parker said, her voice breathy. "Looks like rain." Yes. Rain tended to look like rain. She stood up, her legs still tingly, her hand feeling cold and empty. "We better hurry."

Careful not to look at him, she grabbed a few things at random, a plate, a glass, a napkin. Then the heavens opened, and she raced up the stairs, as much a coward as Beauty.

The cold rain on her shoulders was almost a relief.

WHEN JAMES GOT UP to the house, he was soaked. And the power was out. Looked as if all of Gideon's Cove had lost power, in fact. He put down the things Parker hadn't managed to grab and ran his hands through his wet hair.

"James, leave everything, okay?" Parker's voice came from down the hall. "I'll clean up in the morning. Uh, Beauty's scared, and she's hiding under my bed, so I'll stay in here. Good night."

Beauty wasn't the only one who was hiding. "Good

night," he said. Another bolt of thunder crackled across the sky.

He'd almost kissed her. Which was a dumb idea, no matter how much he wanted to.

It would be a long time till he fell asleep, he knew. Rather than fight it, he opened the quiet fridge and groped around for a beer, took it out onto the back patio and sat, watching the storm roll and flash over the harbor, the pine trees black in the harsh flashes of lightning, the lobster boats starkly white.

What do you think's gonna happen, idiot? his conscience chided in the harsh voice of his father. *She's already blown you off once. Think you measure up to the Paragon? And what happens when she finds out what you did?*

James took a long pull on his beer. There were plenty of women out there who'd be a lot easier than Parker, that was for sure. Leah back home would *love* to see more of him. It's just that there wasn't a lot to Leah. Sweet girl. Fun to hang out with, fun in bed. But while she tended to talk…and talk…and talk, she never seemed to say anything. Which was cute for a while, that chattering. Cute for about two hours, at which point they'd fool around, then she'd chatter some more, then he'd leave.

So no, not Leah. But surely there was someone else out there. Someone who was not Parker. For crying out loud. One time, three years ago, and he was still hung up on her, even though she'd made it very clear that he was a drunken mistake.

Stupid. Men were stupid, and he was no exception.

The storm was moving down the coast, the bulk of the thunder south of them now. He wondered if Mary Elizabeth was getting any of this weather, even though they were inland a bit. She hated storms. He fished out his phone and hit her number. "Hi, honey," he said when she answered. "How you doing? Getting any thunder down there? Well, you have Spike with you, right? All right, then, you're all set. He won't let anything bad happen to you, you know that….Because he's an angel, that's why."

CHAPTER THIRTEEN

"GOOD. YOU'RE HERE. And oh, you brought your dog." Lavinia knelt down to pet Beauty, who ducked her head and hid behind Parker's legs.

"She's shy," Parker explained. "She'll warm up to you eventually." She set down the coffee she'd brought for her cousin and took a sip of her own.

Vin twisted around, cracking her vertebrae. "Heard you got Dewey's nephew working over there with you. That your family friend?"

"Mmm-hmm." Less said the better on that subject.

"You two doing the nasty?"

Parker choked on her coffee. "Um, no. He...he works for my father. He's just helping."

"All right, if you say so. Seems like a waste, though, not doing that cute boy. Anyway. You know anything about flower arranging?"

"Well, I took a class once. At camp."

Lavinia surveyed her through squinted eyes. "Did you? Well, the first rule is, you're going to get dirty. That shirt of yours...silk?"

"Oh." Parker glanced down. "Yes."

"Well, it'll get ruined. You need to dress more like me."

Please, God, never that. Lavinia was dressed in aqua-blue stirrup pants and a green-and-red flannel shirt. "Come on, then," her cousin said. "Let me give you the tour. This here's the cooler. We get a delivery maybe once a week, less in the winter, when business slows down."

With Beauty practically attached to her leg, Parker looked into the case, where there was a small variety of flowers: carnations, roses, lilies, baby's breath. "Over here," Vin continued, "we've got the containers, vases, angels, a few boxes of chocolate. I wouldn't eat those if I were you—can't tell how old they are—but if someone wants them, buyer beware, right?" Lavinia coughed and lit up another cigarette.

"Think the smoke is bad for the flowers?" Parker asked, waving her hand.

"Probably. At any rate, cards are over here. Rolls of tissue paper, cellophane, all the tools you might need, and be careful with those scissors, 'cause those'll cut you faster than a cat can lick its ass."

The kitty cat licked its cute little bum. Oh, those worms were so itchy! "*If only someone would adopt me, I could get these pesky intestinal parasites taken care of!*" Another winner.

"You listening to me?" Lavinia pointed to a heavy oak door with a large pane of frosted glass. "This here's the greenhouse. Don't go in there, got it? It's temperature controlled. That's why there's the lock on the door."

"What do you grow back there?" Parker asked. She could see a blur of green, a few splotches of pink. Beauty was sufficiently interested to sniff at the door.

"Rare orchids, shit like that. Wicked particular about hot and cold. Okay? I'm the only one what takes care of those."

"Got it." Parker turned back to the older woman. "Lavinia, I really appreciate you letting me work here."

"Oh, hell. That's what family's for." She smiled, her

face crackling into an array of wrinkles that Parker found quite attractive. Althea, who was roughly the same age as Vin, didn't sport *any* wrinkles, having had her face paralyzed by Botox far too many times to count.

"So you and my mom played together as kids?" Parker asked.

"Ayuh. Back when we were really little. Couple, three times is all. Then we moved to town, over by the fisheries plant."

Lavinia was quiet for a moment, and Parker wondered what her silence meant. Once, Lavinia had lived in a mansion; now, she chain-smoked and wore stirrup pants.

"Vin, why do you think Julia left the house to me? Instead of you or my mom? You were her nieces. I'm just a grand-niece."

"Ah, Julia was always mad at someone or another," Vin answered, lighting another cigarette. "She was furious when my brother sold the Pines, even though he gave her that little cottage. Pissed that he got himself into financial trouble and whatnot. As for your mother, Julia didn't approve of divorce, so I guess that's why she picked you. Not many of us to choose from."

"And you never got married? No kids?"

"Nope. Always wanted a kid. Never a husband, though. I'm too fickle. You, too, from the look of it."

"Oh, I don't know about that."

"What are you? Forty?"

Parker winced. "No. Thirty-five."

"Nothing wrong with being fickle when it comes to men. Keep those options open, I always say. Anyway, most of our orders are pretty basic. Got your bible right there." She picked up a huge and faded book and swiped it against her butt, a shower of gray flakes falling to the floor. Between the dust and the smoke, Parker could practically feel her lungs shriveling. "Oftentimes, we don't have the right stuff in stock, but we do our best. Folks understand. Well, hello there, Maggie."

Beauty crouched behind Parker's legs as Maggie came in. "Hi, Lavinia! Hi, Parker!" she said. "How are you? Oh, you have a dog! Hi, puppy! Can I pet her?"

Ah, love. The woman's happiness was palpable, and heck, it *was* awfully romantic, the way her guy had popped the question in front of everyone.

"She's pretty shy," Parker said, but Maggie knelt down, and to Parker's amazement, Beauty's tail wiggled a little bit.

"Shy is fine," Maggie said. "Nothing wrong with shy." Beauty sniffed Maggie's hand, then offered a lick.

"She likes you," Parker said.

"I'm a dog person. You should bring her over sometime. She can play with Peaches. That's my dog. Malone gave her to me." At the name of her honey, Maggie blushed. "And speaking of Malone, I'm here to talk about the wedding. It's a quicky job. Not in that sense of the word—I'm not pregnant, at least not to my knowledge. It's just, you know, Malone, he'd rather get it done, plus his daughter's only here for a month… Crikey, listen to me." She smiled sheepishly. "Anyway, we're getting married a week from Saturday. Sorry it's such short notice."

"Well, it's not like people are lined up around the block. And for you, Maggie, no problem, sweetheart." Lavinia's face melted again into wrinkles as she flashed some browning teeth. "What kind of bouquet were you thinking?"

"Oh, heck, I don't care. Whatever you think is pretty. My dad said he'll pay for the wedding, but I don't want to drain him dry, either. Hydrangeas are in season, right? Those are nice. Whatever's easy."

"What's your budget?" Vin asked.

"Three hundred dollars sound okay?" Parker tried not to wince. Three hundred was nothing.

"Oh, ayuh," said Vin. "We can do real nice for three hundred."

Wow. Parker could honestly say that she'd never met a bride like Maggie. Lucy had been pretty easygoing, but they'd had a girls' night with Corinne, Lucy's sister, and pored over *Martha Stewart Weddings* magazines, drank wine, and it had been a blast. As far as Esme, please. There'd been more tantrums during that engagement than at a day-care center during a full moon. Bloodlust and fury over things like flowers and seating arrangements and limos. Even her own mother, who had weddings down to a science, got religious with details; Althea's last bouquet had cost three *thousand* dollars—just the bouquet, which was made of rare lavender roses and vivid pink orchids flown in from South America, all wrapped in satin ribbons embroidered with *Althea and Maury* and studded with Swarovski crystals.

Maggie smiled at Parker. "You helping Vin out this summer, I heard?"

"That's right," Parker said.

"Cool. I bet you have great taste. I love your clothes. You always look so nice."

"Thanks," Parker said, feeling a blush.

"Hey," Maggie blurted, "you should come to Dewey's tonight! We're having a girls' night out. I think it's sort of my bridal shower, too. Just bring something for the food pantry. No gifts. Want to? Vinnie's coming. You can meet everyone."

Parker opened her mouth to pass—she barely knew Maggie—then realized her standard excuses were not going to work. No kid to go home to. No manuscript to work on.

And if she didn't go out, she'd be home with Thing One of the eyes and the hands and the smile. "Thanks. I'd love to."

WHEN PARKER PULLED INTO the short driveway of her place, Thing One was up on the roof.

Shirtless. Again.

At the sight of him, every egg in her ovaries leaped to attention and started banging their tiny fists against the wall. *Let us out, Parker! Now!*

He wore carpenter-style shorts and a tool belt and work boots and nothing else but sweat, and Parker suddenly realized her mouth was dry.

Thing One. Was. Beautiful.

"I'm back," she croaked, and he turned, wiping the sweat from his forehead.

"Hey." He started toward the ladder.

"Don't come down! I brought sandwiches from the diner."

"Great." He disobeyed her order, jumping the last few rungs. And now he was getting closer, and she could smell that nice, clean sweatiness of him.

"Did you put on sunscreen?" she heard herself ask.

He smiled. Her knees tingled dangerously. "Thanks for bringing lunch."

Parker swallowed. "Oh, you're welcome. You know. The least I can do is feed you."

His arms were most…unlawyerly, curving with muscle, glistening. No shirt. Had she mentioned that? And he was standing approximately four inches in front of her. Should she choose to lean in and taste him just for the hell of it, it wouldn't be hard at all.

"What?" she asked, realizing abruptly that he was talking. "Sorry. Um, Beauty, stop, honey."

That's right. Use the dog as an excuse. Good play. Not that the dog was doing anything other than cowering behind her legs.

"I said I'll be up on the roof most of the day. There's a part of the floor in the kitchen that's rotted out, thanks to a leak, so I figured the roof was a priority."

"Good call." As if she knew anything. "Okay. I'll get going, then. Cleaning. And I might get started doing the, um, prep stuff. For painting. Cleaning and taping. I need to sponge down the walls in your room." Did that sound dirty? It sounded dirty to her. *Sponge down. Sponge bath. Your room. Your bed.* "Um, is Apollo locked up?"

"Yep." He was smiling at her, that knowing, faint smile. The *I've seen you naked* smile.

Without another word, she went into the house.

Parker managed to avoid Thing One for much of the rest of the day. He went to the hardware store; she talked to Nicky twice, once after lunch, once after he'd seen a deer and wanted to tell her about it. Mostly, though, she cleaned.

Parker found that she liked hard physical labor. The last time she'd worked this hard, she'd been pushing out a baby; her housework at home didn't usually entail more than making Nicky's bunk bed—which was awkward, let's give credit where it was due. But this stuff, this schlepping and bending and wiping and sweeping... forget Zumba or Pilates. Body by Hoarding.

She didn't get to James's room. It felt a little...personal. But the living room and kitchen walls had been washed with bleach and water, and she'd taped all around the windows, cupboards and doors. Tomorrow she'd start painting. Rolly and Ben were coming over to help.

That would be good, having some people there. People other than Thing One.

He's awfully cute, the female Holy Rollers said.

"Shush, you guys." But maybe James needed a drink. Parker filled a glass and went outside, where James was coming down from the roof. "How's it going up there?" she asked, handing him the glass and gazing out at the harbor—not at his shirtless glory, no, of course not.

"Good." He took a long pull of water, then dumped the rest over his head and ran a hand through his thick, wavy hair. God. She was going to need a pulsating showerhead, and soon.

"Um, I'm gonna take a shower," she said. *That sounds like an offer,* the HRs advised. "I'm going out tonight. With the girls."

"Maggie and Chantal?" he asked.

She kept forgetting he had roots here. "Yeah. Well, Maggie. I don't know about Chantal."

"Have fun."

"Thanks. You all set for, um, everything? Dinner?"

"All set."

Pretty soon, Parker told herself, she should confront the elephant in the room. *James, we slept together once,* she'd say. *Not gonna happen again. We're both copacetic with that, yes? So even if you look like a chocolate lava cake and I haven't had dessert in three years, it's not gonna happen. I'm almost positive.*

An hour later, Parker was clean and sweet-smelling and surveying the dark interior of a shabby little bar decorated with wooden lobster traps and the occasional lobster claw. There were about ten tables, a few booths and a counter.

"Parker! Over here!" There was Maggie, at a table in the back. Or it was the other one, her twin. They waved in unison. A busty redheaded woman was nursing a baby, and four or five men watched unabashedly. Beth, the woman from the animal shelter, was also there.

Parker went over. "Hi," she said, suddenly feeling shy.

"I'm so glad you could come!" Maggie said. Parker assumed it was Maggie, because she had on a Hello Kitty tiara. "Have you met my sister? This is Christy, and she refuses to get a big *C* branded onto her forehead so people can tell us apart. Really, Christy, you're so difficult sometimes. This is Beth, who says you've already met her, and Chantal, our sister-in-law, and Luke, our nephew. Isn't he beautiful?"

"Oh, he is," Parker said, though admiring the child would mean staring at Chantal's boob, which apparently was the thing to do.

"Glad you're nursing, Chantal," one of the men said. "Best for baby."

"Oh, ayuh," the others murmured from their trance.

"How's Beauty doing?" Beth asked Parker.

"Oh, she's good. Very shy, but she's getting there." Parker smiled. "Couldn't let the poor thing be put down."

Christy gave Beth a look. "I thought you never put animals down."

"Sorry, Parker. I lied," Beth said with a grin.

"Ah, well. She's a great dog," Parker said.

"Okay, girls," Christy said, "let's get our new pal here a drink. Dewey!" Parker jumped at the bellow. "Bring our friend a mojito!"

"Coming up!" Dewey was apparently the large man behind the bar. Didn't look much like James, not that she could tell, anyway.

Christy leaned forward. "While we wait, ladies, let me tell you something. I saw the hottest guy in the *world* today, outside of my own husband, of course—"

"And Malone," added Maggie.

"And your brother," added Chantal.

"Disgusting," chorused the twins, and all three of them laughed.

"Anyway, as I was saying," Christy went on, "the *hottest* guy. Now, Parker, you don't understand. This town is rather difficult. I had to import my husband from away. But locally, if you like surly alpha males, we had one, and sorry, Maggie got him."

"It's true," Maggie confirmed, sucking up the last of her mojito. "He's my surly alpha male."

"And if you like irritating, lazy, annoying but cute guys," Christy went on, "there was exactly one, and he's our brother, and for some ungodly reason, Chantal married him. Otherwise, there's Crazy Dave, named that for a reason, Pete Duchamps, our local alcoholic, and Mickey Tatum, our sixty-year-old fire chief. So a cute guy in town…this is big news."

"This is incredibly exciting," Beth said. "I can tell he's my soul mate already."

"Yes." Christy nodded sagely. "Who is he, and how can we get him to marry Beth?"

Parker had a feeling she knew who the hot guy was. How many gorgeous new strangers could be bopping around a town of 1,400 people? "Dark hair? Red pickup truck?" she asked.

"Yes! You know him? Is he yours?"

"He's mine. My nephew," said the bartender, who'd arrived with a round of drinks. He looked down at her. "Hello. You must be Parker."

She stood up. "Hi. Are you Dewey?" He nodded. "It's really nice to meet you, and thanks for your help with the house. You've been great."

"My pleasure, dear," he said. "The least I could do for Jamie's friend."

"Oh, my gosh! *That* was Jamie Cahill?" Christy said. "He turned out *so* nice!"

"He's a good kid," Dewey said. "Not married. Drink up, girls, and have fun. Nice meeting you at last," he added to Parker, then lumbered back to the bar.

"I've already seen Jamie Cahill, hugged him and copped a feel," Chantal said. "Sorry, Christy, old news." She popped the baby off her breast and covered up. "Show's over, boys," she said to her audience. "Who wants to burp him?"

"You take him, Maggie. I have my own little burp machine at home." Christy smiled at Parker. "I have a two-year-old and a two-month-old, and I couldn't get out of the house fast enough tonight. Shoved both of them at my husband, got in the car and floored it."

Maggie practically lunged for the baby and kissed his fat little cheek before assuming the position and patting the baby on the back.

"So how do you know Jamie?" Christy asked.

Parker took a sip of her drink. "He worked for my dad, and he's helping me flip a house. Over near Douglas Point."

"The hovel just before the Pines," Chantal supplied.

Parker gave a painful laugh. "That's the one."

"Is he seeing anyone?" Beth asked.

Parker paused. "Um, not that I know of." *Though I almost kissed him the other night and have dirty thoughts of him hourly.*

"If I weren't happily married, et cetera, et cetera," Chantal said, lifting an eyebrow.

"Sorry I'm late." Lavinia plunked herself into the chair next to Parker. "I was watching Jim Cantore on

The Weather Channel. *When Storms Kill* or some-such. I would do him in a New York minute. So. Who're we talking about?"

"Dewey's hot nephew," Chantal said. "Jamie Cahill."

"Little young for me," Lavinia said.

"So what's he like, Parker?" Maggie asked.

Yes, said Spike. *Do tell.* "Well, he's...he's very handy."

This set the women off in gales of laughter. "Speak of the devil," Chantal said, adjusting a breast. "Jamie! Over here!"

Parker's ears began tingling as James walked over. Christy gave him a hug; apparently he'd seen Maggie at the diner, knew Lavinia from his summers here and shook hands with Beth, which caused her to blush a fire-engine red.

"Jamie, this is my son," Chantal said, reclaiming her little bundle. "Admire away."

James looked at the baby, who gazed back, then spit up. "Very, um...well fed," he said, smiling at Chantal. Then his gaze shifted to Parker, and Lady Land stirred. Bugger.

"Pull up a chair and charm us, James," Chantal commanded. "It's sort of Maggie's shower."

"I'll make your drinks instead," James said. "I told Dewey I'd help out tonight. But have fun, girls." He turned and went back to the bar.

"Tell me you don't want a bite of that," Chantal said, watching him walk away.

"Preach it, sister," Beth murmured.

"So, Parker, I have to ask you," Christy said. "Are you the Parker Welles who writes those books about the angels?"

Parker took another healthy sip of her mojito. "Afraid so."

"Someone gave me a few Holy Rollers books when Violet was born."

"I'm sorry. You don't have to pretend you like them," Parker said easily. "They're pretty nauseating."

Hey! We have feelings! The HRs pouted.

No, you don't. You're imaginary, Parker countered.

"Was that the one where the kitten gets crushed by the tractor?" Maggie asked.

"That was my favorite one," Lavinia said. "Cried like a baby." *Thank you!* the angels chorused. At Parker's questioning look, Vin added, "Hey. You're my cousin. I did a Google search on you."

Parker finished her drink. "Anyway. The series is over, thank God."

"So what are you working on now?" Beth said.

"Um, I'm not really sure yet," Parker said. "I have a few ideas." *That's great news!* the Holy Rollers cheered. *Yay, you!*

If only.

"That dear boy is looking at you, Parker," Chantal said. "You guys doing each other?"

"Ignore her," Maggie said. "Chantal has sex on the brain."

"It's true. Your brother is a happy man," Chantal answered, raising a perfect eyebrow.

"No more sex talk about our brother!" Christy ordered.

Parker laughed. "No, it's not like that. He's my father's lawyer."

"So?" Chantal asked. "He's living with you. Have you seen him naked yet?"

"No! And even if I was interested—" *which you totally are* "—he's got the triple crown of no against him," Parker said. "Younger, unemployed, um…"

"Impotent?" Christy asked.

"Prison record?" Beth offered.

"Married to the church?" Maggie said.

"Oh, he's not impotent," Chantal murmured, raising an eyebrow. "At least—" she paused for effect "—he wasn't."

"Oh, Chantal. Are you kidding?" Maggie asked.

"Hey, somebody had to do it. He was seventeen, and *so* cute." Chantal grinned, and Parker felt an odd twang of…something. Another sip of mojito fixed that.

"Okay, time for a subject change," Maggie announced. "Let's leave poor James alone and talk about something else. I wear the crown of Kitty, so I'm the boss."

"And such a lightweight," Christy added.

"True. So, Parker, are you married? You have a little boy, right?"

"Nope, never married," she said. "My son is five. Nicholas Giacomo Mirabelli." She fished out her phone so Nicky's sweet face could be admired.

"Is there a story of forbidden love here? Or did you get knocked up, like me?" Chantal asked, peering at the photo. "He's beautiful."

"Nothing wrong with getting knocked up," said a male voice. "Chantal never would've married me if I hadn't knocked her up, right, babe?"

"Jonah, shush," Maggie and Christy said in unison, then laughed.

"You shush, girls," he retorted. "You're both love children, too. I'm the only child Mom and Dad really wanted." He turned to Parker. "Hi. Jonah, long-suffering brother of the idiot twins here. I've seen you out on your dock."

"Go away, Jonah," Maggie commanded. The pink-beaded tiara she was wearing was slightly askew. "Go to the boys' section. This is for women only. Shoo."

"You two are ugly when you drink." He bent down and kissed Chantal. "See you at home, gorgeous."

"Bye, honey." Chantal beamed up at him and patted his ass as he walked away.

"Disgusting," Christy said.

"So gross," Maggie added. "So anyway, you were telling us, Parker, before my brother so rudely interrupted?"

"Well," Parker said, "let's say I have this thing for emotionally unavailable men."

The table burst into laughter. "Please. You have no idea who you're talking to," Maggie said. At Parker's questioning look, she added, "I was in love with a priest."

"Okay. That's hard to top," Parker acknowledged.

"And I shtupped my best friend's baby brother. Have I mentioned Jonah is thirteen years younger than I am?" Chantal said, smiling. "Cougar, baby. The only way to go."

"And I slept with a certain married Massachusetts senator whose last name starts with *K*," Lavinia said. "Wasn't really worth the effort, I'd have to say."

"So how was your guy emotionally unavailable?" Maggie asked.

"It sounds worse than it is, but he was in love with someone else," Parker said. "And I didn't figure it out until after Miss Egg and Mr. Sperm met, so I have a five-year-old, and we have joint custody, and it's all very friendly and civilized."

Huh. Her second mojito was gone. *The last time you had two drinks and Sweet Baby James was around, you did the drag-and-shag,* Spike, now in his early twenties, pointed out. *Speaking of cougars. Just sayin'.*

"So have you dated at all?" Beth asked. "It's hard to find a decent guy these days."

"Nope, haven't really dated. Maybe a first date every few months, but nothing real," Parker said.

"You haven't had sex since your five-year-old was born?" Chantal asked, her mouth hanging open in horror.

This was, of course, the moment that James brought another round of drinks over.

"That's awful," Lavinia said, shaking her head. "Thank you, James, darlin'."

Parker didn't answer. James put a glass in front of her. "Thanks," she said, not daring to look at him.

"Anything else, girls?" he asked, his voice warm and smiley.

"Would you take off your shirt?" Christy asked. "We didn't get Maggie a stripper."

He laughed, and the sound scraped something deep down in Lady Land. Something that *liked* being scraped. James had almost kissed her the other night. Right? It had seemed to her that a kiss had been possible, there on the dock, before the thunder, when she'd bolted like a scared little baby horse.

Okay. No more mojitos. Who referred to themselves as scared little baby horses? Mojito-enhanced people, that's who.

James looked down at Parker, who decided that now would be an excellent time to drain that mojito. The straw stuck her in the eye, but she squinted and managed a swallow or two.

"I'll walk you home when you're ready," he said.

"No need, Thing One," she said sweetly. "I'm fine. I can canter on home all by myself."

He laughed, and there it was again, that scraping. *Meow.* "I'll do it anyway."

All righty, then. If he insisted. He could walk her home. He was paid by Harry to walk her home, she reminded herself. No matter how cute he was, no matter how smiley were those eyes, he was in Harry's pocket, and Harry was in jail and not a nice person, and James was here to babysit her and assuage Harry's conscience. Sex would not be part of the equation.

A while later, the party broke up. Maggie had to open the diner early, Christy's baby didn't yet sleep through the night, and Jonah was giving Chantal the look of love, according to her. Parker stood, too. James was nowhere to be seen, but after the sobering thoughts earlier, she really didn't want to wait. She was thirty-five years old, for heaven's sake. Didn't need an escort.

The air was surprisingly chilly, thick with the salty smell of the ocean. The bar had been loud, and as Parker walked toward the harbor, the quiet of the night settled around her companionably. Mackerly was pretty quiet, too, and also surrounded by water, but it wasn't like this. This was a place where livelihoods were still made on the sea, a town that was remote and craggy. So far, she hadn't seen any condos or McMansions on the water; the Pines was it as far as it went for posh real estate.

Waves slapped briskly against the hulls of the lobster boats in the otherwise quiet night. In the far distance, Parker heard an eerie, laughing noise; a loon, perhaps, not that she'd ever heard one before.

She fished her phone out of her bag and hit *Ethan*. Then, before it could connect, she hung up. She'd talked to Nicky three times today, and while she knew Ethan and Lucy wouldn't mind one more call, it seemed… needy.

And sleeping with James—not that she was thinking about it (cough)—would be needy, too. A lonely older woman who was in the midst of financial ruin and a career crisis should not have a fling. No matter how chocolate lava cake was her housemate.

"Parker. Wait up." Speaking of cake.

She turned as James loped down the half block that separated them. "Thing One," she said.

"Miss Welles. I believe I'd said I'd walk you home."

"Part of your duties for Harry?"

He gave her a measured look. "No. Just a concerned citizen who doesn't want you falling into the ocean."

"Please. I could drink you under the table."

"That's probably true. But since we're heading to the same place, why not?" He grinned, and she looked away quickly.

"Fine. Thank you, James."

"So were you girls talking about how handsome and strong I am?" he asked.

She snorted. "Little bit," she admitted. "I hear you and Chantal have a history."

"She kindly relieved me of my virginity," James answered. "And I will forever be grateful."

"You spent summers here, Thing One?"

"I did. A few, anyway." He hesitated, and Parker got the sense he was going to say more, but he stayed silent as they walked past the little diner, the dock, the harbor itself.

There were no streetlights on Shoreline Drive, and though it was past ten, the sky was just now deepening from indigo to black, the stars brightening overhead. The loon called again.

"So, Parker, any thought of maybe staying up here for a while?"

She shot him a puzzled look. "What do you mean?"

He shrugged. "You can work from anywhere, right?

You have some family up here. You could have the house winterized—"

"I'd never take Nicky away from his father." Her posture stiffened to Miss Porter's Finest.

"Didn't Ethan live away for most of Nicky's life?" James asked, his tone mild.

"No! No, he traveled a lot, but he was home every weekend. And then he switched careers so he could live in town. We're five minutes apart."

"I see."

There was something in his tone that grated on Parker's nerves. "Ethan's a wonderful father."

"Of course he is. Isn't my tone hushed and reverent enough? I'm sorry."

"What's your problem with Ethan?" she snapped. "I mean, really, Thing One. You barely know him."

James nodded, then picked up a rock and threw it out into the sea, where it hit the water with a hollow dunk. "How long were you with him, back when you were dating?"

He probably already knew the answer. "A couple of months," she answered, her tone icy.

"And why'd you break up?"

She walked a little faster. "Is it any of your business?"

"No, probably not. But he sounds so very perfect in every way. It's a little confusing as to why you didn't snatch him up."

"Your dubious charm is wearing thin."

"He married your best friend, right?"

"It wasn't like that! I barely knew Lucy when he and I were dating. We only got close after I broke up with him. And *I* broke up with *him*."

"Of course. So sorry, Majesty. Didn't mean to criticize the Paragon."

"The what?"

"Ethan. The Paragon of Perfection."

Well, bugger. She was either going to smack him or—or agree with him. "Oh, look, home sweet home. Sleep tight, Thing One." With that, she jerked open the front door of the little house, got Beauty and went out the back to go sit on the dock.

She didn't slam the door.

But she wanted to.

CHAPTER FOURTEEN

"So you got this? You can hold down the fort, and all?"

"Sure, Vin. You go. Have a great time." Parker smiled at her cousin. She couldn't wait till Vin was gone so she could start cleaning. The shop was filthy.

"Thanks. 'Cause I haven't been laid in God knows how long." She sighed. "That's where I'm going. A sex date. And I cannot wait."

"Thanks for sharing."

"This guy? Knows what he's doing," her cousin continued, squinting appreciatively as she took a long drag on her cigarette, her face contorting into a sea of wrinkles. "Some men, it's just in and out, right? Nawt him."

"That's…that's great."

"Does this little circly thing. Makes me crazy." Lavinia stubbed the cigarette out on her palm, then fished her bra strap up from where it had slid down her crepey, mole-encrusted arm. "He might be hairy, God knows, but once you get used to the friction, it's all good."

Parker had never thought of herself as a prude, nope, but damn if she didn't throw up in her mouth a little bit. "Well, then. Maybe you should get going. Um, traffic and all that." Yes. The fabled traffic of Gideon's Cove, Maine, where once in a while you had to wait four or five seconds to make a left-hand turn onto Elm Street.

"Good point, kid." Lavinia punched Parker on the arm

fondly. "Have a great day. And thanks. I'm off to have my orgasms."

"You go, girl," Parker said, swallowing. Would definitely be throwing away that cranberry muffin from Joe's, no matter how good it had looked a half hour ago. Lavinia saluted as she left, hitching up the waistband of her drooping shorts.

As soon as her cousin was down the block, Parker opened the windows. She liked Lavinia, sure, but the smell of cigarette smoke was nasty. Made Parker look forward to her swim later on even more than usual.

Funny thing about that swim—the water seemed to do wonders for Beauty, who acted like a normal dog, leaping off the dock, retrieving whatever happened to be floating, joyfully paddling after Parker, making her funny little woofing breaths. But James…James clearly didn't like it. Wherever he was, he'd stop and watch her go. It wasn't the bikini thing—though she had to admit, his reaction upon seeing her that first time was very gratifying. No, he ignored her as she went out, and as she came in, but the whole time she was in the water, she could feel his eyes on her. Must've seen *Jaws* too many times as a kid.

But the swims were glorious as far as Parker was concerned. The icy bite of the water, the tang of salt, the sure, strong strokes as she swam. Maybe she could get a job as a swim coach or something. Not that she could support Nicky on that, but it was a thought. She'd been on the swim team in college, after all. Had been the third Olympic alternate, which by Olympic standards meant she was a loser, but by normal human standards meant she was pretty great. Swimming was one of the few times she felt as if she knew exactly what she was doing. That, and being Nicky's mother.

At the thought of Nicky, she glanced at the calendar. Thirteen more days.

The house was shaping up, as James had predicted. A week and a half, and he had on a new roof. Chimney fixed, most of the old shingles off the side. He worked like an ox, she'd give him that.

But it was still…uncomfortable, being around him. There were definitely moments where she really, really liked Thing One. And then she'd remember how he'd known she and Nicky were about to be financially ruined. How he'd known they'd have to move. How he'd taken care of his own interests and not said a word to her, even knowing that she and Nicky were completely dependent on that stupid family trust. Well, Nicky had Ethan to support him. There was that.

But even as those things seemed to matter less, there were those phone calls from Harry. Oh, yes. She'd over-heard them. The easy camaraderie between the two men. Practically father and son. BFFs till the end of time.

Harry hadn't called her once. She made her own duti-ful weekly call, but they never talked for more than three minutes.

"It's the old wound," she said, quoting the dying Lancelot. Paternal rejection left a mark on a girl. A woman. Bugger and damn, she was thirty-five. Hardly a girl anymore. Half a decade older than Thing One. Ethan, too for that matter, which had never seemed to be an issue. He had an old soul. James did not.

Time to whip out Mr. Clean, her favorite male these days. Lavinia didn't really seem to care much about where things were in the flower shop, but Parker had been itching to rearrange. It was a tiny little space, jammed with all the detritus of the business. Not that there was a lot of business. Maggie and Malone's wedding was coming up. Otherwise, there'd been a couple of get-well arrangements, one sheepish-looking husband in for a bouquet, two new babies. So far, if Parker was at the shop, Lavinia let her handle every job. Vin seemed oddly detached from the flower arranging. The only thing she really seemed to care about was the small greenhouse that housed the orchids, where she spent hours each day, misting, watering, checking soil pH. Parker had offered to help and was immediately waved off.

"You like doing the flowers? Run with it," she'd told Parker. "This back here is my baby."

And Parker *loved* doing the flowers. She'd spent a summer down at a finishing school of sorts, where she'd learned helpful things like how to pour tea, make conversation without expressing an actual opinion and yes, walk with a book on her head. The flower arranging had been the only thing she'd really enjoyed. At night, there had been other lessons—how to buy drugs, water down your parents' alcohol so they wouldn't realize you were drinking, give a blow job, demonstrated on a banana by Caitlynn Swann, whose father owned most of North Carolina. Obviously, these nighttime lessons weren't on the curriculum, but the older girls had taken it upon themselves to share. Parker had been fourteen at the time.

At any rate, she'd always liked flowers. Back in her Grayhurst days, she'd cut a bunch every Monday from the vast garden and put together something for the kitchen table, her nightstand, Nicky's room—though he had a tendency to pick off any red petals and glue them on his *Star Wars* figurines to represent blood. She'd even put an arrangement in the bathroom. It always felt nice, flowers in the loo. Made brushing your teeth seem much more pleasant.

Four hours later, Parker was dusty, sweaty and more

than pleased with her efforts. She'd dragged the card display to be near the cash register and rearranged the shelves with all the little tchotchkes. The shop was now much easier to navigate, the dusty porcelain figurines and candles wiped clean and placed in the corner. She put the houseplants on the wide shelf in the front window—Lavinia had them against the back wall, for some reason—and made a gorgeous arrangement of gerbera daisies, larkspur, irises and ferns for the counter, the colors all in shades of pink and purple. Beautiful.

She hoped Lavinia would let her do Maggie's wedding bouquet. Maggie had been so nice to her, so welcoming. Parker had gotten an invitation to the wedding, even. And Malone had smiled at her the other night. Maybe. It was sort of hard to tell, but Parker had a bit of a soft spot for him, as he was the first resident she'd met. She liked looking out for his boat each night, knowing he was safely back home and on his way to Nice Maggie.

"You'd think I'd be cynical," Parker said aloud to Beauty as she swept the floor. "But I'm not. I love love. Gross, huh?"

Beauty's tail swished in agreement, her eyes never leaving Parker.

It was too bad they couldn't keep the cottage as a summer place. It was hard not to fall in love with this town.

Well. Maybe someday.

The bell over the door rang, and Parker looked up to see who it was. An older man in a suit, not someone she'd met before. Beauty fled to her hiding spot under the worktable behind the counter.

"Hello," Parker said. "How can I help you?"

"I'd like a potted plant for my mother," he answered.

"Sure. Take a look around. Is it a special occasion?"

"Well, we had to put her in a nursing home, poor thing."

"I'm sorry to hear that."

"And I don't make it up here too often." He gave her a once-over. "I live in Winter Haven. Ever been?"

"Can't say that I have."

He reminded her of Harry; his suit was expensive, and his leather briefcase gleamed. Parker would bet he drove a German car and lived in a house on the water. He glanced dismissively at the Boston ferns and African violets, the jade plant and the cheerful yellow primrose. "Got anything else? Something a bit more…"

"Exotic?" Parker supplied.

"Exactly," he answered, smiling. "You read my mind." Another glance at her chest. In a way, flattering that he was checking her out, as she was filthy from cleaning and dressed in a once-white T-shirt and jeans. On the other hand, he exuded that entitled vibe—*I can look at your boobs because I'm rich, and you're a serving wench as far as I'm concerned.*

"Well, what you see is pretty much it," she said.

"What's in the greenhouse?"

"Right. Um, we have some rare plants back there."

"Would you mind showing me those?"

Parker hesitated; it really was Vinnie's domain. Then again, her cousin grew them to sell, ostensibly.

"I don't mind paying extra," the guy said. "My mom deserves the best."

And Vin could use the money. "Sure. Let me get the key. We have some orchids. Does your mom like those?"

"Doesn't everyone?" he answered. "They're almost as pretty as you. Dan Jacobs, by the way."

Yep. A Harry. Dan Jacobs had to be sixty-five if he was a day, complete with wedding ring, but it seemed that once a man passed forty, he suffered some kind of acute stroke that affected his mathematical abilities, encouraging him to hit on women young enough to be his daughter. The Hugh Hefner School of Nasty.

"And you are?" he asked.

"Parker. Nice to meet you."

"*Very* nice to meet you."

Beauty growled, very softly. *Indeed, sweetie.* "Let's see what we have," Parker said, her voice brisk. She took Vin's key from the drawer, opened the padlocked door and pushed it open.

She hadn't been in here yet. There were orchids, all right. About ten of them were in rather sparse bloom, a couple of blossoms here and there, but nothing really striking. More of the orchids were dormant—unremarkable, rubbery green leaves in pots. But the other plants, maybe fifty in all, looked like houseplants—densely growing, delicate leaves, almost like a miniature green Japanese maple. Some of them had fluffy white flowers akin to something Dr. Seuss might've drawn. They were very pretty, though Parker had no idea what they were.

"I like those," Dan Jacobs said. "Are they orchids, too?"

"I don't think so," Parker said. She checked one or two of the pots for an identifying plastic stick. Nothing. No sticker on the bottom, either.

"Well, I'll take one," the guy said. "Wrap it up with some pretty foil, if you would."

"Sure." Parker could find no price tag…well, she'd charge him seventy-five dollars. Looked as if he could afford it.

As she wrapped the pot and tied some ribbon around it, Dan Jacobs leaned forward, the thick smell of his cologne enveloping her. "So I wonder if a beautiful woman like you would like to have dinner with me," he said, showing a whitened grin.

"I'm pretty sure your wife wouldn't like that," Parker answered, smiling to soften the blow.

"My wife has nothing to do with this," he said.

The guy was *just* like her dad. Hey, what did marriage mean when you could bang a younger woman, right?

"No thank you," Parker answered. "You're a few decades too old for me. That'll be seventy-five dollars, please."

"Bitch," he muttered, very softly. He put down four twenties and walked out of the store without waiting for change.

"You're disgusting," Parker sang out once he was out of sight. Well, at least it was a good sale. Vin would be pleased; the African violets were six bucks apiece.

The rest of the afternoon passed quietly. By two o'clock, Parker found herself wondering what James was doing. If he was doing it without his shirt. No, no, that's right. He wasn't at the house today. She'd given him the day off. Ordered him to take the day off, more like it.

They'd been skirting each other the past few days... polite, pleasant, but not intimate. Not since that first dinner on the dock, when he'd taken her hand. Since he'd almost kissed her, and she'd almost let him.

But there was something about James. The memory of his hard, naked body against hers at Esme's wedding— that tawdry, smokin'-hot, porno memory, yes, that was something indeed. He'd done incredible things with the cottage—that was for sure—a steady and hard worker, completely uncomplaining about the amount there was to do. But there was something else. Something quiet. Something a little bit sad, maybe.

Today was the first day they'd been apart since he arrived. And let's face it. It wasn't because he deserved a day off—which he absolutely did. It was because if she had to keep seeing him shirtless, her thin resolve not to climb him like a tree might crumble, after all.

Just then, the bells rang out in alarm as the door was jerked open, and there he was, Dan Jacobs, her customer du jour. "That's her," he said, his face florid.

"Is there a problem?" Parker said. Holy crap, was that a cop with him? It was.

Dan pointed. "She's the one. The one who sold me the drugs."

"What?" she yelped, getting an answering yelp from Beauty. "I did not!"

"Ma'am, you have the right to remain silent," the cop began.

"What? Why? What did I do?"

The Harry-clone jammed his fists on his hips. "You sold me a marijuana plant! For my mother, no less!"

CHAPTER FIFTEEN

"I DIDN'T KNOW it was marijuana!" Parker protested for the fifth time as the cop led her inside the police station.

"You probably don't want to say anything till your lawyer gets here," the cop said. His nameplate said Bottoms.

"Are you related to Billy Bottoms?" Parker asked, her voice a little tremulous. Because hell, she was handcuffed! And she was being *processed!* Holy halos, they were pressing her fingers into ink! For fingerprinting!

"He's my father," the cop replied. "I'm Young Billy."

She took the wipe he offered and cleaned her hands. "He's nice. Your dad." *Please let that show that I'm a good person!*

"Ayuh. Hold this number and look up."

"Why? Are you taking a mug shot? I don't need—" The bulb flashed. Her mug shot had been taken. The cop put the cuffs back on—*This is horrifying!* the female Holy Rollers whimpered. *What's happened to you?*—and led her across the room to the curious stare of the secretary, a middle-aged woman who was talking on the phone.

"Listen, Billy—"

"I go by Young Billy, actually."

"Oh, okay. Well, um, Young Billy, I'm a mother. I would never sell drugs, I swear."

"Welp, you sold a marijuana plant, sweetheart. I'd say

that's selling drugs, mother or not. It's a little hard to believe you don't know what pot looks like. Haven't you
ever seen a Bob Marley T-shirt?"

"I thought it was bonsai or something!"

"Ayuh. Well. Come on down here, watch your head."
He led her down a set of medieval-looking stone steps
into a dank cellar, lit by a flickering fluorescent light.
"In you go. You sit tight. No need to worry."

No need to worry? She was in *jail*. The clanking of a
cell door…not a sound she was likely to forget.

*Little Pup whimpered as the cage slammed closed
behind him. Note to self: must not poop on the Evil King's
yard.*

Speaking of little pups… "Young Billy?" she called.

His head appeared around the door. "What is it, sweetheart?"

At least he was nice. "My dog's still at the flower
shop."

Billy frowned. "Anyone you could call to come get
her?"

Parker thought for a second. "Maggie Beaumont,
maybe? She runs the diner."

"I know who she is," he said. "Sure, I'll swing by, ask
her."

"Do you have to tell her? About this? Is it public
record?"

"It's probably all over town by now."

Great. "When can I make my phone call? I get a phone
call, right?"

"Ayuh. We have to process the contents of your purse,
then we'll be right in." He disappeared again.

She was alone. In a cell. In a basement. Like the place
Hannibal Lecter was kept.

"'Half a league, half a league, half a league onward.'"

The flat monotone voice echoed off the stone walls, and Parker jumped, squeaking, hands fluttering. Oh, God. She *wasn't* alone! That was much worse! Someone was in the cell with her—no, no, the cell next to her. Parker looked over, her heart convulsing in her chest. A man. A criminal, staring at her through the bars.

She looked away, and fast.

"'Half a league, half a league, half a league onward.'"

She should *not* be here. She didn't know it was pot! Oh, and speaking of pot, Lavinia was *growing* it! Where was *she,* huh? Being shtupped by a hirsute man with hidden talents and not available to clear up this misunderstanding! Because if anyone should be in jail, it should be Lavinia.

"'Half a league, half a league, half a league onward.'"

Why was he chanting that? Like a spell or something. A whimper escaped her throat. She looked around the cell, which was, well, rather spacious, actually, bigger than her bedroom in the cottage. A bunk bed with steel mattresses was on the far side of the cell. A steel toilet with no seat. A steel sink.

"'Half a league, half a league, half a league onward.'"

Oh, God. Her son's mother was in *jail.* The Mirabellis would die! This actually might bring on the heart attack Gianni kept threatening to have. And what if this affected her custody of Nicky? What if he had to live with Ethan all the time?

No, no. That couldn't happen. It was an accident. She didn't know it was pot!

Nevertheless, Parker had been processed. Processed! What if this got on the news? What if Nicky saw it? *Daughter of Convicted Wall Street Baron Harry Welles Arrested on Drug Charges.* The Coven would be thrilled.

Former Children's Author Turns to Marijuana. Save the Children would give all the money back. Oh, God!

If Harvard could see her now. She, who'd never even had a speeding ticket, who'd never done drugs, never so much as inhaled—and at Harvard, please, there should've been a special award for that—was in jail.

"'Half a league, half a league, half a league onward.'"

And another thing. The man in the next cell was batshit crazy, that was clear. Hopefully harmlessly crazy. Then again, he was in *jail.* Parker swallowed, glancing over again at her…companion. His gray hair was matted, and he looked very, very dirty. Dirtier even than Nicky after a day of making meatballs and sauce with Gianni and Marie. He was still staring at her as if she was a Thanksgiving turkey and he was coming off a hunger strike.

"'Half a league, half a league, half a league onward.' Hello. You're very pretty."

Oh, dear Jesus. "I love that poem," she said, her voice cracking. Yes, yes, make friends! In case he was thinking about shivving her. Was that the right term? "'Charge of the Light Brigade,' right?" *Thank you, Miss Porter's!*

"'Half a league, half a league, half a league onward.'"

Young Billy was back with her cell phone. "One call," he said.

Her hands were shaking, she noticed. There. *Thing One.* She hit his number, very, very grateful that she'd saved it.

"You've reached James Cahill. Leave a message, and I'll get back to you as soon as I can."

No! No no no no no.

"James, it's Parker. Um, I'm in jail. In Gideon's Cove? Next to the town hall? I, um, seem to have sold a marijuana plant by accident. Could you come here as fast as you can? Thank you so much. Please hurry, James. I really need you to get here. Fast." She glanced at Young Billy. "Okay. I guess that's it. Drive safely. But fast, okay? Bye." She clicked off. "My attorney."

Young Billy took the phone back. "All righty, then, we'll bring him right in when he gets here. In the meantime, you sit tight. Want a magazine?"

"Okay," Parker whispered.

"We got *Hemmings Motor News* or *InStyle.*"

"*InStyle,* please," she said, feeling her lips quiver. The cop handed her a magazine, soft with age. "Young Billy, is that guy...sane?" She nodded toward the Tennyson fan.

"Who, Crazy Dave?" Billy asked. Guess that answered *that* question. "Well, he's a little off. Hears voices. But he's harmless. We keep him here once in a while, make sure he eats some dinner. Right, Dave?"

"'Half a league, half a league, half a league onward.'"

Young Billy laughed. "You bet, buddy." With that, he left Parker and Crazy Dave alone.

Parker looked at the clock across the hall from her cell. She'd been in here fourteen minutes. Childbirth had flown by compared with this.

She thought of Harry, who was in an actual prison, not just a holding cell where the police officer was as nice as pie. Did he have a roommate? Those kinds of details didn't come up. She'd asked how it was, and his answer was abrupt. "It's prison, Parker. How do you think?"

What that meant, she didn't know. Gangs? Homemade tattoos? Probably not, as it was one of those white-collar, minimum-security places. But still. Prison was prison.

Where was James? Why had she insisted that he take today off, of all days? Why hadn't he answered his cell phone? God, what if he hadn't taken it? What if it was sitting in his room or on a windowsill? Holy halos, what if he'd gone to Rhode Island for something? It could be hours before he got here! It could be tomorrow!

Parker noted that she was hyperventilating. "Settle down, settle down," she whispered, trying to get her breathing under control. *Dude, chill,* said Spike. *It's jail. You're just killin' your number.* Great. Now he talked like a gang member.

"Excuse me," said a voice. Parker looked up. Crazy Dave had pressed his face against the bars that separated their cells. His eyes were red-rimmed, and his filthy nails were way too long. Like a werewolf's.

"Yes?" she managed.

"I wanted to tell you something."

"Oh."

"I've been a little bound up lately."

"Oh. Okay. Um, sorry to hear it."

"But that seems to be resolving now. I'll be needing the facilities."

Without turning her head, she glanced at his steel toilet, which was, alas, in full view. "Oh."

"But I don't wish to use that one. Can I use yours?"

"No! Nope. Um, that's your cell, and this is mine, and I don't have a key or anything."

"That's fine." His voice was pleasant. Not as if he were about to shank her.

Then Crazy Dave pulled down his pants and squatted, and Parker leaped back to the far wall of the cell, grabbed her copy of *InStyle* and buried her face in great dresses from the 2007 Emmys.

"You really are quite pretty," Crazy Dave said between grunts.

Where the hell was James?

CHAPTER SIXTEEN

"I'LL SEE YOU SOON," James said into Mary Elizabeth's hair. "Love you."

"I love you, too. Why don't you live here?" she asked, smiling up at him. "We could be together all the time."

She always asked, and it always sliced him right open, that question. "Well, I have to work," he said, tucking some of her curly hair behind her ears.

"Work here." Her blue eyes were as innocent as the sky. "You should work here, James."

"I wish I could. I'll see you soon, okay?"

"Bring me a present."

"Don't I always?"

"A big present. I want a present, James."

"You got it."

He kissed her cheek and walked to his truck.

Parker had been right. It was good to take a day off. First he'd gone to see Harry, a helluva drive, more than four hours across the state of Maine, just over the New Hampshire line. His boss had been nicely surprised. He looked fairly awful, though, gray-faced and a little slack. The wages of sobriety, at least at first. They'd talked for an hour or so, shooting the breeze, talking about the Red Sox and their excellent fielding, sure to collapse when hopes were high, as usual. Harry had some funny stories about some of his fellow inmates, most of whom, like him, were in for white-collar crimes or too many petty misdemeanors. There'd been a Ping-Pong tournament. Movie night.

Harry didn't ask about Parker, not directly. About Nicky's trip, and the progress on the house, yes. But nothing more. As ever, James had the impression that while Harry loved him like a son, the subject of Parker was off-limits.

Then, on the way home, James stopped by to see Mary Elizabeth, which was always a painfully happy occasion. As ever, she was overjoyed to see him. Luckily, she'd had no other visitors today, because God knew, that made things awkward.

As he left Mary Elizabeth's, James checked his phone. No service, that was right. They were in East Boonies, Maine, after all. Still, it was a beautiful place. And only forty minutes from his parents'. But that was a stop he wouldn't make, though he supposed eventually he'd have to.

Once back on the interstate, James's phone chirped. *One missed call...Parker.*

Well. That was kind of nice. Maybe she wanted him to pick something up for dinner, as it was now after six. Unlikely, but maybe. They'd been in this war of supreme pleasantness since the night he'd dared to mention St. Ethan.

He pulled over and listened to her message. Listened to it again. And a third time.

Well, holy crap. He'd better put the pedal to the metal. Unfortunately, he was still an hour and a half away.

James couldn't help laughing as he pulled back on the highway. Parker Harrington Welles, in a holding cell. He couldn't wait to see it.

WHEN HE WALKED INTO the Gideon's Cove Police Department, it was eight o'clock. James had been on the phone most of his drive, first with Dewey, then with Lavinia, who was out of town herself, then with Maggie Beaumont, who knew everything. James had called the local judge, set up an arraignment, took care of Parker's bail and left a message for the prosecutor's office.

"James Cahill," he said to the sergeant on duty. "Attorney for Parker Welles."

As Officer Dewitt led him down the stone stairs to the holding cell, James could hear Parker...crying? His heart lurched. But no, not crying. Singing? And my God, that smell!

"'Half a league, half a league, half a league onward,'" someone—a man—chanted.

"'All in the valley of Death rode the six hundred,'" Parker answered back.

"'Forward, the light brigade,'" the man shouted triumphantly.

She was lying on the steel bunk, an old magazine with a picture of Cameron Diaz covering her face. "'Into the valley of Death rode the six hundred,'" she said, definitely a panicky edge to her voice.

"Your attorney's here," Officer Dewitt said, unlocking the door.

Parker jerked upright, hitting her head on the top bunk. "James!" She hurtled across the cell, and before he knew it, she was in his arms, hugging him hard, and though she smelled a little dank from her time in the basement, it was sure better than that other smell, and *man,* he hadn't felt anything this good in years, her hair silky against his cheek, her body pressed against his.

"Parker. Always lovely to see you," he murmured, hugging her back.

"James, oh, James, thank God you're here," she blurted into his shoulder. "That man over there, he pooped on the floor, and holy halos, there was so much of it! He hasn't stopped chanting that horrible poem for hours, and if I don't stop reciting 'Charge of the Light Brigade,' I'm going to kill myself."

"I'm afraid you have to stay overnight," James said.

She pulled back, eyes wide with horror.

"Just kidding," he said, grinning. "You're free to go."

Those beautiful eyes narrowed. "You're a horrible man."

"Hey. I'm not the drug dealer here."

"My cousin is growing pot in her greenhouse," Parker said. "That's another thing. Pot, James."

"More on that later," he said, taking her hand and leading her up the stone stairs. "Let's get you home. Thanks, Officer."

"You're welcome," he said, sitting at his desk and picking up a newspaper.

"Yes, thanks for nothing," Parker echoed. "What happened to Young Billy? He would've come down here and cleaned up that mess, I bet. I only called for you a thousand or so times."

"You know how many drunks we get bellowing for us all the time?" the cop said, turning a page of the newspaper. "A lot."

"I'm not a drunk! I should never have been in here. I thought it was a fern!"

"Right."

"It looked like a fern." The officer rolled his eyes. Parker turned to James. "It looked like a fern, James. Or a miniature Japanese maple tree. It was actually quite pretty. And since I'm not a drug dealer and in fact made it all the way to the ripe old age of thirty-five without ever having smoked marijuana or even a cigarette, I can tell you, I had no idea what it was!"

"And yet a ninety-nine-year-old lady in the nursing home ID'd it immediately," the cop said.

"So maybe she's a pot smoker! I'm not!" Parker snapped.

"Okay, settle down, honey," James said.

At the term of endearment, she glanced at him sharply. Then she took a deep breath and flicked the cop's newspaper. "Thank you so much for your hospitality, Officer," she said. "Have a wonderful day."

"You're that rich chick, aren't you?" he said, finally looking up. "The one whose father is in jail?"

"Yes."

"Runs in the family, I see."

She straightened into princess posture and tilted her head slightly. "And inbreeding must run in yours."

"Okay, Parker, let's go," James said. "Don't get into more trouble." He took her hand more firmly this time and led her out into the cool, clear night.

"We need to get Beauty," Parker said. "She's at Maggie's—at least I think she is. Young Billy Bottoms—"

"I already picked her up. She's in the truck."

James held the door for Parker, and at the sight of her dog, she seemed to melt a little. "Hi, honey," she murmured, burying her face in the dog's neck. Same as she'd done to him.

"So. Jail," he said. "I guess you can cross that off your bucket list."

"Yes. That and amputating a toe, just for fun."

He glanced at her as he backed out and headed past the diner. "You okay?"

"Peachy."

"That hug was nice," he said mildly.

She didn't answer for a minute, though her cheeks flushed slightly. "Did you have to…arraign me or whatever? Put up bail?" she asked.

"Yep."

"I'll pay you back."

He sighed. Emphatically.

"Any word from Lavinia?" she asked, looking out the window.

"I talked to her. Says she wants to grow medical marijuana, fully intended to get a license one of these days. Doesn't seem really concerned about prosecution. She said she slept with the D.A. back in the seventies."

"Beautiful. So what happens next?"

James glanced at her profile. "There'll be a hearing. You'll tell the judge that you didn't intend to sell an illegal substance. Maybe a fine, some community service. I wouldn't worry about it. Lavinia will have to give her plants to a licensed marijuana grower." He was already going through a mental Rolodex to see if he had any friends from law school practicing in Maine who might be able to do him a favor.

They were home within minutes. Parker jumped out of the truck, Beauty on her heels. The dog had been friendly enough when James had picked her up at Maggie's house, where she'd been rolling around on the floor with Maggie's much bigger yellow Lab, but now that Parker was back, he was once again persona non grata.

"I'll make you something to eat," James offered.

"That's okay. I have to call Nicky," she said. "I haven't talked to him all day."

"You gonna tell him what happened?"

She gave him an odd look. "No, James. He's five."

"Right." Stupid question.

"But first, a shower. I thought Crazy Dave was going

to throw poop at me, like the gorillas do at the zoo." She shuddered, gave him a grin and disappeared into the bathroom. A second later, the door popped open, and for one ridiculous, wonderful instant, he thought she was about to invite him in.

"Thank you, James. For the bail and whatever else you had to do. And for getting Beauty."

"You're welcome," he said.

Another smile, and she closed the door, leaving him standing there.

A half hour later, Parker was down on the dock, though it was now fully dark, laughing on the phone as she told Mr. and Mrs. Paragon about her day in the clink, no doubt.

Her hair was about the only thing he could see now. It had brightened in the sunlight; she'd been working outside, hacking the long grass, digging up the scrubby bushes that overhung the stairs to the water. She hadn't complained once since getting the news, hadn't blinked at the backbreaking work. She really hadn't even complained too much about spending six hours in a cell.

Harry would be proud of her, James thought. Or he should be.

Why Harry could barely tolerate his only child was a mystery. James had seen that unique look of hers leveled at Harry so many times—that jaded, knowing look, the same one she'd given James himself so often, though less lately. But sometimes, when she was looking at Harry, James was almost sure he'd seen something else. A flash of hope. Regret. Sorrow.

Then again, he knew jack about relationships and people and certainly nothing about fathers and daughters. But if he ever did have a daughter—unlikely, but still—a look like that would kill him.

Her laughter rang out against the shushing of the waves against the rocky shore.

Damn Ethan Mirabelli. Parker would smile at James, thank him—oh, yes, she was wicked polite—but she would never let him in her inner circle. He couldn't blame her, not really. He wasn't good with kids. His father liked to tell him he didn't take life seriously enough, disgusted that he hadn't done more—more what, he wasn't sure. More penance, probably. He'd done well enough in college and law school, but it wasn't as if he was brilliant. Once, a professor had written a comment on one of James's papers: "Well written but lacking substance." Kind of struck a chord. Then James took a boring desk job for the money, and now he was unemployed.

James finished his beer and went to the stove. Took some bread, cut a hole the size of a fifty-cent piece in each slice, added some olive oil to the pan, then the bread. Cracked an egg. Toad in the hole. Comfort food for the woman who'd been in prison, whether she wanted his comfort or not.

As he approached the dock, he could hear her talking. A story, actually. He paused before stepping onto the creaky wooden dock, not wanting her to know he was there.

"Mickey never forgot what it was like to be left out," she was saying. "From that day on, he shared all the calls with Wensley, and in time, Wensley became a great fire truck, too, same as Mickey, and the two were great friends. Mickey was a legend, and all the children of New York knew his story, and whenever he went racing through the city, little kids and their parents, grown-ups going to work, rich people and poor people, police officers and tourists...all would stop and watch as the bravest fire truck there ever was went out to do the job he loved so well. The end." She paused. "You still awake, sweetheart? Nicky? I love you, honey."

There was a pause. "Hey, Ethan. Guess he was pretty worn-out. Okay. You guys have a great day tomorrow. No, I won't. I'm a model citizen from now on." She laughed. "Good night, buddy. Give Lucy a smooch from me."

She clicked off and stroked Beauty's cheek; the dog was lying with her head on Parker's lap, and gave a little wag. James stepped onto the dock, and Parker looked up.

"Hey."

"Hi. Thought you might be hungry," he said, setting the plate down next to her.

"I'm starving, actually. Thank you, James. It smells great. What is it?"

"Toad in the hole."

"I've never had that before."

"Get outta town."

"Nope. It's the sad truth." She smiled and took a bite. "Goes great with this sauvignon blanc I stole from Harry's wine cellar. Want some?"

"No, I'm good." He sat next to her, though the rocking of the dock was a little unsettling. Beauty moved closer to Parker's chair, though not to the other side. Progress. "So was that the tail end of *Mickey the Fire Engine* I overheard?"

She looked up sharply. "Yes. How'd you know that?"

He shrugged. "Harry asked me to double-check Grayhurst one more time. I found a box in the attic. It's in the house somewhere. I meant to give it to you before. Anyway, it's got some of your papers from college. *Mickey the Fire Engine,* too." He glanced at her, shrugged. "I couldn't help myself."

"Did you also read my essay on the significance of language in *The Sound and the Fury?*"

"Passed on that one. Too many big words."

She went back to her toad. "*Mickey* was my first manuscript," she said. "Couldn't sell it to save my life. That copy is the last one. I burned all the others along with the rejection letters."

"I thought it was great," he said.

"Did you?" Her voice was wry.

"Mmm-hmm. Even got choked up a little."

"Really."

James grinned. "Well, there were fire trucks involved. Doesn't every boy love fire trucks?"

"Not if you work in publishing, apparently."

"How's the writing coming along?" he asked.

She sighed. "I haven't hit on the right idea yet. Guess the Holy Rollers burned me out a little bit."

They were quiet for a few minutes. The sky was completely clear, and the stars so brilliant they looked almost like a thin veil of clouds. Taking care not to move too quickly, or to look at her, James reached down and stroked Beauty's head. The dog allowed it. Taking that as a sign, he decided to go for it.

"Can I ask you a personal question, Parker?"

"How is it that a Harvard grad can't recognize marijuana?" she said, offering the last bite of toad in the hole to her dog, who took it delicately.

"Why don't you and Harry get along?"

She didn't move for a second, just let Beauty lick her fingers. Then she poured herself a little more wine and looked up at the sky. Sighed. He could smell her soap from here.

"I don't know, Thing One," she said quietly. "Maybe he wanted a son."

"Do you think that's it?"

Another pause. "No." She cleared her throat. "So I guess I owe you a real answer, huh? Since you bailed me out and chose to spend your summer up here, working like an ox."

"You don't owe me anything."

"No, I do. I do." She shifted in her seat and looked at him, then back out at the water. A loon called from past Douglas Point. "Okay, here's the deal. When I was little, I worshipped Harry. I mean, what little girl doesn't love her dad?"

"I guess they all do."

Parker took a sip of wine and petted her dog, her hand very close to James's, though she didn't appear to notice. "It was hard not to. He had the whole package—looks, charm, brilliance. If Harry had you in his sights, you felt like the most amazing, interesting person in the world."

James grunted. True enough.

"And I don't know, it was a long time ago, but he seemed to adore me, too. I used to—" She broke off for a second, not choked up as much as lost in a memory. "I used to go running into Welles Financial and his whole staff would treat me like a princess. And it didn't matter if he was on the phone or in a meeting, he'd tell whoever it was that his daughter was here and kick them out, or he'd introduce me, pull me onto his lap and then keep talking, like I was smart enough to understand."

"So what changed?" he asked.

"The summer I was ten, I caught him in bed with my babysitter."

James flinched. "Ah, shit."

"Indeed." She stroked Beauty's ear, not looking at him.

"I'm sorry, Parker."

She didn't say anything for a minute. "Keep that to yourself, okay? Nobody else knows. Well, my mother. And the babysitter, but she was paid off." She finished her wine. "It's been a long day. Thank you for everything, James." She stood up, and he lurched to his feet, blocking her path.

"Is that it?" he asked.

She tilted her head. "What more should there be?"

"I don't know, Parker. You drop an announcement like that and then hike off to bed?"

She didn't answer, just looked at him, her brows drawn together.

"I've known you for years," he heard himself say with a sinking sense of dread. *Shut up, idiot.* "We slept together once. You could talk to me, Parker. You could… we could be friends."

Yeah. Chicks loved when you begged. How about if he went ahead and handed her his balls and said, *Do what you will.* Any second, she was going to smother a laugh or roll her eyes or call him Thing One, and—

She leaned forward and kissed him on the cheek, her lips a soft, sweet press, her summery dress swishing against his arm. "Thank you, James," she said, her voice softer now.

Then she stepped around him, Beauty scuttling past, as well, and went up the stairs to the house.

CHAPTER SEVENTEEN

PARKER LAY AWAKE for a long, long time, Beauty a silky ball of warmth at her side. James didn't come in for a good hour, and she was glad.

She couldn't figure him out. He'd spent years attached to her father like a remora attaches to a shark. She knew he was here under Harry's command and on Harry's payroll, because while her father might not love her, she was his only child, and he'd damn well keep tabs on her. She didn't appreciate James's little digs about Ethan, and she didn't appreciate that sleepy, hot, knowing look he sometimes got around her. The *I slept with you* look. He'd ingratiated himself to Harry so that Harry couldn't even visit his grandson without his sycophant tagalong.

That's what she used to think, anyway.

But for the past ten days, James had been a prince. No getting over that. When she'd seen him there outside her cell, her heart had leaped. And not only because he was getting her away from the Excrement King, either. It was because she felt something for him. Something beyond garden-variety cougar lust.

Maybe.

As for his offer of friendship, well, hell. She thought for one second that she was going to cry. Because though she was pretty good at sounding cavalier and worldly, the fact remained that one doesn't tell another person about the day one's childhood died an abrupt death without feeling it.

She hadn't thought about Lila for a long, long time.

It was during what would be her last childhood summer at Grayhurst, though she didn't know that yet. Lila wasn't a real nanny—Parker was ten, after all. No, Lila was a Mackerly girl who'd just finished college and came every day to keep Parker company, take her to tennis lessons or swimming in the ocean. Parker liked her a lot…Lila didn't read magazines or talk to her friends on the phone or pump Parker for details on how much money her family had, like most of Parker's babysitters. She was twenty-two but treated Parker like an equal. Even when they were drawing fairies and unicorns, Lila seemed to think Parker was cool. She was always up for a swim, no matter how cold the water was. And she'd make fun snacks, too, the kind that Althea would've never allowed: s'mores and raw cookie dough and orange macaroni and cheese that, fascinatingly, came from a box.

Sometimes, Lila would complain about her college boyfriend to Parker, and Parker would be almost breathless with the coolness, the adultness of the conversation. No one talked to her like that. Her cousins had become a closed circle, and her mom was prickly this summer. And Daddy…things were different with him these days, too. Lately, he'd been distracted, less interested in hearing about school trips and grades. Her parents had been arguing a lot lately, so Parker had tried to be at her best— smart, charming, cheerful—then find something else to do. Ten going on thirty, her father liked to say, and she knew it was a compliment.

At any rate, that particular day was hot and clear, the best of a New England summer, a hearty breeze off the water and the sun baking the air. Althea had gone into Boston for the day to do some shopping; Harry was working in the house. Parker and Lila had been making sand castles on the beach, with moats and tunnels and turrets and everything, and Lila had seemed just as interested as Parker. But after an hour or so, Lila had to go to the bathroom. As long as she was in the house, she said she'd make them a snack, too. Root-beer floats, maybe. Parker would be okay on her own, right? She wouldn't go in the water.

"Of *course* not," Parker said. "I'm not an idiot. Plus, I can swim better than you."

"I know, I know," Lila answered fondly. "But I had to say it. Back in ten."

Parker added some seaweed to a turret. Daddy would appreciate how much time they'd spent on this little fiefdom—she'd only recently learned that word, and she was going to use it, because he always loved when she used words that most grown-ups didn't know. Yes. This *fiefdom* would win back his approval, most def. Which would be nice after yesterday.

Harry had come to her swimming lesson the day before, and they were teaching diving off the high platform. All the other kids had done it, but when it was Parker's turn, she froze, quite unexpectedly. The water looked so far away, so shallow. How long would it take to hit the water? What if she flubbed the dive? Her legs began to shake.

"Come on, Parker," her dad called, his voice already tinged with irritation. Even so, she couldn't move, picturing the crack of her back as she slammed the water, sinking to the bottom, paralyzed, dying, blood floating in a cloud. *Just do it,* she whispered to herself. *Go. Jump.*

She couldn't. She couldn't even climb down the ladder

herself. One of the teachers had to come up and go down first, his arms gripping the bars around her, his voice kind and reassuring, telling her it happened to him, too, his first time.

Didn't matter. Her father was peeved. She'd stared out the window all the way home so he couldn't see her tears, listening to a heated lecture on being brave, taking chances, how his valuable time had been wasted.

Well. Today was a new day. She'd make him forget her cowardice with a few smart words. He always loved that kind of thing. She sat back in the sand. Maybe, if he wasn't irritated anymore, they might watch a movie or take a sail. Not to be disloyal to her mom, but it was always fun when Althea was away on a shopping trip. Harry traveled a lot, so time alone with him was precious.

"Fiefdom," she said, so she wouldn't forget.

The seaweed flag looked great. She stuck a few more seashells on the side. Perfect. A fiddler crab for the moat, and the thing was really a work of art.

However, Parker had sand in her bathing suit, and *that* did not feel very good. Though she wasn't supposed to go in the water alone, she wasn't going to sit there with a lump in her suit, either. She glanced up at the house—no sign of Lila—and went to the water's edge. It was high tide, but the water was calm and flat. No big waves today.

She went in up to her waist and pulled out the edge of her suit. Much better. Then she went back to shore and waited a little more. The crab wasn't happy. Would it die if she left it there? She didn't want to kill anything. She might become a vegetarian, in fact, having recently learned where veal came from.

Where was Lila? She'd been gone so long that Parker had to pee now, too.

With a sigh—grown-ups, so irresponsible—she went up the forty-two stairs that led from the beach to Grayhurst's backyard. Across the thick, lush carpet of grass, onto the hot slate patio, into the kitchen.

No sign of Lila.

Parker used the loo—she'd come across that word in an Agatha Christie novel, and it sounded vastly superior to *bathroom* or, as Althea said, *little girls' room*. Another word to drop in front of her father.

Grayhurst was huge, but to Parker, it was an old friend. Her grandfather had died three years ago, but Parker would try to summon his ghost once in a while, feeling equal parts melancholy for Granddad and terror in case she succeeded. Right now, the house was quiet. *Dead* quiet, like in that movie *Demon Seed* that Lila had let her watch, where it got really quiet right before all the killing.

Feeling the abrupt need to find someone, Parker went to her father's study. Empty. She headed upstairs. Maybe Lila was sick. Or maybe she wanted to use one of the fancier bathrooms. Besides, Parker wanted to change. Having a soggy bottom was getting yucky.

The thought dawned that maybe Lila was stealing something. They'd fired two people this year for stealing. Parker's heart sank. The last thing she wanted was to lose Lila.

She made a deal with herself. If Lila was stealing, she'd tell her to put it back and she wouldn't tell on her or anything.

As Parker got to the wing that held the family bedrooms, she heard a noise. A…grunt or something. As if someone was sick.

There it was again.

"Daddy?" Parker whispered. She knew her father was

rich and important. Would someone try to kidnap him? Had they already knocked Lila out? This would explain why there were no root-beer floats. Why Parker had been left out on the beach for longer than ten minutes. Both parents were very strict about her being left alone by the water.

She tiptoed down the hallway. Past her own room, which had just been redecorated and was, in her father's words, "the prettiest room for the prettiest girl," awash in shades of pale green with light pink trim.

Another sound. She wasn't about to stop for dry clothes. Not when her father might be hurt or tied up. She'd be brave and save him. She'd need a weapon or something, though. Like a knife. Or a gun. Her father kept guns in his study. One of them used to belong to Teddy Roosevelt. Should she get it?

Parker's mouth was sticky and dry, terror nailing her to the floor. Something bad was happening in that room. She knew it. She didn't want to see it, though. But her *father* was in that room, and if she went downstairs for the gun, she might miss the chance to save him.

Don't be so chicken, she told herself. She'd been a chicken yesterday on the high dive. This time, no. She'd be brave. And smart. She'd peek and then if there were bad guys, she'd run really fast and quietly and call the police and *then* she'd get TR's gun, and she'd hold the bad guys off until the police came, and her father would be amazed at her courage, and it totally would make up for her not jumping off the high platform.

Her parents' bedroom was at the end of the hall. There was that grunt again. Oh, God. Her heart thudding, nerves stretched so tight it seemed as if she was floating, Parker opened her parents' bedroom door.

At first, she thought they were strangers. Naked

strangers, wrestling, that was her first thought. But no, they were having sex. Gross! In her parents' bedroom!

Then in a flash that also seemed to last a full minute, she realized that one of the people was her father, moving on top of someone. They were *both* making those moaning hurt noises.

"Oh, my God, Mr. Welles, don't stop," said the other person.

It was *Lila*.

"Daddy?" Parker asked, her voice small.

The word was electrifying. Both Harry and Lila jumped, scrambling for covers, but not before Parker had seen Lila's boobies, and her father's graying chest hair.

"Jesus, Parker, get out!" her father yelled.

"Oh, God, I think she peed herself," Lila said, her face twisted with sympathy.

"I did not!" Parker shouted, her face broiling hot. "I did not, you…you…slut!"

"Parker, this is not what you think," her father said sternly.

She was downstairs, feet flying so fast she wondered how she didn't fall, almost wished she would fall, crack her head open on the marble floor, go to the hospital; that would punish them. Down another flight, through the wine cellar that had always creeped her out, into the garage where her father kept his fancy cars. She climbed into the Porsche and curled up on the floor of the passenger seat.

Hours later, Esteban, one of the gardeners, found her and lifted her out. Althea was back, white-faced with fury and screaming at Harry. She grabbed Parker and half dragged her upstairs, yanked out some suitcases and began hurling clothes inside.

"Althea, don't be ridiculous," Harry barked. "It's not

what she thought! She's read too many books, that's all. She misunderstood." He didn't even bother looking at her.

Maybe that was the worst part. She was ten going on thirty, after all. Her father was…what was that expression Lila the Slut used? Throwing her under the bus.

It's not what she thought. "Bullshit," she whispered.

"Parker, don't swear," her father said automatically. "It's crass."

"Bullshit!" she yelled. "It *was* what I thought. It was gross! You're disgusting, Da—" No. He didn't deserve to be called *Daddy*. "You make me sick, Harry."

Althea yanked the suitcase closed. "You had to screw the babysitter. That's your legacy to your child. Rot in hell, you bastard," she said. She grabbed Parker by the hand, and an hour later, she and her mother were in a suite in the Devon Hotel, her mother already on the phone with her attorney.

Parker sat in the bed, ostensibly watching TV. Piercing her heart was an icicle of fear.

Their family had ended. And her father…her father didn't love her anymore.

Romance Reading...

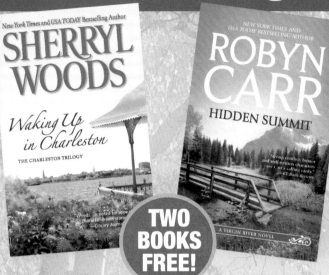

New York Times and USA TODAY Bestselling Author

SHERRYL WOODS

Waking Up in Charleston

THE CHARLESTON TRILOGY

NEW YORK TIMES AND
USA TODAY BESTSELLING AUTHOR

ROBYN CARR

HIDDEN SUMMIT

A VIRGIN RIVER NOVEL

TWO BOOKS FREE!

Each of your FREE books will fuel your imagination with intensely moving stories about life, love and relationships.

We'd like to send you **two free books** to introduce you to the Reader Service. Your two books have a combined cover price of $15.98 in the U.S. and $19.98 in Canada, but they are yours free! We'll even send you **two exciting surprise gifts**. There's no catch. You're under no obligation to buy anything. We charge nothing – ZERO – for your first shipment. *You can't lose!*

Visit us at
www.ReaderService.com

YOURS FREE!

We'll send you 2 fabulous surprise gifts (worth about $10) just for trying "Romance"!

The Reader Service — Here's How it Works:

CHAPTER EIGHTEEN

"Everyone has left us. Everyone. You, Nicky, Lucy and that Ethan. We're bereft. Bereft, Parker."

Parker grinned. Ethan's mother didn't believe in Skype, and therefore couldn't see Parker enjoying the melodrama. "I'm sorry, Marie. I miss you and Gianni, too."

"Our grandson! Six weeks without him! I don't know if Gianni's heart can take it."

"Well, Ethan will be back soon, Marie."

"Who takes three weeks for a vacation? And then Ethan's taking that precious boy to see *you*."

"Well, he is my son."

"We're so alone. To think we left Valle de Muerte to be abandoned by our family."

Parker bit down on a laugh. She got quite a kick out of the Mirabellis, who'd always been good to her, so long as she could ignore the many, many, many nudges, hints and suggestions on how to raise Nicky and why she should've married Ethan—at least that battle hymn had stopped since he married Lucy—and how Parker should eat much, much more.

"So what's new up there? In *Maine?*" Marie said the word suspiciously, as if not quite certain Maine was a true part of the United States.

"Oh, not too much." Parker opted not to mention her

stint in the clink. "Lots of work to do before Nicky gets here."

There was a gusty sigh. "You could come home," Marie suggested. Parker had told her and Gianni about her father—hard to miss when CNN had done a special on him—and the change in her finances, but Marie didn't always pay attention to facts she deemed unpleasant.

"As soon as I get this house ready to be sold, I'll be back. Nicky and I will be home at the end of August at the latest." She had to be; Nicky started kindergarten after Labor Day. All-day kindergarten. The thought caused her heart to spasm.

"August. I could be dead by August."

"True, true. Well, I have work to do, so I should get going, Marie," Parker said, having fielded enough guilt for the day. She loved the Mirabellis. She was also very grateful not to be their daughter-in-law and could therefore hang up, whereas Lucy could not. "I'll call you soon."

"You're eating enough? You're too skinny."

"Aw! Thanks! I've gained eleven pounds this year."

"Well, it's not enough. We love you, sweetheart. Gianni says hello. You know how he is—he won't talk on the phone. Bye-bye."

Parker hung up and went outside. It was two days after her inadvertent drug dealing, and before Marie's call, she'd been working at improving the house's curb appeal, mainly by hacking up the roots of the sumac trees and scrubby pines. She'd buy some hanging baskets, since she knew the wholesalers now, and put out some pots of geranium and sweet-potato vine. Who knew? Maybe it would trick someone into buying the place.

James had been right about her sentence of community service. Yesterday, when the judge had found out that she was a children's author, he ordered her to do a library program on the Holy Rollers, the favorite books of His Honor's six-year-old grandchild. Frankly, Parker would rather have spent another day in jail with Crazy Dave (who was out with no fines at all, go figure). Lavinia had been told to file for a medical-marijuana-growers' license, and would also be having dinner with the judge on Saturday with a possible session of "slapping uglies" afterward.

As for James, he was on the roof right now, doing God knew what. Looking beautiful, apparently. Killer tan, too, no matter that she'd bought him his own 100-factor sunscreen. His hair was curling from sweat, and the skin on his back glistened. She did love a sweaty man.

That's icky, said Golly.

"You'll appreciate it when you're older," Parker muttered. Yes, she was thirty-five years old and hadn't been laid in three years. Time to look away. Time to focus.

Funds were running low. A part-time job at the flower shop was not doing much other than covering groceries. To her own eyes, the cottage didn't look much better. In fact, it looked worse. The sides were stripped and covered in Tyvek, the shingles having yet to be delivered. The grass, which she'd hacked away at like some Amazon explorer, was uneven, rife with weeds and dry, thanks to a notable lack of rain this summer.

"Don't worry so much," James called, reading her mind. "It's getting there. It looks worse before it gets better."

"I know, I know," she said, a bit irked that she was so transparent. An electrician had put in a few more outlets and given them a discount, as he was an old schoolmate of Dewey's. The bathroom shower no longer leaked onto the floor; the Three Musketeers had come over to supervise her caulking. She couldn't change the fact that the tiles were pink, but she was working on how to make that look cute and retro, rather than hideous and dated.

So this was what house flipping was like. Backbreaking, ever more expensive, built on a frail hope, but kind of fun anyway.

Especially with Thing One. He was eternally patient with her dopey questions—she hadn't been able to figure out how to change a vacuum-cleaner bag the other day—and he never made her feel useless, the way Harry did. And when he smiled at her, she felt a rush of something so sharp and sweet, it actually hurt her chest. Add to this the fact that he walked around half-dressed all the time, and heck yeah!

James knelt down to check something on the roof, then stood and crossed his beautiful arms over his beautiful chest. "Put up or shut up," he said with a wink.

"Jeesh, Thing One! Such an ego." She paused. "But you are fun to look at."

"You look nice, too," he said. "I'm on fire. Stunned with lust." Her beige carpenter pants were grubby, the T-shirt from Gianni's Ristorante Italiano was torn, and her hair was stuffed under a Yankees baseball cap—one didn't forget where one was born, after all, and Parker had been born at Columbia Presbyterian, New York, New York, thank you too much. She was sweating like a racehorse and could only imagine the shade of red her face had taken on: beet or boiled lobster. Either way, she was not flushed a delicate pink; she knew that. The bathroom had a mirror, after all.

Well. She'd cool off with a swim in another hour or so, and hopefully James would be the one ogling then. Seemed only fair. She knew he didn't like her swimming—he watched her like Nana watched the kids in

Peter Pan when she was out there—but she also knew he couldn't take his eyes off her, eleven pounds be damned.

So. Mutual lusting. Always fun.

"Parker? Oh, dear God, tell me that isn't you, sweating like an Ecuadoran stonemason."

Parker's eyes widened in shock at the sound of the voice. She turned. Oh, Lord. It was true. "Mom? What are you doing here?"

Althea Harrington Welles Foster Brandheiser Levinstein was staring with openmouthed horror at Parker, the house, the yard. She wore Jackie O–style sunglasses, a long silky scarf and a white linen suit. The car was a red BMW with rental plates.

"This?" Althea said. "*This* is what Julia left you? Oh, the old shrew! I'd kill her if she wasn't already dead! She always made it sound like... Oh, Parker, you poor, poor thing. And that father of yours. I'll kill him, too. I hope he's someone's girlfriend in prison. I hope he's on a chain gang. I hope—"

"Mom! Wow. I can't believe you're here." Parker wiped her forehead with her sleeve and walked toward Althea.

"Neither can I. I'm rather hoping this is a bad dream or a hallucination. Tell me I'm wrong. Tell me you inherited the Pines. Please."

"This is it. It's all I have in the world, Mother dear."

"Oh, my God. You may as well throw yourself off that dock and hope to drown quickly. The smell in this town! How can you bear it?"

Actually, Parker had gotten used to the smell of baitfish. She gave her mother a robust hug, which Althea accepted, daintily patting Parker's shoulder. "It is what it is, Mom. But what are you doing here? Why didn't you call me?"

Her mother removed her sunglasses and gave Parker a level look. "When one hears that one's daughter has been in prison, one hops on the next plane. Apparently, you're following your father into a life of crime."

Parker sighed. "Yes, Mother. That's it exactly. I'm a drug dealer. It wasn't prison, by the way. It was just a holding cell. And the charges were dropped."

"Just a holding cell. Dear Lord, what have we come to? Have you gained weight? You look beefy."

Only Althea would call a size ten beefy. She herself had the scrawny size-four physique of the desperately middle-aged—those women who were liposuctioned and implanted and had tans applied and paid a personal trainer to deny Nature its due. "And calling me? Why was that a bad idea?"

Althea stared. She might've been scowling, but Botox had frozen her eyebrows into that shiny, plasticine look, as well as given her a permanent half smile, so Parker could never tell.

"I wasn't sure you could get phone calls, dear. I thought time might've been of the essence."

"How did you know I was in trouble?" Parker asked.

"Lavinia tracked me down on Facebook, then called. My goodness, the woman sounds like Yul Brynner on his deathbed."

"Since when do you and Lavinia talk to each other? She told me she hadn't seen you since you were kids."

"Well, I *appreciated* the call, Parker. I'm here because I thought you might need bail money."

"Thanks, Mom." Althea would never win Mother of the Year, but her heart was in the right place.

"What is *that?*" her mother asked, squinting as best she was able. Beauty stood on the steps, not quite ready to defend the place, not quite ready to back down from a stranger, either. Progress, in other words. "Is that a *dog?*"

"Shoot, I thought it was a pony. No, you're right, it's a dog. Dang."

"Sarcasm is the lowest form of humor, Parker. Did Harvard teach you nothing? And who on earth is *that?*"

James was coming down the ladder. He walked over, all sweaty male glory, and extended his hand. "Hi. James Cahill. We've met a few times."

Althea deigned to look at him. "Have we?" she asked.

"Yes. At your grandson's christening and again on his third birthday."

"He works for Harry, Mom. He's helping me out."

"Is he? How fascinating. Put a shirt on, young man. If I wanted to see a naked man, I would've stopped at Chippendales."

James smiled that wonderful, achingly wide smile, causing Parker's Lady Land to squeeze hot and hard. He gave Parker an amused glance and went off. He did not, she was pleased to see, put his shirt back on.

Althea huffed. "Well, this ruins my plans. I thought we might spend some time together, do a little redecorating, but I see it's hopeless. I absolutely cannot stay here."

"Actually, you could have my room, and I'll—"

"No. I'll find somewhere. Surely there's a B and B around this godforsaken area."

"It burned over the winter."

"Small wonder. Well. Give me some time. I'll see what I can find. Dinner tonight, darling? I'll pick you up around six." She put her sunglasses back on and climbed back behind the wheel, then gunned the motor, leaving Parker in a cloud of dust.

"What a happy surprise," James offered.

"So happy," Parker said.

"By the way," he added, "I think you look great, beefy or not."

"I'm not beefy," she snapped.

"You're beautiful," he said.

There was that knowing grin, the *I've seen you naked* look. "Just…just pipe down, you," she said.

"Gorgeous."

"Stop it, Thing One."

"Stunning."

"Okay, you've pushed your credibility enough for one day. I'm going swimming. Want to come?"

That shut him up. "No thanks. Be careful."

And as always, she felt his eyes on her as she and her little dog swam through the cold water.

AT SIX O'CLOCK that evening, Parker heard the purr of an expensive car coming down the road.

"Here comes trouble," she said, opening the front door. James came up behind her, smelling of soap and laundry detergent and sun. So good it should be illegal. She could feel his warmth behind her, and if she stepped back a little bit, she'd be nicely cozied up against his—

"Who's that?" James asked.

"My next stepfather?" Parker guessed.

"Sweet ride," he murmured, his breath stirring her hair. And not only her hair. Lady Land perked right up. She cleared her throat and stepped forward a little bit.

Her mother was sitting in the passenger seat of a chocolate-brown Porsche convertible; at least it wasn't black or red, so points to the driver for not living the total midlife crisis cliché. He was blond, maybe forty years old and wore aviator sunglasses.

"Hello, darling!" her mother called, vaulting out of

the car, her half smile as unchanging and disturbing as Jack Nicholson's Joker. "Guess into whom I ran."

"'Into whom I ran'?" James echoed. "That is some very impressive grammar."

Althea hustled to the door and, ignoring James completely, whispered, "This is Collier Rhodes, he owns the Pines, he's loaded, don't blow this. Husband material, Parker."

"For you or for me?" Parker asked.

"For you! Don't be ridiculous! I'm blissfully happy with Maury. Let's go! Hurry up. I don't want him to see this pigpen any more than he already has." She glanced back. "Collier, we'll be one second! Oh, damn, he's coming in."

"Now, now, Mother," Parker murmured. "Hi," she said to the man. "I'm the daughter." She was positive the man had already been briefed on her blue blood, education, career and fertility.

The man removed his sunglasses, revealing very blue eyes. Nice. He smiled. "Hi. I'm Collier. I guess we're neighbors."

"Parker Welles. This is my friend, James Cahill."

"Good to meet you, man," Collier said as they shook hands.

"He's not her *friend* per se," Althea chirped. "He's the help."

Parker raised an eyebrow. "Actually, he's—"

"Darling," Althea interrupted, widening her tightened eyes with great effort. "Collier has been *so* sweet! I wandered up to the Pines, a little nostalgic, and there he was, and before I knew it, he'd invited us to stay for a few days!"

Mmm-hmm. A little nostalgic, her ass. It wasn't surprising Althea had tracked down the town's biggest landowner. She had a nose like a drug-sniffing bloodhound when it came to rich men.

"And he's having a little dinner party tonight for us. Isn't that wonderful? So let's go." She gave Parker a quick scan and apparently found her dress acceptable, though she unsubtly tucked her finger into her own neckline and made a downward motion, sign language for *Show more boob and he'll pop the question faster.*

"James, you free? You're more than welcome," Collier said.

"Oh, I'm sure he had other plans," Althea said. "My ex-husband sent him to do a little work for Parker, that's all."

Parker glanced back at James. His hair was still damp from the shower. "Why don't you come, James?" she asked, suddenly quite aware that she really, really wanted his company.

"The more the merrier," Collier said enthusiastically. "I'd love it!"

"Oh, are you sure, Collier?" Althea said, laying a hand on his arm. "James wouldn't want to put you out. You've already been so, ah, generous with the locals."

"I'd *love* him to come," the man said, his blue eyes blazing. Gay, maybe, Parker thought. "What do you say, James?"

"Sounds like fun," James said. "Thank you."

"Great!" Collier said. "Off we go, then."

"Parker, you simply must sit in front," Althea said as they walked down the path to the Porsche. "It's such a darling car. Parker's father loves Porsches." Translation: *She comes from money, too.*

"Oh, no, Mother. You know what they say. Age before beauty." Smiling at her mother's murderous look, she slid into the backseat with James.

CHAPTER NINETEEN

Two hours later, James was fairly sure he hated Collier Rhodes.

Apparently, Collier knew every famous person on the face of the earth, from Lindsay Lohan to the president. He couldn't stop talking about his famous pals, his money, his career, his travels, and all with such false modesty that it was making James ill. At least Harry was honest about his own self-admiration.

Maggie Beaumont and her fiancé, Malone, were here, in addition to Lavinia. And thank God for that, because otherwise, James was pretty certain Althea would've locked her daughter in a bedroom with Collier until consummation occurred. Between her references to Parker's suitability as a bride and Collier's name-dropping, James was feeling quite homicidal. He took another sip of whatever wildly expensive wine Collier was serving and tried not to roll his eyes as Collier dropped the seventh celebrity name of the night.

"You're kidding!" said Maggie. "You actually went rock climbing with Aron Ralston? The guy who cut off his own arm?"

Collier considered the question. It wasn't a hard question, but he seemed to need time to answer. "I guess I don't really notice a person's disabilities. It's not my way of seeing people."

"You didn't notice that he only had one arm?" Parker asked. "That's kind of a big thing to miss."

Atta girl. She was sitting next to James, as ever so close and so out of reach.

"That's how I'm made," Collier answered thoughtfully. "To me, we were just two kindred spirits communing with nature. It was the same when Steve and I—Stephen Hawking, that is—were having drinks one time. I mean, yeah, he's in a wheelchair, but to me, that stuff's invisible."

The invisible wheelchair. Like Wonder Woman's plane.

"How do you have drinks with a man who's completely paralyzed?" Lavinia asked. "Feeding tube? Straw?"

Good question, Vin. "Go on, Collier," said Parker's mother, staring at her cousin with her creepy frozen face. "Tell us about the, ah, climber."

"Well, that Aron can really fly when it comes to free-climbing. He almost beat me to the summit."

"That's so neat," Maggie said.

"It's *amazing*," Parker's mother seconded. "Collier, the stories you have! Such a fascinating life you've led!"

"Wait a minute, wait a minute," Lavinia barked. "Who just said he cut off his own arm? Maggie, are you shitting me?"

"Let's not discuss that at dinner," Althea said. "Collier, tell us about that novel you mentioned. Parker, Collier wants to write a book, too!"

Oh, kill me now. Just one more reason Collier was perfect for Parker. James closed his eyes.

"*Another* thing you have in common," Althea said brightly.

"You don't really want to hear about my little idea," Collier said, gazing upon each guest in turn.

"Most authors don't like discussing their work," James offered.

"I've heard that, too," Malone said, giving James a commiserating look. At least James wasn't the only one suffering.

"I just read a book," Lavinia said, leaning back in her chair. "Pretty steamy stuff. Written by some Chinese chick. Very dirty. I enjoyed it."

"Please tell us, Collier! I know *I'm* dying to hear about it," Althea said.

"Well, Jim there has a point." That was another thing. Jim. "But if you insist."

"We do!" Althea chirped. Malone sighed.

"Okay, okay," Collier said, holding his hands up in mock defeat. "It's about this retired Microsoft executive."

"Like you?" Parker asked innocently.

"Well, not really. But maybe. He's a little like me in that he retired young after making his fortune." Making his fortune? Did people talk that way? "And then he comes across this painting by Picasso. But there's this code in it, and no one's ever deciphered it before. But coding is what the Microsoft guy does. His name is Wolfe, Wolfe Shepherd, and he's the only one who sees that this code is actually a treasure map, so then he embarks on this amazing journey that leads him to the secrets of the Vatican."

"Sounds like *The Da Vinci Code,*" James said.

"Never heard of it," Collier said a bit sharply. "I only read literature. Anyway, when the Vatican finds out he's on the trail…"

The guy went on. And on. And on. This was hell.

Worst of all, Parker seemed totally into it. Laughing, asking questions.

Then again, he was from the same world she was. Maybe she liked him.

"But enough about me," Collier said. "I was thinking about maybe getting a boat and doing a little lobstering, like you, Malone. Cowboys of the sea, right?"

James would bet both lungs that Malone had never thought of himself as a cowboy of the sea. For crying out loud.

"I wouldn't call it that," Malone said. Maggie elbowed him in the ribs. "But it's a good life."

"Exactly!" Collier said. "Hey, you guys want more wine? It's from a little vineyard I'm part owner in, this sweet place in the Loire Valley. Now, not to brag, but Robert Parker gave this a score of ninety-eight. You can't get it here in the States, but, well, ownership has some privileges. Hey, Parker, your dad has quite the wine cellar, doesn't he?"

"Had," Parker said. "His defrauded investors own it now."

"Right, right. Sorry to hear about that."

"Oh, he had it coming," Althea said. "Always was a cheater."

James glanced at Parker. Her expression was pleasant and composed.

He hadn't been horribly surprised to hear her story of Harry and the babysitter. He knew how Harry was with women, after all. But he winced at picturing Parker at age ten, walking in on her father. And though his boss had been a complete and utter shit, he could well imagine Harry's panic on being discovered. Harry didn't like people knowing he had feet of clay; he tended to fire them if they found out. But you couldn't fire your kid. It sure explained the origins of the father-daughter cold war.

"So you two kids are getting married this weekend?" Collier said, turning those freaky blue eyes on Maggie and Malone.

"It's true," Maggie said. "You should come! We'd love it." Malone winced, then coughed to cover.

"Man, I wish I could," Collier said. "I have a meeting with my portfolio manager, then have plans to pop down to Maryland to look at a sailboat. But hey! Where are you going on your honeymoon? You'd be welcome to use my place in Aspen. I'll call the caretaker, and it's yours. Or New York! I have a little apartment there on Central Park."

"How little?" Althea asked. The woman practically had dollar signs in her eyes. "Parker loves the city. Of course, she grew up there. You two should get together sometime! Parker, wouldn't that be nice?"

James was suddenly aware his jaw was aching, he was clenching it so hard.

"Well," Parker said, "I don't get down there too often."

"No, your mom's right," Collier said. "We should! But, Maggie, if you'd like to use it, feel free, anytime. It's only three bedrooms, but I like it. Minimalist, a little Japanese flair. The view of the park is very nice."

"That's really sweet, Collier, and thank you," Maggie said. "We'll probably go away in the winter, when it's not so busy around here. But we'll keep your offer in mind."

An older woman James recognized from Dewey's came out with a platter of something. "Bananas Foster," she said, setting the tray down with a clatter. She groped in her pocket for a match, and set fire to the dish, making Collier clap like a little kid.

"We supposed to eat that now?" Lavinia asked. The

woman rolled her eyes and began serving the dish once the flames burned out. Rich people. Always looking for more ways to gild the lily.

"So, Jamie, I haven't really had the chance to talk to you," Maggie said. "Chantal says you're a lawyer?"

"Yes," James said. "I worked for Parker's father."

"May he rot in prison," Althea added, sucking down the last of her martini. The cook put a plate of slimy, burned bananas in front of him. Nasty.

"I thought you were a carpenter," Collier said.

"No. But I worked on a construction crew in college." He met Collier's eerie gaze.

"And are you and Parker dating?" Collier asked.

"Heavens, no!" Althea cried. "No, Parker's *completely* unattached."

Collier looked at Parker. "Is that right?" he asked with a small smile.

James stared at the tablecloth. *Good question, Parker. You've been ogling me since I got here, you worship the Paragon...are you unattached?*

Out of the corner of his eye, he saw her glance at him, as if feeling his thoughts. He didn't look up. "Well," she said, "I'm a single mom. Not much time for dating."

"Please. Nicholas is four years old," Althea said. "He's hardly aware of your comings and goings."

"He's five and a half," James said.

"Thank you, James," Parker murmured.

"You have to think of yourself first," Collier said, folding his hands.

"Actually," she said, "it's the other way around. Child first, parent second. In most cases, anyway."

Collier shook his head as if coming out of a daydream. "Anyway, Jim, with Harry Welles in jail, you must be looking for a job. Want me to ask around? I know a lot of people."

As you've told us. "I'm fine on my own, but thanks," he said. "It's James, by the way."

"So why did you retire from Microsoft?" Althea asked, pushing around her charred bananas.

"It's hard to say," Collier answered. "I guess I wanted to be more than Bill's right hand. Not that he isn't one of my closest friends, right? I mean, just last week, he and Melinda and the kids and I had the nicest time. Have you been to their place? It's beautiful."

"Well, it's getting a little late," Maggie said. "We're getting married in two days, and we have a ton to do. Thanks so much for a wonderful night, Collier."

"It's always great to see you, Maggie," Collier said. "Best wishes for a long and fruitful marriage. See you in a week or so. I'm sure you'll make a beautiful bride."

And off went the happy couple. The rest of the dinner guests weren't so lucky. Althea insisted they stay longer, Vin was working on her third plate of bananas Foster, and Parker seemed to be having a fine time.

The thing was, the idiot known as Collier was the answer to all of Parker's financial worries for several lifetimes at least. Richer than God. Richer, perhaps, than Harry had been. And with Althea pushing Parker like a broodmare...

"No, she was only in labor for a few hours. Born to be a mother."

"True," Parker said, smiling. "Want to see a picture? Not of childbirth, but of my son?" She pulled out her phone and handed it to Collier.

"Oh, he's beautiful!" Collier exclaimed. "Wow. What a cute kid." He slid his finger on the screen to view another shot. "Aw, man! Adorable. I love kids."

Of course he did. The guy was flippin' perfect. He and Parker should have a double wedding with Maggie and Malone.

"Parker, I'd love for you to stay here, at least for a few days," Collier said now. "Really! Come on, let me show you the guest suite. Well, it's one of three, actually. Your mom took the Osprey's Nest, but the Loon and the Puffin are both available. They have Jacuzzis, too, if you like that sort of thing. Me, I like to start the day off with an early-morning swim, and man, that tub feels incredible when you get back."

See? Perfect. The Paragon might've been taken, but here was another one, dying to hook up with her.

"That's okay," Parker said. "I'm fine—"

"Parker, don't be silly!" Althea said. "Go see the suite! Go! They're beautiful! And this is, in a way, your ancestral home."

"At least see what you're turning down," Collier said. He stood up and took her hand. "Come on, it's really pretty!"

Parker hesitated. James said nothing. "Okay," she said. "Then I really have to go home."

"That shack is not your home, dear," Althea said. "This is much more what you're used to. I'll come, too."

The three of them left the room.

"You want another drink, Vin?" James asked.

"Nah, I'm good." She leaned back in her chair and cracked her knuckles. "You gonna sit on your ass, son, and let him take your girl?"

"She's not my girl."

"Seems like you'd like her to be."

He gave her a dark look. She shrugged. "How's the judge?" he asked.

"He's still got it," she answered. "Been a few decades,

and things have all dropped a few inches, if you know what I'm saying, but he's still got it."

James couldn't help laughing.

"How about you, sweetheart?" she asked. "What are your plans after this summer?"

Excellent question. "Not really sure, Vin. Gotta find a job."

"Ayuh. It's been nice having you back around. You sure were a sad sack back then." She reached over and squeezed his hand. "I dated your uncle for a while, remember?"

"Uh...no."

"Well, it was one of those fast-and-furious love affairs, you know? Burned out pretty fast. It was hot while it lasted, though."

"That's... Yeah. Okay."

Lavinia sighed fondly. "Oh, good, here they come. I gotta get home and put some Bengay on my back."

Althea, Collier and Parker came back into the dining room.

"You sure?" Collier was saying. "Tell me that bathroom didn't tempt you."

"It's beautiful, Collier," Parker said. "But I'm fine in the cottage. It's very cute."

"I think you're being silly," Althea said. "But do what you will! You always do. She's got her own ideas, Collier."

"Which I totally respect," he said.

"I'll drive these two back," Lavinia announced cheerfully. "No need for you to get in the car again, Collier. And hey, thanks for inviting me. It was great to see the old place again."

James offered Collier his hand. "Thanks for including me," he said.

Collier squeezed hard and stared at him with his vivid eyes. "Absolutely, man."

Ten minutes later, they were back at the cottage. Cute, Parker had called it. Right.

She was down on the dock with a glass of water, talking to her kid and the Paragon, while James stared at her, his hands jammed in his pockets, from the back porch, irritable as a hungover porcupine.

He was mad. Jealous and mad and an idiot.

Collier. What an ass. And Althea, pimping her daughter. And his own stupid self, sulking like a teenager. And Parker, constantly…just…whatever. She was sitting, dog at her side, feet in the water, her white dress glowing in the darkness. God forbid she decide that now was a good time for a midnight swim, because he'd have to go in after her, no matter how good she was. No one should go in the ocean in the dark, alone. Currents, tides, drowning. Daylight was bad enough. Seriously, who the hell swam in the ocean up here?

But knowing her, she'd do something like that. Midnight swim. Midnight skinny-dipping, even. Yep. She'd take that dress off and jump in, half to torture him, half because she was the type to jump in dark, freezing water and come up laughing. Right before some drunken Masshole mowed her down in a powerboat.

It could happen. Plus, it gave him the excuse he needed. He was halfway down the stairs before he'd even finished the thought.

At the sound of his footsteps, Parker stood up, Beauty, too, her tail wagging a little.

"Hey," Parker said. "Entertaining night, didn't you think?"

He only stopped walking when his arms were around her and his mouth was on hers. She made a surprised little squeak, but oh, God, her lips were so soft, and he kissed her hard, too hard, maybe, one hand sliding through her silky, cool hair, gripping the back of her head, a kiss that reached right in and clamped his heart in a fist...the taste of her, the smell of her, her softness melded against him. The kind of kiss that ruined a man.

Then he let her go, turned around and left her standing on the dock, one hand over her lips, her dog standing at her side.

CHAPTER TWENTY

PARKER WAS GONE when James woke up at the late hour of 6:38 a.m. the next morning. There was a note next to the coffeepot:

Early delivery @ flower shop, library thing at 10.
If you go out, make sure you shut Beauty in my room, okay?

Nothing about last night, of course. Parker Harrington Welles was not the type to leave a note saying, *Thanks for the kiss, it changed my entire perception of you, let's get it on, shall we?* or *Never kiss me again, Thing One. Don't even look at me.* Nope. He'd bet his left nut she'd never bring it up again.

And look. He was stroking the words as if he was that idiot Romeo, the prince of poor planning, and little Miss Capulet had sent him a lock of hair. Totally whipped. With a hearty sigh, he started making breakfast.

Parker's dog was watching him from the doorway of the bedroom. He had yet to convince the scared little thing he wasn't about to kick her. "Want some bacon?" he said. She didn't move. He dropped half a piece on the floor and glanced over at her. Beauty wagged her tail and licked her chops but didn't move from her spot. Another female who wanted nothing to do with him.

Yep. Whipped.

Well. Nothing a little hard labor and some headbanger noise wouldn't cure. He went outside, flipped the radio on to the metal station. "Dream On" by Aerosmith.

"Point taken," James said.

The tin roof was on, the chimney repaired. Time for some deeply satisfying physical labor. Forget the nail gun for now. James picked up his hammer in one hand, a cedar shingle in the other and got to work.

Too bad his father couldn't see the tidy job James had done. Of all four boys, James had always been the one most interested in their father's work. The best at it, too. Tom was a general contractor, like their dad; Matt worked at a factory that made Adirondack chairs, and Pete did finish carpentry. If he'd thought there'd been a chance in hell they'd have come up here, James would've asked for the help. Sure. At the end of the day, they'd get a six-pack and take turns flirting with Parker, and his brothers would bust his stones over his crush until their father told them to knock it off, at which point Parker would give him a sweet smile as she passed, and Dad would agree that yes, James was pathetic, and the ribbing would start again.

Dream on was right. What had his father called him the last time they'd spoken? A slick little bastard. Which had not stopped dear old dad from cashing any of the checks James had ever sent.

Helping Parker was a way to do Harry a final favor, after all the man had done for him. Not just the healthy salary, either. He'd given James a place in the world when James had had none, given him a father figure, and when your own father hasn't looked you in the eye since you were twelve years old, that meant something. Harry was the only person James had ever told about Mary Elizabeth, and one of the few who saw him as a loyal, decent person.

The irony was so thick, James would need an ax to cut it.

So yeah. He owed Harry. And he owed his own family. He sure as hell owed Mary Elizabeth. And Parker. And her son.

But it got tiring, owing everybody everything all the time. Living in a debt of guilt. Trying to look at yourself in the mirror.

He felt a tickle at the back of his leg and looked down. It was Parker's dog, standing next to him, looking up at him with those big brown eyes. Her tail gave a tiny, noncommittal wag.

"Hey, Beauty," he said. She wagged again. "Are you a sweet girl?" She bent her head, seeming to acknowledge that yes, in fact, she was. Very slowly, he knelt down. She didn't run. "Are you a pretty girl, Beauty?" The wagging grew more constant, though still tentative. "You got any pointers for me, dog?"

When James was a kid, they'd had a dog. Brandy, a big old Irish setter. After what happened, it seemed as if she was the only one left who still liked him. She died two years later, and the Cahills had never gotten another.

Slowly, James reached out to pet Beauty's head, but just as he almost touched her, a car came roaring up to the house, and the dog bolted, disappearing around the front and down the stairs toward the dock.

Collier Rhodes. Why not Jay Gatsby, right? Same overall message. The Porsche purred to a stop, and James threw his hammer down with more gusto than was perhaps necessary and walked over to the driveway.

"Hi, Jim! How's it going here?"

"Collier."

"So, is Parker around?"

Why don't you go step on a rusty nail, huh, pal? "She's either at the flower shop or the library."

"Awesome." Collier glanced around the cluttered little yard. "Think she'd be interested in having dinner on my boat tonight?"

Yep. Lockjaw would definitely improve you. "Better ask her."

"I will." The guy looked at him for a second. "So this buddy of mine and I were talking the other day."

"Sebastian Junger?"

"No. Though he and I did shoot the breeze at a fundraiser a few years ago. Why? You know him?"

"No."

Collier frowned. "Anyway, this buddy of mine happens to work at the SEC."

Oh.

James gave him a long look, noting the smug gleam in the alien blue eyes. "I have to get back to work," he said. He turned and walked back to the side of the house.

"Does she know?" Collier called.

James didn't answer, and a minute later, he heard the snug thunk of the sports-car door closing, then the expensive thrum of the motor as Collier left.

"Poor Little Kitten went through the pearly gates into heaven, where there were rainbows and butterflies and flowers and fields, and so many friends! Poor Little Kitten was not poor anymore, nor was she squished from the tractor. 'It's beautiful here!' she mewed happily.

'I know,' said Spike. 'Now, don't forget, you have to choose a heaven-name.'

'I choose Princess,' said the sweet little cat, and all the other cats cheered. With that, Spike kissed the little

*kitten on her soft, fluffy head, then sped back to earth
on his magical roller skates.*

*'Her heaven-name is Princess,' he told the children
as their tears dried in the sunshine, 'and she's very, very
happy. Now, who wants some angel food cake?' And with
that, Golly, Polly and Molly, Ike, Mike and Spike brought
the mortal children to their special tree house, ate cake,
and everyone felt much, much happier. The end."*

Un-fricking-believable that these books had made a
fortune.

Parker swallowed the familiar bile that had crept up
her throat during the reading and looked at the assem-
bled children. Collier and her mother stood together in
the back, and Lord have mercy, Collier was wiping away
tears. *Grow a pair, pal,* she thought, even as she nodded
with a smile.

James wasn't here.

Just thinking his name made her heart speed up. But
James was absent, despite her note telling him exactly
where she'd be. So what was that about? A guy kisses
the stuffing out of you, you'd think he'd accept a blatant
invitation to come see you. But he hadn't. And it was a
bit surprising how disappointing that was.

"Any questions?" she asked.

"Did you write *Harry Potter?*" asked a cute little
blonde girl. Judge Freeman's granddaughter, if she wasn't
mistaken.

"No, honey, I didn't, but I sure love those books, don't
you?"

"Are you gonna go to Hollywood and see the movie
of your books?" asked another little girl.

"No, not to Hollywood. But my son and I will see the
movie, sure. He's five. Anybody else here five?"

Several hands shot in the air, and for the next hour,

Parker took questions. Which Holy Roller was her favorite? Why did Mike have blue eyes and Ike have brown? Did she draw the pictures? Why not? Was she rich? Why not? Had she ever met Harry Potter? Why not?

Was she writing more books?

The little bloodsuckers always asked the hard questions.

"I'm taking a little break this summer," Parker said. "But I'm reading a lot. What are some of your favorite books?"

There. Truth deferred.

The truth was, Parker still had nothing. Every day, she'd tried, and yet every idea had been so ridiculous that she couldn't bear to go on. Fairies, leprechauns, gnomes, dwarves, giants. Farm animals, wild animals, domestic animals. City kids, country kids, kids from the future, kids from the past, kids on drugs—that was going to be a young adult novel, which had petered out after sentence number four. Horses with wings, horses with horns, horses with psychic powers. Wild cats, domestic cats, long-haired cats, big cats, blind cats who formed a penal colony and ruled using their heightened sense of smell.

Yeah. The only decent things she'd written this summer were the postcards to Nicky, so he'd have something from her every day.

"Well, kids, hasn't this been wonderful?" the children's librarian said. "Can everyone thank Miss Welles for coming in today?"

"Thank you, Miss Welles!" they chorused, and Parker gave out hugs and autographs. Being with the kids made the Nicky-ache swell, but the hugs were so sweet, given with unhesitating affection. Maybe she could get her master's and teach.

At the moment, though, she couldn't afford to go back to school.

When the kids had left, Althea approached, her arm through Collier's.

"Parker, I'm really, *really* moved," Collier said, his eyes still wet. "I'm so moved. Wow. That was beautiful! Such a statement of faith and simplicity. Truly touching, Parker. Where on earth did you get the inspiration?"

A pair. Grow one. "Oh, heck. You know how it is, right? I mean, you're a writer, too."

Collier gave a pleased shrug. "I guess I do. Yes. Yes. Hard to put a finger on exactly where ideas are born. The muse strikes when she chooses. Well said. You're right."

"Darling." Althea put a bejeweled hand on Parker's bare arm. "Let's have lunch, shall we? Collier knows a wonderful little place in Bar Harbor. He's friends with the owner."

Of course he was. "Actually, Collier, do you mind if I steal my mom so we can have a little time alone?" she asked, smiling up at the guy. "I'm going on Skype with my son, and he'd love to see his mimi's face."

"Mimi. That's adorable. Of course. I understand completely. Your son comes first." He winked, as if showing her he'd Truly Been Listening last night, then kissed Althea on the cheek. "See you later, beautiful ladies."

"I really think you have a shot with him," Althea said as they watched him leave.

"I really don't want one," Parker said. "Come on, Mom. I was serious about Nicky. Over here." She waved to the librarian, who was used to Parker coming in every day, and sat in front of the computer. A few minutes later, she was looking at her son's beautiful face, his twinkling brown eyes, that adorable nose.

"Hi, baby!" she said, the sight of him filling her with a bubble of joy.

"I have a loose tooth!" he announced. "Look!" He grabbed his top front tooth and leaned closer to the computer screen and wiggled. Nothing seemed to move, but Parker cooed anyway.

"Oh, Nick! That's so exciting! Hey, buddy, look who's here. It's Mimi!" She slid over and gestured for her mother to get closer to the screen.

"Hello there, Nicky," Althea said.

"Hi, Mimi! My tooth is loose! See?" Again he demonstrated the alleged looseness of the tooth. "Guess what? Daddy got me a knife. I whittle now. I'll make you a bird, Mimi. Or a worm. A worm's easier because I'm not too good yet. Also, my knife isn't sharp. Daddy says he'll sharp it up when I get better."

As her son babbled on, Parker felt almost dizzy with love. Sweet, sweet Nicky. He didn't think it was strange that Althea rarely visited; it was simply the way it was. Faraway Mimi, Close-Up Nonny, he'd once said.

"My goodness, you're such a handsome boy," Althea said, and her frozen smile seemed to grow a bit. "Are you having fun in…"

"Yosemite," Parker supplied in a low voice.

"Yosemite?" Althea added.

"It's great. I'm gonna live here when I'm a grown-up."

"Is that Althea I hear?" came Ethan's voice. A second later, his face appeared next to Nick's on the screen. "Hello, you gorgeous creature."

"Oh, Ethan, you devil. How are you? I hear you got married. Such a shame."

Parker rolled her eyes. Ethan had a way with the hot-flash crowd, it was undeniable. Part of his appeal. As her mother chatted with Nicky and Ethan, Parker checked her phone. No messages.

Not that James would call her. Not when they lived in the same house.

Not when he was steaming mad.

That kiss last night…she'd never been kissed like that, just grabbed and…and…*owned*.

She swallowed. Hot. It was hot in here.

"Mommy! I found a rock this morning. Wanna see?"

"Yes! Hold it up," she said. Rocks were Nicky's thing. Ethan had already shipped a box back home, he'd told her, since clearly Rhode Island didn't have enough.

When she signed off from Skype after blowing twelve kisses to Nicky, she turned to her mom. "Want to have lunch at the diner? It's really cute."

"That diner was here when I was a girl," Althea said.

"Yeah, it's a classic, isn't it? Let's go. I'm starving."

"And you wonder why you're getting beefy."

"Mmm, beef. You're right. I'll get a cheeseburger."

A half hour later, Parker was eating her beef with gusto as Althea picked at her salad, low-fat dressing on the side. "How is everything?" Maggie called as she came out of the kitchen.

"Fantastic," Parker called back. "Um…aren't you getting married tomorrow?"

"I most certainly am." Maggie smiled.

"Shouldn't you be doing something other than working?"

"Nah," Maggie said. "It's a low-key thing. How are the flowers coming? Have you started?"

"They'll be beautiful," Parker said. She hoped that was true. Lavinia hadn't seemed too concerned over what they were making.

Maggie checked her watch. "Oops. Gotta fly. I have

to pick up my dress in an hour. I ate so much last night, I'm not sure it'll fit." She waved and bopped into the kitchen. The woman seemed perpetually happy. Then again, with tall, dark and smokin' as her fiancé, why wouldn't she? Plus, she was a twin, which Parker had always thought would be so cool. A brother, too, Chantal's husband. Nice, to have siblings. Or so Parker imagined.

"She's back there *cleaning,*" Althea said incredulously, craning her head. "She's getting married tomorrow, and she's cleaning!"

"She seems pretty laid-back."

"Hey, Parker, guess what?" Georgie said, stopping by their booth. "I got a tux. I'm the best man. For Malone."

"I heard that, Georgie. That's really great. Are you nervous?"

"A little bit. I've been practicing." He solemnly pantomimed reaching into his pocket and handing over the ring.

"Looks like you've got it nailed," Parker said.

"Thanks! It's a nice day, isn't it? Well, I have to mop the kitchen floor. Bye!"

"Bye, pal."

Althea was frowning. Sort of. Must be time for another shot of botulism if Parker could read her expression. "Parker, how do you know all these people?" she asked.

"Small town, Mom."

"Well, you fit right in, don't you?"

Parker paused. "I guess. Lavinia helps. I'm related to her, can't be too bad, that sort of thing."

Althea shrugged.

"So what's going on, Mom?" Parker asked gently, taking a sip of her milk shake.

Her mother didn't answer right away, choosing to examine her water glass for smudges. Finally, she spoke. "I thought you inherited the Pines."

"So you said."

"And I thought you might be able to loan me some money."

Parker's head jerked back.

Her mom sighed and nudged a cherry tomato with her fork. "Parker, I know it seems like I'm well-off, but the truth is, I'm not. Maury is, and the shriveled old bastard keeps me on a budget. A *small* budget. He wants me to look good, so things like clothes and jewelry, that's fine. Anything else, anything that's just for me, forget it."

"I thought you were really happy," Parker said. "Bliss incarnate and all that."

Her mother rolled her eyes. "No. I was embarrassed. Fourth husband, you'd think I could get it right. But it turns out that he has control issues, in addition to that bowel thing. Honestly, I should be getting hardship pay."

Parker set down her burger, appetite gone. "Why don't you leave him, Mom?"

Althea blushed. "I'm sixty-two years old, honey. I need to stay married. How would I support myself? Really?"

Parker swallowed, her eyes stinging. "I wish you'd told me earlier. I would've given you money, Mom." She reached across the table and held her mother's hand. Crap. Two months ago, she could've given her mother as much as she needed. Not anymore.

"I was holding out hope that Maury and I would be happy again. I was in denial, whatever." She paused. "Aunt Julia told me years ago you were going to inherit her place, and for whatever reason, I thought she meant the Pines. You know I never kept in touch with them once you were out of high school. Then Lavinia called me and said you'd been in jail, and I really did want to help. But I also thought…well. I thought I could leave Maury and start over."

"You'd really leave him, Mom?"

"I think he's going to divorce me for a younger model, and with that prenup he made me sign, I don't have much."

"Oh, Mom. I'm sorry. I can't help there. But you have three ex-husbands, Mom. Didn't you save anything? And what about the Harrington money?"

Another huge sigh. "The Harrington money was gone before I was born. All that was left was the memory of what it was like to be rich and a little set aside for my education. At least there was that. And when this all happened with your father, and I heard about your trust fund, I wanted to kill him, because I know how you gave all your book money to the World Wildlife Fund—"

"Save the Children."

"Same thing. So now we're both stuck, it seems." Althea sighed and rubbed her forehead. "At least you're young. Ish. You could probably get Collier to marry you by the end of the year. He's clearly not the sharpest tool in the shed. Me, I'll have to look for someone even older than Maury."

"You could always…" Parker's voice trailed off.

"I could always what, dear? Become a party planner?"

She had a point. Althea had never worked, outside of the tremendous efforts she put into husband hunting and wrestling Father Time. "I don't know, Mom. We could figure something out."

Her mother snorted. "Well. Being dependent on a man seems to be the way of the world. My world, anyway.

Father or husband, you and I have always had some man paying the bills."

Ouch. "Guess those days are done."

"I guess so. I hope you'll be all right. I'd feel so much better if you did marry Collier."

Poor Althea. She seemed completely unaware of her contradictions. Being dependent on men had gotten her where she was, but she wanted the same thing for Parker.

"I'll be fine, Mom. I'm doing okay. I can get a job, I have a great education, and I'll even have a little nest egg when I sell Julia's house."

"That shack?"

"That shack."

Althea nodded. "I do have a little squirreled away, honey. If you need it. If Nicky needs it."

Parker's heart softened in a rush. "Thank you, Mom. But we'll be okay. I promise."

Althea opened her eyes. "Yes. You always were a tough little customer." She smiled more broadly. "And Collier is definitely interested, if you need a backup plan."

"He's not my type."

"Do you have a type, dear?"

An image of James grinning at her, all dark hair and tanned skin and sweat and smile. "I don't know."

"Well, if you want more children, you'd better get on it. Those eggs don't last forever."

"Thanks for the reminder." Parker couldn't help a laugh, and after a second, her mother smiled.

"I only want what's best for you, Parker. Whatever that might be."

"Right back at you, Mom."

Underneath the table, her mother's foot nudged hers. It was the most genuine gesture of affection Parker could remember. "Do you want to stay here?" she asked. "Nicky's coming up a week from Sunday. He'd love to spend time with you."

"I can't, honey. I need to get back and see what I can squeeze out of that cadaver before he serves me with divorce papers."

"Jeesh, Mom." Parker laughed.

"Anyway, I have a flight out of Bangor at six. Tomorrow's our charity fashion show. I'm walking the runway. Can you believe it? Part of the tryouts for *Real Housewives.*"

"I thought you were afraid Maury's divorcing you."

"What does that have to do with the show, sweetheart? Half those marriages are shams. More than half, I'm sure."

"Right. Well, good luck," Parker said, grimacing. "What are you wearing?"

"A gown. Feathers. It's a Christian Siriano."

"Cool."

"You don't even know who that is, do you?"

"Nope."

"Yet I claim you as mine." Althea stood up. "Lunch is on me, darling. Back to the coal mines. Don't marry an older man, Parker. I can't remember the last time I was properly laid."

"You should talk to Lavinia. The woman is a walking sex education."

Althea smiled. "She always was. Maybe I'll stop by her shop. Well, take care, darling." She air-kissed Parker on each side, but Parker pulled her bony little mother against her and hugged her properly, getting a little contact high on Chanel No. Five.

"Love you, Mommy."

Althea squeezed her back. "I love you, too, honey. By

the way, Pilates will do wonders for that little tummy of yours. And trust me, in five years, this—" she pinched Parker's ass "—will be three inches lower than it is now. Tempus fugit. Bye! I'll call soon."

Bemused, Parker watched her mother leave, seemingly resigned to her fate with Maury. For the moment, anyway. Odd, that she'd come to Parker for help. Odd, but nice.

CHAPTER TWENTY-ONE

"Don't know why your panties are in such a twist," Lavinia said a few hours later. "It's not your wedding."

"Well, I like Maggie. And Malone." She wound a blue ribbon around the stem of a bouquet, fingers flying.

"So do I," Lavinia said. "Just don't see what's so awful about them there." She gestured toward the Teleflora book, circa 1972, at the arrangements she'd told Parker they'd be reproducing.

"Orange chrysanthemums, Vin? We're not doing orange chrysanthemum centerpieces. Trust me. We can do gorgeous."

"Well, for three hundred bucks, it's gonna be only so gorgeous." Lavinia did her trademark stub-out, and while Parker's own hands had developed some calluses these past couple of weeks, the sight of ciggie against palm still made her flinch.

"It'll be gorgeous. You'll see. Get here early, okay?"

"No way in hell I'm getting up at 5:00 a.m., Parker. I got a date with His Honor tonight."

"I'm sure what he's doing is illegal."

"Oh, it is, all right. In some states."

Parker laughed. "I meant, making you go out with him instead of fining you for growing pot—"

"Medical marijuana, please."

"—without a license."

"Whatever, Parker. I'm just scraping by with the

flowers. Figured the pot would help. I'm hardly a drug dealer."

"No. That's me." Parker set down the flower-girl bouquet and started on the bridesmaid's.

Vin laughed. "Look at you, Miss Busy Bee. Want my help with anything?"

Parker straightened up and looked around. The shop was a mess. "You can do the boutonnieres, okay? A little bitty sprig of hydrangea, and a piece of ivy, like this."

"I think I can make a boutonniere, Parker," her cousin said. "I've been in business for thirty years."

"Got it. Sorry, Vin."

Lavinia gave her a grudging smile. "Ah, well. I admit…you're not half-bad at this."

By four o'clock, Parker's back was aching, and they still had miles to go. But Lavinia was growling about the judge, and honestly, everything that could be done today was done. She'd take care of the rest in the morning.

"Vin, you go ahead. You have a date. I'll clean up."

"It's more of a sex date. What do you kids call that these days?"

"Booty call?"

"Ayuh. Don't get me wrong, my eyes are wide open. Men would fuck a fur-lined knothole, you know what I mean? I'm just glad to be getting a little some-some at my age."

Parker grinned. "I'm so glad we're related," she said honestly.

"You're a good cousin," Lavinia said. "Not much like your mother, are you?"

"Mom's not so bad."

"That branch of the family never got over being rich. We had more practice, over on my side. Ah, well. Gotta go pluck some hairs and shave my legs," Lavinia said. "Thanks, kid."

"You bet."

Parker cleaned up the mess of stems and bits of blossom and ribbon, then swept the floor. *Admit it,* Spike said, stubbing out a ciggie the same way Lavinia did. *You're avoiding him.*

It was true.

James was five years younger than she was. Did he want a serious relationship with a single mom, or a roll in the hay? Did *she* want more? James always seemed so much like Harry...slick, insincere. *Parker, always lovely to see you.* She couldn't help feeling as if he was mocking her, that lifted eyebrow, that gleam in his eye. His compliments on her books always stung a little, as if she didn't already know they were nauseating and fake.

And yet, James had spent the past two weeks working like a draft horse. There had been moments between them, sure. Chemistry and all that. But the truth was, she really didn't know what kind of a man he was, and...

She paused in her sweeping, a little surprised at the thought that was forming in her brain.

...and if James ever found out just how lonely she really was, it would be horrible.

Because nobody knew that.

She wanted a husband. She wanted more kids, maybe, and yes, she was thirty-five. She wanted someone who loved her the way Ethan loved Lucy, who looked at her the way Malone looked at Maggie, and let's be honest. She'd never had anything even close.

James was here under orders from her father. He wanted her, sure. But Nicky was coming in nine days.

Well. She couldn't avoid him forever. She locked up the shop and headed for home. The Volvo was comforting, the smell of Goldfish crackers and old leather, the indentation in the backseat from Nicky's booster, reminding her who she really was.

A mom. With a sigh, she pulled into the driveway.

James was shirtless, sweaty and doing stuff for her house. Parker's knees weakened. *He's beautiful,* said Golly. "Preach it, sister," Parker muttered. She forced her attention to the house. Her purpose in being in Maine, after all. Flip the house. Earn a little money for a place back home.

She dragged her eyes off Thing One's arms, those lean, muscular, capable arms that had crushed her against him last night, a kiss so fierce and angry and hot that— *House, Parker, house!*

James had reshingled the entire western side of the house. For now, the color was creamy-cedar, but the salt winds and water would turn the shingles to gray. He didn't look up as she got out of the car, but Beauty came bounding over, her plumy tail wagging, her nose cool against Parker's leg.

"Wow, Thing One. You've been busy," Parker said as she bent to pet her little dog. Yes. Adopt a casual attitude. Definitely the way to go. "It looks great."

"Thanks." He didn't look at her.

"You're welcome. Thank *you.*"

"My pleasure." Still no eye contact.

Beauty lay down in the grass and put her muzzle on her paws, watching the two humans avoid meaningful conversation.

"So the library thing was kind of fun, as debts to society go," Parker said, reaching out to touch a shingle with one finger.

"Good." Bang! The sound of the air gun made her

jump. James bent—his ass…perfect—and picked up another shingle. Bang!

"Collier was there," Parker said. No comment. "I reduced him to tears as the Holy Rollers helped bury the squashed kitten."

"He's a sensitive soul." Bang!

Was James jealous? Please, she wasn't *that* desperate. Still, perhaps clarification would be in order. "Yeah, well, he's very nice and all, but I don't think I could be friends with a man who took those books seriously."

No comment. His neck glistened with sweat.

"So, James, you kissed me last night."

"Yes." Bang!

Parker reached out and put a hand on his warm, hard shoulder. "Would you please stop for a second and talk to me?"

He put down the nail gun and folded his arms across his chest and looked at her with those dark, dark eyes. No smile. It was a little intimidating. In a very hot way. In a smoldering, brooding, alpha way. Heck yeah!

"Put a shirt on, Thing One. Cover up all that male beauty and stop distracting me."

He smiled at that, and crap, it was worse than ever, because that smile *melted* her, and the idea that she could make him look that happy had her heart swelling. It felt *good,* earning that smile. James obeyed, getting his T-shirt from the railing of the porch and pulling it over his head. "There. Can you think straight now?" he asked.

"Better," she said. "So."

"So. I kissed you." He stared at her, the wind ruffling his thick hair.

"Yes."

She cleared her throat. "And while it had a certain effect, I don't think it should happen again."

"I think it should."

Bang! No nail gun this time, just her rabbity heart. Nine days. Nine days till her son came back. "Well, things are uncertain in my life, as you're aware, and even though you're very cute, and yes, we've done the deed before, it's a bad idea."

"Why?"

Not sure, actually. "Um…it just is."

A smile began at the corner of his mouth and spread slowly. Parker's skin actually broke out into goose bumps. *Get a grip, Parker,* she told herself.

Fling! Fling! Fling! chanted Lady Land.

"You're scared," he said.

"Could be, Thing One. Or it could be that I'm smart. Either way, not gonna happen again. Okay? I'm flattered, and as I said, you're quite cute, but no. Thank you. Now, I'm going inside to start painting your bedroom. Can I get you a drink of water?"

The smile was full-blown now. *Devastating* smile. Two more seconds of that smile, and James would find himself flat on his back with her on top of him.

"That'd be great, Parker. Thank you."

She stood there another second. How could she have thought he looked sulky and brooding when he had the most wonderful, open, generous, happy, genuine smile in the whole world?

Crikey.

"One ice water, coming up for my hardworking boy." She smiled, too—*See? We can get along just great!*— and went inside, stuck her head in the freezer and told Lady Land to pipe down.

An hour later, Parker paused outside James's bedroom, which would soon be Nicky's bedroom. His was the last room to be painted.

She'd discovered that she loved painting rooms. Painting was good for the soul. It was soothing and exciting both, the invigorating smell and luscious texture of the paint, the hissing of the roller as she zipped it against the walls. Pulling off painter's tape, the revelation of the perfect line, the tidiness of it all, had become one of the great thrills of her life. Pathetic but true.

She'd chosen a very pale green for her bedroom—Sage Mist—and repainted the trim bright white. Amazing how it perked up the room. Her quilt was green, blue and pink, and the other day, Maggie had taken her to World of Curtains—Maggie was moving in with Malone, who had no curtains, which both women had found stunning and inexplicable. Parker had found some pale green drapes a shade or two lighter than her walls, lined with pink, *and* they were eighty percent off. Bargain shopping, another new experience for Parker, was also proving quite thrilling.

The kitchen was a nice sunny-yellow—Northern Sunrise—the battered cupboards much improved by a glossy red. With the Formica-and-steel table and the funny yellow chairs, it now looked pretty nice—if you could overlook the linoleum, which was the color of dried blood. A new—and cheap—floor was next on her list.

Maggie had had a tag sale a few days ago, so there was finally a little furniture in the living room—a couch and a pretty nice-looking Mission-style chair. One day, while out walking Beauty, Parker had come across a great hunk of bleached driftwood and hefted it home as the dog tried to chew on it. Ordered a piece of beveled glass from the boys at the hardware store, and voilà. A coffee table was born.

The shack was becoming pretty cute, and completely unrecognizable from the hoarder's hell she'd first seen.

It was almost too bad she had to sell it.

At any rate, it was time to paint James's room.

It felt extraordinarily intimate, for some reason, opening his door. Also, her father's snake was in there. She paused, then went back to the kitchen, where she could see him through the open window. "I'm going to start painting your room now," she said. "Want to move your porno stash first?"

"It's all up here," James said, tapping his temple.

"Okay. Hope your diary's not open. I'd hate to see how you yearn for me."

"That's hardly a secret," he said, his tone cheery, his smile killer.

"Is Apollo's cage locked?"

"Sure is." Then he hefted the ladder, his biceps bulging most attractively, and moved past the window.

Lady Land was getting downright hostile. She sighed, then went back down the hallway.

She hadn't been in here since Day One. It contained almost nothing: bed, night table, battered old bureau, the glass tank containing her father's beloved. Had she mentioned the bed? A sudden image of James's tanned skin against the white sheets made her mouth dry. *Down, girl.* On the night table was a battered paperback by Harlan Coben. A clock.

The room was as neat as a pin; neater than her room, which always seemed to have a towel or a pair of shoes lying around somewhere, no matter how she tried to keep it tidy. His room was like a monk's quarters. No porno stash anywhere that she could see. She got a towel from the bathroom and draped it over Apollo's tank so she wouldn't have to see the creature.

There was a single framed photo on the bureau. Parker went over and picked it up. It was of James hugging a woman with dark hair. The woman's face was buried in his shoulder, but Parker could see enough of her face to tell that the woman was laughing. James was smiling, his chin resting on the woman's head, his eyes crinkling. A happy, happy picture.

Had James ever been married? The thought lanced Parker with an abrupt arrow of shame. She'd never asked. Was he divorced? A widower? Or was this laughing woman his sister? He had mentioned a sister, as well as three brothers, but Parker couldn't see enough of her face to tell if they looked like each other.

But she could see that the woman had curly hair, beautiful skin and that she loved James. And he loved her back.

Very carefully, she put the picture back and started on the taping. When she was done with that, she pulled the bed away from the wall. There was hardly enough room to get past, as James's room was significantly smaller than her own. A thought occurred to her. "Hey, James?" she called, going back into the hallway. He was right there, and she jumped back. "Oh. You're in. I thought you were, um, still outside."

"I'm gonna shower and head for Dewey's," he said.

"Oh."

"It's Malone's bachelor party," he added.

"Right. I knew that." Too bad they couldn't shower together. Save time and all. Wet, naked, soapy James and her own wet, naked self—holy halos, Batman. Her knees softened, then thunked into place, locked. Great. She was staggering without even taking a step. "Well, have fun, Thing One." Her voice was brisk. "Don't drink and drive, of course."

"I never do." He leaned against the wall and looked at her. He hadn't shaved today. He was still fairly baby-faced, in fact, not one of those men who could grow a beard in a couple days, like Malone or, um, what's-his-name. Ethan.

"What did you need?" he murmured.

What indeed. She felt her cheeks warm. God, this was just not her, all this swooniness and blushing! "Well, if I start painting tonight, the fumes might bother you. So maybe you should sleep at your uncle's house. Or on the couch. Or something." *Your bed is pretty big, Parker,* the Holy Rollers pointed out. Great. Now her angels were becoming pimps.

"Okay. Want me to move Apollo while you're painting?"

"Sure. Your call. Whatever. It's all good." *You babble when you're nervous,* the HRs noted. "Thanks," Parker added, then closed her eyes. "So who's the woman in the picture?" She inclined her head toward his bureau.

"My sister."

Oh, goody. Sister. Not wife. "You guys are close?"

"Yes." His mouth pulled up on one side, and her knees wobbled again.

"Well. You have fun tonight, James."

He smiled and went past her, and the brush of his arm against hers was enough to make her entire side tingle.

Fling.

CHAPTER TWENTY-TWO

JAMES WAS POSSIBLY a little bit drunk.

The thing was, he never really could hold his liquor. His father and brothers, man, those guys could pound beers like coal miners or teamsters or some other group who drank a lot of beers. And these lobstermen, damn, they were drinkers, too. But James had been working in the hot sun all day; he hadn't slept much the night before because of *that kiss,* and he might've been pretty dehydrated and fairly exhausted before those beers hit his system. Three beers, one cheeseburger, a very loud bachelor party with guys making toasts to things like "not being a priest" and "Maggie's desserts" and stuff like that.

Jonah, the brother of the bride and Chantal's husband, lucky bastard, was sitting next to him, talking about nothing the way men do—why Boston could beat the Yankees in practically every game this season yet still be in third place. Guy stuff. Same sort of nothing James talked about with his buddies in Providence.

All in all, James felt slightly dizzy, pretty foggy and generally happy. "I got a question for you, Jonah," he said, watching as Malone won another game of pool. "How'd you get Chantal to marry you?"

"Got her pregnant," he said. "Then I kept bugging her till she said yes. Why? Oh, hang on a sec. Georgie's calling me."

"Here's the deal," James said, possibly slurring a little, "I have a thing for this woman, right? A big thing. But it's like her heart is…I dunno. Made outta Plexiglas. Stuff bounces off Plexiglas, right? And that shit's hard to break, know what I mean?"

"Dude, you are whipped," a female voice said. James blinked. He thought he'd been talking to Jonah, but this was not Jonah next to him. No. It was a woman. A very, very, veryveryvery beautiful woman who could even give Perfect Parker a run for her money. If you liked black-haired, blue-eyed Liv Tyler type of princesses, that was. Which guys did.

And you know what? He was a guy. Who probably should look for a woman whose heart wasn't made out of Plexiglas. She looked like…what was that thing that turned into a seal? Mary Elizabeth loved that book. A selkie. That was it.

"Hi, I'm James. You are so beautiful, I shouldn't even look directly at you or I might go blind."

She smiled, growing even more beautifuller, if that was a word. "Hi, I'm Emory. Malone's eighteen-year-old daughter."

"Shit. I take it back and apologize, and if we could pretend this conversation never happened, that'd be great." He looked at her glass. "Also, I hope that's soda, because I'm an officer of the court." Yep. Drunk.

She laughed. "It's root beer."

"Why are you here? Aren't women banned from these things?"

"Nah. I hardly get to see my dad, so I got to come. Dad! Come over here!"

"No, no, that's fine," James said, but Malone turned, his eyes locking on James in an unmistakable look—*If you touch my daughter, I will kill you, cut up your body and use it as bait.* James shoved his chair a little farther away from the Liv Tyler selkie thing as Malone approached.

"Is he bothering you?" Malone growled.

"No!" James said. "No. I'm not. Absolutely not. I barely even know her. Besides, I like someone else."

"Father dear, James was telling me his romantic woes. He's in love with someone who doesn't love him back. It's really tragic."

Malone's face creased a little. "I know."

"You do?" James asked. Malone here was psychic or something. Cool.

"Ayuh. Parker, right?"

"Right! Parker," James said, nodding. Nodding made him feel a little sick, so he stopped. "You guessed? Is it really obvious?"

"Ayuh."

Okay, here was a guy who had spoken maybe three sentences that James could remember, but he was marrying the cutest girl—woman—in town. There was Jonah, who wasn't even as old as James, and he'd dated and mated Chantal the Delicious.

"So how'd you do it, man?" James asked. "'Cuz I'm trying my best, and she doesn't seem to even notice. Her heart is like Plexiglas. Or cement. Something really hard, whatever."

"Jeezum crow," Emory said, taking a sip of her soda. "It's like watching a puppy being put to sleep. Help him out, Malone."

"Yeah. Help me out, Malone," James said. "'Cuz you got Maggie, who's so cute." Another glare from Scary Lobsterman Guy. "Sorry. She's not. I mean, she is… I'll stop now. Good job, is what I meant to say."

Emory laughed. "Yeah, well, it wasn't that easy, James. My dad was as pathetic as you are. Right, Dad?"

Malone took a sip of his beer. "Ayuh."

"So whatja do?" James said.

Malone shrugged. "Waited her out, I guess."

Emory shoved his shoulder. "He didn't wait. He kissed her, and according to her, he's a great kisser, which made me throw up in my mouth. I mean, ew! We have to have a talk about boundaries, since she's gonna be my stepmother and all. And why anyone would want to kiss that ugly mug…"

Malone slid his arm around his selkie's shoulders and smiled.

"I tried the kissing," James said. "Didn't work."

Malone grinned. "Try again."

James leaned back in his chair and pretended to fire a pistol at Malone. "Good advice, partner," he said, just before the chair tipped over.

An hour or so later, James followed his uncle upstairs to the little apartment.

"You have fun, kid?" Dewey asked.

"Definitely," James answered. "Thanks for letting me crash here." He'd switched to water after Beer #3 and was feeling much improved.

"Your mom called today," Dewey said, pulling a blanket out of the closet and handing it to James.

So much for feeling improved. "How's she doing?"

"Good. Worried about you. She saw something on the news about your boss and whatnot. Figured out you're unemployed."

James nodded. "I paid Beckham for the next few years. She doesn't have to worry."

Dewey folded his arms across his massive belly. "I

think she was worried about you, Jamie. When was the last time you saw them?"

"It's been a while."

"Ayuh. Well, they're your parents."

"Yep."

His uncle sighed. "I know it's tough, kid. And for whatever it's worth, you're welcome to stay here as long as you need. Wouldn't mind having you around more. You were always my favorite nephew."

James gave a halfhearted smile. Staying was a nice thought. Find a sweet, easygoing girl, do some blue-collar job. Carpentry, maybe. Those options, however, had died when he was much younger. "Thanks, Unc. But I can't. Gotta make the big bucks. Or at least as big as I can manage."

Dewey nodded. "Right. Well. You're a good kid, you know that?"

"Sure."

"All right. Sleep well."

He probably wouldn't. The clock was ticking on getting a real job, taking care of his responsibilities. He couldn't play house with Parker forever, and the thought of leaving her, of not seeing her anymore—ever, maybe—made his chest hurt.

Tomorrow, he'd be helping Dewey set up for the wedding, basically transporting the bar over to the town green, serving drinks, cleaning up. Parker would be doing the flowers and whatnot.

It occurred to James that the last time he'd been at a wedding with Parker, they'd ended up in bed.

A guy had to wonder if he might get that lucky again.

As he lay there on Dewey's lumpy couch, James felt

the beginning of a smile. Weddings had always been good to him.

Maybe there was reason to hope tomorrow's would be, too.

CHAPTER TWENTY-THREE

PARKER WOKE UP at five—the curse of a parent. Nicky had always been an early-to-bed, early-to-rise kind of kid. He could sleep through fireworks, thunderstorms and alien invasions, but he was bright eyed and bushy tailed long before the sun came up.

Well, the one small benefit of having him with Lucy and Ethan for three weeks was that at least she didn't have to answer his endless stream of questions before having two cups of coffee. She stretched, and her little dog did the same.

"Sleep well?" Parker whispered, petting the dog's silky head. She'd have to make sure Nicky understood how shy Beauty was, as the little guy tended to charge toward whatever caught his fancy. "You'll be sweet to Nicky, right?" Parker asked the dog, and Beauty's tail gave a slight wag.

Today was the wedding, and she had a ton to do. She got out of bed, pulled on jeans and a Joe's Diner sweatshirt—because prior to this month, she hadn't *owned* a sweatshirt, for heaven's sake.

James wasn't on the couch; Parker figured he must've opted for his uncle's place instead.

Or maybe he'd found some cute woman who didn't have so many hang-ups and suspicions. That was a definite possibility. Sure, he'd kissed her the other night. And she'd told him not to do it again.

You really need to figure out what you want, Spike advised sagely.

"Shush," she told him.

When the coffee was finished brewing, Parker filled a travel mug, clipped a leash on Beauty and got into her car. She drove through the silent town, past the lovely brick town hall, the more modern and uglier police station, where she'd been a guest. Across the diner was a paper banner—Congratulations, Maggie and Malone!

The couple was getting married by a justice of the peace right on the town green, in the little gazebo next to the flagpole and war memorial. A potluck reception— Parker had never been to one of those—would be held under the white tent. The tables and chairs were already there, Parker could see, though not yet set up.

They might not have much in the way of a flower budget, and Maggie was definitely a casual bride, but there was something really touching about the two of them—lovely, outgoing Maggie and the quiet, honorable Malone—and Parker wanted to make their day beautiful. Going to all those wildly expensive, over-the-top weddings of her cousins and family friends and college mates…well. She knew something about floral arrangements.

A short way out of town she pulled off the road. A field rich with lupine was just past the scrubby pines that lined the road. Parker had never seen the cone-shaped wildflowers in bloom before, but last week, she'd nearly driven off the road at first glimpse.

She pulled over, got a few buckets out of the back of the Volvo and started cutting.

By THREE O'CLOCK that afternoon, Parker was finally satisfied. Everything looked…well, stunning; she really had
to give herself credit here.

The gazebo was twined with garlands of ivy and hydrangea blossoms, most of which she'd, er, appropriated
from a lush bank at the edge of the Pines property. Collier wasn't around, but Parker figured that he wouldn't
mind—or even notice. On the wide steps leading into
the gazebo were two huge arrangements of pine, lupine,
twigs and more ivy and phlox, a riot of color and deep,
dark green. Parker had filled eight tin buckets with
smaller versions of the arrangements and set them out
at intervals along the makeshift aisle.

Inside the tent, she'd strung up fairy lights; Vin had
had some in a closet, and last week, Parker had emptied
a going-out-of-business craft store of its cache. All the
supports and poles were lit up like the old Tavern on the
Green in Central Park and twined with more blossoms
of hydrangea, wild roses, baby's breath and lupine. For
the centerpieces, Rolly had helped her drill holes into
split white birch logs, into which Parker had put tall
white candles, then set that into a bed of pine, roses and
fern.

It was magical and lush and uniquely Maine, and she
couldn't wait to see the look on Maggie's face.

Lavinia was delivering the bouquets and boutonnieres
to the bride and groom, so Parker was free to go. She
took one more smug look around the tent. Time to go
home, shower and change. Good thing Lucy had convinced her to bring a really nice dress in case of a fling.

And speaking of flings and weddings, it was hard not
to remember Esme's big day, when Parker had ended
up with James. He'd been little more than a stranger
back then.

This time, she had reason to like him.

The thought made her knees wobble a bit.

LIKE MOST MEN, James wasn't crazy about most weddings. Ceremonies were mostly the same, give or take. Brides looked pretty. Food was mediocre and took too long to be served. The expense always seemed a little grotesque. Single women tended to eye him the way a starving coyote might eye a plump, blind baby bunny, then make their predictable and unsubtle advances. In fact, that's how he and Leah had met. A New Year's Eve wedding. She'd been cute, she eyed him, she kept positioning herself closer and closer, till she could accidentally bump into him and apologize, with plenty of hand laying and hair tossing.

Parker's wedding pass had been, by far, the least subtle ever. She'd been no sneaky coyote, no. More like a strike from a great white. Didn't see it coming, was completely stunned.

Not that he'd complained.

This wedding, he acknowledged, was nicer than most. Parker and Vin had done a great job on the flowers; in fact, Maggie's mouth had dropped open when she got out of the limo, and people couldn't stop talking about how pretty everything looked. Every time he heard someone gushing, he felt a little rush of pride for his housemate.

And speaking of, she looked…perfect. Wearing a long blue dress cut low in the front and low in the back. Hair up in a twist. She wasn't wearing shoes, and the sight of her toes peeping out from under the silky fabric was getting him a little aroused. Didn't take much where she was concerned. Whether she wore that horrible Yankees cap and stained jeans or a gown, she was beautiful.

She was also avoiding him. She'd waved. He'd waved back. She seemed to be arming herself with babies; first Chantal's fat little package, then a smaller baby, then one that could walk.

The bride herself appeared. "Jamie, you don't have to stay glued behind the bar," she said, her cheeks flushed with happiness. "Eat something! We can pour our own wine."

"You sure look pretty, Maggie," he said.

She smiled, and for a second, she looked exactly like the cute waitress he'd had a crush on way back when. "Thanks," she answered. "But go. I'm the boss of today, right? Go eat something. Dance with someone. Parker, for example. Malone said you have a huge crush."

James shot Malone a look. "Thanks, pal."

Maggie leaned forward and kissed him on the cheek. "I'm so glad you came up this summer."

"No kissing other men," Malone said. "Wife."

"Oh, that's right, we're married," Maggie said. "I forgot why I was wearing this white dress." She slid her arms around Malone's waist. "Go, James. I am queen and therefore dismiss you. Have fun. Oh, hang on, there's Parker. Parker! Over here!"

"She's really bossy," James muttered to the groom.

"Ayuh," he agreed.

Because Maggie was queen, Parker came over, and James felt his nerve endings do the now-familiar howl.

"Parker, these flowers are amazing! I can't get over it!" Maggie said, hugging her.

"Thanks, Maggie. So glad you like everything." She paused. "Hi, James."

"Parker. Always lovely to see you," he said. Her cheeks grew pink. James smiled. Used to be, he could only make her ears turn pink. Now he had the whole face. Progress.

"Oh, I love this song," Maggie said. "Come on, Malone, let's dance." Malone grimaced—what straight guy wouldn't—it was something by Beyoncé about all the single ladies.

"You have to obey her," James said. "She's the queen…"

"Thanks for nothing," Malone muttered, following his wife as she dragged him onto the dance floor. Poor slob. Well, he wasn't that poor. He was smiling.

James turned to Parker. Her blush deepened. "Did you have fun last night?" she asked.

"Sure."

"You stayed at your uncle's?"

"Yep." She smelled so good. "You look beautiful," he said quietly.

"Thank you," she answered, then cleared her throat. "You look very…um, nice to see you dressed." She winced, closing her eyes. "Dressed up, I meant. In a suit. More like yourself. Whatever, don't listen to me. Nice wedding, don't you think?"

She was nervous; he could feel the electrical current radiating from her. She licked her lips—*God*—and the blood made the cheerful and familiar flight from James's brain straight to his groin. "The flowers look great."

"Thank you."

Such pleasant chitchat, when what he really wanted to do was…her. Yeah. That was right. Just clear off this table and tip her back on it, and let nature do its sweet thing.

A lock of her hair slipped out of its twist, brushing against her cheek. James reached out and slowly tucked it behind her ear, his fingertips brushing her silken skin, touching her earlobe. Her lips parted. He looked in those green eyes, which had grown soft and unguarded, and felt his heart slow to thick, solid beats.

The Beyoncé song ended, and something slow came on. "Want to dance?" he murmured.

"Excuse me?" she whispered.

"Would you like to dance, Parker?"

She blinked and seemed to come out of the trance that had wrapped around them both. "Oh, I should— I have to check something. Um, rain check?"

"Okay."

With that, she turned and fled, like a scared little horse or something, stopped and fussed with an arrangement, and glanced back at him, then looked quickly away.

James felt a smile begin in his chest. Parker was afraid of dancing with him. Had to be a good sign.

He looked over the guests. There were a couple of age-appropriate women there, giving him the coyote stare. *Not today, ladies,* he thought, and approached a tiny, ancient old lady who was looking at the group on the dance floor with a bit of longing on her face. Bingo. His date for the evening. "Would you do me a favor and dance with me?" he asked.

"Oh, my *word!*" she exclaimed. "I can barely *stand,* let alone *dance,* sweetheart!"

"I'm extremely handsome and strong," he said. "You sure you want to turn me down?"

"Fine. You've *convinced* me," she said, standing with the help of her cane. She came up to his chest. "What's your name, young man?"

"James Francis Xavier Cahill."

"Oh! What a *lovely* name! I always did love the name James! I was so sorry when they shortened James Stewart to Jimmy." She patted his shoulder fondly. "You can call me Bess. Do you know it's been at least a *dozen* years since I danced?"

"I think you're lying," he said, maneuvering very carefully among the other dancers. "You're too pretty to be on the sidelines. You must have at least three boy-friends." He grinned as she laughed.

Parker had made herself scarce.

Well. They happened to live together, so she couldn't hide forever.

James also danced with Lavinia, danced with Maggie's mother, dodged a pass from a woman he didn't know, and made his way back behind the bar and stayed there, watching the crowd. Parker stayed on the sidelines, though she did dance with one of the Three Musketeers, the guy whose wife died earlier this year.

She didn't come his way again.

A while later, his uncle approached, sweaty from having danced with Maggie's twin. He sat down in front of the bar and eyed James. "Why don't you go home, kid?" he said, wiping his forehead. "We're all set here."

"No, I'll stay, Unc. Help you pack things in later on."

"Nah. You did all the setup. Don't worry. The McConnell kid will do it. He needs a little money. Going off to Dartmouth this fall."

James hesitated. "Okay." He started to walk off, then stopped. "Dewey," he said, "I wanted to thank you."

"What for?"

"For letting me come stay with you when I was a kid. When things were tough."

Dewey's expression changed. "Sure, kid. Now go home. Go. Git. I'm gonna see if Chantal will dance with me for old times' sake."

LITTLE MONKEY WATCHED the other monkeys swinging through the vines. Gosh, it looked like fun! But what if she missed the vine? She might fall, breaking her bones as she crashed through the branches, possibly rupturing some organs as she fell to the jungle floor, where Hungry Jaguar was waiting to gobble her up. On second thought, maybe she'd stay in the tree instead, make a martini and call it a day.

Parker sighed, put aside the red notebook and sat back in the old wooden chair. She'd slipped away from the wedding and was down on the dock, still in her dress. Beauty lay at her feet, contentedly staring out at the water, which was a purplish-blue under the darkening sky.

Lovely wedding. Just lovely, all that happiness so palpable. She'd laughed and eaten and truly enjoyed sitting with Lavinia and watching the bride and groom. Little Violet Jones fell asleep on her lap, an achingly wonderful moment, the sweet smell of the little girl's head, her limp, warm weight so welcome.

But mostly, she'd felt James. Felt his every smile, directed at her or not. When he'd touched her face, his eyes so dark, she'd been unable to even breathe. Thought he might kiss her for a second. So, in typical fashion, she bolted, but from that moment on, she'd *felt* him. His laugh hit her in the stomach in a warm, aching squeeze, and each time those smiley, dark eyes met hers…well, hell, there it was again, that strong, tingling pull she'd only ever felt around him.

Music from the reception drifted down from the green and out over the water, the thump of bass and occasional roll of laughter easily heard from the dock. The music changed from fast to slow…something by Norah Jones, the words just out of reach.

The tingling pull started again. She turned her head, and there he was, the sleeves of his dress shirt rolled up, his tie loosened, standing at the foot of the dock, watching her. Beauty's tail swished.

"Hey, James," she said mildly.

Mildly, right. Her heart was shuddering, it was beating so fast. *Jump him,* Spike advised. *He's a guy. He'll love it.* In her mind, the former child angel wore a black leather jacket and squinted through a haze of cigarette smoke. She should look into medication for this.

James came over to her, the dock rocking gently. He stood in front of her and held out his hand. "Come on, coward," he murmured. "You owe me a dance."

His hand was warm and sure. He pulled her to her feet, right against him, and Parker thought she might actually swoon, because he smelled so good, was so warm. Her entire body seemed to melt into his as his arm slipped around her waist. Her hand went to his shoulder, and James tipped his head and smiled at her, just a little. Parker swallowed, then put her cheek on his solid shoulder.

Norah Jones's smoky voice floated across the water, and the waves lapped against the dock, and she and James stood there, barely moving. *Do something, James,* she thought. *Help me out here.*

Slowly, slowly, he slid his hands down her bare arms, threading his fingers through hers. His hair tickled her neck as he bent his head, his lips warm as he kissed her shoulder, and the relief was so immense that her knees wobbled. He smiled against her neck.

Parker slipped one hand against his chest, feeling the solid thumping of his heart, such a sweet, intimate feeling that the ache in her grew sharply. His lips moved higher up her neck, his beautiful mouth smooth and warm against her skin.

Beauty suddenly decided that James was all right, because she chose that moment to stand, putting her paws against his knee, as if she was cutting in. James smiled down at the little dog, then looked at Parker, and honest to God, she was actually dizzy, his smile was that good, crinkling his eyes, changing his face.

He leaned in a little closer, still smiling, still not kissing her, but please, it'd better be soon or she might die. She closed her eyes, and thank goodness, his lips were against hers, the softest brush, so smooth and warm. Another brush. Then he did kiss her, a gentle, soft kiss that she returned carefully, almost shyly.

This was so different from that first time, so long ago, when she'd barely been thinking, when she'd used him to distract herself from loneliness. This was slow and tender and meltingly wonderful, James's mouth against hers, waiting for her response. Then he cradled her head in his hands, angling for better access to her mouth, and kissed her more fully. Her hand slid into his thick, curling hair, and he held her closer, that beautiful mouth kissing hers as if there was nothing more he wanted to do other than stand out here and do exactly what they were doing.

Beauty whined, and James smiled. He pulled back a little and smoothed Parker's hair back from her hot face.

"The blackflies are starting to bite," Parker whispered.

"Maybe we should go in," he said, that smile still playing at his mouth.

"Okay."

Then he took her hand and led her off the dock, up the stairs and into the house, and Parker went with him as if it was normal, not as if her legs were watery and her whole body was pulsing with a warm, honeyed glow; as if this was old hat, no big deal, when the truth was, she felt something akin to terror here, all that warm, glowing stuff aside. Beauty leaped neatly onto the couch, ditching them, the good dog. James led her down the hall, past his room. There was her bedroom. Yep. Terror.

James stopped outside her door, tilted her chin up and kissed her again. He stopped almost immediately this time, pulling back to look at her. "You okay?" His voice was gentle. Which made sense. He was a gentle man.

The thought somehow made her more scared than ever.

"Yeah! No. It's just…I'm a little…nervous," she heard herself say.

Yes. The woman who'd given birth to an eight-pound, nine-ounce bouncing baby boy in a total of three hours. No drugs, either. Not really virgin-bride material.

His eyes were dark. "We don't have to do anything, Parker," he murmured, and his voice alone made Lady Land croon.

"Right. No, I know that. Which, thank you, by the way." She took a shaky breath. "No, James, it's just the last guy I was with was…" She felt her head wiggling around like a bobble-head figurine and managed to stop. She looked at his chest, which seemed like a safe place to park her eyes. "You. You're the last guy I was with."

He didn't answer. She continued looking at his chest. Fascinating shirt, all white and, um…cottony. Then he cupped her face so she really did have to look at him.

His eyes were soft. And he was smiling. He looked so relaxed, how could he be relaxed when she was about to jump out of her skin?

"And that was… But this…" she said. "It feels—it feels different." Her voice was a whisper now.

Very slowly, as if she were a skittish fawn—Why a fawn? Why not a skittish mule or ferret? Oh, Lord, her brain was going to explode—James kissed her, just a soft brush on the lips. "Maybe because we're friends now," he murmured.

And that was it exactly. Whether it was good or bad, she didn't know.

It was probably good.

He leaned in, so slowly, and kissed her again, and without quite realizing she'd moved, she found her hands were sliding against his lean rib cage, up to his chest.

"Is that a yes?" he whispered, pulling back the slightest bit.

"It's a yes," she breathed.

"Good."

"Yes."

He reached behind her and opened the door, his mouth finding her again, hot and slow and sweet. Backed her into the room, one hand undoing her hair clip, sliding his fingers through her hair, down her back. Her dress was suddenly looser—he'd unzipped it, clever lad—and his tongue brushed hers, and suddenly her hands remembered what they were for. They were for unbuttoning his shirt, even if they were shaking a little. His skin was hot and smooth, and she jerked his shirt open, exposing that beautiful torso, and pulled him down on the bed, suddenly desperate to get him on her, in her.

He captured her hands in his and pinned them gently above her head, his fingers twining with hers. "Not this time," he whispered, kissing just below her ear. "This time, we take things slow."

Then, his mouth hot and sure as he tasted her neck, his hands releasing hers to slip her dress off her shoulders, James proceeded to show her why some things in life shouldn't be rushed.

And you know what?

The guy had a point.

CHAPTER TWENTY-FOUR

WHEN JAMES WOKE up, the sun was at an odd angle, shining right into his face. The bed felt different.

He bolted upright. Reality, or really, really excellent dream? Nope, this was her room. Clock said 8:13 a.m. The latest he'd slept in months. He turned his head, and sure enough, a gorgeous female was looking at him.

Just not the one he expected.

"Hey, Beauty," he said, and the dog wriggled closer and rolled on her back, offering her stomach, which he rubbed obligingly.

Man. Best night of his *life*. Parker Harrington Welles, with him. All night. For a few seconds there, when they'd come up from the dock, he'd thought she might bolt and they'd have to start all over again. Or never.

Nope. The Fates smiled on him, and if she wasn't the most beautiful, softest…the way she'd said his name with a little gasp of surprise as she came, and the sweet, soft sinking afterward, as if her bones had dissolved and all she could do was curl against him, her hair cool and smooth against his shoulder.

Shocking. It was shocking, how good it had felt. Maybe it was years of unrequited imagining, but James could honestly say that there was sex, which was always a good thing.

And then there was last night. Which was unbelievable.

Where was she, anyway? He didn't hear anything going on in the rest of the house. No shower running, no noise from the kitchen.

He got out of bed and pulled on some clothes, an image of Parker on top of him actually making him stop in his tracks.

Best. Night. Ever.

She wasn't in the kitchen. Wasn't on the dock. Wasn't painting in his room, wasn't outside in the little yard. Wasn't swimming, thank God.

No note, either. Odd, because she'd been leaving him little notes as to her whereabouts lately.

At that moment, his cell phone rang. *New Hampshire Correctional.*

Shit. "Hey, Harry," he said.

"James. How are you?"

Great, Harry. Just shagged your daughter. A few times, actually. "I'm, uh, I'm good. How are you?"

"Not bad." There was a pause. "How's Parker?"

So, so good. James grimaced. "She's excellent. I mean, uh, very good. She's fine. I mean, she's looking forward to seeing her son next weekend." He closed his eyes.

"Good. How's the house coming along?"

"Pretty well."

"She hasn't been to see me. You think you could get her to come down?"

James paused. "Well, I think you should ask her yourself, Harry. It'd probably mean more, coming from you."

"Is that right? And now you know my daughter better than I do?"

Oh, most definitely, boss. "Something wrong?"

"It would be *pleasant,* James, if my only child decided she could get her ass in the car and visit me."

"Okay. I'll pass that message on."

"Thank you." Harry's voice was curt.

"So how's sobriety?" James asked.

There was a long pause. "It's harder than I thought," Harry acknowledged. "Sorry if I'm being a prick."

"No, Harry, you're fine. You're in prison. You're supposed to be in a bad mood. Maybe you should join a gang, make some friends."

Harry laughed. "You're the only friend I have, kid." There was an unfamiliar note of sincerity in his voice. "All right, James. Take care."

"You, too, Harry."

Bringing up Harry was not really on James's list of top ten things to talk about with Parker. Especially now, when she'd apparently bolted. Her car wasn't in the driveway, so she must be either at the diner or the flower shop. Or on the Interstate.

A note would've been nice.

Parker, warm and sleepy in bed next to him, would've been even better.

With a sigh, James took a shower, fed the dog and walked into town. She wasn't at the diner, which was packed with pretty much the same folks he'd seen at the wedding yesterday. He said hello to a dozen or so people, got two coffees to go and headed for Lavinia's.

As he walked in front of the open window of the shop, he heard Parker curse. "Tell him I'm on a delivery," she hissed, completely audible. James rolled his eyes and went in.

"Hey, Lavinia," he said, setting one cup of coffee on the counter and taking a sip of his own. "Brought you a coffee. Didn't think you were open so early. On a Sunday. And look at you, here all by your lonesome."

Lavinia stubbed out her cigarette on her palm, looking somewhat like a creased and grumpy badger. "I don't *usually* open so early on a Sunday morning, you're right. But as you might know, I live upstairs, and some crazed idiot was unlocking the door at six-fuckin'-thirty. To clean up the shop, she said." Lavinia picked up the coffee and took a sip. "Thanks for this, by the way."

"You're welcome. So this crazed idiot, I guess she's on a delivery, huh?"

"Ayuh. Something to that effect."

James nodded. "Well, I'd like to send her flowers."

"Sure. Your money."

"Okay, here's what I want the card to say. You ready?"

Lavinia picked up a pen and grinned. "Go for it, kid."

"Dear Parker, thank you for the best sex I've ever had, even counting the last time you did me, which was also fantastic. Still, last night was even better. I'd love to have these encounters more than once every few years, and as we are currently living together—"

The door to the back room opened. "Okay! Fine! I'm here. Stop embarrassing yourself."

"Parker, hi, what a shock. I thought you were on a delivery." He grinned at the sight of her flushed face.

"I'll leave you two lovers alone," Lavinia said with a rusty chuckle. "Eavesdropping the whole time, of course."

Parker waited till Lavinia went into the back room. "James, I'm sorry I had to leave so early. I, um, had to clean up."

"No, you didn't. You're avoiding me."

"Okay, yes, I'm avoiding you." She shoved a piece of hair behind her ear, pinched her pinkie, then folded her arms over her chest and looked at the floor, Princess Agitation. "I wasn't sure what to say."

"I missed you," he said.

She pinched her pinkie again, biting her lip, as well. Very agitated indeed. "I— Can we—" She stopped herself, looked down for a second. Sighed, then raised her eyes back to him. "Last night might've been a huge mistake. I don't know. I'm not really sure what I want here, or what you want, or what... Anyway, I need to think a little bit, and I'm not ready for a conversation yet."

He was not going to let her shovel some wrongheaded story again. "Well, for what it's worth, last night *wasn't* a huge mistake, as far as I'm concerned. And I don't believe you think it was, either."

"Well, I— You might be right. I don't know."

"Yes, you do," he said, his voice containing a hard edge. Good. "You blew me off the last time, Parker. You really gonna do that again?"

She looked at the floor again. "No," she whispered. "I'm just thinking. Okay? I'm not blowing you off. And I'm sorry that I bolted this morning. As you might be aware, I'm not really good at relationships."

She looked so miserable that he wanted to leap over the counter and kiss her stupid.

"Give me a few hours, okay?" she asked.

Well, shit. He couldn't really say no, could he? Still, he couldn't suppress a sigh, either. "Fine."

"Thank you for finding me," she whispered. "It was very sweet."

That was the thing with Parker. Made him crazy on one hand, made him crazy on the other, but for two entirely different reasons. Plexiglas heart vs. gooey caramel center.

"I'll be at home," he said. "And I'll be thinking of you the whole time."

"My Gawd, that's wicked romantic," Lavinia called. "Nice one, Jamie."

"Thanks, Vin," he called, not looking away from Parker.

Then, what else could a guy do? He went home.

"FIVE YEARS? PLEASE. Jonah's thirteen years younger than I am. Jamie's what? Twenty-nine? Thirty? That's totally legal. So he's your beautiful boy toy. Run with it."

"Beats the electronic solution," Lavinia added.

Parker sighed. Advice from Chantal and Lavinia—probably not the best role models.

"There doesn't seem to be a good ending here," she said, trying yet again to explain. "When I thought about a summer fling, it was with someone I barely knew."

"Trashy," Vin said admiringly.

"So he's not just a fling. But he's not stepfather material, either. He's…I don't know. Glib."

"Is he glib? What does glib mean, exactly?" Lavinia said, scratching her head.

"It means insincere and shallow," Chantal answered.

They were drinking cheap white wine at some odd little structure in the middle of nowhere, half bar, half restaurant and the only alternative to Dewey's in a forty-mile radius. Chantal had dropped by the shop to chat that afternoon, and Lavinia, claiming Chantal was an expert on all things male, had spilled out Parker's deeply personal issues. A girls' night had been deemed necessary, and as Parker wasn't really sure about going home, here they were at Jason's Taverne.

Parker sighed. "See, he's only here this summer because my father told him to come. He's being paid. Not to have sex with me, maybe, but still. I can never tell if he's sincere or jerking my chain. And half the time, I think he's only nice to me because it's part of his job."

"But your father's in jail, so James doesn't have a job, does he?" Vin asked. Parker shrugged.

"And he might be glib," Chantal said thoughtfully, "but he has the best ass in town since Father Tim. Hey, I'm married, not blind."

"So have a fling," Lavinia said. "God knows you could use one."

"Thanks, Vin. You're so sweet to say so." Parker sighed.

"Why not, Parker?" Chantal agreed. "Lavinia's right. Have a fling. He's there, he's edible, you're horny—"

"Okay, okay. What if *I'm* not fling material?" Parker said, cheeks hot. This whole conversation was extremely uncomfortable.

"Don't sell yourself short," Chantal said, eating some popcorn and waving to some guy at the bar who was eye-balling her. "Sorry," she called. "Happily married." She refocused on Parker. "Call it a summer romance. What are you afraid of? If James was good at seventeen, I can only imagine—"

"And again, I'm so uncomfortable talking about this," Parker said, leaning her forehead against her fist. The cheap wine was doing its trick. "What if I break his heart or something? What if he breaks mine?"

Lavinia drained her Seven and Seven. "Then you'll both be older and wiser and write a song about it or something. I don't know, sweetheart. He seems like a guy who's been around a bit. Looking like that, hell, he probably has to hold women off with a bowie knife."

Where Lavinia came up with her expressions was a mystery.

"When does your son come up?" Chantal asked.

"Sunday. A week from today," Parker said. Thank God, Nicky would be back in her life. Her little rock.

"So have a fling for a week, Parker. Enjoy yourself. Live a little." Chantal patted her hand. Just then her phone rang. "Speaking of boy toys," she said, clicking on. "Hi, babe. Don't bother me. I'm out with the girls. Oh, really?" Her expression changed to a sex-kitten purr. "Is that right? Uh-huh. Go on. You did not. You did? Ooh. The whole thing? Well, I love you, too. I'll be home in twenty minutes." She hung up the phone. "Baby's asleep, Jonah did the dishes and washed the kitchen floor." She stood up and smoothed her dress over her lush hips. "My husband is about to get laid. Parker, my advice is, go for it. See you, girls."

Lavinia drove Parker back to Gideon's Cove. "Want me to drop you off?" she asked as she came up to the flower shop.

"No, I'll walk. I could use the air. Thanks, though." Parker sat for a second. "You've been really good to me, Lavinia. I appreciate it."

"Ah, shit, it's nothing."

"It's a lot. I wish I'd known you when I was younger."

"Well, you're hardly in the grave now, are you?"

"Guess not. You're gonna love Nicky."

"I'm sure I will, sweetheart. Now get outta my car."

The stars were blazing overhead. No light pollution up here, that was for sure. The town was quiet, as it was after 9:00 p.m., and the smell of pines and salt filled the air. The shushing of the water in the cove was soft and lovely tonight.

She could do a fling. Sure. Maybe. Probably not, actually. Last night hadn't felt like a fling. The first time, at Esme's wedding, yes. That was porno-movie sex. Definitely flingish. But last night had been slow and long and tender, and there'd been smiling, even.

Bugger.

I fail to see a problem here, Spike said.

Parker stood for a minute, looking at the little cottage. It was a far sight better than her first glimpse. The new shingles and roof had perked it up. The back porch had been fortified, the grass cut. She'd paint the doors and railings this week.

She could never have done this without Thing One.

Going inside, she stopped to pet Beauty, who must've heard her and was waiting at the door. "Hi, sweetie," she whispered. "Sorry I left you all day." Then she straightened up. "I'm back," she said more loudly.

James stepped out of the bathroom, his hair damp. He was brushing his teeth.

"Okay, here's how it'll be," Parker said, shoving her hands in her pockets. "I can't have a real relationship, because my life is very unpredictable these days, first of all, and more importantly, I don't think that would be fair to Nicky, since Ethan and Lucy got married six months ago, and with the move out of Grayhurst and starting kindergarten in September, he's got a lot of change going on, so me having a, um, boyfriend, it's not gonna happen. And I can't have you here when Nick is here, so you're going to have to either go back to Rhode Island or find somewhere else, because I'm really sorry, but you can't stay—it's not the example I want to set. But obviously I find you attractive, so if you agree, then I would say let's enjoy each other's company this week, and when my son comes on Sunday, we can part as friends."

Crap. That was long. Palms sweaty, face burning. But yeah, she thought she covered everything.

James was staring at her. "Can I spit now?" he asked thickly.

"Oh! Sure. Sorry. I'll be, um, in the living room."

He raised an eyebrow, then closed the bathroom door and turned on the water.

Rolling her eyes at herself, Parker went down the hall and sat down hard on the couch. Beauty came up to her and pushed her nose against Parker's hand. Such a soft little muzzle, the nap of her fur so deep and velvety. "How'd you think that went?" Parker whispered. The dog wagged her tail. "Good. Me, too." The dog jumped neatly onto the couch and curled against her side.

Nice to have a pet. She should've gotten one long ago.

The water stopped running, and James appeared, smelling of soap and mint. Kind of hard to look him in the eye after her speech. But he was smiling, and her stomach flipped as he knelt in front of her. "Okay," he said.

Parker swallowed. "Okay to what?"

"To everything."

Then he was kissing her, his work-roughened hands under her shirt, hot against her skin, and without further ado, he pulled her to her feet and did her against the wall without even bothering to take off all her clothes.

Meow.

CHAPTER TWENTY-FIVE

ON DAY THREE of the Seven Days in Paradise, as he was thinking of it, James called Lavinia and asked her if she'd look after Beauty for the day.

"What for?" she asked.

"I want to take Parker out of town."

"You two gonna elope?" she said, coughing that rusty bark. "She's been all smiles the past few days."

James laughed. "We're not eloping. I'm not that lucky."

"Aw, listen to him. Sure, I'll watch the dog. Bring me a present. I'm low on ciggies."

"Thanks, Vin."

Parker was in the shower when he got back. She was singing. He tilted his head. "Wheels on the Bus." Maybe it was because her kid was coming up this Sunday, but she did seem happier.

He sure was.

For years now, Parker had been in the back of his mind—and in the front a lot of times, too. Though he'd had the expected hookups with Leah on and off for the past year, as well as a few before her, James hadn't really been in what he thought of as a real relationship. He'd never met a girl's parents. Never thought of himself as wanting more, except for a few hours at the cousin's wedding, that was.

Last night, he and Parker had gone down to the dock

with a bottle of wine and the dog. Spread out a blanket and just lay there, looking up at the stars, Parker's head on his shoulder as she pointed out constellations he pretended he could see, blinded by the perfection of the moment. The water lapped gently at the rocky shore, and his fingers had played in Parker's smooth hair, and it occurred to James that he'd never even imagined a moment like this happening to a guy like him.

"And right there, see? That's Orion. See the belt?"

"Sure," he said, seeing nothing. "It's Armani, isn't it?"

"Okay, okay. You don't have to mock me. It's just that Harvard had a fabulous planetarium, and until now, I haven't had anyone to impress."

He held her a little closer. "In that case, impress away."

She'd rolled on top of him instead. And hell, he'd been very impressed at what she'd done next.

"Come on, Parker!" he yelled now, thumping on the bathroom door. "You rich girls take forever in there."

"I'm not rich anymore," she said, opening the door. Wearing a towel, her wet hair streaming down her back.

"Let's get out of here," he said. "Hurry up. We have a long drive."

She smiled and padded into her bedroom. She sat on the edge of the bed. "You sure we should go anywhere?" Those green cat eyes were inviting.

"Actually, we can wait a little," James said.

And so it was that they were a little late in getting down to Machias. "Why are we here?" Parker asked.

"I thought we could see a movie," he answered.

"Which movie?"

"Oh, come on."

"What?"

"Parker. *The Holy Rollers in 3-D!* opened a few days ago." He glanced at her.

"Oh, crikey," she said, putting her hand over her eyes. "Dang. I knew there was something great about having spotty internet." She peeked at James. "How'd it do?"

"Fourteen million, second only to the alien flick." He was well aware that she'd been paid quite a bit for the film rights, all of which had been donated to Save the Children.

"Do we have to see it? I'm taking Nicky as it is."

"Let's get it over with. You can make gagging noises with me. With him, you'll have to behave," he said.

"Good point."

Twenty minutes later, they were in the little theater, along with about twenty rowdy kids between the ages of chair kicking and squealy texting. The previews began—Smurfs, gnomes, wizards, dogs. The kid behind him spilled his popcorn and started to cry. The tweenie girls in front of them giggled shrilly. "Mommy? Mommy? Mommy? Mommy?" one kid chanted over and over while her mother ignored her and talked to another kid's mom.

Even Dante couldn't have imagined this circle of hell.

He glanced at Parker, whose face was a little gray. "Hey," he whispered. "It'll be great."

"It'll suck, James," she whispered back.

"Terrible attitude. Put on your glasses, it's starting."

The lights lowered completely, and the movie began. Parker was right. *The Holy Rollers in 3-D!* was ghastly. Obvious, blatant, manipulative and all wrapped up in more sugary coating than Lucky Charms cereal. Could there be any more shades of pink in the Holy Rollers' tree house? One angel's voice was so high that James imagined every dog in a two-block radius was howling. Rainbow-colored butterflies floated out at them in 3-D effect, as did bubbles, bluebirds and the glittery rush of angelic roller skates.

James glanced at his watch. Fifteen minutes had passed. This felt longer than a problematic colonoscopy.

He sighed and put his arm around Parker, who was staring, horrified, at the screen. He kissed her temple, but she was mesmerized. "I can't believe people paid money to see this," she whispered.

Golly, Polly and Molly, Ike, Mike and Spike whooshed in and out of regular kids' lives, ate angel food cake and soothed mortal children. A cat died and went to heaven. A dog learned that his limp wasn't so bad. A bat, previously thought to have rabies, was accepted by the owl family, and throughout it all, the Holy Rollers delivered squeaky messages of mercy and good cheer.

A lifetime later, the Sappy Six had earned their sparkly wings—which seemed to flutter right into the audience. A few kids clapped. The tweenie girls pronounced the movie "so, like, totally stupid" and the audience filed out. Parker and James sat there, watching the credits.

There. *Based on the bestselling children's book series by Parker Welles.*

James looked over at her. Even wearing 3-D glasses, she was beautiful.

She was also crying.

"Hey, it wasn't that bad," he said, taking her in his arms.

"No, it was," she said unevenly. "And the thing is, I hate the Holy Rollers, James, but somehow they're the best thing I ever did, and how rotten does that make me feel? I can't write anything else, I'm completely tapped out for ideas and this is my legacy." She tucked her face against his shoulder, her back heaving in little spasms. "Meanwhile, Nicky's having the best summer of his life, Lucy's the world's greatest stepmother—she bakes cookies every *day,* James. Every day! They have this cute little family, Ethan is perfect, and you know they'll have kids of their own pretty soon, and Nicky will have siblings. He'd probably miss me if I died, for a couple weeks, anyway, but Lucy would be a great mom, and the only thing I'm good at is being fake. Those squeaky little bastards were the best I could do, and now even that's done."

She pulled back, her face wet and blotchy, and looked at him.

"Wow," he murmured. "So much self-pity in one big sloppy breath. I can't believe I slept with you." Then he grinned, and she gave a little surprised snort of laughter and smacked him on the shoulder. Hard.

"You're no help. I shouldn't have said anything. You're just my boy toy." She swallowed and wiped her eyes with a napkin.

James looked at her for a long minute. "Come on, princess. I want you to meet someone."

IT TOOK TWO HOURS TO GET from Machias to wherever James was taking her. They didn't talk too much on the way. They did hold hands, though.

Parker couldn't remember the last time she'd held hands with someone other than Nicky, who always grabbed on without thinking. It was admittedly the sweetest feeling in the world, his warm little hand in hers. But James holding her hand so firmly, so naturally…this was pretty great, too.

Around four, they slowed down in front of a long, solid-looking rock wall. The sign said Beckham Institute in brass letters. James pulled up to the guardhouse, which sat in front of an iron gate. "Hey, Bert," he said.

"Hey, James, how's it going?" The guard looked into the window. "Hello there," he said, smiling.

"Hi," Parker answered, feeling suddenly shy.

Bert punched a code, the gate swung open and James drove in.

The grounds were lush and beautiful, carefully landscaped, dotted with robust beds of red and white impatiens, well-placed trees and brick pathways. It looked like a college campus, the old brick buildings in good repair, window boxes overflowing with ivy and geraniums.

But it wasn't a college. There were a lot of staff members identified by the red shirts they wore, *Beckham* written in white letters across the back. There were also quite a few people in wheelchairs. Parker saw one man on a bench, wearing a helmet, rocking, as a staffer chatted with another client, this one on the type of metal crutches that bespoke lifelong use. Some of the clients were older, with white hair and spines bent from osteoporosis. Others were heartbreakingly young.

Someone was kicking a ball. Parker could hear snatches of music. There was a large playground with wider-than-usual swings and pathways—to accommodate wheelchairs, Parker guessed. She'd seen one such playground before.

James parked in front of a more modern building and got out. "Come on," he said, extending his hand.

Parker would've asked who was here, but the lump in her throat was too big. She had a good idea, anyway.

"Hi, Carol," James said to the woman at the front desk.

"Hi, honey!" she said. "How are you?"

"I'm great. This is my friend Parker." He bent to sign a book, writing Parker's name, as well, she noted.

"Hello," the woman said.

"Nice to meet you," Parker said.

"I think she's in her room," Carol said. "They just got out of music therapy. She'll be thrilled to see you."

"Thanks." James went down the hallway, and Parker followed.

How had she never known?

Then James stopped in front of room 111, knocked once and opened the door to a dorm-style room: a twin bed, posters on the wall, stuffed animals. Parker hovered half in the doorway, half in the hall.

"Hi, sis," he said, smiling.

"James!" the woman exclaimed. "Hi, James! Hi!" She launched herself into James's arms, laughing with joy. "You're here!"

It was the woman from the photo on James's bureau. The blue-eyed, dark-haired woman.

She had her brother's smile.

"How've you been?" he asked, kissing her on the forehead.

"I had art. I made a bird. It's not so good. I kept it, though. It's drying. Pete sent me a teddy bear." She picked up a bear from her bed and handed it to James, then twisted her fingers together.

"Oh, that's a really nice bear," James said. "What's his name?"

"Duh. Teddy. It's a teddy bear, James. Pete sent it."

He gave her a look. "I know what it is, Mary Elizabeth. But you don't have to name them all Teddy. James is a great name for a bear. I'm just saying."

Mary Elizabeth found this pretty funny, because she stopped twining her fingers and laughed, a big open-mouthed laugh that ended in a squeak. "James! That's your name!"

He smiled and reached up to smooth her curly hair.

"Hey, Mary Elizabeth, I brought someone to see you," James said. "This is my friend, Parker. Parker, my sister."

Mary Elizabeth looked at her a bit warily.

"Hi, Mary Elizabeth," Parker said.

"Hi," she said, glancing back at her brother. The finger twisting began again. "Okay, bye, James's friend."

"She's gonna stay a little while," James said. "You know the Holy Rollers, right?"

"Duh, James. *The Holy Rollers and the Blind Little Bunny.* You gave me a Spike doll. He's the head angel."

"Well, Parker here, she wrote those books," James said.

Mary Elizabeth's eyes widened. "You did?" she breathed. "You wrote those books? You wrote the Holy Rollers books?"

"I did," Parker said.

The girl's—woman's—mouth dropped open, her fingers moving faster now.

"You like those books, right, Mare?" James asked.

"I like those books. I love those books! I have a Spike doll! They live in a tree fort!"

"We saw the movie, Mare. It was great. I'll take you next week, okay?" James offered.

Mary Elizabeth Cahill had all the Holy Rollers books on a shelf. James had given them to her, she said. For the next hour, Parker fielded the girl's—woman's—questions as best she could, agreeing that yes, *The Holy Rollers and the Big Mean Bully* was the best of all the books, and yes, angel food cake was her favorite dessert, too, but no, she had never had a tree fort.

Throughout the interrogation, Parker kept looking at James, who sat on the window seat, his face neutral as Mary Elizabeth chattered. Occasionally, he made a joke, but mostly he was quiet.

Finally, an aide of some kind knocked on the door. "Sorry to break this up, guys. Mary Elizabeth, it's time for dinner, hon. James, you and your friend gonna stay?"

James glanced at Parker. "Not this time."

"I'm starving," Mary Elizabeth announced. She stood up and looked at Parker. "You're my best friend now."

"Thanks, Mare," James said with an exaggerated sigh. "I thought I was your best friend."

"You're my brother. You can't be best friends with your brother."

"So true, Mary Elizabeth," Parker said. "Don't listen to him—he's just grumpy."

Mary Elizabeth seemed to like that. "You're just grumpy, James," she repeated. "You're grumpy." She looked at Parker, a gleam of conspiratorial delight in her eyes. "I love you, James's friend," she added, hugging Parker hard.

"I love you, too," Parker said. Then Mary Elizabeth detached and hugged her brother. "Bye, James! See you tomorrow!"

"Bye, Mare. I love you." James hugged his sister back, kissed her twice, then waved as she and the aide walked from the room.

"See you tomorrow?" Parker asked.

"She doesn't really have a sense of time."

"Oh."

James stood up and put his hands in his pockets. "Well. Thank you for making her life." He grinned, but it was a pale imitation of the usual. "Want to take a walk?"

"Sure."

James clearly knew the place well, and several people, clients and staff alike, said hello, calling him by name. They walked through the campus, down a wide brick pathway to a little garden. There was a fountain in the middle, and two sparrows were taking a bath. The grounds were quieter now, and Parker could smell garlic and roast chicken.

"Food's pretty good here," James said, as if he heard her thoughts.

"That's a plus."

He was staring at the birds. "The technical term is *anoxic brain injury.* Deprived of air during a near drowning."

Parker bit her lip. "I'm so sorry," she said.

He leaned back, took a deep breath and ran a hand through his hair. Then he told her the story.

Mary Elizabeth had been a surprise baby—the four Cahill boys had been born within six years of each other, with Mary Elizabeth coming five years after James, the youngest son. She'd been as spoiled as a little girl could be; if one brother failed to obey her command, surely another would. She had them all wrapped, James said. Especially their father, who viewed Mary Elizabeth as a reward for enduring four boys. Her brothers would give her piggybacks, ride her on the handlebars of their bikes, even play princess tea party with her. She was the light of the family, everyone's favorite.

Then, when James was twelve and Mary Elizabeth was seven, Tommy graduated from high school. The school gave out only four tickets per family, so James volunteered to stay home and babysit. *The Terminator* was on, and his mother hadn't let him see it when it was in the theaters. The rest of the family went off to the high school. Mary Elizabeth asked to go swimming; the Cahills lived on a lake, and the kids swam almost every day.

James said no. Gave her some popcorn, made her a fort out of blankets in her bedroom, left her there playing with her dolls. Then he went into the living room and sat in front of the TV.

By the time he realized she was in the lake, she was already way too far out. He yelled for her to come in, and she turned and headed for shore. All the Cahills were excellent swimmers. But she was tired. When her head slipped beneath the surface, it took him a second to realize what was happening. There was no splashing, no yelling, no flailing. She just disappeared.

"I remembered what my dad always told us—row, throw, go. Row out, throw them something or go for help." James's voice was horribly quiet and calm. "We had a little dinghy, and I don't even remember getting in it. I was pulling the oars as hard as I could, and I could hear myself screaming her name…."

He jumped in where he thought she'd gone under, but the lake was murky, and it was hard to see anything. He swam around, eyes burning, chest aching, resurfaced for air and went under again.

And then he saw his sister's hand, floating there, white against the green murkiness. He grabbed and pulled, kicking for all he was worth.

"They make it look so easy in the movies," he said. "We were barely moving. She was a chubby little thing, weighed almost as much as I did back then. Then we broke the surface, and I held her face up, but the boat had drifted off in the wind, and I couldn't make it. But I couldn't let her go, either."

"Oh, honey," Parker whispered, wiping her eyes.

"We both went down, and I thought that was it, we were dying. I could see the light getting farther and farther away, and I felt so bad for my parents, to have to find us in the pond. But at least Mare and I would die together."

Parker pressed her hand against her mouth, but a sob slipped out.

He gave her an oddly wry look. "I know. It's a horrible story, isn't it?" She squeezed his hand, unable to talk. "So, next thing I knew, my father had me by the arm, pulled me up, tossed me in the boat and went back for Mary. Got her to the dock, did CPR, all that. My mother was screaming, my brothers…well. It was a nightmare."

"James, I'm so, so sorry," she said in a shaky voice, the words pathetically inadequate.

He shook his head. "The TV was still on when I went back in the house. That's what I remember. I wanted to watch the movie, and my sister almost died because of it."

"James, you didn't know what would happen! You told her not to go in, and you thought she was playing. It's not your fault."

"Oh, sure it is. My father grabbed the wrong kid first, that's all."

Parker's heart seized. "No, James, you can't think like that. You can't."

He gave her a bleakly rueful grin. "It's what he used to tell me."

Jesus. Parker squeezed his hand, unable to speak.

"So." He took a breath, and his voice became more brisk. "Mare was in the hospital for weeks, then a rehab center. Mom started drinking, my brothers blamed me, and my father couldn't stand the sight of me. That's why I got shipped off to Dewey in the summers. And that's the end of the tragic tale. I guess every family has one, and that's ours."

"You can't hold yourself responsible for that, James. You were twelve years old," she said.

"I was in charge. I knew she wanted to go in, and I

knew she usually did what she wanted, but hey. *The Terminator* was on."

"No, James. You were only a little kid yourself. It wasn't your fault."

He didn't contradict her, but she could tell he didn't believe her, either. The little birds were done with their bath, and a breeze rustled the leaves of the willow tree behind them.

"Do you pay for this place?" she asked, wiping her eyes on her sleeve.

He nodded. "Shitty consolation prize. 'Hey, Mary Elizabeth, I'm sorry I almost let you drown, but at least you can live in a nice institution.'"

No words were going to help here. Parker scootched onto his lap and wrapped her arms around him, kissed his head, her throat tight, and held him close, smoothing his hair, not saying anything.

"Parker?" he said eventually, his face against her neck.

"Yes?"

"I turned your father in to the SEC."

The words took a minute to sink in. She blinked. "Excuse me?"

James pulled back to look at her. "He let something slip about a deal one night. Something that would be as good as Apple. I wasn't sure at first, but it sounded... off." His eyes were sad. "A drug company had a product really close to FDA approval, and he sank everything into it. He was absolutely sure it would be huge. But it didn't pass its final trial. When he came to me and asked to liquidate your trust funds, I knew he'd screwed up."

"Oh." She took a deep breath, utterly stunned.

James was quiet for a minute. "The law says if an attorney suspects a client is committing fraud that results in financial loss for other people, he has to turn him in.

And even though I owed Harry everything, because I could never afford this place without him, I had to do it. I called the SEC, and they took it from there."

Parker blinked. A sparrow landed on the back of the bench, then flew off. "Does he know?" she asked.

"He might. He probably does—he's not an idiot—but he's never said anything. He knows about my sister and how I pay for this place." His dark eyes were full of so much—guilt, sorrow, regret. "I'm sorry, Parker. I knew you and Nicky would be collateral damage, but I couldn't say anything without breaking the law. If I lost my license or got indicted with Harry, I wouldn't be able to take care of Mary Elizabeth."

Parker looked at him for a long, long moment, then put her hand over his heart. "Oh, James," she whispered. "I would've done the exact same thing."

IT WAS NOT GREAT TIMING, falling for someone four days before a relationship was scheduled to end. Parker admitted that. But that night, James asleep on one side of her, Beauty on the other, both of them sound asleep, she had to acknowledge that it was true.

She was in love.

She studied him as he slept. Cheekbones of an angel, perfect, smooth skin.

They would make beautiful babies, that was for sure.

Oh, holy halos. Where had that thought come from? Now was not the time to be thinking babies. She *had* a child. That child—and reality—were returning in four days.

And James had never said anything about wanting kids, or a future, or anything other than getting exactly what he was getting now. The *L* word had not been exchanged. Given the horror he'd lived through, having kids was probably not on his list of things to do.

But hearing about James's past, seeing him with his sister…it changed things in her heart, if not in the world.

James stirred, frowned, then opened his eyes. "Hey," he muttered.

"Hi."

He looked at her, his eyes softening. "Everything okay?"

"Yes." Then she leaned over and kissed him on the cheek, on the chin, on the temple, until he was smiling, and then she kissed him on the mouth, and the feeling was so overwhelming, so right and wonderful, she thought her heart might come right out of her chest.

Four days. Four more days of this.

It didn't feel like enough.

CHAPTER TWENTY-SIX

ON SATURDAY NIGHT, their last night together, James sat on the dock as ordered. He could hear Parker rattling around in the kitchen, putting the final touches on dinner. She'd already brought down a bottle of wine—the last one from Harry's wine cellar, she'd said—and it was sitting in a bucket of ice next to him. The picnic blanket was spread and set. She'd even put a little vase of flowers in the middle.

James didn't hate being on the dock anymore, despite the gentle rocking and deep water. Nope. It was growing on him, better late than never. The evening was warm and clear, the sun taking its time to set, lighting up Gideon's Cove in a clean, golden glow.

It was almost insultingly romantic.

His bag was packed; his bed, in which he hadn't slept for seven nights running, was now made up with fire-engine sheets for Nicky. James would be moving to Maggie Beaumont's old apartment for the next week or so; all he had to do in exchange was check in on Maggie's little old lady neighbor.

What happened with Parker after tonight, he had no idea.

A fling, she'd said. A weeklong summertime fling, at the end of which, they'd part as friends. Except he didn't want her as a friend.

But she already seemed to be pulling away. Putting

out her son's stuffed animals on the bed, a few books in his room, making a sign that said, Welcome, Nicky! I missed you! He was getting the message. She was shifting back into mommy mode, and he couldn't blame her. She had a lot to do back in Rhode Island—get a job, find a place to live, adjust to a new lifestyle, get her kid settled in school.

Didn't stop the wanting, though.

But he had his own stuff to deal with. His own bills to pay, his own job to find.

"Okay, here we are," Parker said, walking carefully with the tray. Beauty bounded onto the dock and flopped down expectantly, making Parker laugh. "It's not for you, girl. It's for him. Ta-da!"

Lobster. Drawn butter, mashed potatoes, green beans. "There's peach cobbler for dessert, but it was too hot to bring down just yet," she added.

"Wow," he said. "This is really nice, Parker. Thanks."

"Well. I owe you. For all you've done."

Ah. He was being relegated back to the help. Got it.

The food was fantastic. Hard to really love your kiss-off meal, though. Parker chatted easily about town things…a little gossip from the flower shop, the busload of Canadians that had stopped at the diner today, Stuart from the hardware store dropping by with a "blonde with sand" for her today, which apparently was a cup of coffee with cream and sugar.

All very pleasant conversation, same as she'd have with the mailman.

"Why wouldn't you go out with me back then?" he asked, setting down his fork. "After your cousin's wedding?"

His question surprised James nearly as much as it surprised Parker. Her mouth opened, then closed, and she began stacking the plates neatly onto the tray, where Beauty surreptitiously gave them a few licks. Then, finally, she looked at him. "Well, at the time, I didn't want to date you, James. You were Thing One. My father's minion."

"But you were okay with using me for sex."

She flinched a little. "I guess so. It wasn't like I'd planned anything." She looked out over the water. "I figured you slept with me because my last name is Welles."

"I slept with you because you dragged me into a bedroom and mauled me, Parker, and no straight single guy in his right mind would say no to that." He smiled a little to soften the words.

Her ears grew pink. "Right. I did drag and maul. It's true. But then you went off with my father, and it seemed very…convenient. You were already in my father's back pocket—now you had his daughter, too."

His smile dropped. "So you really thought I was complete scum, in other words."

"You were my father's favorite person. My father is complete scum. You were scum by association." She studied her hands. "I was wrong, if it helps."

He said nothing.

"I figured if you really wanted to date me," she added quietly, "you would've tried harder."

Women. Honestly. James leaned back in his chair. "I brought you flowers. I came to your house, and you squashed me like a bug. You weren't going to date me, Parker. I was the help."

"No. It wasn't that. It was more like…" She sighed. "I don't know. I didn't think you were sincere. I figured you came over to see Harry's daughter. Not me." Her cheeks were flushed now, so at least there was that, a little shame thrown in. "If you really wanted something with me, I thought you'd try again. But you didn't." She was pinching her pinkie finger. "I guess it was a test or something."

"See, to me, it didn't seem like a test. I came over with flowers, and you were armed and ready with the Paragon and your kid and told me I was a drunken mistake. Kinda hard to feel the urge to call you again."

"That was a rotten thing to say. I'm sorry for that."

"Well, shit, Parker. I'm sorry I assumed you knew that you were an adult who knew what you wanted. I'm sorry I didn't read your mind."

She blinked. Then she swallowed. "You've made your point, James," she said, her voice husky. "And for the record, I wasn't drunk. I knew what I was doing."

There it was again, her way of saying something abruptly honest. She was so careful all the time, so vigilant about what she'd tell him, and then bam, she'd say something like that, and it was a sucker punch to the heart.

Also, her eyes were wet.

Their last night together, and he was making her cry. Shit.

"Don't cry," he said, his voice soft.

"I'm not," she lied. "I'm sorry for how I acted back then. I really am."

"It's just that I thought about you. A lot." He reached for her hand, ran his fingers over the back of it. She didn't look at him. "For years, if I'm being honest."

That made her glance up. "Really?"

"Yes. Many thoughts." He grinned a little.

"What kind of thoughts?" she asked, a smile of her own starting.

"Dirty."

"Really?"

"Filthy."

"How filthy?" She was smiling in full now.

"Extremely."

"Any interest in pursuing those now?" she asked, raising an eyebrow.

He stood up. "Race you to the house."

LATER, AFTER SEX and peach cobbler and another—and possibly last—round of lovemaking, James was still awake, Parker's head on his shoulder, his fingers in her hair. She was asleep, her breathing soft and slow.

This was it, he guessed. Tomorrow her son would be here, and she was a great mom. She'd focus on him, make Nicky's transitions easier and all that. The kid didn't need his mother's boyfriend in the mix. He couldn't argue with her there.

It was time to let her go. He'd finish what he started with the house and head back to the real world. Parker had a lot in front of her, and she deserved this time with her son to be uncomplicated and happy.

And if that meant being Thing One again, so be it. The last thing he wanted was to make her life more difficult any more than he had already.

He just hadn't imagined it would be this hard.

CHAPTER TWENTY-SEVEN

NOTHING FELT AS good as having her son back in her arms. Nothing.

"I missed you, Mommy," he said, wrapping both his arms and legs around her.

"Oh, sweetie, I missed you, too. Felt like I was going to pop without you."

Nicky laughed at that, and Parker breathed in his good Nicky smell, kissed his sweet little neck again. He'd gained two pounds in the three weeks they'd been apart. She could tell. "Let me see your beautiful face," she said, pulling back. "Oh, my gosh. The handsomest boy in the universe—am I right, Ethan?"

"The image of his father," he agreed with a grin.

"There's a dog! You have a dog! Hi, doggy!" He wriggled out of her arms to investigate, and Beauty, who was crouched in the corner, trembled at his approach.

"She's a surprise for you, honey, but she's really shy," Parker said. "Just hold out your hand and let her sniff it."

Nick obeyed, and, wonder of wonders, Beauty's tail wagged. "She likes me!" he announced, kneeling down, and sure enough, Beauty licked his hand, then came closer. "Mommy, she's kissing me! What's her name? Is she mine? Can I keep her?"

"Her name's Beauty," Parker said. "And yes, we're keeping her."

"Hi, Beauty! You're licking me! Do you think I'm

lunch?" He petted her on the head as the little dog licked his face. "Ew! She licked my mouth. Mommy, when can I go swimming?"

"We can go later on. Do you have to go to the bath-room?"

Nick thought about that, then bolted, slamming the door of the loo behind him. "Sorry!" he called.

Parker and Ethan shared a smile of child-adoration. "I've literally been counting the hours," she admitted. "You want some iced tea? You're staying here tonight, right? It's a long drive."

"It sure is."

"Nicky and I can sleep in his room, and you can have mine," she said. A great excuse to snuggle with her son all night.

"Anywhere's fine," Ethan said. "I have to say, the place looks great, Parker. It's really cute. A lot better than I pictured."

"Thanks. Um, James…you know, Thing One? My father's attorney? I told you he was here, right? Harry made him come. Anyway, he's been doing everything. I just clean and paint." Her ears started itching.

"Is he around?" Ethan asked.

"Nope. Not today." James had said he wouldn't be by today so she could have some time alone with Nicky. He'd even left Apollo, remembering that her son loved the snake, and had offered to take the creature when it was time to leave Maine for good. The thought gave her a pang; not of parting from Apollo, of course, but of the summer ending.

"I always thought he was a good guy," Ethan said.

She was spared from having to comment with Nicky's return. "Mommy, Elephant loves it here! He already found a fort!"

"Elephant! You are so good at finding forts!" She kissed Nicky's favorite stuffed animal on the nose. "So who's hungry? I have enough food for an army, or, in the case of the Mirabelli men, two people."

Ethan had pictures of the big trip on his iPad, and Parker admired them, as well as Nicky's collection of rocks, which he'd brought with him. "This one's quartz," he told her. "And this one is I don't know what. And this one's shale, right, Daddy?"

It was amazing, how much Nicky seemed to have grown up in the three weeks without her. But after lunch, he climbed into her lap and rested his head against her shoulder, and he fit just as well as he ever had. Parker called Lucy, who was fending off the elder Mirabellis and doing a mountain of laundry. She offered to go check on a house Parker had found online; it was a rental in a nice neighborhood—not that Mackerly had slums, exactly—and it was close to Nicky's school.

That night, when Nicky was asleep in his room—it didn't seem like James's room at all anymore, not with Nicky's rocks and Legos and stuffed animals scattered about—Ethan and Parker sat on the small back patio.

"Want to go down on the dock?" Ethan asked.

"Nah," Parker said, feeling her cheeks prickle with heat. "Here's good. The blackflies get pretty fierce on the water."

They sat in the comfortable silence of two people who'd been friends for a long time. But it was a little different now. Maybe it was the three weeks apart, but Ethan seemed…older. A little preoccupied.

"So I have to ask," Parker said. "Is Lucy pregnant, Eth?"

His head snapped up. "Wow."

"Ethan! You dog!" She jumped up and hugged him. "Congratulations, buddy."

He smiled, his mouth curling in what Lucy called his elvish smile, and his eyes were bright. "Thanks. It's really new. She started puking on the trip, and that tipped us off."

"It's wonderful. I'm so happy for you guys." Remembering Lucy's loss of her first husband, as well as her adoration of Nicky, brought a lump to Parker's throat. Lucy and Ethan deserved every happiness. They'd both waited a long time. "What do I have to do to be godmother? Diaper coupons? Free babysitting for life?"

"I'm pretty sure you have it locked down," Ethan said.

Parker sighed happily. "That is the best news. So. New restaurant, new baby. You'll have your hands full."

"In all the best ways. We figured we'd wait to tell Nicky, if you're okay with that. It's early days, and nine months is a long time."

"Good idea." Ethan had never made a misstep as a parent, not so far as Parker could tell, anyway.

"So are you doing okay, Parks?" he asked gently.

"Yeah. I'm actually really good. The house is listed, and now that it's spruced up a bit, I'm hoping to get an offer."

Ethan nodded. He was quiet for a long minute. "How's your father?"

Parker paused. "I don't know. We've had a few tortured conversations in which neither of us says much. According to James, he's fine."

"Have you been to see him yet?"

"No. It's a long drive. About four hours from here, maybe more."

"Nicky was asking about him. Wanted to know if he could visit."

Parker paused. "I'd have to check the place first."

"Your call. But he's curious." Ethan stood up. "Okay, I'm gonna hit the hay," he said. "I was alone in the car with your son for eight hours today. I'm whipped. Your son can talk, Miss Welles."

It was their habit to refer to Nicky as "your son" whenever discussing his, ah, less-than-stellar moments. *Your son put my phone in the washing machine today* or *Your son sang "Wheels on the Bus" for thirty-nine straight minutes.* "Like he doesn't get that from your side of the family," Parker said with a smile. "He's Marie's grandson."

"And Althea's, let's not forget. You guys have a good visit, by the way?"

"We really did. It was different. Nice."

"Glad to hear it. See you in the morning."

As Parker washed up, she could hear Ethan talking to Lucy. She went into Nicky's room, and the sight of his little form there in bed filled her with such a rush of love that her knees went weak. Beauty was snuggled at his side, her muzzle on his hip. "Good girl, Beauty," Parker whispered. She wondered if Beauty sensed that Nicky was hers. The dog hadn't let Ethan near her, slinking behind something when he approached. But she already loved Nick, thank goodness.

Three weeks was too long. She made a mental note never to be away from her son that long again until he was, oh, maybe forty-five or so.

Nice that he'd be a big brother. She'd known it would come, that announcement, and the familiar pang of envy bounced around in her heart with her genuine happiness.

She lay down next to her little guy, stroked his silky hair. The band of worry and loneliness that had been tight around her heart loosened as she listened to his breathing. He was back with her, and all was right with the world.

Even so, she wondered how James was doing tonight. He'd seemed pretty chipper when he left, his duffel bag in hand. Hadn't seemed melancholy at all, whereas she... well. This was a dopey train of thought to pursue.

She got under the covers and snuggled closer. Nicky didn't stir. The kid could sleep through a monsoon and not wake up; had in fact slept through a pretty fair hurricane last year and then had been quite confused as to why so many leaves and branches were on the ground the next morning. She kissed his neck, breathing in the smell of baby shampoo and boy.

They were back together, mother and child. She shouldn't want more.

THE NEXT MORNING, Ethan made breakfast as Nicky explained how many tricks he was going to teach Beauty. "She could jump through my hula hoop. She could catch mice for Apollo. She could jump off the diving board! She can swim with me in the pool all winter long!"

Ethan and Parker exchanged a look. "Well, we won't be living in a house with a pool anymore, remember, honey?" Parker said.

Nicky's face fell. "Oh. Yeah." He looked around the kitchen. "Is this our house now?"

"Nope. This is just for a couple weeks. A little vacation. Then we'll go back to Rhode Island and live near Daddy and Lucy."

"We'll move in with you, Daddy," Nicky said as Ethan put a plate of scrambled eggs and toast in front of him.

Parker gave Ethan a look that said, *Help me out here, pal.* He got the message. "You and Mommy are going to have your own house, and you'll spend half the time there, and half the time with me. Just like always, Nick."

"I want to live with Beauty all the time."

"Well, Beauty can meet Fat Mikey, and maybe they'll be friends." Ethan grinned at Parker; the enormous cat would be more apt to eat Beauty than befriend her, but there was always hope.

"They will be," Nicky pronounced. "They'll be best friends. Except Beauty's scared of you, Daddy. You have to be nicer to her."

At that moment, a knock came on the door, and Parker's heart seemed to roll over in her chest. "Come on in," she called.

"Morning," James said as he came down the hall.

At the sound of his voice, Beauty left Nicky's side and streaked over to him, wagging her tail and whining happily, putting her paws against his leg, the better to get an ear scratch.

"Hey, Beauty." James knelt to pet the waggly little dog, then stood up. "Ethan. Good to see you again." The men shook hands. "How was your trip?"

"It was great, thanks for asking. How are you?"

"No complaints." James's gaze dropped to Nicky. "Hi."

Nicky stared back solemnly.

"Honey, you remember James, right?" Parker asked. "Mr. Cahill? Grandpa's friend?"

"Yes," Nicky said suspiciously. "I remember."

"Can you also remember your manners?" she prodded.

"Hi, Mr. Cahill."

"Did you have fun on your vacation?" James asked, rather solemnly.

Nick nodded.

Not his usual chatty self. Of course. Maybe her son sensed something. Ethan did, apparently, as he was gazing steadily at Parker.

James cleared his throat. "Well, I figured I'd get to work on the stairs to the dock."

"Oh, okay. Um, would you like some coffee?" She was abruptly aware of the little tableau she, Nicky and Ethan made.

"No, thanks. I got some at the diner."

"Want some help, James?" Ethan asked.

James glanced at Parker. "No, no, that's fine. But thank you."

"Parker says you've been great," Ethan added as Nick climbed into his lap. He dropped a kiss on Nicky's head.

"Yes. You've really been...um, great," she blurted. Lordy, this was uncomfortable.

"Well. My pleasure." He paused. "I can come back later, if that would be better."

"No, no. It's fine. Whenever you want, James," she said.

"Do you have a nail gun?" Nicky asked.

James looked at Nicky. "Yes."

"Can I use it?"

"No," she and Ethan said at the same time.

"They're the bosses," James said. "Okay, I'll get to work." With that, he went out the back door, and a few seconds later, the screeching sound of wood being pried up could be heard.

"I wanna help. I wanna use the nail gun," Nicky declared.

"No, Nicky. It's not for kids," Ethan said. "Why don't you work on teaching Beauty a trick? Maybe in your room, so you can surprise us?"

"Okay." Nicky scrambled off Ethan's lap and ran down

the hall. "Come on, Beauty!" he bellowed, and Beauty trotted obediently after him. "Come see Apollo. Do you love Apollo? Mom, can I let Apollo out of his case?"

"No," Parker said. "It's locked, and it's gonna stay that way."

"He wants to come out," Nicky argued.

"He's not coming out," she said. Nicky grumbled but dropped it. Seemed as if he'd gotten a little more willful than she remembered.

"So," Ethan said.

"So." She took a bite of toast. Didn't look at Ethan.

Right from the birth of their son, Parker and Ethan had agreed to share information that might affect Nick. Dating was one of those topics; when Ethan and Lucy had taken up with each other, he'd come to her and made sure she was okay with it. Things like vacations and work schedules, family events, any kind of change that might impact Nick had always been discussed. ·

The subject of Parker having a boyfriend had never come up. She sensed it was about to.

"Are you and James seeing each other?" he asked quietly.

Bingo.

"Not really," she whispered. She was actually more afraid that James would hear; Nick was chanting the word *Jump* over and over in his room. "We, um…we had…" *Jump. Jump.* "He was staying here." *Jump. Jump. Jump, Beauty, jump.* "It made more sense, with all the work we had to do. We hung out a little bit. But it's done now." Ouch. Saying the words out loud…it hurt. She cleared her throat. "I didn't want Nicky to be over-loaded."

Ethan sighed, then looked at the ceiling and scratched

his chin. He was quiet for a minute. "James always struck me as a decent guy."

"Yeah, no, he is. Very decent." She paused. "I didn't always think so, but I do now." *Jump. Jump. Jump, Beauty.*

"So?"

"So nothing. We had a little summer fling, at the recommendation of your wife, I might add, and it was fun. It's also finished."

"Why wouldn't you want it to be more than a fling?"

She took a sharp breath, an unexpected flare of anger arrowing through her. "Well, Ethan, I guess because Nicky's got a lot on his plate right now. Grandpa in prison, new house, new school, new stepmother, new sibling on the way. His mother having a boyfriend doesn't seem fair."

Ethan didn't say anything for a minute. "You have a point. It's a lot. But I'd hate for you to think that your job was to just serve Nicky. If you were in a relationship, he'd adjust, and happily, if it was the right person. I mean, do you think he's less happy because Lucy and I are married?"

"No. He's probably happier. He adores her. But that's different. He's known her his whole life."

"He's known James his whole life, too."

Heck. That was true. And she was tremendously hung up on James; that was also true.

But a real relationship? She had no idea what James had planned for the future. She could ask, of course. Or wait and see, maybe. That seemed safer.

Ethan cleared his plate. "Well, it's obviously up to you. Just don't martyr yourself on the altar of motherhood."

Her mouth dropped open. "Ethan Mirabelli! Bite me." She flipped him the bird.

He grinned. "I'd rather hug you. I should hit the road, anyway."

"Good, because you're a pain in the ass. Get out of here." She hugged him, then smacked him on the side of the head. "Tell your parents I miss them and I'll be home in a couple weeks."

"Tell them yourself."

"You're a cruel man."

He grinned, then went down the hall to say goodbye to their boy.

CHAPTER TWENTY-EIGHT

JAMES WAS BEING watched. For the second day in a row, Nicky Mirabelli was staring him down, sitting at the top of the hill that led down to the dock, idly digging a hole with a gardening spade. Parker was planting flowers, and Nick was allegedly helping. More than that, he was staring at James. Occasionally, he'd announce a fact: *I can swim a mile. I can eat five pancakes. I'm stronger than you.*

It was making James nervous. He'd never felt comfortable around kids, not that he got much chance. The natural, automatic affection that flowed effortlessly from both Parker and Ethan toward their kid...he couldn't imagine that. Maybe it happened when it was your kid. Maybe he wasn't the kid type. That seemed more likely.

"I can use the nail gun," Nicky said now. "My mother said so."

"Really?" James said. "Well, if she tells me that herself, I'll show you how."

"Mommy!" the kid bellowed. "Mr. Cahill said I can use his gun!"

"I did not say that."

"James," Parker said, appearing at the top of the hill, sweaty and beautiful, a red bandanna around her blond hair, "he can't use the nail gun."

"I know, and I didn't tell him he could."

Nicky scowled at James and flung a little dirt down the stairs.

"Come on, Nick, leave Mr. Cahill alone. Why don't you fill up Beauty's water dish, huh? Make sure it's nice and cold."

The kid trotted off obediently.

"You better have a talk with him about going in the water," James said, turning his attention back to the ancient, splintering staircase. "He tells me he's a great swimmer."

"He is, and he already knows."

"Maybe you should get one of those leashes they have. Make sure he doesn't decide to jump off the dock, like his mother."

"I'm not going to leash my child, James." Her voice was sharp. "He won't go swimming without me. He grew up at Grayhurst. He knows the rules."

"So did my sister."

Parker looked away. "I'm sorry," she said in a gentler tone. "I'll talk to him again. But please don't tell me to use a leash on my son. He's a good boy."

James nodded, tore up another chunk of wood. "So how are Mr. and Mrs. Paragon?"

"Are you jealous? Is that what this is?"

"Hey. I'm just the help."

"You're not the— You know what? I think I'll strangle you. With a leash. How would that be?"

"I'd die happy, so long as I was in your golden presence." He smiled at her, perversely happy to see her irritation.

She rolled her eyes and turned to go.

"Parker."

She stopped.

"I'm sorry. I just—" *Your kid is giving me chest pains.* "Your kid doesn't like me."

Her face softened. "Sure he does. He likes everyone. Nicky! Come here, honey!"

"Shit," James muttered. The kid cantered over.

"Do I get to use the nail gun?" he asked, chewing on the ear of a stuffed animal.

That stuffed animal…

"No, you don't get to use the nail gun. Mr. Cahill might stay for lunch. We can have a picnic on the dock and maybe go swimming after that. How would that be?"

"Could I use the nail gun then?" Nicky asked.

James was only half listening. The stuffed animal was familiar. "I like your rabbit," he said.

Nicky spit out the ear. "His name is Elephant. 'Cuz he has big ears."

"I see."

James looked at Parker, who suddenly felt the need to look out to sea. "I think I gave you that rabbit. When you were born," he said.

"No, you didn't."

"I'm pretty sure I did."

"No. Someone else gave it to me."

"Mr. Cahill's right, Nicky," Parker said. "He brought you that in the hospital."

So she remembered.

"You brought me Elephant?" Nicky repeated.

"Yep."

"Can I use your nail gun, then?"

Parker laughed, but Nicky was serious. "Sorry, pal," James said.

"Come on, Nicky. Let's finish the flowers." Parker turned and walked back toward the house.

"I don't like you," Nicky said.

"Sorry to hear that," James answered. It was more mature, he was almost sure, than saying, *I'm not sure I like you, either.*

"How's THAT, MRS. K.?" James asked, wiping sweat from his forehead. Maggie Beaumont's ancient tenant was a tyrant; this was the fourth time James had rearranged her bulky living room furniture in three days.

"It's *wonderful,* honey!" she chirped. "I'm *finally* getting the hang of feng shui!"

Or James was, as the muscle of the operation. "Great," he said. "Can I do anything else for you?"

"No, you've been an *angel!* It's true! Besides, I'm having *dinner* with Maggie and that nice husband of hers tonight. Do you know him? Mahoney?"

"Malone. I was at their wedding, remember?"

"Of *course* I do, dear. You're quite a good dancer. Malone, you're right, that's his name. For some reason, I can *never* remember!"

James smiled. Mrs. K. was a sweetheart, even if she was a despot. And a spy. Still, it was kind of nice to have someone caring when he came and went.

He went upstairs to the tiny apartment, got a beer from the fridge and sat on the floor. The only furniture left was a bed, a little kitchen table and two chairs. But he'd be leaving soon, so it didn't really matter.

The kid had been here for five days. Parker's stairs were nearly finished. And that was a problem, because James was running out of things to do.

He'd gone to see Mary Elizabeth yesterday and sat through *The Holy Rollers in 3-D!* for the second time, which definitely registered him for sainthood. Had a near miss with his father, but luckily, he'd caught a glimpse of his father's battered truck from Mary Elizabeth's window and said his goodbyes before dear old Dad had appeared.

He'd told Dewey he'd help with a few things at the bar. The door to the men's room stuck, a windstorm had blown the gutter off, a faucet leaked in the kitchen. If James was slow and lazy, he maybe had a week's worth of excuses to stay in Gideon's Cove. Real life was waiting. It was time to get back to work.

This morning, he'd had a phone interview with an old crony of Harry's, who was a partner at Goldman Sachs. James was fairly sure a job offer would be coming, the old-boy network in play, despite—or perhaps because of—Harry's felony. He'd have to move to New York, not that he really wanted to, but a job was a job. A buddy from law school had even offered to sublet his Brooklyn apartment for a year. It would be stupid not to take it.

Except he didn't want to leave Parker. Even the kid had his moments. Well, one moment, anyway. James had been at the hardware store this morning, shooting the shit with Rolly and Ben, and picked up a pair of lobsterman gloves for Nicky. The kid had gone wild. Wore them all morning, chasing the dog around the yard, digging with them, trying to eat lunch with them.

"You give really good presents," Parker observed. Then, as if realizing this was too intimate a thing to say, now that they weren't together anymore, she'd sidled off to start the dishes.

That was about as close as they'd come to a conversation lately.

A knock on the door startled him.

Speak of the devil. "Hey," he said, opening the door. "Everything okay?"

"Everything's fine." She smiled. "Can I come in?"

"Sure."

"This is really cute," she said, looking around at the empty rooms. He was going to have to buy a bottle of the shampoo she used and keep it around for an occasional hit, because he was incredibly pathetic. He glanced at her; she was staring at him expectantly.

"Yeah. Um, how's Nicky?"

"Since you left him two hours ago, you mean?" She grinned.

Okay, so it was a stupid question. "Yes."

"He's excellent. We had an early dinner at Lavinia's, and the two of them are playing Nintendo."

"'Soldier of Fortune'?"

Parker laughed. "She does own that one, but no. This is Mario Brothers or something. Anyway." She sat down on one of the two chairs. "How are you?"

Ah. So this was a booty call. There was nothing wrong with being used for sex. Right? So why was he pissed off?

"I'm fine. You want a beer, Parker?"

"Sure. Thank you."

He got her a Sam Adams and poured it into a glass. This was Parker Harrington Welles, after all.

"So what are you doing here?" he asked, handing her the glass.

"Um, just went for a walk. Thought I'd check on you."

"Want to fool around, then?"

"What? Oh. Uh…" The tips of her ears flushed. "I thought we could talk."

"What would you like to talk about?"

She set her beer on the table. "Are you mad at me, James?"

He didn't answer. Because the answer was, of course, yes. He hadn't realized it until now.

"Something on your mind?" she asked.

"Not really."

"Do you want me to go?"

"No." Funny, he used to know how to talk to women.

"Well, what do you want, then?" Her voice was sharp.

You. All I want is you. I want what I saw in the kitchen when Ethan was here. I want your kid to like me. I want you to love me. "Sex would be great, if that's what you're here for."

"Okay, you're being an ass. I'll go now." She got up and went to the door, and if James had a pin, he would've stuck it in his eye, because he was an idiot.

"Parker, wait." She stopped by the door, turned and folded her arms over her chest. Not exactly conducive to soul-baring, but who could blame her? "Look," he began, running a hand through his hair. "I know you and Ethan have a kid together. And I know what a great guy he is."

"What's your point?"

"I also know that when he was with you, he was in love with someone else."

Her jaw tightened. "I fail to see why—"

"I don't have that problem."

Her mouth opened a little, and her eyes widened.

"I don't want to be nothing to you, Parker. I don't have to be…ah, hell, I don't know. But I miss you. I'm with you every day and I miss you, and I hate being near you and not being able to… This summer's been so…"

This was careening toward idiocy. Talking sucked. He took her by the shoulders and kissed her. Hard. Pushed her against the door and kissed her, that beautiful, soft mouth, just kissed her with all the pent-up frustration that had been building in him for the past week. He slid his fingers into her cool, smooth hair and tilted her face for better access to her mouth, his kiss softening as she opened her lips and let him taste her, and please, God, he wanted her so much that his damn heart was about to burst.

She pulled back, her breathing shaky. "Does this place have a bed?" she asked, and James could definitely see why people believed in prayer.

"JAMES! JAMES, DEAR! I need a *tiny* favor!"

Mrs. Kandinsky's peeping voice came clearly through the heating vent, piercing the warm, drowsy fog.

"Is that your other girlfriend?" Parker whispered.

"I was trying to keep you two apart," James said. He leaned over the bed and shouted, "Be there in a few, Mrs. K.!"

"Thank you, dear! You're an *angel!*" she chirped.

"I should get back, anyway." Parker propped her head on her hand and looked at him a long moment, her face serious. "You're not nothing to me, James," she said gently, and the words felt like a gift.

"Glad to hear it," he murmured, pushing a strand of hair behind her ear.

"I do want something with you," she said. "But to be honest, I have no idea how to do this. Whatever it is, it's going to be glacier-slow, okay?"

"I like glaciers."

She smiled, and there it was again, that aching pressure in his chest. Love, or a heart attack. Kind of the same thing.

They pulled on their clothes. James followed her to the door and kissed her, and watched as she blushed and then made her way down the stairs. She waved from the sidewalk, then walked briskly away.

He closed the door, smiling like a fool. An hour ago, he'd been moody, horny and glum.

He wasn't any of those things anymore.

Life was good. Wicked good.

"James, dear! The pretty blonde is gone! Could you help me find the remote?"

"Coming, Mrs. K."

CHAPTER TWENTY-NINE

CHANTAL HAD SHOWN the house twice, and the second couple had seemed genuinely interested. It was August now, and Parker had to face facts. Her time in Maine was winding down. She sighed, sitting down at the kitchen table, the sun streaming in through the windows.

Two nights ago, she and James and Nicky had gone to Dewey's, along with half of Gideon's Cove. Nicky had shown off his impressive belching abilities, though Lavinia had him beat in that area; Parker had held little Luke Beaumont while Chantal and Jonah danced; Maggie sat on Malone's lap to make room for Collier Rhodes, who'd come in to mingle with the locals.

And every time she'd glanced at James, he seemed to be looking at her, a little smile playing on his face.

They hadn't slept together since she'd gone to his apartment. There'd been some very hot groping on the couch after Nicky had fallen asleep one night—the things her boy toy could do with his hands, without even taking off her clothes, should be documented and sent to men everywhere—but James didn't seem to mind that it hadn't gone further. "Another satisfied customer," he'd murmured against her neck, and if she hadn't been so weak and trembly, she would've smacked him. Ended up kissing him instead. He'd left with a grin on his face.

During the day, James was around, putting on some final touches to spruce up the little house. The fresh shin-

gles, green tin roof and the pots of flowers had sweet-
ened the place; it might not be a jewel, but it definitely
looked like a house. Not a shack.

As for Nicky, well, if he didn't adore James, he didn't
hate him, either. But while James did have a knack for
bringing her son great presents—the lobsterman gloves,
a key chain flashlight and a shovel that folded—he
wasn't exactly comfortable around her boy. She caught
him watching Nick a lot, almost the way a person once
bitten by a dog might watch a puppy, as if he wanted to
like her son but wasn't quite sure how to.

But real life was waiting. Parker had to get a job. Since
the ridiculous Ark Angels, she hadn't managed to send in
another idea for a series, and the weekly prodding emails
from her editor only made her sweaty. The creative part
of her brain felt utterly empty.

We were your one and onlies, Spike informed her.

The truth was, she didn't really miss writing—*Thanks
a lot!* the HRs said, pouting. She loved working with
Lavinia, though; Vin had passed most of the duties off
to her and spent her time smoking and reminiscing on
the great loves of her life. Her cousin adored Nicky, and
the two of them spent a lot of time drawing pictures of
swords and maces, Nicky's latest passion.

Another thing to miss about Gideon's Cove. Lavinia.

But Parker missed Mackerly, too; missed Lucy and the
sweet little town, the bakery, the Mirabellis. And now,
she actually had a place to live. The rental deal had gone
through, according to the email she'd gotten earlier.

"Nicky!" she called. "Come see our new place. The
internet's back up." James had brought her an antenna
for her Mac, so she no longer had to traipse to the library
to go online.

Nick came running into the kitchen; James followed,

smelling sharply of wood and paint. "Where is it?" her son demanded.

"It's about three blocks from Daddy's restaurant."

"I'm gonna be a chef," Nicky announced. "Like Daddy. Or a spy."

"Or both," James said.

"Yeah! Both! Which one's my room, Mommy?"

She clicked on a photo. "I thought you'd like this one. See the slanty ceilings!"

Nicky's eyes widened in a most gratifying manner. "It's like a fort! Or jail! Like where Grandpa Harry lives!"

Okay. Change of subject called for. "And here's the yard," she said, clicking on another picture. Tidy and tiny, filled with flowers.

"I could definitely hide there," Nick said. "Mommy, put my room back on, okay?"

"Sure." She clicked on the photo of his room again. A whole lot smaller than his room at Grayhurst, not that he seemed to care. "When are we going back?" he asked. "I miss Daddy."

"Probably next week, honey. Right, James?"

She glanced up at him, feeling a pang already. But he'd be heading back to Rhode Island, too, so they'd still see each other. They just hadn't worked out the particulars.

"Yeah, we're pretty much done," he confirmed. His face was somber.

"Can I try the nail gun? Please? I'm really careful," Nicky said.

She raised her eyebrows at James, who shrugged.

"Only with James holding it, too," she told her son.

"Yes! Let's make something, James! Come on, come

on!" He grabbed James's hand and towed him outside. James glanced over his shoulder.

"Be careful," she said.

"Got it," he answered. He smiled, and her heart lurched. Her guy, her son, together. She sneaked outside, camera in hand.

James was kneeling behind Nicky, putting on safety glasses. "You don't want to shoot your eye out, so you always wear these," he said.

"I love these," Nicky answered reverently.

"Good. Now we're gonna hold the nail gun up like this—nope, I'll hold the shingle, okay? You put the gun right there, where the nail's gonna go…good boy, now squeeze—"

Bam! The nail went in and Nicky flinched, dropping the gun. James caught it. "Good job, kid."

"I did it!" Nicky's face was alight with joy. Men and their tools, Parker thought with a smile. She raised her camera and took a stealth picture.

"Can I do more?" Nicky asked James.

"Sure. Nice and careful, now, and try not to drop the gun."

"It makes a loud noise."

"It does. You're right."

Parker went back inside, feeling a wicked case of the Warm Fuzzies. Nauseating term, excellent feeling. Her menfolk, bonding. It'd be good for them both.

The photo of Nicky's attic room was still on the computer screen.

A jail, like where Grandpa Harry lives.

A bit hesitantly, Parker picked up her phone.

James hadn't mentioned Harry lately. She herself hadn't talked to her father for a while. Well. Being a minimum-security place, inmates were allowed to get phone calls pretty liberally. She figured she'd give it a shot.

"Harry Welles, please? This is his daughter speaking."

A few minutes later, her father's commanding voice came on the line. "Parker. Is anything wrong?"

"Hi, Harry. No, everything's fine. I had a second, figured I'd call." A breeze blew in from the cove, fluttering the kitchen curtains.

"Oh." There was a pause. Another bang from the nail gun came from the side of the house. "How's my grandson?" Harry asked.

"He's wonderful. He's here, in Maine with me. He had a great time in Yosemite."

"Good."

Another breeze. Nice day, the sun shining, temps in the upper seventies.

"So how are you, Harry?"

"I'm fine."

"Got enough to read?" It was the only question that came to mind.

He sighed. "Yes."

Parker glanced at the computer. "Nicky and I found a place to live. In Mackerly. We'll be heading back next week."

"I see. He's starting school?"

"Yes. After Labor Day."

"Wish him luck for me."

"I will."

There didn't seem to be anything else to say. She waited to see if her father would offer any other subject, but there was only silence. "Well, take care, Harry."

"You, too." He hung up.

A memory of her father picking her up from Stanhope Academy on the Upper West Side came to her. She'd been in second grade, wore a white shirt and green plaid skirt as a uniform. Her father rarely came to get her from school, and the sight of him there, so unexpected and so impressive, had practically lifted her off the pavement. "Daddy!" she'd said, running to him, and she remembered how small her hand felt in his. How safe Harry had made her feel.

Back then, her father had been her favorite person in the world.

She swallowed the unexpected lump in her throat.

Parker went back outside. "Boys," she said, "I think we should go on a picnic."

TWO HOURS LATER, Parker, James, Nicky and Lavinia were at a lake somewhere west of Gideon's Cove. Beauty and Nicky were already wet, having dashed in the second they'd gotten there. Nick hurled sticks as far as his little arm would let him, which wasn't terribly far, but Beauty charged in each time. James and Vin were sitting on a blanket, laughing. Those two were BFFs, practically.

Pine trees surrounded the lake in a dense wall, broken only by the occasional boulder. There was a dock about thirty yards out, and three teenage boys had canoed out there. They were shoving each other and laughing, falling in occasionally, diving like otters, constantly in motion. She snapped a few photos. Maybe this could be her new job—photographer. Or, given her actual skill set, cashier at Wal-Mart, if Wal-Mart would kindly hire her.

"Mom! Mommy! Watch me! I'm a dolphin! I'm dolphin diving!" Nicky yelled. She watched, laughed and snapped a few shots. "Now I'm a shark, Mommy! See? See my fin! I'm eating a seal!" Nicky thrashed around, causing Beauty to yelp in ecstasy.

The sun beat on her hair. No need for highlights after this summer, though she probably had a few new wrinkles after all the wind and sunshine. A few more muscles, too, though the eleven pounds hadn't gone anywhere.

"I'm hungry," Nick said, sloshing onto shore. "Vinny, can I please have some chips?"

"Sure, gorgeous," Lavinia said, offering Nick the bag. Parker looked out at the deep blue lake, so pure and inviting.

"Vin? Want to go swimming?" she asked.

"Hell, no," her cousin answered.

Parker sighed. "James, that leaves you."

"Hell, no," James echoed.

"Hell, no," Nicky said, falling to his knees and digging in the sand like a dog. Beauty joined the effort.

"Come on, James," Parker said. She took off her sweatshirt and slid out of her shorts.

"That bathing suit is not fair," he murmured.

"You look like one of those whatchamacallits," Vin said, taking off her post-cataract-surgery sunglasses. "*Sports Illustrated* models."

"Right. Just with stretch marks and the cellulite I got for my last birthday."

"You're perfect," James said.

"Aw," Vin said. "Go with her, Jamie. Buddy system and all."

He shook his head.

"Are you scared, James?" Nicky asked, pausing in his digging.

"Yep," he answered.

"Really? But you're a grown-up, aren't you?"

"Grown-ups can be scared, too."

"I swim a lot," Nick said. "I could probably swim ten or thirty miles. It's not scary."

"No, it's not scary. I only think it is," James said.

Parker studied his face. "Have you been swimming at all since…then?" she asked quietly.

"Nope."

"Will you come now?"

He hesitated. Glanced at Nick.

"Whoever goes swimming with me gets ten kisses," Parker announced. "Nicky? Want ten kisses?"

"No," he said. "You kiss me all the time. I want ten dollars. Or ten lobster claws. Or ten nail guns!"

"Lavinia?" Parker asked.

"I'm with the kid. Ten bucks, maybe. For fifty bucks, definitely."

"James?"

He looked out to the water. "How far do I have to swim for these ten kisses?" he asked.

"To the raft."

"She won't kiss *you,* James," Nicky explained, his tone tolerant. "She's not your mommy."

"Go on, you two," Lavinia said. "I'll watch the kid."

James glanced at Lavinia, then back at Parker. With a sigh, he pulled his T-shirt over his head.

"Now we're talking perfect," Lavinia said, lighting up a cigarette and squinting appreciatively. "Very nice, Jamie."

Parker took his hand and towed him to the water's edge, where he stopped. "Come on, James. You can do it."

"I hate the water."

"I know." She went in up to her knees, still holding his hand. "Come on."

His jaw was tight, and no smile lightened his face at

the moment. Took a few steps in. "You're doing great," she said, going in a bit deeper, not letting go of his hand. He followed, reluctantly.

When they were waist deep, Parker stopped to let him get acclimated. His face was a little pale under his tan. She swam out a few feet, then turned to look at him. "Harvard Varsity Swim Team, James. Third Olympic alternate. Red Cross certified in lifeguarding."

"Very impressive," he murmured, his eyes on the raft. The three boys had gotten back in their canoe and were now fishing in the middle of the lake.

"You can do it," she said. "You have to someday."

"Do I?"

"Yep." Parker swam out a little farther and started to tread water. "Swim to me, beautiful man," she said. "I'll take care of you."

His eyes were dark and a little tormented. "Not fair," he said, and with that, he dived under the water. He surfaced just past her and swam, steadily, if a little desperately. One yard. Four. Ten. Parker kept pace easily off his right, her eyes never leaving him. When he reached the raft, he grabbed onto the ladder and waited for her to get up first, then followed, water streaming, his hair nearly black with the wetness, drops of moisture sliding down the planes of his face. He didn't look at her, just sat, breathing hard.

Parker slipped her hand in his. He was shaking. Probably not from cold.

"You did it," she whispered.

"Hated every second."

"And you did it," she repeated.

He still didn't look at her, just stared back at the shore. Nicky waved. "See? It's not scary!" he yelled, and James waved back.

The planks of the raft were dry and gray, and the water lapped softly at the edges. A seagull called from overhead. Lavinia coughed, then said something to Nicky. The sound of his laughter floated out to them.

"Shit," said James. "I have to swim back, don't I?"

"'Fraid so," she answered.

Finally, he looked at her, squinting a little in the sun, and studied her face. "When do I get to collect my prize?" he asked.

She glanced at Nicky, who was occupied with digging. "Now works for me," she said, her legs tingling a little.

He leaned over and kissed her, a long, lingering kiss. "That's one," she said when he pulled back.

"Ew! Gross!" her son yelled from shore. Shoot. Busted.

"You're right, Nick," James yelled back, grinning. "I should've asked for ten dollars!"

"I told you so!"

"I woulda held out for at least twenty," Lavinia called.

James looked back at Parker, the drops of water sliding down his brown skin. His smile faded, and his eyes were serious. "I love you," he said.

Then he pushed off the raft and was in the water, swimming back to the safety of the shore, leaving her feeling fragile and precious and completely new.

FROM WHERE HE LAY on the dock back home, James could hear Parker singing "Home on the Range," which was apparently her son's favorite bedtime song. Lavinia had left an hour or so before, and Parker's voice and the gentle slap of the waves were the only sounds. Overhead, the sky was a dark purple, a sliver of crescent moon slicing through the clouds that slipped past.

Happiness wasn't a feeling he was used to. He'd been

pretty content the past few years, grateful to Harry, glad to be able to provide for Mary Elizabeth. He'd had fun, sure—Leah had been fun, as had been dinners with Harry, playing basketball with the guys on Saturday mornings, catching the occasional baseball game.

But that was nothing compared with this. Today, he'd been part of something.

A family.

The kid wasn't his, but the little guy's wriggling delight at finally being able to use the nail gun, the way he'd grabbed James's hand…it had touched some part of James he'd thought had been erased eighteen years ago.

But now, the time before the tragedy kept running through his head. Christmas mornings, fishing trips, running for the school bus with his three brothers, telling Mary Elizabeth stories well past her bedtime. He'd been part of a family once, and when that family fell apart because of him, he'd assumed that was it. When you're told over and over by the father you once worshipped that you don't deserve to be loved…it sinks in. It seems true.

James had simply thought that some people were cut out for family life. Others, like him, were not.

Until today. Today, he'd had a family—Lavinia and Parker and her son. Today, a kid had held his hand. By the time they'd gotten back from the lake, Nicky had been sound asleep in his booster seat, and James had lifted him out, cradling the little guy's sweaty head, shifting his limp weight onto his shoulder and carrying him inside as Parker held the door. The four of them had had hot dogs and salad for dinner, and he and Vin had done the dishes while Parker and Nicky fished off the dock.

It felt better than he could have ever imagined.

Maybe, he thought, maybe it was time to let the past go and stop blaming himself for Mary Elizabeth. Maybe being an irresponsible twelve-year-old kid didn't warrant a life sentence.

Earlier today, he'd gotten the call from New York. The job offer had been finalized, the package details had come through today; the pay was close to what Harry paid him, signing bonus, sweet benefits…all thanks to Harry's recommendation. Last month, he would've taken that job without hesitation. Last week, even.

Things were different now. For him, certainly. For Parker, too. Whatever she wanted, however she wanted it to be, that was all fine with him, so long as he could be near her.

Mine.

Kind of a caveman word. It fit, though. She was his. He'd seen it in her eyes today on the dock.

He heard the back door close, and Beauty came trotting down the new stairs and flopped down next to him on the blanket. Then the dock rocked a little harder, and the other beauty came, her long hair down, wearing a white dress, her feet bare. "Shoo, puppy," she said, and the good dog obeyed. Parker sat down next to him. "Nicky's asleep. Tired from all that swimming." She paused. "He wouldn't wake up if there was a buffalo stampede through his room. I'm just mentioning that." She was smiling.

"Good to know." He felt himself smiling, too, and reached up to touch her cheek.

Parker reached down and started unbuttoning his shirt. Yep. Best day ever.

But next week was looming; New York wanted an answer by Friday, and today was Wednesday. He put his hand over hers. "Parker, I should tell you something."

She lifted her eyes to his. "So serious, Thing One. You're not pregnant, are you?" She grinned.

"Uh…no. Are you?" He jerked into a sitting position, the same icy rush of terror he'd felt today just before diving under the water washing over him.

"Me? No, no, I was…I was kidding." She frowned.

"Okay. Great. Try not to kill me, Parker."

Her eyes narrowed a little. Shit. "But if I was—I'm not, don't worry—would that be horrible?"

"Uh…" These were the conversations that doomed many a man. "I don't know. I mean, no. Not horrible."

Beauty, maybe guessing that James had given the wrong answer, crept closer to him and curled at his side.

"Not horrible." Parker glanced out at the water. "Okay, maybe this isn't time for a big conversation, but maybe it is, too. Look, obviously the summer-fling idea has grown into…more. And this afternoon at the lake, I believe you made a certain declaration." She raised an eyebrow.

"Yes. I did."

"I'm not proposing or anything, James." She squeezed her little finger. "I just assumed you meant in a long-term, monogamous kind of way."

"Yes. Absolutely."

"You weren't just drunk with fear?"

He grinned. "Well, there was that. And the sight of you in your bikini. Though, admittedly, you look better out of it."

She smiled, then looked down at her hands. "Well, someday, maybe, I could see possibly having another baby. Adopting, maybe. Or the other way."

"With me."

She closed her eyes. "No, James, with the guy who rotates my tires. I mean, I'm not asking for anything carved in stone, okay? But I like children. And I don't want to rule out— Well, I'm thinking someday in the distant future, I mean, not too distant, since I'm thirty-five. But not tomorrow, either." She was squeezing her little finger half to death. "You know what? I shouldn't have said anything. I have no idea how we got on this subject. Can we forget I ever said anything?" She pulled her hair onto one side of her neck and looked out at the lobster boats.

"I'm in."

Now who the *hell* said that?

She blinked a few times. Looked back at him. He didn't look away.

"You're in. Like, you'd be interested in a family. Maybe. Someday."

"Yes."

He remembered the first time he'd seen her, holding her son.

Pictured the scene again. This time, though, the baby was his, too, and he was the one at her side.

Mine.

He took her hand and kissed it, then looked at her face. "I want to ask you something."

"Okay," she breathed.

"You wearing anything under that dress?"

She burst out laughing, the sound bouncing out over the water. "Why don't you find out, Thing One?"

CHAPTER THIRTY

THE RUMBLE OF A TRUCK in the driveway the next morning made Parker's heart lift. The sight of James, clad in jeans and a Joe's Diner T-shirt, had her break into a little trot. "Hey," she said, ruffling his hair.

"Hey," he echoed, grinning the *I've seen you naked* look. Heck yeah!

Nicky was in the yard with Beauty. "James! Watch this. Beauty, roll over! Roll over! Roll over! Like this!" He demonstrated rolling in the grass as the dog yelped happily.

"So," Parker said, surreptitiously brushing James's hand with her fingertips, "I thought I'd go see my father today."

"That's great," he said, his smiley eyes so dark and happy. "He'll be glad to see you. But listen, when you get back, I want to talk to you about something."

"Oh, right. We never did get to that last night."

His smile flashed again. "No. We didn't."

"Can it wait till I get back?"

"Sure." His eyes dropped to her mouth. *He's totally into you!* the female Holy Rollers sighed. "You guys have a good time," he said, still looking at her mouth.

"Actually, I figured I'd leave Nicky with you."

His smile dropped. "Isn't Lavinia around?"

"She's around. If you need help, you could give her a

call. But I figured you boys could hang out. Pee outside, hammer things, do what men do."

James ran a hand through his hair. "Okay. But I...I don't have a lot of experience with kids."

"Well, feed him once in a while, and if he asks if he can drive your truck, the answer is no."

"Parker, I'm not sure if I'm, um, qualified."

"You are," she said softly. "James. He's the person I love most in the world. I wouldn't leave him with just anyone." He didn't look convinced. "Besides," she added, "it'd be good for him to spend some time with you."

He hesitated, then nodded. "Okay. Thank you."

"Thank me when I get back. If you still have the capacity for speech, that is." She turned to the yard. "Hey, Nicky! James is going to stay with you today while I run a few errands, okay?"

Nicky bolted up from the grass. "Yes! Can we use the nail gun? Can we? Huh? Please, James? Please? Yes? Is it yes? We can do it now, if you want. Do you want to? Let's go."

Parker's mood was light as she drove the Volvo southwest. Where the talk of babies had come from last night, she had no idea. *Oh, please. It was totally Freudian,* Spike said. *Your subconscious wanted to have the baby talk, and bang. The baby talk occurs.*

"I love babies," Parker said aloud.

No matter what, though, it was nice to think about the future. *Their* future. *I'm in,* he'd said. Parker could see where he'd be hesitant and unsure. But she'd seen his face as he lifted her sleeping child from the car. She'd also seen what it took for him to swim to the raft yesterday. James might not have any idea how big his heart was, but she did.

She caught a glimpse of her face in the rearview mirror. She was smiling.

So this was love. Funny how it had crept up on her, this feeling. Sure, Thing One had always been attractive, and yes, they'd had that shag three years ago. But it was odd; she almost couldn't remember him before, when he was her father's puppy. Now when she thought of him, she pictured his smile, his big, work-roughened hands and kind eyes. Now, she was thinking of him as...well, hers.

Yep. Hers. Nice word. Aware that she was now not only smiling but also humming, and possibly purring, Parker pulled off the highway. She had time for a stop, and Harry would appreciate the gift. Maybe. Hopefully.

New Hampshire North Side Correctional Facility looked like a big box store. The men wore blue work shirts and pants, resembling custodians more than convicts. The visiting room was a cafeteria-like space, the tables and chairs bolted to the floor.

When Harry came in, Parker almost didn't recognize him. No power suit, no sleek haircut, his gray hair now thinner and a bit scraggly. He'd lost a little weight, too, and his face was slack. "Dad," she said, standing up. The word surprised her.

"Parker. How are you?" They looked at each other for a second, not sure what to do next.

"No touching," the guard said, relieving them both of the awkwardness of expectations. They sat. There were several other families in the room—a man and his wife and three children were playing backgammon; a couple murmured in the corner, leaning toward each other so that only an inch or two separated them.

"So this isn't too bad, is it?" Parker asked.

"It's not the Drake," Harry said.

"No." She pulled the envelope from her bag. "Brought you some pictures."

Harry's face softened as he looked. They were of Nicky; she'd stopped at a CVS on the long drive in and had them printed. "He's gotten big," Harry murmured.

"Yeah." She tried to remember the last time Harry had seen her son and couldn't. Easter, maybe. "He says he has a loose tooth."

"Is that right?"

"I can't tell, but he says so."

Her father smiled faintly, still gazing at the photos. "He looks like you."

Parker snorted. "No, he looks like Ethan. Almost exactly."

"No. Very much like you at that age." Harry glanced at her, suddenly wary, as if he'd crossed a line. "Well. A good-looking boy, that's for sure." He put the photos back and passed them to her. "Thank you for showing me."

She slid the packet back toward him. "They're for you, Harry."

"Oh. Well. Thank you even more." He looked at the envelope, resting his fingertips on it. "Have you told him I'm in jail?"

Parker gave a half nod. "I told him you were in a time-out for grown-ups."

"Maybe I could talk to him sometime."

"Sure. That would be nice. Um, I did tell him you were in here for being greedy and breaking some rules."

"True enough," Harry said, studying the table. An awkward silence fell.

Okay. So they'd covered Nicky, and it was reassuring that Harry had wanted to talk to him. He might not be the best grandfather in the world, God knew, but he wasn't the worst, either. Maybe his time in here would help her father figure out some priorities.

On to the next topic. Parker racked her brain for something neutral to talk about. "So what do you do in here to pass the time?"

Harry shrugged. "I read. There's a gym. Sometimes we have television privileges. Go to meetings."

"What kind of meetings?"

"Alcoholics Anonymous."

Wow. Okay, yes, she knew her father could put away the wine and scotch. Once, when Nicky was a baby, James had driven Harry to Grayhurst and put him to bed, but Parker'd been too busy with trying to soothe her colicky child to really take note. Figured it was a case of overindulgence, not really *alcoholism.* "Are you... Is it really a problem? Your drinking?"

"No, Parker, it was AA or cribbage, and you know how I hate card games." He lifted an eyebrow. "My name is Harry, and I'm an alcoholic. Didn't really realize it till I had the DTs in here, but yes, I have a problem. I hid it well," he added, reading her mind.

"So how long have you—"

"Oh, probably since college, technically, though I suppose it got worse after your mother left me."

Parker shut her mouth, which was hanging open. "This is a bit of a bombshell, Harry."

"Really? You didn't know?"

"Nope."

"Well. I suppose that's good." Harry drummed his fingers on the tabletop.

"Speaking of Mom," Parker said, still a bit stunned. "She came to visit."

Harry pursed his lips. Parker wasn't sure, but that

might've been regret in his eyes. "And how is she?" he asked.

"She's good."

"Glad to hear it."

Another silence fell. She glanced at the clock; she'd been here ten minutes.

"How's James, by the way?" Harry asked.

Parker felt her face warm. "He's good. Um, he's been fantastic this summer." Should she tell her father they were together? Or maybe that should come from James. She wasn't really sure how to handle that topic.

"Has he started yet?" Harry asked.

"Started what?"

"His job."

She felt her stomach tighten as if against a blow. "His job?"

"Yeah. Mitch Stravitz, remember him? At Goldman? No? Well, he's been to the house a number of times. Came for that wine tasting where we went through the case of the '82 Margaux." Harry smiled in fond remembrance. "Anyway, he was happy to do me a favor. This whole insider-trading charge was completely blown out of proportion. Once I'm back, it'll be like nothing ever happened. Sort of like the Mafia. Everyone does their stint in the joint." Harry laughed his client laugh, that low, insincere Hollywood laugh.

Parker was finding it hard to draw a deep breath. "Hang on, Harry. James is working at Goldman Sachs? In New York?"

"In the legal department. Yes."

"Do you know when he starts?"

"Next week, so far as I know." Harry frowned at her. "He didn't mention it, I gather?"

"No," Parker said calmly. "It didn't come up."

"Huh. He got an apartment and everything. I figured he'd have told you. Is he still in Maine?"

"Yep. Still in Maine. For now." She forced herself to smile. "How's the food here?"

THE DRIVE BACK to Gideon's Cove was much longer than the drive down had been. Or so it seemed.

So while Parker had been talking about a long-term monogamous relationship with a possible baby in the future, James had been planning to trot down to Manhattan. He had a job waiting for him. He had an *apartment*. On the one hand, he said he loved her. On the other, he was moving. And he'd never said a word. Maybe that's what tonight's talk was about.

She could see the future spreading bleakly in front of her. She'd get a job, share Nicky with Ethan and Lucy. James would come up a weekend or two, but he'd be busy. Time together would be harder to manage. In the end, he'd feel guilty and burdened, and she'd feel bitter and resentful.

"I'm an idiot," she said aloud.

It's just that last night, out on the dock…it had seemed so… Oh, crikey, how many women read into these things? How many men said what a woman wanted to hear, simply to make the moment easier?

Well. She and James were going to have that talk when she got home, that was for sure. She checked her phone. No new messages. Just as well. This was a talk to have in person, and besides, she was entering the area where cell-phone service started to cut out.

The Holy Rollers were silent. Polly patted her shoulder, but no one had anything to offer.

When she finally came into Gideon's Cove, the town seemed oddly vacant. No one was in front of Dewey's, and almost no cars lined Main Street. The sun was sinking into the sea, one last ray cutting right into her eyes as she drove past the fisheries parking lot and onto Shoreline Drive

Then she saw the lights.

Fire trucks, the ambulance, a dozen pickup trucks and cars, in front of…in front of…in front of her house.

Malone saw her coming, opened the door for her before she'd come to a complete stop. She got out, but her legs buckled, and he caught her. "Nicky," she managed to say.

"He's missing," Malone said in his rumbling voice. "Whole town's looking for him."

SHE COULD SEE EVERYTHING, but nothing had any impact. The fire chief had sad eyes. Maggie was holding her hand so hard it hurt. Lavinia choked on sobs, sitting on the runner of a fire truck. Rolly, Ben and Stuart stood to one side, saying nothing. James was wet. Jonah Beaumont pulled on his scuba gear, his face white. Collier Rhodes was on his phone.

Parker could hear herself answering questions, but she felt so deep inside herself that it was like looking out from the bottom of a deep, dark mine shaft. She was feeling for her son—*feeling* for him, reaching for him. *Where are you, sweet boy, come to Mommy—*

"A blue T-shirt with a dinosaur skeleton on the front. It glows in the dark. Brown shorts," she said in answer to a question. *Please, God. Please. Please. Anything but this.*

Her son had been gone for two hours. Two hours, and she hadn't even known. They'd tried calling her, but the damn cell-phone service sucked up here in this miserable, godforsaken county.

The dive team was in the water.

The dive team was in the *water*.

Please, God, don't let him be in there, but the images were too clear, his little body being pulled up, limp and white, a tiny casket, Ethan devastated, their beautiful boy, gone. Parker choked, started to gasp, her breath yanking in and out of her chest. Maggie hugged her, hard. "Easy, Parker, easy," she whispered.

That's right. She didn't have the luxury of her own feelings. Her son needed her. She would not fall apart now.

"Give me a minute," she said, her gaze glancing off James, who looked decades older. She put her hands over her ears, muffling the sounds of radio and talking. Closing her eyes, she thought.

"Where's the nail gun?" she asked. The chief glanced at someone else, a look that clearly said, *She's losing it.* "Is the nail gun around?"

James bolted into the darkness. A second later, he was back. "It's not in my truck. That's where I left it."

"Okay, so he took it. The nail gun is with Nicky, so he probably went off to make something." He could've gone down to the dock to drive nails. He could've fallen in. "Has anyone talked to Ethan? Maybe Nicky called him?"

"I did," James said. "He hasn't heard from Nick. He's getting a flight up."

"Where was he the last time you saw him?" she asked James, forcing herself to look at him, and in that moment, she *hated* him, God help her, and hated herself, as well, because she'd left her *baby,* her boy, her son, with him, and James had lost him.

James flinched, as if he knew what she was thinking.

"I was making dinner. Macaroni and cheese. He was on the couch, playing with his little computer thing—"

"Nintendo." God, she'd left her son with a man who knew *nothing* about children, who'd *told* her he knew nothing about children, and she wouldn't listen, she did what she wanted—

"—and then he was…gone." His voice broke. It didn't matter. He didn't matter. Only Nicky mattered.

"Did you go anywhere today? To the hardware store? To the harbor?"

"No."

"Maybe he went to the Pines," Lavinia suggested in a wobbly voice. "I told him his great-great grandfather built the place."

The chief dispatched a crew to go up the street. Collier squeezed Parker's shoulder and went with them.

It was fully dark now.

What did Nicky love? What would make him go off…?

"He's hiding," Parker said abruptly. "He hides all the time. He loves forts, and he took the nail gun and he's hiding in a fort somewhere. Where's Beauty? Maybe she's with him."

Beauty, who never barked at strangers; Beauty, who hid when people came into the house.

"Call the dog," the chief instructed. "People, quiet down!" The crowd, which had grown to maybe fifty or so, grew silent. "Cut the trucks." The growl of the town's three fire trucks died abruptly. "Go ahead, Miss Welles."

"Beauty!" Her voice was quavering and weak. "Beauty, girl! Come on!"

Everyone was silent, listening.

"Beauty! Come on, girl! Let's go for a swim! Come on, Beauty!" Better, if edged with hysteria.

There was nothing but the sound of wind and water.
Oh, please, God, please. She tried again. "Beauty!
Come on, sweetie! Let's go for a swim!"

Then she heard it—the whine of her faithful little dog.

"Over here!" someone yelled, and Parker was running. People were shining lights at the bottom of the
house, where James had put up latticework so no skunks
could get under there. But there was a shallow scraping
in the dirt, enough so that a child and a dog could fit
under there. James ripped off a great chunk of the lat-
tice, and Parker grabbed a flashlight and wriggled under,
spiderwebs veiling her hair, sand in her pants. Then her
light caught the reflection of her dog's eyes, and she saw
Nicky's head, the cowlick he got from Ethan. "Nicky?"
she called, reaching out to touch him. He was warm. He
was breathing. "Nicky, sweetheart?"

Her son opened his eyes. "Mommy! You're back."

"I got him," she called over her shoulder, and a cheer
went up from the crowd. "Nick, we've been looking for
you, baby."

"I fell asleep in my fort," he said, rubbing his eyes.
"Mommy? Why are you crying?"

LATER, WHEN EVERYONE had patted her son, when Chief
Tatum had given him a plastic fire hat, when the yard
and road had cleared, when Ethan had been called, when
Nicky had been fed and bathed, Parker just held her son
on her lap.

"I'm sorry," Nicky said for the millionth time.

"This is why you tell me if you're going to hide,"
Parker said, kissing his head.

"You weren't here." There was a hard edge of resent-
ment in his little voice.

No. She wasn't. "You should've told James, then."

"I don't like James," Nicky said sullenly, and Parker knew he blamed James for all the fuss, for Mommy being scared and crying. "I want to go home and live with Daddy."

"We're going home in a few days."

"Good. Because I hate it here. And I wanna live with Daddy." He started to cry.

She kissed his head and held him a little tighter. "Listen, honey. Everyone makes mistakes. It's what you do after the mistake that really matters. You don't hide without telling a grown-up, and you never go somewhere you don't know is safe. Promise me, Nicky. It's really, really important."

"Fine. I promise." He took a shuddering breath and snuggled closer. "I love you, Mommy."

"Oh, sweetheart, I love you, too. So, so much."

She held him until he fell asleep, breathing in the scent of baby shampoo. Then she put him in her bed and got in beside him, calling quietly to Beauty to jump up next to them.

Thank you, God. She could've been in the E.R. right now. She could've been watching a boat drag the harbor. She could've been picking out a little casket. *Oh, Jesus, thank you for sparing me that.*

Little sobs jerked out of her as she smoothed Nicky's hair. Beauty put her muzzle on Nicky's leg and watched with her mournful eyes as Parker wept.

Her cell phone buzzed, and she looked at the screen. Ethan.

"Hey," she whispered. They'd already spoken twice since Nicky had been found.

"How is he?"

"He's asleep."

Ethan exhaled slowly. "Good. He sounded scared before."

"Yeah. It was…intense."

They were quiet for a long minute. "It'll be good to have you both home," Ethan said eventually.

"I can't wait," she said honestly.

"Me, neither." Ethan sighed. "This hiding thing…it can't happen again. He did it in Muir Woods, ducked behind a tree, didn't answer when we called, and I almost lost it. Gave him a mammoth lecture, took away dessert, made him go to bed early. I thought he was over that phase."

"Well. Seeing everyone looking for him drove the point home, I think." She traced the outline of their son's ear.

"Good." There was another silence. "Poor James. He must've been scared shitless."

"He was."

"Well. I hope you get some sleep tonight, Parks. Here, Lucy wants to say hi."

"Hey, sweetie," Lucy said, and the sound of her voice caused more tears to flow, but when Parker hung up sometime later, she was calmer. These things happened. Parents lost years off their life simply by being parents. The vision of the dive team in the water, looking for her son…that would haunt her forever. But Nicky was safe, and nothing else mattered.

The exhaustion of the day caught up with her in a wallop, and suddenly her eyes burned. She turned out the bedside lamp and cuddled her son close.

Just before she fell asleep, something clicked.

James had been wet because he'd gone in the water, looking for her son.

CHAPTER THIRTY-ONE

JAMES LAY AWAKE all night, adrenaline still flying through his veins, his heart stuttering and racing in fits.

The day with Nicky had been pretty okay, up until then. They'd gone for a walk on the beach and climbed the rocks exposed by low tide. Had peanut butter and jelly sandwiches for lunch. James had read *Hungry, Hungry Sharks* four times in a row. They'd played hangman and tic-tac-toe. Drew pictures. Told knock-knock jokes.

The whole time, James had watched the kid like a hawk. Didn't let him out of his sight. Said no to every dangerous activity the kid suggested, which had ruled out climbing trees, jumping on Parker's bed, a game of hide-and-seek and swimming.

"Let's use the nail gun," the kid had suggested.

James had considered it. Pictured taking Nicky to the E.R. because he had a nail through his hand. "Maybe tomorrow."

The kid pushed out his bottom lip. "You kissed my mom." It was an accusation.

James took a slow breath. "Right. I did."

"Why?"

What do you say to that? "Well, she's nice."

"She's *my* mother."

"Oh, definitely. Your mother."

And the kid had seemed satisfied with that. Then he'd

asked if he could play his little handheld computer game, and James said sure, he had to make a quick phone call. Went into the kitchen, called Goldman Sachs and told Mitch Stravitz no thanks.

Because Parker Harrington Welles loved him, and he wasn't going to move a hundred and fifty miles away from her. No way.

He hung up, gave the mac and cheese a stir, glanced into the living room. The kid was gone.

At first, James had thought Nicky had gone to the bathroom. A minute or two later, he knocked. No answer. Opened the door. No kid. "Nicky?" he'd called.

Not in either bedroom. Not in the kitchen. Not on the patio. Not in the yard, not in the truck. James heard his voice growing louder, then more desperate.

The dock.

The water had been as cold as death, and it was hard to see, the salt stinging his eyes. Rocks. A beer can. A school of fish, darting away into the dark, deep water.

The lake water had been much clearer the day Mary Elizabeth had almost drowned. Her little hand, so peaceful almost, no resistance left in it, like an underwater plant, drifting in the current—

"Nicky!" he heard himself yell, his voice hoarse with terror. "Nick!"

Two more dives before he realized he needed help. Called 911. Went back in the water until the dive team came and James was shaking so hard with cold that he couldn't speak.

Then Parker's face, utterly white in the deepening gloom of the night. *You lost my son,* her eyes said. *You killed my baby.*

And then she found him. All by herself, she figured out what the entire fire and police department and twenty-five volunteers couldn't.

The little bastard was hiding.

"Didn't you hear James calling you?" she'd asked sharply, even as she clutched him against her.

"We were playing! It was a game!"

"Now, now, don't be too hard on the little guy," the fire chief had said. Easy for him to say. In that moment, James was so, *so* glad he wasn't a father, because honestly, he could've killed the kid, he was so relieved.

Parker hadn't spoken to him for the rest of the night, too focused on her son. A doctor was there—Maggie's brother-in-law—and he'd checked Nicky out for any concussion or whatnot. Hard to believe the kid had slept through fire sirens and all, but Parker confirmed her son slept like a rock. Her eyes slid off James's face as if she hated him.

Twenty-four hours from love to hate.

He couldn't blame her. He'd lost her son, and the kid could've just as easily gone into the water and died, all because James had no fucking clue. *You should've paid attention,* his father had screamed at him in the hospital after Mary Elizabeth had been whisked away. *You stupid, selfish little shit,* each word a bullet.

No. Family life was not for him.

This whole thing with Parker was over. That was clear.

WHEN THE SUN HAD FINALLY risen and a decent-enough hour approached, James got dressed. Dockers, blue oxford with the sleeves rolled up. His carpentry work was finished.

He looked in the window; Lavinia was already here, playing cards with Nicky on the floor of the kitchen. James knocked.

"Hey there, Jamie," Lavinia said. "Come on in, sweetheart."

"I'm looking for Parker, if she has a minute," he answered. "Hi, Nick."

Nicky didn't answer. Refused to even look at him.

At that moment, Parker came into the kitchen, and the sight of her hit him like a truck.

"James. Hi," she said warily.

"Hi. Sorry it's so early." It was after nine, not really early at all. "Got a sec?"

"Sure. Um, Nicky, I'll be right back. Vin, you don't mind keeping an eye on him, do you?"

"Not a bit," Lavinia answered. "See you, James."

So Lavinia already knew he was toast.

Parker came out and walked around the house to the street side. Not down on the dock, thank God. She stopped and folded her arms.

"Parker, I'm so sorry," James began.

"It's okay. Nicky hides all the time. All's well that ends well. It wasn't your fault."

Sure it was. He could feel it.

"Thank you for trying to find him," she added, finally meeting his eyes. "It must've been horrible for you."

"No. I mean, it was... I thought he—" The thought was too unspeakable to finish. "I'm glad he's okay."

"Yes." She looked at the yellow and orange lilies along the fence, which she'd liberated from a bank of weeds a couple of weeks ago. "I heard you took a job in Manhattan."

Harry must've told her. "Yeah."

"It sounds perfect for you. Congratulations."

And there it was. "Thanks. They just called. Last week."

She nodded, glancing at him, then away again.

"James, I'm sorry about the conversation the other night. I was...I don't know. Caught up in the whole summer-romance thing. Sorry if I seemed like another desperate single woman talking babies. The truth is, I don't want any more kids. One's enough, right?"

"Yeah. Sure, he's a great kid." He glanced at the house. "Anything else you need me to do here?" he asked.

"No. Thank you. You were so helpful, James."

He nodded. "Well, I'll probably see you before you head back for Rhode Island. I have to help Dewey with a couple things, so I'll be around. I'll...I'll pick up Apollo before I go."

"Thank you."

And with that, he went back to his truck and backed out of the driveway.

CHAPTER THIRTY-TWO

IT DIDN'T FEEL RIGHT, having the summer end like this.

Three days after Nicky's incident, and Parker was still tense. She hadn't seen James, though he'd come by when she was out and taken Apollo, leaving her a note that only said to call if she needed anything. On the house front, there'd been only one solid offer, so she supposed she'd have to take it, though it wasn't a heck of a lot. Another couple had made a higher offer, but they had to sell their own place first, and time was of the essence for this sale. She and Nicky needed to get back to Rhode Island, settle into the new place. Two college friends said they could hook her up with a job—insurance or technical writing.

She really couldn't picture doing either one. Then again, she hadn't been able to picture fixing a leaky toilet before this summer, and she'd managed to do that.

They were leaving on Monday; today was Saturday. There'd be less traffic—more time to pack, not that there was much to pack up. Maybe she was stalling. She didn't know.

Nicky, on the other hand, couldn't wait to go. He'd been sullen since the night he hid, kept asking when he could go back to Daddy, and was generally rubbing Parker's last nerve to a bloody nub. She found herself counting the hours till bedtime, then feeling like a horrible parent because she was so eager for her child to go to sleep.

It was Parker's last day at the shop. There was a funeral in the next town, and she and Vin were making huge, somber arrangements. Well, Parker was; Vin was having a smoke, watching Nicky draw on the sidewalk with chalk through the window while Beauty kept him company.

"You gonna forgive that boy?" Lavinia asked abruptly.

"Nicky?"

"No, Parker. Jamie Cahill."

"Oh." She paused. "There was nothing to forgive. It really wasn't his fault."

"Well, he sure looks miserable. Saw him at Dewey's last night. You dumped him, didn't you?"

Parker glanced up, then resumed stripping the leaves from a stalk of gladiola. "No. It ended. He took a job in New York. I'm going back to Rhode Island. That's all."

Vin took a deep drag on her cigarette. "Coulda fooled me. The kid looks like what's-his-name. Spartacus?"

"Spartacus?"

"What's-his-name. The guy who turned in Jesus."

"Judas."

"Ayuh. That one. Guilty."

"Well, he has nothing to feel guilty about. Here. I'm done."

Lavinia turned her attention to the arrangement. "Shit, that's real nice." She frowned, her face creasing like a shar-pei's. "I'll miss you, Parker. Nicky, too."

Parker's eyes suddenly filled with tears. "I'll miss you, too, Vin. I don't know what I would've done without you this summer."

"Ah, you would've figured something out. Don't get all mushy on me now."

Parker hugged her, trying not to breathe in the scent of smoke. "Will you come visit me? Maybe for Thanksgiving?"

Lavinia tilted her head. "That'd be great, Parker. You mean it?"

"Absolutely. Please come."

Her cousin smiled. "Then sure. Being as we're family and all. Okay, gotta get this over to the church. I'll see you for dinner tomorrow. I'm making clam hash. Don't make that face—you'll love it."

That afternoon, as Parker was reading *David Gets in Trouble* to Nicky, he suddenly pulled on her sleeve. "Mommy?"

"Yes, honey?"

Her son's face was somber, his hands clenching his Obi-Wan and Darth Maul figurines. "I heard James calling me, and I didn't want him to find me."

She closed the book. "Why not?"

"Because I dunno." Nicky looked at his lap and made Darth Maul take a stab at Obi-Wan.

"You must know a little. Weren't you having fun together?"

"Sort of. Not really. He told me I couldn't use the nail gun. And I already did use it, and I know how."

"Well, if James said no, that was the end of it, Nicky. You don't run away and hide because you didn't get your way! Daddy and I have both talked to you about this."

"He's not you or Daddy. So he's not the boss of me." Nicky slammed the figurines together, his mouth obstinate.

Ah. "No, he's not Mommy or Daddy," she said, gently turning his face so he had to look at her. "But he was the grown-up in charge, and, Nicky, you scared him! Did you know he thought you were in the ocean? He went swimming to look for you, honey. In the cold, cold water."

Nicky's eyes filled with tears. "I didn't *mean* to scare him. I wanted to hide and have him be sorry he bossed me. I took the nail gun, but I didn't even use it. I listened. And then I felled asleep. It was hot under there." His mouth wobbled and two tears slipped down his chubby cheeks.

Parker took a deep breath. "Okay, honey. Thank you for telling me. Will you tell James you're sorry?"

"He doesn't like me."

She didn't think that was true, but it was a moot point. He was heading for New York. The end. "You still have to apologize. You can write him a note and draw a picture if you'd rather do that."

"Okay." Nicky scrambled off the couch and ran into his room, slamming the door. "Sorry!" he yelled.

Parker sat for a moment, stroking Beauty's head. Maybe Lavinia would babysit for an hour or two after dinner. Because despite the job in Manhattan, despite the fact that she'd made a fool of herself with talk of babies to a man who clearly didn't want any, Parker didn't want James to think that Nicky's disappearance had been in any way his fault.

Vin came over for dinner and was more than happy to babysit. Parker smiled, watching the two of them; Vin was teaching her son poker. Her cousin was definitely an unexpected benefit of this summer.

She decided to walk into town, realizing abruptly how much she'd miss Gideon's Cove, the constantly changing sounds of the ocean, the rush of wind through the sea grass, the sweet smells of Maggie's baking that drifted from Joe's Diner each morning. She'd miss the cries of seagulls and the rumble of the small fleet coming in each night.

She'd miss the people, who'd welcomed her without a second thought, without judgment.

Mostly, she'd miss James.

She never thought she could be that type of woman, who blushed when a man smiled at her. Who felt a man's presence before she could see him.

That moment at the lake when he'd said he loved her… that was one of the happiest moments of her life. It was shocking, the impact of those words.

Well, hell. She seemed to be crying a little bit.

She wiped her eyes and peeked inside the window of Dewey's. James might be there, after all. Apparently not. Seemed as if the rest of the town was, though. Parker could see Maggie talking animatedly, her hands flying, as Malone looked at her, a faint smile on his face, radiating Satisfied Alpha Male. Chantal and Jonah were there, cuddled against one another, and Christy and her husband. The waitress from the diner who never seemed to wait tables. Beth Seymour, who'd tricked her into taking Beauty. She owed Beth a drink, that was for sure. There was Dewey, squeezing between tables, pausing at the table to talk to Rolly, Ben and Stuart. Collier Rhodes was with them, no doubt getting his fill of local color, schmoozing with—and probably boring—the working class.

Was that how she'd been in Mackerly? Gracing the masses with her presence, swooping in from Grayhurst occasionally to buy a round at Lenny's? That wasn't how it felt, but it might've been how it seemed. She'd always been grateful to live in Mackerly; grateful to have an in via Ethan and Lucy and their families. She lived in Grayhurst because it was there, and it held some happy memories. Some bad memories, too, but more of the happy variety. She hoped she hadn't seemed like a snob, or worse, an idiot.

Well. Time to see James and say goodbye.

The thought hurt so much it pushed the air from her lungs. She didn't *want* to say goodbye to James. She didn't want him to go to Manhattan and become a Harry. He was better than that.

Besides, she loved him. The incident with Nicky—she was past that. They could both get past that, hopefully. In her pocket was Nicky's note: a drawing of Beauty holding Apollo in her mouth—it looked as if Beauty was eating the python, but no, Nicky had informed her Apollo was simply getting a ride—and the words *I'm sorry James from Nicholas Giacomo Mirabelli.*

She went onto the porch of the two-family house where he was staying and paused, looking in the window of the first floor; the little old lady who lived on the bottom floor of the house was sleeping in front of her huge TV, where a slasher flick was playing in gruesome detail. Parker smiled a little, then went up the stairs to James's apartment.

She knocked, albeit very quietly. Her heart was pounding rather erratically in her chest. Crikey, it was terrifying, this…this vulnerability. But he'd said he loved her. That had to count for something.

There was no answer to her knock, and she couldn't see anything through the little window. Maybe he'd already left town. The thought made her mouth dry.

The door was unlocked. Parker went in, biting her lip. "James?" she said quietly, setting Nicky's drawing on the counter.

The bedroom door was closed, but light shone from under the door, and she could catch a few strains of music. Okay, great, he was here. She ran a hand over her hair, swallowed, then knocked and opened the door at the same time.

"Hi, baby!" said a voice.

A woman's voice.

A woman was in the bed. Naked. A very surprised-looking, very well-endowed, very *perky* young woman. Wow. No cellulite there—or anywhere—that was for sure. Candles flickering on the windowsill. Harp music coming from an iPod speaker.

James had left. He was gone.

The two women stared at each other, frozen for a horrible second. Then Boobalicious jerked the sheet up to her chin. "Oh, my gosh! I'm so, so sorry!" she spluttered. "I thought you were someone else!"

"Oh, no, me, too," Parker said. "I'm really, really sorry."

He'd moved out. She'd missed her chance. Her throat tightened as if Apollo was wrapped around it.

"I—I'll go," Parker said. "My friend used to live here. I didn't realize he already... I'll— I'm so embarrassed. And so sorry."

The woman smiled sheepishly. "No, no, I should've locked the door. My bad, totally. I'm waiting for my boyfriend. Obviously. Duh, right?"

"Well." Parker half grimaced, half smiled. "You have a good night."

"Thanks." Beautiful girl. Woman. Whatever.

Parker turned to leave, then froze.

Apollo's glass tank was in the corner, complete with the python curled up inside.

Then the bedroom door opened, and there was James, a six-pack of beer under one arm.

"James," Parker breathed.

"James!" the naked woman said at the same time, albeit much more enthusiastically. "Hi, baby!"

CHAPTER THIRTY-THREE

THIS COULDN'T BE HAPPENING. His luck wasn't *this* bad. A guy goes to Jason's for supper, comes home to find… this?

James's eyes ricocheted from one woman to the other. Nope, his luck really, really sucked, apparently. And what do you say in a situation like this?

"Hi," he ventured.

"Surprise!" Leah said. "Um, this nice lady came to see her friend, who, like, lived here before and just moved. Awkward! Right?"

Oh, indeed. James seemed to be paralyzed. *Speak, idiot,* his brain commanded. But Leah was in his bed— *Leah,* for God's sake. How the hell had she found him, even, let alone wound up in his apartment, in his bed, naked? Because yeah, there was her left breast, and while it was a completely excellent breast, he could've sworn they broke up, and she and her fabulous rack really had no business being here.

But here she was. Her pretty red hair was curled, she was all made up, there were candles burning—he didn't even have candles…hell, she must've brought them herself—and it was clear what Leah had in mind.

And in this corner, there was Parker, wearing jeans and a Joe's T-shirt and flip-flops, her hair in a ponytail. And if—just if—she'd come over to offer the proverbial olive branch, James sensed his odds were falling. That instead of a branch, she might whip out a chain saw and cut off his arm. Or another body part.

He was so screwed. "Uh...Parker, this is a friend from home. Leah, this is Parker." Yes. What was the etiquette in a situation like this? Last names? No?

Leah sat up straighter, finally pulling the sheet over her breast. "Parker? Parker, like, Welles? I'm *so* happy to meet you! You're Harry's daughter, right? Cool! James has told me a lot about you! You're an author, right? Really cool."

"A pleasure to meet you, too, Leah," Parker said, her rich-girl drawl in full glory. "I gather you're James's girl-friend."

If looks could castrate...

"Well, yeah." Leah's voice was charmingly sheepish. "We've been together since, oh, man, that wedding on New Year's, right, James?"

He didn't answer.

"Eight months. That's great," Parker said. Her expression and tone were completely pleasant. "Obviously, my business with James can wait until after you two catch up. Welcome to Gideon's Cove. Have a wonderful night."

She walked past James, not touching him. "She's *totally* nice!" Leah said. "I thought she'd be so stuck-up!"

"I—I'll be right back," James said. "Stay here." The door to his apartment closed as Parker left. Way too classy to slam it, of course.

"I wanted to surprise you," Leah said, a hint of a pout creeping into her voice.

"And you did," he said over his shoulder. "Be back soon."

He bolted out the door, clattered down the stairs. "James!" said Mrs. Kandinsky, opening the door.

"There's a very *pretty* young lady here to see you! And I believe that children's author just left!"

"Thanks, Mrs. K.," he said, not stopping.

"Always in such a *hurry,* you young people," she commented.

Parker was already a block ahead of him. "Parker! Wait up!" he called. She didn't slow down. He didn't blame her.

He caught up to her in front of Dewey's and grabbed her by the arm. She shook him off. Already, people inside were watching them. "Parker, it's not what you think."

She gave a bitter laugh. "Wow. That was *really* the wrong thing to say."

"I didn't know she was coming! I had no idea! You heard her. It was a surprise."

Parker tilted her head and looked at him, her expression calm. "How old is she? Just out of curiosity?"

"Um, twenty-two? Twenty-three?"

Clearly that was the wrong answer, because Parker jerked the door open and walked up to the bar. "Hello, Dewey," she said pleasantly. "I'd like a glass of your best scotch, neat, if you don't mind."

"You bet, Parker." He winked.

"Parker." James came up beside her. "I really need to—"

"Hey there, Parker!" said one of the Three Musketeers…Stuart, who'd helped Parker paint her bedroom. "How's it going?"

"Well," she said, smiling at the old man, "I've been better, Stu. How are you? How's your knee?"

"Not so bad. You look upset, sweetheart. Anything I can do?"

"If you could keep James here from talking to me, that'd be great."

James flinched. "Parker, please let me explain."

"The lady doesn't want to talk to you," Stuart said pleasantly. "Sorry, son."

Dewey placed the glass in front of her, and she drained it in one gulp. His uncle's eyebrows rose.

"Parker—"

"James, I do not wish to speak to you at this time. Please leave me alone." Her voice carried through the bar quite clearly, especially as everyone had stopped talking.

James glanced around. Chantal shot him a smile, and her husband made a sympathetic *Dude, you're screwed* grimace. Malone was less friendly, giving him the Stare of Death.

"I had no idea she was coming," James said, turning back to the subject at hand and doing his best to ignore the nearly silent bar. "I had no idea *you* were coming. You could've called, Parker. You have my number."

"I definitely wish I *had* called, believe me," she answered, not looking at him. "Then I might've learned that you have a girlfriend. Dewey, can I have another one? Thanks, buddy."

"Parker, I don't have a girlfriend. I broke up with her. Months ago," James said.

"Well, I'm pretty sure the fact that she came all the way up here, lit all those candles, took off her clothes, got into your bed and called you 'baby' shows that she, at least, thinks you have a girlfriend." Her eyes were diamond-hard.

"That's really not honorable, man." This from the rich guy. Great. Collier Rhodes, there to pick up the pieces.

"Parker, Leah is not the… She's not my girlfriend. We

hung out a few times. I told her I was going to Maine for the summer— Do we have to discuss this here?"

"You know, it's ironic. I used to think you were just like my father, but you changed my mind this summer. But here you are, exactly like him. The son he never had. Twenty-two, huh? Twenty-two. Wow."

"Parker," James ground out, "please tell me why you wanted to see me."

Parker swallowed her second scotch and turned to look at him fully. "I came to tell you this, Thing One." Great. He was back to Thing One. "Nicky told me today that he hid on you. On purpose. He heard you calling and he didn't want to come out. And I was concerned about you, James, because I knew you felt responsible for losing him." Her voice thickened with tears. "So don't. Don't feel guilty about that." Her voice took on an edge, rising in volume. "But the fact that you were planning to move to New York while I was thinking about babies and long-term relationships? Feel guilty for leading me on."

"Parker, I wasn't—"

She cut him off. "Oh, and the naked woman in your bed with the candles and music? Yes. Go ahead and feel guilty about *that,* Thing One!"

There was a moment of absolute silence in the bar.

"Unattended candles are a leading cause of house fires," someone said, and there was a ripple of nervous laughter.

"It's not what you think, Parker," James said.

"No," she agreed, looking at him, and for a second, he saw hurt flash across her eyes. "It's not." She reached into her pocket and fished out some bills.

"On the house, honey," Dewey said, giving James a dirty look.

"Let me take you home." Collier Rhodes stood next to James. "Buddy, I think she's done with you."

"Thanks, Collier." Parker stood up and looked over the bar patrons. "Guys, it's been absolutely lovely being here this summer. Thank you for all your help and hospitality. I hope to come back and visit. Sorry for the drama."

"Oh, no, it's nothing," Chantal said. "Don't even worry about it."

"Come to the diner for breakfast tomorrow," Maggie said. "Bring your little cutie."

"I will. Thanks."

And with that, she left, not looking back at him. Collier held the door.

When James got back to the apartment, Leah was dressed, her little overnight bag sitting by the door. "Hi," she said wetly.

"Hi," he murmured.

"I guess I'll go. I'm really sorry. I should've called."

James sighed and glanced at his watch. He sat heavily in the other kitchen chair and scrubbed a hand through his hair.

"Leah, I have to say, I'm really surprised to see you."

"I stopped in at the hardware store, and some old guy told me where you lived." She looked like a pinup girl, all chest and hips and little rosebud mouth. Pretty as anything. She bit her fingernail, then folded her hands. "James, I know we put things on hold, sort of. Well, you did. I was pretty into you. I thought if I could surprise you and remind you that I'm really fun, then maybe you'd want to get together again." Her voice faded to a whisper as she spoke.

He sighed. God, he was tired. He hadn't slept much since Nicky disappeared. "You *are* fun, Leah. You're really nice and sweet and fun."

"Just not what you're looking for." A tear dropped onto the table, and she smeared it with one fingertip. "You're a really good guy, James. That's not easy to find."

He looked at her a long minute, then took her hand. "I'm sorry."

She swallowed and shrugged, trying to smile. "So you and Parker finally hooked up, huh?"

He nodded. "Hooked up and broke up."

"You in love with her?"

Another nod.

"Figures. I'd probably be, too, if I was a guy. Or a lesbian."

He had to smile at that. "Leah, I meant what I said. You're great, and you're gorgeous, and someday, you'll—"

"Meet the right guy someday and have babies and a dog."

"Exactly. But I'm not the right guy."

She surreptitiously wiped away a tear. "At least you never led me on. Never pretended it was more than it was."

No. He'd used her and let her use him, and somewhere along the line, she'd fallen for him, and he hadn't noticed.

"Stay here tonight. You can have the bed. It's a long drive."

"Okay. Thanks."

He sighed, squeezed her hand and stood up. "You hungry?" he asked. "I make some killer pancakes."

CHAPTER THIRTY-FOUR

TWENTY-*TWO*.

Maybe that wasn't what should've stuck with Parker, but hell. Twenty-two. Thing One's girlfriend was *thirteen* years younger than she was. Thirteen years! No stretch marks there. No droopage. No crow's feet when you're twenty-two.

"Here you go, Parker," Maggie said, setting down a plate of French toast and bacon. "Mind if I join you?"

"No, not at all." Her son was washing the floor with Georgie, apparently the greatest activity on God's green earth.

"So how are you today?" Maggie asked gently.

"Well, I'm pretty embarrassed. I don't usually go to bars and screech at people."

"No? A pity." Maggie smiled. "Once, I got drunk at a church supper and told our priest I was in love with him."

"I feel better," Parker said. She squeezed Maggie's hand. "Everyone has been so nice to me in this town."

"We like you," Maggie said simply. "So tell me about home."

Parker did, describing Mackerly and its many charms, the Mirabellis, Lucy's little café, the beautiful library where she and Nicky had spent so many hours, the bridge over the tidal river.

It would be so good to get back. Back and safe from

the vagaries of love and lust and whatever else was mucking up her life.

"Maybe we'll come visit sometime," Maggie said. "I haven't been to Rhode Island in ages."

"I would love that! Malone was the first person I met here. I'm very…fond of him. Is that okay to say?"

"He's hot, what can I tell you? Women love him. And he has no idea, which only makes him hotter. Oh, hey, speak of the devil. Matthew Malone, come sit with your bride. Our friend's leaving tomorrow."

Malone sat next to Maggie, who immediately popped up. "Oops. Tavy's giving me the evil eye. Better get back to the kitchen. You two talk. If I don't see you before you go…well, I have your email." She reached down and hugged Parker, and Parker hugged her back.

"You married well," she said to Malone as Maggie went back into the kitchen.

"Ayuh." Malone watched his wife, a smile playing around his eyes, then looked at Parker. "You okay?"

"Ayuh." She grinned. "I've been wanting to say that for two months now."

He smiled in full. Damn. The guy was hot, all right. Good for Maggie.

From the corner, Nicky laughed at the wonder of the mop bucket. "Mommy! I want to be a bubble boy when I grow up! Like Georgie!"

"Sounds like a plan," she said, smiling over her shoulder. "Thanks for watching him, Georgie."

"You bet, Parker."

"He's not watching me, Mom! I'm his helper!"

Parker winked at Georgie, who was clearly enjoying having a protégé. "My bad." She turned back to her breakfast companion, who seemed utterly content never to say another word. Made him seem wise. "So. Fun doings last night, huh?"

He gave a half nod. "I've seen worse."

Twenty-two.

She believed James. Well, she believed that he *thought,* kindasorta, that he'd broken up with the Playboy bunny in his bed. But men were often vague, weren't they? They might not be real clear, in case things with someone else didn't work out. They might make promises they didn't really mean—*I'll call you when I get back from Maine,* he might've said to the bunny. Or, *I'm in* when asked if he might want to settle down and be part of a family.

Yes, men had their little escape hatches. If life got boring, they could always screw the babysitter, for example. Weren't entire chapters of *The World According to Garp* devoted to screwing babysitters? Men always had ways of keeping their distance. Jobs, another example. They had to work hard in big cities and spend their free time with twenty-two-year-olds while their wives raised their kids and hoped they'd come home.

You never knew.

Malone was looking at her. She took a sip of coffee. After last night, she felt she'd spilled more than enough.

"Hey, good morning. How are you? I was really concerned." Malone sighed as Collier Rhodes sat next to her in the booth.

"Hey, Collier. Thanks again for the ride," she said.

"Oh, my pleasure, of course. Damsel in distress, right? I'm so sorry that you were victimized."

Parker suppressed her own sigh. Her own fault for stomping into Dewey's and making a scene—though it had been somewhat satisfying. "I wouldn't call it victimized, but I appreciated the ride."

"Of course. Hey, Judy," he said, calling to the heavyset waitress, who appeared engrossed in a crossword puzzle. "I'd love the house special today! Except, maybe instead of eggs, it could be egg whites? With a little fresh cilantro, if you have it? And no bacon…maybe some turkey bacon if you have that. Some OJ, no pulp, and a flaxseed muffin, if Maggie made any of those?"

"I don't even know what flaxseed is," Judy said, not looking up from her paper. "Why don't you ask Maggie yourself?"

"Okay! Will do, Judy! Gosh, this is the best place, isn't it? I love it here. I come in every day."

Malone raised an eyebrow at Parker, and she stifled a smile.

"Say, Parker, I saw the for-sale sign in front of your house," Collier said, turning to look at her. "Why is that?"

She glanced at Malone, who rolled his eyes. "Because it's for sale?" she suggested.

"Excellent! I was thinking it'd be a great house for a caretaker. Because, like, my travel schedule is a little crazy. Did I tell you I'm booked on a speaking tour? It's called 'Living the Life Fantastic.' Now, I didn't pick the name, trust me, my agent did, but I thought, yeah, I need a caretaker. Back before I retired, I'd close up the house for the winter, but since I plan to pop back and forth between gigs, I'd like to have someone keeping an eye on it, turn on the heat, stock the fridge. Is your place winterized?"

"Uh, it needs a little work." *A furnace, for example. A cellar.*

"It's a jewel," Malone said gruffly.

Parker blinked.

"Malone, my man, you're so right!" Collier exclaimed.

Parker suspected he had a man-crush. "It really is a jewel."

"Historic, too," Malone said, taking a sip of coffee. "Built as a companion house to your own."

Historic companion house, her ass. It was a fortified shed. She felt the wriggle of laughter trying to force its way up her throat. The creases around Malone's eyes deepened.

"It's really not winterized, Collier," she said, unable to lie.

"That's okay! Have you had any offers?"

"Actually, I'm, uh, considering a couple right now."

"Shoot," Collier said. "Well, what would I have to offer to beat it?"

Parker paused. "Well, Chantal is handling—"

"Double it," Malone suggested. "You want the house, go for it."

Holy halos. Malone was pimping her house. Even so, doubling it was crazy, and Collier had been nothing but nice, if somewhat vacuous. "Well, Collier, doubling it would be a bit—"

"You know what?" he interrupted. "Malone's right. I want the house. I'll double the higher bid. I'm sure I can swing it."

"I'm sure you can, too," Malone said. "A man of action." He toasted Collier with his mug and smiled at Parker.

"Fantastic! This is so great! Thank you, Parker! I'll call Chantal and get you a cashier's check right away." Collier beamed, then got up to harass Maggie about his omelet.

Parker sat there for a minute. "Malone," she said, "don't take this the wrong way, but I love you."

He winked. "Take care, Parker."

"You, too, hottie." Then she got up, tousled his hair and fetched her son from the wonders of the storage room.

SHE PACKED UP NICKY and left at dawn the next day, not wanting to see anyone on the way out. It was hard enough. Beauty was curled up next to Nicky's booster seat, and her son was chattering away.

She'd deposited half of Collier's check into her bank account yesterday afternoon. It would be a pretty good nest egg, enough to carry her and Nicky until she settled into a job, enough to put a little into savings. She planned to make a donation to the lobstermen's society in honor of Malone, and another one to the Gideon's Cove Animal Shelter.

The other half would go to James. Parker had given Chantal instructions to give him a cashier's check. He'd certainly earned it. And aside from that, she wasn't going to think about James Francis Xavier Cahill.

There was a lump in her throat as she turned past Joe's. You're Leaving Gideon's Cove, a sign announced. We Hope You'll Come Again!

CHAPTER THIRTY-FIVE

"IT'S THOSE IDIOT parents of hers," Lavinia said at Dewey's on Sunday night. "They screwed her up and good. And the father of her kid, he's no help. Mr. Perfect."

"Thank you," James muttered.

"So what are you gonna do, sweetheart? I got the impression she was pretty fond of you."

He sighed. "Not so much anymore."

"Love sucks."

"I'd have to agree." He looked at Lavinia's face. "I thought you were pretty happy, though. You and the judge?"

"Ah, that ran its course. Just physical. We broke up last night. Think he coulda told me before we played two rounds of 'Spank Me, Nanny,' but no."

James choked. "Men," he managed.

"Exactly." She gave him a long look. "So what are you gonna do, hon?"

"I'm gonna go home, get a job, keep on keeping on."

"Well, Jamie Cahill, you come visit me when you're in town. You're a good egg."

James smiled. "Thanks, Vin."

He said the rest of his goodbyes the next morning; his uncle hugged him and messed up his hair, Maggie and Christy and Chantal all kissed him and fussed over him, so it was apparent that no one really held the Leah issue against him.

No one but Parker, of course.

The cashier's check for his half had been like a kick in the groin. And while he could've used it for Mary Elizabeth's fees, he didn't want to. "Tell you what," he'd said to Chantal. "Make it out to Save the Children."

He had almost nothing to pack—just a duffel bag with his clothes and his tools.

First stop, Mary Elizabeth's.

As always, seeing his sister lifted his spirits. They took a walk. She didn't ask about Parker, but he saw that her room was filled with Holy Rollers crapola—a big poster from the movie, Manga versions of the book and several stuffed animals, including a kitten that could flatten out as if roadkill, then pop open again, with wings coming out of a zippered compartment in its back. Sick, really. Carol at the front desk told him it had come from New York the week before.

"I'm drawing a horse," Mary Elizabeth announced now, reaching for the crayon box.

"I'm drawing a cow," he said.

"Don't draw a cow, James," she chided. "You can't ride a cow."

"This is a riding cow," he said. "You'll see. It could beat your horse in a race any day."

His sister looked up at him, her eyes so blue, and laughed her squeaky laugh, then went back to her artwork.

What would life be like if she'd listened to him that day? If he'd been a better brother, a better babysitter, paid more attention? Would he have left Dresner, or stayed and become a carpenter? He'd probably be married by now. Maybe a couple of kids, even.

He remembered Nicky's warm, sweet weight as he'd

lifted the boy from the car. The joy on his face when James had let him use the nail gun.

"You think I'd be a good father?" he asked his sister.

"Aren't you a little young for that?" she asked, sounding for the life of him like a normally functioning adult.

"I'm thirty, Mare."

She looked up from her drawing. "You are?" He nodded. "Is that old enough to be a father?"

"Yep."

"You give good presents. That's important. Presents are important." She bent back over her drawing.

He smiled.

"You always take good care of me," she added, and her words clamped like a vise around his heart.

"You take good care of me, too," he said unevenly, leaning over to kiss her cheek.

She glanced at his picture. "That's the worst cow I ever saw."

THE LAST TIME HE'D BEEN in Dresner had been two Christmases ago, at his brother Peter's house. He'd stayed out of the way, gave all the kids the latest model of iPod and counted the minutes till he could leave. Only Mary Elizabeth, who left Beckham Institute for holidays and one weekend a month, had been really happy to see him.

He hadn't been to his parents' house in, oh, maybe seven, eight years.

The place looked the same. His father's pickup was in the driveway, along with Mom's old Buick. Not that she drove much anymore.

He knocked on the door, heart pumping in slow, heavy beats. His mother answered. "Yes?" she said.

"Hi, Mom," he said.

"Oh, *James!* Hello! Come in, honey! What a nice surprise." She was slurring, and her hair was matted on one side, as if she'd just woken up.

He kissed her cheek dutifully. Yep. Thems were Jack Daniel's fumes.

"Frank, look who's here! It's James!" Mom weaved into the kitchen and sat down. "You want some coffee, honey?"

"No, I'm good," James said. "Hey, Dad." He extended his hand; his father shook it, not looking him directly in the eye.

"So what brings you here?" Mom asked, taking a sip of her own doctored beverage from a mug.

"I'm on my way home," James said, sitting down.

"You still working for that Ponzi-scheme guy?" his father asked.

"Actually, I'm unemployed at the moment."

"So your brother tells us." Frank Cahill looked both pissed off and pleased.

"It's good to see you, honey," his mother said, smiling. She'd always been the kind of drunk who thought she covered well.

"You, too, Mom." He shifted in his chair, the same worn vinyl chairs they'd had since he was a kid. "I just saw Mary Elizabeth."

"My angel," Mom murmured, her mouth wobbling. His father rose to leave.

"Dad, wait. Please. I need to ask you guys something."

"Frank, sit down!" Mom said. "James is hardly ever here."

His father sat back down. "What?" he growled.

James took a deep breath and looked at his parents, his bleary- and blue-eyed mother, his angry, bitter father. "I want you to forgive me," he said.

"Ah, Jesus," his father said.

"Dad, Mom, I wish—"

"You wish! Who cares what you wish? You were supposed to take care of your little sister!" his father barked, slamming his hand down on the table. "You said you'd stay home and watch her, and instead I come home to find her half-dead! All because you wanted to watch the fucking television!"

"I know."

"And look at her now!"

"I know."

"So how dare you ask us to forgive you? Your mother's never gotten over it. Neither have I. And Mary Elizabeth…" His voice choked off. "She has to be cared for the rest of her life."

"I know," James said. "And I'll always take care of her. I'd have her live with me, if you'd let me. I've asked you that before."

"Right. So you can ignore her again? She's got the mind of a seven-year-old, James! You can't take care of her!"

"Yes, I can. And I would. I'd—"

"No. You can't."

James looked down at the table. "Okay. She's your daughter."

"Damn straight." Frank sat back in his seat and folded his arms.

James sighed. "I'd still like you to forgive me."

"Let's not talk about this," his mother said, pulling a tissue from her pocket and wiping her eyes. "This is not pleasant."

"Look," James said, looking at the scarred tabletop. "I screwed up. But I was twelve years old, and you know how she was. She did what she wanted, and we all let her get away with it. I told her not to go swimming, and she didn't listen, and yeah, I should've watched her better. But, Dad...kids screw up. I tried to save her. I did my best. I did everything I could, and I'll always be sorry it wasn't enough. I would've given my life for her. But I can't keep living under what happened when I was twelve. It's killing me, Dad."

"You don't look dead to me," his father said coldly. "You destroyed this family."

James nodded wearily. "But I love my sister."

Frank gave a disgusted snort. "I think it's time for you to go."

How easy, James thought, staring at his father's face, to pin all the blame on someone else. His father had spoiled Mary Elizabeth most of all, had made excuses for her not listening, had let the rules change according to what Mare wanted. His father had been the decision maker in the family, the one who deemed James old enough to watch his sister for the day.

Maybe Frank blamed him because to acknowledge that he'd failed Mary Elizabeth, too...maybe that was more than his father could bear.

It had been worth a shot. James paused, then stood up. "Take care, Mom," he said, kissing his mother's head. She sniffled in response. He dropped a hand on his father's shoulder. "See you, Dad." He removed his hand before Frank could shrug it off and walked through the house.

There was the funky little closet where Mary Elizabeth always hid during hide-and-seek; James and his brothers would have to pretend to be stumped, wandering around the house, saying, "Where could she be? I can't find her anywhere," as she giggled wildly inside. There was the railing Pete had encouraged him to slide down, neglecting to warn against the ball-busting newel post at the bottom. The dining room, which had always looked so magical at Christmas, filled with Grandma's cut-glass bowls, the candles and the good china, which only came out on holidays.

Once upon a time, this house had been a happy place.

It'd be good to be back in Rhode Island, where nothing had ever been too complicated. Saturday-morning basketball games, the occasional bike ride, beers with the guys, flirting with some girls.

Maybe he'd call Harry's friend from Goldman. It might not be too late.

He opened the door and went out, closing it quietly behind him. Crossed the tired yard.

"Jamie. Wait."

It was his mother, shielding her eyes from the sun. "What is it, Mom?"

She came up to him. "Your father's sorry. It's hard for him."

"I know."

"You know how he is. He's strung so tight, and your brothers, well, they're not much better. Tom's exactly like him—they're peas in a pod. Petey's not bad. You should call him more."

"Sure, Mom."

"Good!" His mother beamed.

"I should go. It's a long drive." He opened the truck door.

"You'll be her guardian, you know. Once your father and I die."

James froze.

"We signed the papers when you graduated from law school. You've always been a good brother."

"Mom—"

She waved her hand. "And this problem of mine, the

drinking… That started before. Long time ago." She gave a shaky smile, then ran a hand through her hair, making it wilder than ever. Then her eyes filled with tears. "Honey, that day…as horrible as it was, my God, and it was…I thought I'd lost you both. We'd just pulled into the driveway, and I happened to look over at the lake, and there you were, trying to save her, screaming her name. When you went under, I thought you were both dead." His mother wiped her eyes, then smiled apologetically. "Sometimes, afterward, I'd wake up at night and think you really did drown, and I'd sit by your bed at night and pet your hair and just look at you. My baby boy."

"Mom…" His voice broke.

"I know you tried, honey. I watched you try. Without you, she'd be dead. Don't you forget that."

James rubbed his forehead, looking at the ground. "Mom, if you ever wanted to come live with me—"

"Oh, honey, why would I want to do that? I love your father. Even if he can't get over what happened with Mary Elizabeth. He's very good with her, you know. He visits her twice a week, Wednesdays and Sundays."

"I know. I see the visitors' log." He paused. "Well, you don't have to live with me, but I sure would like it if you visited."

His mother smiled, looking her age and then some. "Maybe, sweetheart."

"I'd come get you."

"That sounds nice."

He hugged her then, hugged her for a long time, breathing in the scent of whiskey and shampoo and the musty smell of his childhood home.

CHAPTER THIRTY-SIX

SEVEN WEEKS AFTER arriving back in Rhode Island, Parker opened a flower shop.

Blossom was on the far side of Mackerly, away from the little green. It had occurred to Parker that while Ethan and Lucy were hugely important in her life, she probably shouldn't take a storefront on the same block as their restaurant and pastry shop. So over to the other side of the island, next to a pizza place and a shoe store. An old, Lavinia-style flower shop was going out of business, and the timing had been perfect. A little construction for a new counter, made by Gianni, who was grumpy in his retirement and looked for odd jobs to keep him out of the house. A cozy little corner with a wing chair, a love seat and a coffee table, should a bride come in for a consultation. Parker had ordered some giant Georgia O'Keeffe posters and hung them on the brick wall, stocked up on tissue paper in every conceivable color and ribbons to match, and gotten to work.

She loved Blossom, loved Tuesday mornings, when she'd be at the shop at 5:00 a.m. to get the week's delivery from the wholesaler. She loved the waxy, clean smell of flowers, loved Carlotta, whom she hired after the first week to run deliveries and cover some hours. Carlotta had six grown children and seventeen ear piercings, spoke Portuguese and often brought Parker a coffee.

After two weeks, Blossom already had repeat customers, including Ethan, bless his heart, who ordered all the flowers for his restaurant from her, ensuring some continuity. He also stopped by for flowers for his bride about once a week. She'd done one funeral and one birthday party. She had a wedding booked for Christmastime, and had sent out beautiful printed announcements, complete with pressed flowers, to her Harvard and Miss Porter's classmates.

There was a lot of reason to hope she'd do just fine.

The shop was ten minutes from Nicky's school, fifteen from the little Victorian they'd rented. Parker was already hoping to buy the house eventually. It was snug and adorable, more than enough room for her and Nicky. A spiral staircase led to Nicky's room on the third floor, which he called the Bat Cave. Parker's room was on the second floor, along with two smaller bedrooms, and downstairs was a galley kitchen, a dining room and a living room. Her favorite part, though, was a front porch.

Every night, Parker and Nicky sat out there before dinner. He'd tell her about his day, the games the gym teacher came up with, the art classes, his sight words, how Colette was the prettiest girl in kindergarten *and* the nicest, how she sat with him on the bus and they would probably get married.

"Don't worry, Mom," he said, zipping his Matchbox cars over the porch railing. "You can live with us and our eight babies." It was a simple statement, but Parker's eyes filled with tears. It had been happening a lot.

Another plus of the front porch and normal neighborhood: accessibility to other humans. Christina and Louis, the newlyweds next door, talked in baby voices to each other, which, though exceedingly nauseating, was also kind of sweet. Jennifer, the single mom with the beautiful toddler, was lonely and often stopped for a chat.

Sometimes, Parker wondered how'd she'd managed to live at Grayhurst all those years.

One night, when Nicky was at Ethan's, Parker sat on the porch, nursing a glass of wine, one foot on Beauty, who was snoring gently, when Lucy came up the front walk.

"Hey there," she called, smiling. "I left the boys to do manly things. Figured we could hang out."

"Absolutely," Parker said. "Glass of wine?"

"Can't," Lucy said, patting her belly, which had begun to pop. "Those doctors are so mean. Know what they said last week? 'Limit your chocolate intake.' Don't they know who I am?"

Parker laughed, and Lucy sat next to her. They chatted till it got dark—Nicky, Ethan, baby names, work—then went inside, little Beauty padding after them, then curling up in the corner to keep an eye on Lucy. She was still shy, though her abject terror at outsiders seemed to have passed.

"I love this place," Lucy said, looking around. "You've done a nice job, Parker."

"Thanks," she said. She'd painted the walls a soft green, filled the bookshelves and hung some framed artwork by her son. "I never really had a place of my own. I mean, I had apartments and stuff, but my mom would come in with her decorator and take over."

"Did you mind?" Lucy asked.

"Nah. It was her way of taking care of me."

"And how is your mom?"

"Oh, she's fine. She's in the final ten for *Real Housewives of Las Vegas*."

"Dear Lord."

"I know. She might come out for Thanksgiving. But my cousin is a definite."

"It'll be great," Lucy said. They were coming, too, as well as Gianni and Marie. A full house.

Lucy took a sip of her seltzer water, then pulled a throw pillow into her lap. "So."

"Uh-oh. Are you going to lecture me?"

"Yes." Lucy smiled. "You were so good at lecturing me about this time last year."

"Was I?"

"Oh, yeah. Figured it was my turn."

Parker sighed and took a sip of wine. "Okay. Go for it. I'm ready."

"Thanks. Well, it seems to me that on some levels, you've never been better. The shop is fantastic, and you seem to love it."

"I do," Parker said. "Never thought I'd be a florist, but you're right."

"And this house feels so much more like you than Grayhurst ever did."

Parker gave a half nod. "Yeah. Hard to feel at home in a mansion when it's just two of you."

"Nicky's doing great, obviously."

"He's getting married."

"Yes. Colette. Do you approve?"

Parker smiled. "I do. She came over on Sunday and has beautiful manners."

Lucy was quiet for a minute. "You ever hear from James?"

Parker looked down. "No. We…we're done. Summer lovin', and all that."

"Please, no singing." Lucy smiled. "The thing is… well, you've been different since you got back. A little sad."

Dang. There were those ninja tears again, slipping

up on her without warning. "Um, you know. A lot of change."

"Right," said Lucy. "But I know you had feelings for James."

Parker took a sip of wine. "No, you're right. I did."

"And I know that's pretty rare for you."

"Hey. I was in love with John Stamos for quite some time. Of course, I called him Jesse back then."

"Okay, okay, so John Stamos, sure, who didn't love him? And the Old Spice man, we can't forget him."

"He saw me through a lot of lonely hours," Parker seconded.

Lucy smiled again, her soft, gentle smile. "But in all seriousness, Parker, the fact that this guy got to you… that's huge. Isn't it?"

Her words brought a lump to Parker's throat. "He's a lot like my father." Her voice was just above a whisper.

"Really? Because I never got that impression. I always thought James was kind of sweet. And a little lonely, maybe."

Parker swallowed. "He is. Or he's not. I don't know, Luce. I was thinking about a future, a relationship, and the whole time he already had a job lined up in New York. And the girlfriend…"

"Yeah, yeah, you told me the story."

"Right. So at the very best, it was a huge miscommunication. At worst, he was cheating on me. Or her."

Lucy was quiet for a long minute. "Well, let me say something, and don't get mad, okay?"

"I hate when people say that," she grumbled.

"Right, but I'm in a delicate condition, so you have to listen."

"Fire away, Pregnita."

Lucy looked at her hand for a minute, and twisted her

wedding ring. "It's just that sometimes, the right guy seems really wrong. And sometimes, it's easier to grab hold of an excuse, because really going for it, putting yourself out there…that's hard. You know that. You saw me through that last year."

Parker conceded the point with a nod.

"So, welcome to the world, Parker. Loving someone can be terrifying." She set her glass down gently. "And it's worth it."

ON SUNDAY, WHEN THE SHOP was closed and Nicky was with Ethan, Parker got into the Volvo and headed north. It had been a week since the Lecture from Lucy, and she'd been itchy and scratchy ever since.

Life would be much simpler without a relationship.

She had a son to raise.

She had a business to run.

James didn't want what she did. Or so he said. Except for that one time, on the dock. *I'm in.*

He'd gone into the water looking for her son.

As she turned onto the street of dear old dad's correctional facility, a car pulled out of the parking lot. She caught the quickest glimpse of the driver, and before her brain registered who it was, longing surged up so fast and strong that her chest actually ached.

James.

Her hands zinged with adrenaline, and she bit her lip hard. But he didn't see her, turned the other way, didn't seem to glance in his rearview mirror, didn't tap his brakes.

She went in, the guards as polite as the waiters at the Pierre, and went into the visiting room. A few minutes later, Harry appeared.

"Parker," he said. He looked better than last time. "What a surprise."

"Harry. How are you?"

"Good. And you?"

"Fine."

"How's Nicky?"

"He's great. He wants to get married and have eight kids." She pushed some hair behind her ears, her heart thudding sickly, though she wasn't sure why.

"Seems like a lot." Harry gave a small smile, and Parker felt something shift in her chest.

"So I saw James leaving as I pulled in," she said.

Her father nodded. "He comes every other weekend or so. Good kid." Her father paused, tracing an invisible design on the tabletop. "Of course, he *should* come see me, since he's the one who put me here."

Parker's mouth dropped open. "You know about that?"

Harry shrugged. "He told me a few weeks ago, but I already suspected. I was stupid. He did the right thing."

"Doesn't it bother you? That he's the one responsible?"

"Well, the truth is, I'd have probably gotten caught anyway. He jump-started the process, let's put it that way."

Parker shook her head. "Did you *want* to get caught, Harry? Is that it?"

Another shrug. "I don't know. You get to a point where you think you're invincible. That you're smarter than everyone else. Maybe I wanted to see how far I could push things."

You always did.

"I have a question for you, Harry," she said, her voice low.

For the first time during the visit, her father looked uncomfortable. "Go ahead."

She hesitated, her stomach twisting. *Say it,* Spike advised. She swallowed. "How is it that you could be such a crappy father to me and be so…easy with James? The first time I ever saw you two together, you were already closer than you and I have ever been. He put you in here, and you don't seem to hold anything against him." Her voice was shaking.

Harry didn't answer.

"You barely speak to me. We've talked more since you were convicted than we have in a decade, and I'm sure it's because you're bored. But James…James is your BFF, even now. Did you always want a son? Is that my problem? I was born with the wrong parts?"

"Don't be ridiculous," he snapped. He glanced over her shoulder, thinking, then looked at her again. "It's not that at all."

"Well, what is it, then?"

"It's that you've been waiting for me to screw up again since you were ten years old."

"When I walked in on you doing the babysitter, you mean?" Her voice was loud, and several people looked over.

"Yes." His eyes were stony. "Exactly. And ever since that day, you've sat in judgment, just like your mother. You moved into Grayhurst to remind me of that day, to remind me that I was dog shit."

"You were screwing my babysitter, Harry! You *were* dog shit!"

Her father shook his head "See, that's your problem, Parker. Granted, I'm completely to blame for that day. But nothing I could do afterward could ever make up for that one stupid roll in the sack. You wouldn't forgive me. Ever."

"You never apologized," she said tightly.

"You seem to wait for people to disappoint you, Parker," he continued, ignoring her comment. "And guess what? They will. People make mistakes. We're not perfect. You want to know why I like James? Because he likes *me,* Parker. Not many people do, in case you haven't noticed. It was nice to be with someone who wasn't simply kissing my ass or talking behind my back. He didn't sit and judge and wait."

"You paid him well."

"Well, I haven't paid him since May—"

"But he said—"

"—and yet he's the only one who comes to see me, other than one visit from you. Two, counting today, which I gather is for you to vent your spleen and tell me what a shitty father I've been."

"Do you have any idea how much I missed you, Dad?"

The question shocked them both. Harry's eyes widened, but he said nothing.

"When I was a kid," she went on, slowly, as the thoughts seemed to form only as she spoke, "you made me feel like the most important person in the world. I worshipped you, Harry. Everything I did, I did to impress you. But after that day, you could hardly look at me. It was like you hated me."

"I didn't hate you," he said. "I never hated you." His gaze dropped to the table.

Parker looked at her father, the once-powerful legend of Wall Street. For years, it seemed that Harry had a pact with the devil, barely aging, the only change the silvering of his hair. But in prison, the years had caught up. He'd missed a spot shaving, and the skin under his eyes was puffy. His hair was longer, and a lock stood up in the back, same way Nicky's did. Maybe her son's cowlick wasn't courtesy of Ethan's gene pool. Maybe her son looked a little bit like his grandfather.

"I never hated you, either, Dad," she said gently. "I moved into Grayhurst because it was where my happiest times were. Except for that one day."

He looked up, and his eyes were wet. "I'm sorry about your trust fund," he said. "I hope to make it up to you and Nicky both when I get out."

"Don't bother," Parker answered. "Losing it was the best thing that ever happened to us."

There was another long silence. "I'm sorry about the babysitter," he said, so quietly she almost didn't hear.

She reached over and covered his hand with hers. "Thank you."

"No touching," said the guard. Parker squeezed her father's hand, then obeyed.

So that was something, she thought as she drove home. Obviously, you didn't repair a relationship that had been neglected for a quarter century in one conversation. But they'd said more across that little metal table than they'd said in years. Decades. It was a start.

Her father's words echoed in her head. *You wait for people to disappoint you.*

No one had ever called Harry Welles dumb.

Beauty greeted her at the door, wagging vigorously, sniffing her shoes to see where she'd been. Parker bent to pet the dog's soft head. "How was your day? Tell me you didn't just lie on the couch and watch QVC." The dog wagged some more, her eyes filled with love.

Funny, how Parker really hadn't been looking for a dog and now couldn't imagine life without her little pal.

"Come on, sweetie," she said, heading upstairs.

Nick had left his drawing pad on her bed; they'd been

coloring last night. She missed her son in the familiar rush, even though he hadn't been gone for even twenty-four hours. Flipping through his pad, she saw the chronicle of their recent life—a girl with curly hair and blue eyes who could only be Colette, Nicky's love. A brown-and-white dog. "It's you," she said, holding out the pad for Beauty to see. Lots of pictures of swords and maces. Darth Maul, his face distinguishable by the red-and-black coloring. A school bus with smiling faces in the windows. Sweet.

The next one gave her pause. Two smiling stick figures next to a house with a triangle for a roof. The smaller figure had spiky hair and held a gun and a square. The taller figure had curly brown hair.

James and Nicky and the nail gun.

He must have drawn this recently; the drawing pad was the one she'd bought him for school.

So he'd been thinking about James. Remembering him fondly, even, because the stick figures were holding hands.

She put the pad down and, on impulse, went to her closet for the box of stuff she'd taken from the house in Maine. Some rocks her son had insisted they bring. The plastic tomato with the top hat and eyelashes. The red notebook of her wretched story ideas. The manuscript of *Mickey the Fire Engine*. A piece of driftwood Beauty had brought her. Two pieces of blue sea glass.

She wasn't sure what she'd been looking for. Sighing, she opened the notebook. There were the pulverized chipmunks. Swimmy the Shark, being eaten by his mommy. The Lonely Maggot. Nice. Quite a theme of distress here, most def. Oh, crikey, the Ark Angels. That one was really scraping the barrel.

She turned back to *Mickey,* the story Nicky loved.

Now *that* was the book that should've made her famous.
A hardworking but aging fire truck bumped into disservice by the bigger, shinier truck. Only Firefighter Bill
had kept the faith in Mickey, and on that frigid winter
night when the apartment building was on fire and the
newer truck's engine couldn't start, Bill asked Mickey
to come through just one more time.

Wonderful themes about being chosen, being useful,
commitment and friendship. Of showing up when you
were needed the most. Of forgiveness.

James had said he loved *Mickey.*

Beauty rested her muzzle on Parker's shin. "Really?
You think so?" Parker asked, rubbing the dog's velvety
snout. The dog blinked. "Okay. You're the boss."

She brought the manuscript downstairs, rustled
around in her desk and pulled out a manila envelope and
did a Google search of the address. *James F. X. Cahill,
c/o Goldman Sachs, 200 West Street, New York, NY.*

CHAPTER THIRTY-SEVEN

"I'm NOT GOING in there. You're crazy. You're trying to kill me."

"I've hardly killed anyone this year," James said. "Come on. I feel like an idiot as it is."

"'Cuz you *are* an idiot, man. Go yourself. Leave me out of this, skinny."

James could feel his teeth turning to dust, he was grinding them so hard. When he'd signed up for Big Brothers Big Sisters, he'd envisioned taking some cute little kid to the movies, shooting hoops, going out for ice cream. Someone around Nicky Mirabelli's age, for example, or maybe seven or eight. In this scenario, he'd pick up the kid in a poor but respectable neighborhood where the parent(s) would be delighted to see him.

Instead, he'd been greeted by the dead-eyed stare of an enormous man who'd exuded boredom and contempt like a toxic gas.

"Hi. I'm James Cahill from Big Brothers? I'm here for Taymal."

"That right?"

"Yes, sir. Thank you."

"Okay. Let's go, then." He grabbed a jacket, then stopped. "What? You got a problem?"

So yeah. Taymal was fifteen years old, stood six feet three and had the physique of a Patriots linebacker. He looked as if he could—and might—snap James in half.

Nevertheless, James couldn't exactly say, "I was looking for someone cuter and less frightening," so here they were, standing poolside at the Providence YMCA. "Look. I signed us both up," he said.

"That is *not* my problem, skinny."

It was probably a hundred degrees in here, and about a thousand little kids seemed to be having a screaming contest for who could sound the most in peril. James's skin was crawling, his nerves were like piano wire, and he was trying not to let Taymal see that he was fricking terrified.

While Taymal refused to go in the pool, he had nonetheless let James spend $89 on a pair of swim trunks an hour before, since he didn't own any. He also asked if James would buy him a $165 pair of Nike sneakers. When James asked if he liked basketball, Taymal gave him a very loud and eloquent lecture on racial stereotyping, then asked if he could get a Kobe Bryant shirt.

"Just try it, Taymal. It's okay if you don't know how to swim. We're here for lessons."

"Bite me, skinny. I can swim. I don't want to."

"Really?"

"In*deed*. Why? You think black people can't swim?"

"No, I didn't mean that—"

"Hi! Are you James and Taymal? I'm Quinn! I'm your swim instructor!" A *very* beautiful girl bounced up to them. Red bathing suit, blue eyes, brown, curly hair streaked with the greenish-blond of a swimmer. "Are you guys ready?"

"Oh, baby, I am *so* ready," Taymal said, pursing his lips and giving her an appreciative scan.

"Taymal. Stop." This was a really, really bad idea. "Show some respect, okay?"

"Oh, in*deed*. Quinn, honey, I respect you, baby—"

"Yeah, you actually will have to stop or I get to drown you," Quinn said, tapping her clipboard. "It's part of the rules."

Taymal rolled his eyes. "Well, I'm not going swimming. Uh-uh. No way."

"Great," James said. "Well, let's stand here for an hour, then, and listen to the children scream."

"I'll give you two a minute. How's that?" Quinn said, bouncing away again.

"What do you wanna swim for, anyway?" Taymal said.

James thought about the answer he'd prepared: really important skill to have, the importance of wholesome hobbies. They could swim here in the winter and go to the beach in the summer—though whether Taymal would tolerate him for even ten more minutes was dubious. He sighed. "We don't have to. I'll take you out to eat instead."

"Now you're talking."

James looked at all those little kids in the shallow end of the pool, shrieking and splashing. "I almost drowned when I was a kid. My sister, too. She has brain damage because of it, and I've been scared to swim ever since. I thought maybe if I had someone with me, it wouldn't be so hard. But it still seems hard. See?" He held up his hand, which was shaking.

"Shit, man. That is one sad story. Where do you wanna eat?"

"I don't know. Chili's okay?"

"Yeah."

James turned to go. "Sorry, Quinn," he called. "We have to cancel."

"Not a problem," she answered.

When he got to the door, he found that Taymal wasn't

with him. The kid—the Hulk—was still at the edge of the pool. James sighed and went back.

"You really wanna do this?" Taymal asked, jerking his chin at the water.

"No. I mean, I actually do know how to swim—I just hate it. But if you don't want to do this, I'll come back another time without you."

Taymal gave him a long-suffering look. "Dude, you're about to piss your pants as it is. You won't come back. Yo, Quinn! Come on over, beautiful! My man's ready."

WHEN JAMES GOT HOME late that afternoon, he was exhausted, his head was killing him and he was fairly sure there was some nasty-ass pool water lurking in his left lung.

But.

He'd been swimming. Not as rewarding as when Parker had bribed him out to the dock, but he'd done it. Taymal had howled with laughter, shown off his own pretty solid swimming skills and then, at Chili's, eaten a bacon burger, a full order of baby back ribs and the Triple Dipper platter. Extra fries.

"You want to see me again?" James asked as he pulled up in front of Taymal's house.

"What, are you my girlfriend now?" the kid asked. "Dude, this is part of my parole, okay?"

James stared him down. Four hours with the kid, and he was starting to catch on.

"Okay, that was a joke," Taymal said. "Yeah, my mom wants me to have a positive male influence. And that's you, dude. Pretty sad, if you ask me."

"Great."

"I'd rather not have to see your skinny white legs

again, though. Next time, maybe we can do something else?"

James smiled. "Sure. You like baseball? We could go see the Sox, maybe?"

"Man, are you kidding? Take me to Yankee Stadium, hook us up in a hotel for the night, that fancy-ass Waldorf Astoria, get us some box seats. We'll be all set."

"Maybe we can go down for one game. No hotel, and no box seats, though. I don't make that much."

"Too bad. My cousin Louis? His Big Brother took him to the seventh game of the World Series, dude."

"I will never take you to the World Series. You still want me?"

"'You still want me?' Man, you sound like a girl. Later, dude. Call my mother, set something up."

"Okay." The kid heaved himself out of the car and sauntered inside.

So, given how it'd begun, the afternoon had been a smashing success, in a horrible sort of way. He could see Taymal growing on him. He could see—maybe someday—overcoming his fear of swimming.

The condo was quiet, as it always was. He should look into selling it, even with the real estate market in the toilet, because his new job wasn't paying what his old job did, and while he'd paid Beckham Institute in advance for the next four years, that time would be over before he knew it.

Maybe he'd be promoted by then; as it was, he was working entry-level pay and hours, and grateful for it. The firm handled mostly corporate law, a little pro bono on the side. It was nice to work with people again. Actually, it was Stella, his old secretary, who'd gotten him the interview through a lawyer she taught in her jujitsu class. It was a decent firm; one of the senior partners seemed to like him. So four years, sure, he might be on partner track. Could even be married in four years. You never knew.

He went over to the fridge, took out a beer and stared at the photo on the door.

It was a picture of Parker and Nicky, sitting on the dock, taken from behind. The sun shone on Parker's hair. Her arm was around her boy, her face turned slightly toward him. They'd been fishing, and when a miracle happened and Nicky actually caught something, they'd both yelled for James to come down and unhook the fish. Which he'd been happy to do.

It had been nice to be needed.

Well. Taymal might think he was an idiot, but he was needed there. And he'd been calling home more regularly, talking to his mom. He'd even called Pete and talked to his niece, Morgan, who'd answered the phone. She sounded like a sweet kid.

Funny that three months ago, James hadn't wanted much more than he had. Now that he'd had more, though, it was harder to be content.

He touched the edge of the picture, then turned.

There was a FedEx envelope on his table with a sticky note on it: "Signed for this today. Barb from 3G." He'd have to remember to thank her.

The package was from Goldman Sachs. That was odd; maybe he'd been put on their mailing list since almost taking the job. He opened it up to find a note on corporate letterhead, as well as a sealed envelope addressed to him, care of Goldman. No return address. A note said,

This came for you. Took me a while to find your address. Delia Summers, Assistant Director, External Correspondence Department, Goldman Sachs.

No wonder the country's financial system was in danger. The mail room had become the External Correspondence Department.

James opened the package. Inside was the manuscript for *Mickey the Fire Engine*.

The last copy, Parker had told him. The refrigerator cycled on, the only sound in the quiet kitchen. James turned the page. The last copy of the book she loved.

In*deed,* as Taymal would say.

CHAPTER THIRTY-EIGHT

PARKER WAS AT BLOSSOM on a Tuesday morning, lugging buckets of fresh flowers into the cooler, when an unexpected visitor walked through the door. "Mom!" she said, setting down the gerbera daisies with a slosh.

"Hello, sweetheart," Althea said.

"What are you doing here! Again without calling! What a nice surprise!" She hugged her mom, who looked strange...wait, it was that she looked *normal,* actually. The Botox had worn off, and Althea's face had lost that tight, shiny look.

"I know, I know, I should've called. I wanted to surprise you again." Her mother looked around the shop. "This is very pretty, Parker. Oh, you have a dog. I forgot."

"This is Beauty. Beauty, come say hi." The dog declined to leave her little bed, but she granted Althea a small tail wag. "So, Mom. What are you—"

"I left Maury."

Parker blinked. "Oh. Wow."

Althea sighed. "Do you have any coffee? A nonfat vanilla soy latte would really soothe my soul about now."

"I have plain old coffee. How would that be?"

The story was, Althea said, that she got tired of walking on eggshells, trying to please a curmudgeonly old man who was, she suspected, going to dump her anyway. "One day, darling, I said, 'Althea, what are you thinking? You deserve better. You're more than someone's wife.'"

Parker nodded, a little stunned. Her mother had never gone more than eight months without a husband, had been first married at age twenty-one to Harry. Being a wife was her entire *career.* "That's huge, Mom."

"I know. But the truth is, I'm not sure what I'm supposed to do. So I figured the first thing would be to visit my grandchild." She paused. "I didn't call because I was afraid you'd say no."

"Mom! I wouldn't say no! I'm really proud of you. Of course you can stay with us. The new place is small, but we have a guest room. It'll be great!"

Althea smiled. She had lovely crow's feet, Parker noticed. "I was sort of counting on that." Her eyes filled with tears. "I couldn't keep it up, Parker. It's exhausting, trying to be the person someone wants you to be and completely losing the person you once were." She blew her nose. "I promise I won't stay forever. It's just been so long for me, I don't even know where to start."

"Here. Here's where you start." She leaned over and kissed her mom's cheek. "Nicky will be so happy when he sees you."

"You think so?"

"Absolutely. We'll surprise him when he gets off the bus. He comes here after school."

Parker spent the rest of the day showing her mother around the shop, letting her watch as she filled orders, talking about Nicky and the adjustments to their new lifestyle. They got lunch from the deli down the street and ate it in the little sitting area in the shop.

"So you're happy?" Althea asked a trifle suspiciously.

Parker took a bite of her sandwich and thought about the question as she chewed. "I am. I love doing flowers, and even though I thought I'd hate it, I like that

Nicky's in school. Though I did cry a lot the first couple of weeks."

Her mom smiled. "What about—what was his name?"

"Collier?"

"Oh, did you date him?" Althea asked excitedly.

"No. He's a nice guy, but kind of a dope."

"Yes. Well, actually, I meant the other one. The one who was living with you."

"James."

"Yes. Did that ever…?" Her mother raised her eyebrows. So odd to see her with normal facial movement.

"We parted ways," Parker said. She was quiet for a moment. She'd spent the past week berating herself for sending the manuscript. It had seemed cute; in the face of his nonresponse, it now seemed really stupid. She should've been more direct. Just written him a note, or called him and said, "Look, I'm sorry, I miss you, please give me another chance."

"Don't be sad, sweetheart," Althea said, patting her hand. "We're two single women. We can do facials and have movie nights, and I can make your favorite dinner."

"Do you even know what that is, Mom?" Parker asked, smiling.

"No. But you can tell me, and I'll give it a whirl."

NICKY WAS INDEED EXCITED to have Faraway Mimi up close. He wanted to show off the new house, especially the fort he'd made in his room, so Parker switched his booster seat to Althea's rental car and let him go home with her. Her mom beeped the horn and turned at the corner.

Parker watched them go, a little bemused. Aside from a few summers here and there, she hadn't lived with her mom since she was thirteen years old. The cynical side

of her wanted to take a bet on how long it would take
Althea to find another husband. The better part of her
was proud. Althea had never left a husband willingly.
Well. Except for Harry.

Althea had put up with a lot from her husbands over
the years, proving the old saying that if you married for
money, you earned every cent. But she'd married Harry
Welles before he'd become a big deal; she'd loved him
once, and when he cheated on her and traumatized their
only child, Althea walked away. Her mother had pro-
tected her, as best as she'd known how, and that…that
was worth a lot.

Parker sat down at her desk, smiling at Nicky's kindergarten photo. He'd worn a bow tie, at his own insis-
tence, "so Colette will see me as husband material," he'd
announced the night before when they'd all been eating
at Mirabelli's, and Ethan had laughed so hard he'd cried.
Her son looked cheesy and adorable in the photo, all his
baby teeth still present and accounted for.

This was what her life was now—a business to run,
bills to pay, a son to raise. A new home, her friends,
sweet little Beauty curled at her feet and now her mom
staying with her for a while, trying on some indepen-
dence for size.

A nice life. A full life.

She did some bookkeeping for the next hour, the quiet
of the fragrant little shop as soothing as a cup of cocoa.
She had to order more roses; the wholesaler was short on
them this week. She'd work late on Friday for a Saturday
wedding, but the thought gave her a tingle of excitement.
Maggie Beaumont—well, Maggie Malone now—had
emailed her pictures of the arrangements so Parker could
put them on Blossom's website, and the bride had loved
the look.

Maybe, if she could swing it, she and Nicky could go up to Gideon's Cove for a week this summer. See Vin and the rest of the people she'd met. Eat at Joe's, see how the babies had grown.

The phone rang, and Parker glanced at the clock. Five minutes till closing. She could let the machine get it; if it was an order, she wouldn't have time to fill it until tomorrow. Then again, she'd be a fool to turn away business.

"Blossom, can I help you?"

"Hi," said the female voice on the other end. "I need to place an order for my boss? It's his twenty-fifth wedding anniversary."

"I'm just about to close. Are these for today?"

"Afraid so."

Parker paused. "Well, for twenty-five years, I guess I can stay open a little longer. What's he looking for?"

"He said something gorgeous. And expensive."

Oh, goody. Hopefully, he'd remember that she stayed open for him on his special day and use her again. She took out her pen "And the card?"

"Yeah, let me read that—he wrote it out for me. Ready?"

"Yep."

"'I've loved you since the first moment I saw you, and I haven't stopped since. Thank you for our beautiful children, thank you for our life together, and thank you for being my wife. Hope we can fool around later.'"

Parker laughed. "Okay, got it. It'll be ready in about half an hour. Do you have a credit-card number?"

"Can he pay cash when he comes by?"

"Sure. Thanks for choosing Blossom."

Twenty-five years, and the guy was still cheeky, Parker thought, reading the card once more. Poetic, too.

Well. He'd get a beautiful bouquet to bring home to his wife, that was for sure. Not because he was spending a lot, but because he sounded like a good husband. "And let's face it," she said to Beauty, "I'm a sucker for love."

She pulled a dozen yellow roses, some brilliant purple lisianthus, a few deep orange lilies. Four branches of pink phalaenopsis orchid. Some heather and fern. This couple was fun. No mere roses and baby's breath for them. Something extravagant and vivid and memorable.

She pictured the husband as she worked—somewhere in his fifties, probably, an insurance executive or doctor, maybe. The wife would've gotten home a little early, knowing her hubby was not the type to forget their anniversary. The kids were off at college, so the place would be all theirs. He'd come through the door, the beautiful arrangement in one hand, a bottle of bubbly in the other, and she'd be wearing nothing but a smile.

And because he loved her, it wouldn't matter that she wasn't twenty-two or thirty or forty anymore. In his eyes, she was truly the most beautiful woman in the world. The thought brought tears to Parker's eyes. A sucker for love indeed.

"What do you think?" she asked Beauty when she was finished. The dog wagged her tail appreciatively. The bouquet was wildly beautiful, filled with intense colors and odd combinations. She wrapped it in purple tissue paper and tied it with lots of red ribbon.

Then the door to her shop opened, and she looked up, expecting to see her customer.

Instead, it was James.

Her mouth fell open. The rest of her froze.

Beauty, however, had no compunction. She ran over to James, whimpering happily, putting her front paws on his knee. "Hey, girl," he said, bending to pet her, and oh, that smile, it was even better than she remembered. Beauty began crooning in joy, her tail swishing wildly.

Then he straightened up and looked at her. "Hi."

"Hi," she breathed.

"So. *Mickey the Fire Engine.* I'm starting to wonder if it's about more than trucks."

Her heart was jackhammering so hard she'd bet he could see it, fluttering under her shirt. "It's an, um, a metaphor."

"For what?"

Damn if her mind wasn't completely blank. "Second chances?"

"I see."

"How are you?" she managed to ask.

"Good. And you?"

"Good." Crikey. "How's New York?"

"I don't know. I live in Providence."

"You do?"

He nodded.

He lived in Providence. Not New York. "I thought you—"

"I didn't take the job."

"Oh." She sounded like an idiot. Clearing her throat, she said, "Um, James, I'm very happy to see you. And maybe we can have a drink or something, and talk…but I have to wait for a customer. It's his anniversary—"

James smiled, and her heart seemed to leap toward him. "Oh, right, the flowers. Actually, those are for you." He nodded at the arrangement she'd just finished. "I'm a couple decades early, but I'm optimistic, too."

Oh. *Oh.* She glanced at the card. "Are you… Is…is that a proposal?"

He tilted his head as if thinking. "Yep."

"A marriage proposal?"

"Yes."

"I reject it," she said.

He closed his eyes briefly. "Great."

"It's just that I wanted to do the asking." Holy halos. Where was this coming from?

Go for it, the Holy Rollers said. For a nanosecond, she pictured them, the six angels all in a line, smiling and nodding, Spike in his leather jacket, giving her the thumbs-up.

"I'm waiting," James said. He was smiling.

"Okay." Parker's eyes suddenly filled with tears. "James," she said, her voice wobbling, "I'd really like you to overlook the fact that I was a snob and ignored you and thought you were scum, and then, when we finally did hook up for real, basically jumped at the first chance to ditch you."

"Do you have any qualities to recommend you?" he asked, laughing, and she smiled, though a couple of tears slid down her cheeks.

"Yes. I do. Um, I'm smart, and a great swimmer, as you know, and once I love someone, I tend to keep them really close, and I think I have a good sense of humor. I put out, as you also know, and I can do all the voices in *Harry Potter.*" She paused. "Also, I love you. A lot. What do you say?"

"I accept," he said. "Now could you come out from behind that counter and kiss me?"

She did just that, flew across the small space and wrapped her arms around his neck and looked at him for a second, those beautiful eyes, the smile that took up his whole face.

"Thank God you finally wised up," he said, and with that, he kissed her, and Parker had to wonder how she ever got so lucky.

EPILOGUE

Eighteen months later

JUST BEFORE IT WAS TIME to walk down the aisle, Parker peeked into the main part of St. Andrew's. The flowers were amazing—of course, she'd done them herself last night with help from Lavinia. And the place was packed.

The great state of Maine was well represented—Maggie and Malone had come down with their little boy, Aedan, who was happily tugging on his father's hair at the moment. Lavinia and Dewey sat together; according to Vin, they were back together, having dated sometime in the '90s. Parker had invited Chantal and Jonah, too, but Chantal was expecting another baby any minute, so they hadn't been able to make it.

James's mom had come down with Mary Elizabeth—who was holding her Spike doll, Parker noted. James's brother Pete and his wife and two daughters had come, too, which was so nice. Mr. Cahill and the other two brothers had opted not to come, but James had been okay with that.

Ellen, Parker's agent, had come, too. In one of those ironic twists of life, Parker had sent *Mickey the Fire Engine* to her publisher, though they'd originally rejected it years before. This time, however, the story had been deemed a winner. And while the advance had been hefty and the royalties were flowing in, Parker had decided that being a florist and the wife of an up-and-coming lawyer would ensure a solid living. So once again, all proceeds from the book were going to Save the Children.

Lucy's aunts and mother, who'd always treated Parker like another niece, were sitting with the elder Mirabellis, as well as with Althea, who wore a fabulous hat. Friends from town, some of Nicky's schoolmates and their parents. A few Harvard chums, Suze from Miss Porter's. Lucy was matron of honor, so pretty in her lavender dress. Ethan sat in the front row with their daughter, Lily, who was supposed to have been flower girl but had fallen asleep instead. Taymal, James's Little Brother, was best man and looked utterly gorgeous in a tux. He was winking at Lucy's aunts at the moment, causing a ripple of giggles from the two old ladies.

And in the back row, accompanied by a plainclothes guard, was Harry. The judge had granted him a furlough for today. He glanced back, caught her eye and tapped his hand over his heart, and Parker smiled. He was far from perfect, but a woman only got one father.

Well. Time to marry her man. The thought caused a rush of warmth from her toes to her scalp. "You ready?" she asked Nicky.

"Mom, I've been ready for nine minutes," he answered, showing her his watch. Both his front teeth were missing—finally—and the gap gave him an adorable lisp.

Nicky wasn't giving her away, absolutely not. But he was accompanying her down the aisle.

Parker glanced down at her dress—a simple, pale peach silk dress that stopped just above her knee. No white for her. She was thirty-seven, for heaven's sake. But Althea had wept in a most gratifying manner when Parker had emerged from the dressing room, and with the bouquet of apricot, cream and white roses and still-green hydrangeas, as well as a few roses in her hair, she felt quite bridal indeed.

"Then let's get this show on the road," she said, and Nicky offered his arm with a grin, looking as ever like a miniature of his father. But she could see bits of herself, too. His eyebrows, and maybe his cheekbones.

So many people here, and everyone she loved. Malone grinned, Maggie was smiling and teary-eyed, Vin already sobbing into a bandanna. Her mom blew her a kiss, and Parker returned the gesture. Nicky gave a stately nod to Colette and ducked as Ethan reached out to ruffle his hair.

And James. He was so handsome in his tux, his eyes crinkled with a smile, and he looked completely and utterly sure.

She got to the altar and handed her flowers to Lucy. The music stopped, and everyone sat down. Then she bent down and kissed Nicky twice on the cheek, and he smiled and wiped it off, making everyone laugh. "You can go sit with Daddy, honey," she whispered.

"In a sec," he said.

Reverend Covers cleared his throat. "Dearly beloved, welcome to this very happy occasion. Before we get started, the groom has asked if he could say something."

"Be with you in a minute," James said to Parker, and his smile flashed. He stepped around her and took Nicky's hand and looked down at him, his face growing solemn.

Oh, man. The tears came in a rush.

"I, James, take you, Nicholas, as my stepson."

An audible sigh came from the guests. James glanced at her, smiled again and then grew serious as he looked at Nicky. "I promise to love you like you were my own, to always be grateful that you shared your mom with me, never to boss you unless absolutely necessary and to buy you the Lego model of the Death Star that your parents said had too many pieces, which is in my car at this very moment."

"Yes!" Nicky pumped his fist, and everyone laughed.

"I also promise to let you help name any baby your mom and I might have—"

"Mistake," Parker said unevenly. "We'll have a kid named Chewbacca."

James smiled at her again, and honestly, she hadn't known it was possible to feel so much happiness, so much love. Then he looked back at her boy. "And, Nicky, I promise always to remember that you were your mom's son long before I was her husband."

That was perfect, said Spike. The other Holy Rollers had left her bit by bit, but Spike remained, and Parker was kind of glad.

"Amen," Nicky said, mugging for the guests and getting a big laugh. "Okay, my turn. I, Nicholas Giacomo Mirabelli, take you, James, as my stepfather." He pulled a piece of paper from his pocket. "I promise to try eating what you cook, even though your food isn't as good as my dad's. I also promise to try to keep my room clean and not let Apollo out of his cage without asking. And I'm glad you're marrying my mom, because she's really happy. And also, you're nice."

"Thank you," James said, and they shook hands on it, and Nicky got a round of applause as he went to sit in the front row.

Then James took Parker's hands, and without waiting, gave her a long, hot kiss that made her nearly forget there were a hundred people watching. Then he pulled back and smiled that full, wonderful grin, his dark eyes so happy.

"Parker," he said, "always lovely to see you."

* * * * *

Wondering how Ethan and Lucy got together?
Don't miss their story in THE NEXT BEST THING,
available everywhere.

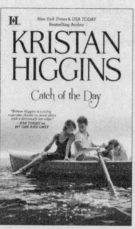

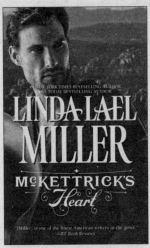

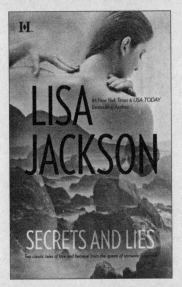

REQUEST YOUR FREE BOOKS!

2 FREE NOVELS
FROM THE ROMANCE COLLECTION
PLUS 2 FREE GIFTS!

YES! Please send me 2 FREE novels from the Romance Collection and my 2 FREE gifts (gifts are worth about $10). After receiving them, if I don't wish to receive any more books, I can return the shipping statement marked "cancel." If I don't cancel, I will receive 4 brand-new novels every month and be billed just $5.99 per book in the U.S. or $6.49 per book in Canada. That's a saving of at least 25% off the cover price. It's quite a bargain! Shipping and handling is just 50¢ per book in the U.S. and 75¢ per book in Canada.* I understand that accepting the 2 free books and gifts places me under no obligation to buy anything. I can always return a shipment and cancel at any time. Even if I never buy another book, the two free books and gifts are mine to keep forever. .

194/394 MDN FELQ

Name	(PLEASE PRINT)	
Address		Apt. #
City	State/Prov.	Zip/Postal Code

Signature (if under 18, a parent or guardian must sign)

Mail to the **Reader Service**:
IN U.S.A.: P.O. Box 1867, Buffalo, NY 14240-1867
IN CANADA: P.O. Box 609, Fort Erie, Ontario L2A 5X3

Not valid for current subscribers to the Romance Collection
or the Romance/Suspense Collection.

**Want to try two free books from another line?
Call 1-800-873-8635 or visit www.ReaderService.com.**

* Terms and prices subject to change without notice. Prices do not include applicable taxes. Sales tax applicable in N.Y. Canadian residents will be charged applicable taxes. Offer not valid in Quebec. This offer is limited to one order per household. All orders subject to credit approval. Credit or debit balances in a customer's account(s) may be offset by any other outstanding balance owed by or to the customer. Please allow 4 to 6 weeks for delivery. Offer available while quantities last.

Your Privacy—The Reader Service is committed to protecting your privacy. Our Privacy Policy is available online at www.ReaderService.com or upon request from the Reader Service.

We make a portion of our mailing list available to reputable third parties that offer products we believe may interest you. If you prefer that we not exchange your name with third parties, or if you wish to clarify or modify your communication preferences, please visit us at www.ReaderService.com/consumerschoice or write to us at Reader Service Preference Service, P.O. Box 9062, Buffalo, NY 14269. Include your complete name and address.

ROM11

KRISTAN HIGGINS

77679	CATCH OF THE DAY	___ $7.99 U.S.	___ $9.99 CAN.
77675	FOOLS RUSH IN	___ $7.99 U.S.	___ $9.99 CAN.
77611	UNTIL THERE WAS YOU	___ $7.99 U.S.	___ $9.99 CAN.
77557	MY ONE AND ONLY	___ $7.99 U.S.	___ $9.99 CAN.
77515	TOO GOOD TO BE TRUE	___ $7.99 U.S.	___ $9.99 CAN.
77514	JUST ONE OF THE GUYS	___ $7.99 U.S.	___ $9.99 CAN.
77458	ALL I EVER WANTED	___ $7.99 U.S.	___ $9.99 CAN.
77438	THE NEXT BEST THING	___ $7.99 U.S.	___ $9.99 CAN.

(limited quantities available)

TOTAL AMOUNT	$ _____
POSTAGE & HANDLING	$ _____
($1.00 FOR 1 BOOK, 50¢ for each additional)	
APPLICABLE TAXES*	$ _____
TOTAL PAYABLE	$ _____

(check or money order—please do not send cash)

To order, complete this form and send it, along with a check or money order for the total above, payable to HQN Books, to: **In the U.S.:** 3010 Walden Avenue, P.O. Box 9077, Buffalo, NY 14269-9077; **In Canada:** P.O. Box 636, Fort Erie, Ontario, L2A 5X3.

Name: _____

Address: _____ City: _____

State/Prov.: _____ Zip/Postal Code: _____

Account Number (if applicable): _____

075 CSAS

*New York residents remit applicable sales taxes.
*Canadian residents remit applicable GST and provincial taxes.

HQN™   HARLEQUIN®
www.Harlequin.com

PHKH0512BL